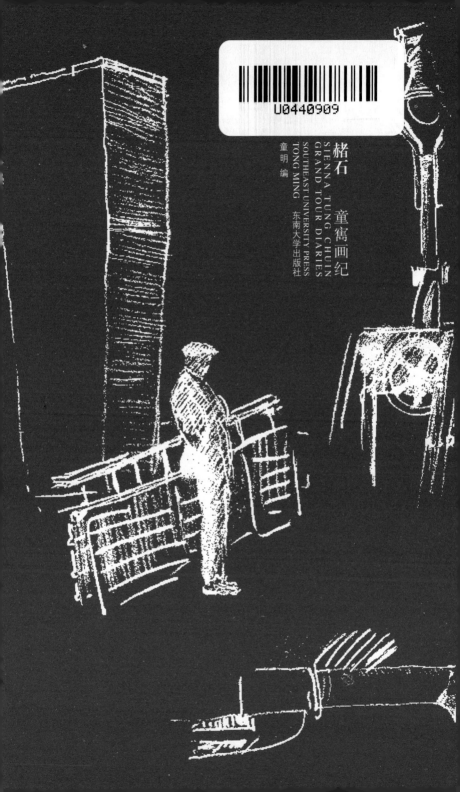

楮石 童寯画纪
SIENNA TUNG CHUIN GRAND TOUR DIARIES
童明 编
SOUTHEAST UNIVERSITY PRESS
TONG MING
东南大学出版社

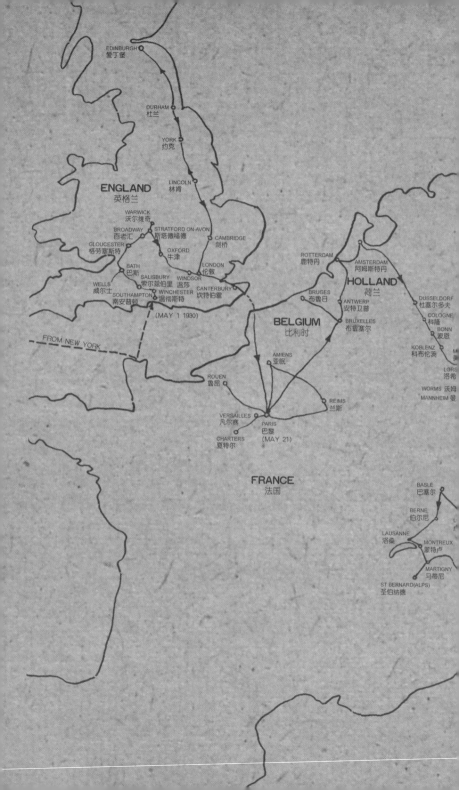

童寯先生修业之旅路线图
1930年5月1日至1930年8月27日

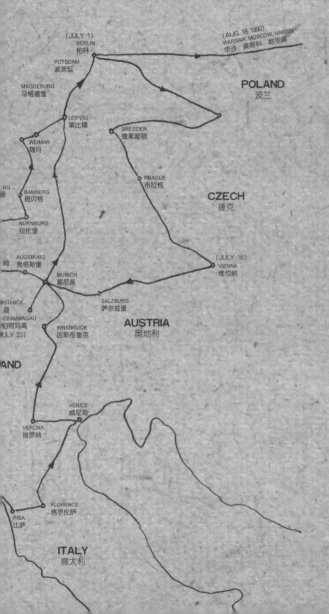

赭石
编者前言

1930年4月26日中午,美国纽约某一港口,一艘名为"欧罗巴"的中型邮轮正在缓缓驶离。船头甲板伫立着一位来自中国的年轻人,身着正装,不苟言笑。尽管对这片即将离别的国土留有深刻的眷恋,也对回到东北家乡的妻儿身旁充满着期待,但是此刻,他可能更加憧憬的则是正要前往的大西洋彼岸。

此前,他已经以令人瞠目的速度从费城的宾夕法尼亚大学毕业,该校的建筑学专业当时在美国被公认为是最具影响和实力的,正处于巅峰时期。而他只花费三年多的时间就已经完成本科及硕士的学业,随后又分别在费城和纽约实习工作一年,深受授课导师以及事务所老板的赏识。

然而,爱国的基因对于那个年代的留学生来说,是一个不言而喻的基本前提。尽早回到仍然处在贫穷落后、百废待兴的故乡,用自己习得的学识去实现出国之前所确立的抱负,这是他在进入大学选择专业时就已经下定的决心,但是,理论上业已完成的学业还有待一次远行来画上一个完满的句号。

作为一条不成文的惯例,在回到故乡之前,几乎所有于美国学习建筑的中国留学生都会从事一次专业目的的欧洲之旅,如庄俊、范文照、杨廷宝、赵深、梁思成等等。对于他们而言,亲身去体验那些平日只能在图像中接触到的经典建筑无异于一道期待已久的圣餐。其实,这不仅对于他们是如此,对于世界上众多刚刚完成学业的年轻建筑师也是必须从事的一次历练。

究其根源，这种针对古典建筑的游历应当沿袭于始自17世纪的游学旅行传统，人们称之为大旅行（Grand Tour）。在欧洲历史上的一些主要城市进行观光旅行，是那些家处偏隅的文人墨客接受教育、触发情怀的一部分。因为若要真正接触、理解西方传统，前往观览文明的发祥之地，置身古典文化的真情实景之中，这是必不可缺的重要一课。随着蒸汽船的发明，出门旅行逐渐变得容易，于是那些较少接触欧洲古典文明的英美年轻人在完成学业后，都需要从事一次历时1~2年的大陆旅行，主要目的地是意大利、希腊、法国，从而有机会充分接触从古典时期到文艺复兴的各类经典文化，聆听古典音乐、研习传统绘画，并且陶练拉丁语。

这一传统对于那些即将从事建筑专业的学生而言更为直接，也更加重要。自文艺复兴以来，雅典、罗马、庞贝、佛罗伦萨等地就已经成为经典建筑的正宗源泉，而巴黎、伦敦、维也纳等等又是新兴城市的杰出代表。它们就像耶路撒冷或麦加那样成为众多建筑学者的朝圣之地，以至于刚刚从学校毕业的学生如果缺少这段游学经历，此前所接受的专业教育就将显得残缺不全，再出色的学业都不能算作完满。

即使在现代，对于那些即将启程的年轻建筑师，建筑游学对他们的未来将会意味着什么？对于他们日后的职业生涯将会影响什么？这一问题可以从路易·康、柯布西耶、安藤忠雄等建筑大师的职业生涯中获得说明，然而我们却很难知晓这类影响是如何形成的，启发是如何获得的。无论对于他们自己，还是对于旁观者，这一过程都依赖于有效的记录。文字是一方面，图像则是另一方面。在某种角度上，其实图像更为重要，因为建筑作为现实场景，从建筑观览中所获得的所悟所思是文字无法进行复现和表述的，于是绘画也就成为建筑师的天然语言。

但他们是另外一种意义上的画家，这倒不完全在于技巧方面的因素，而是在于不同的目的。建筑师的最终目的不在于绘画本身，而是需要通过绘画去通达自身专业的感召之处，并将它们记录下来作为日后重要的知识及修养储备。

相对于繁复的油画，水彩画、铅笔画是建筑专业的常用画种，因为旅途时间往往匆忙而紧促,也不可能允许携带庞杂的设备,因此可以信手拈来的铅笔或水彩画笔成了最好的工具。用他的话来说,"如对某处文化历史环境特感兴趣,触目兴怀,流连光景,又有充裕时间",那么掏出画笔,设好画夹,就可以即兴铺陈了。

当然,即使在20世纪20年代,照相机已经不是一种稀罕物品,与今天学习建筑专业的学生一样,他们在出门游历时,大多数也会携带照相机。但是,在他看来,只有绘画才是一种正规的记述方式,而"照相机是懒汉旅行工具,用机器代替眼睛"。因为绘画并不完全只是为了留影,它同时还伴随着一种严格的操作,"如果要求对建筑物的线、面、体三者加以观察,并在最后明瞭,必须亲自动手画出,经过一番记录才巩固不忘"。

更进一步而言,建筑绘画的价值在于,它可以令研习者必须全力以赴,去真正获得经典建筑可以给人带来的激发和启迪。通过由手操作的绘画,眼睛才能够从事搜索、定焦、捕捉、判断,并把那种蕴含于建造中的智巧与优美进行梳理整合,准确地写绘于画纸之上。

因此,建筑绘画又是与建筑师的修养密切相关的。在画纸上娴熟精准、气度非凡地进行布陈,与在工地上一丝不苟、泰然有序地从事建造,它们之间存有密不可分的关系。诚然,这一问题曾经是不值一问的,因为历史中有许多伟大的建筑师就来自于伟大的画家,如米开朗基罗、拉斐尔、贝尼尼,在中国,也可以列举出王维、李渔、计成等等。但是这一关联并非经由"艺术相通"之类的含糊说辞就能够解释清楚,尤其在计算机模拟、程序建模这个当下的时代中,建筑师的这一传统已经逐渐被淡忘,甚至被质疑了。同时我们所能看到的不争事实就是,当今世界的建筑艺术质量也在普遍下降。

经过这次短暂的欧洲之旅,他回到自己的故乡。在随后的50多年中,无论在建筑创作、建筑理论还是在建筑教育方面,他都取得了非凡成就,成为中国建筑界的一代宗师,为我们留下了众多丰盛的遗产。

我们尚不完全清楚这次旅程为他日后的杰出成就如何奠定了一个坚实的基础,但是可以确信,这对他日后的专业生涯产生过深刻的影响。在这短短不到4个月的研习中,他为我们留下了200多幅的写生绘画和一本详细记录此次旅程的日记,这让我们有机会以一种更为全面的视角来了解他本人，不仅是精湛的绘画艺术，而且包括他的视域范畴和思想轨迹。

于是就有了这一本厚厚的画集和日记，它们究竟可以为我们讲述一些什么？

如果翻开画册中的某一页，可以看见一张描绘着瑞士日内瓦湖畔的西庸堡的水彩画，其内容是古堡内部的某一普通场景。在画中，城堡主塔高耸而立，几乎撑满了画页的上半部，下半部则是一处木结构小屋，也许是马厩，也许是柴房。在这张几乎完全用赭石为主调绘制的水彩画中，我们可以感受到那种历经严格古典构图训练而来的深厚功底：布局方式一丝不苟，建筑形体敦厚结实，细部构造清晰精美，古堡的那种雍容华贵、森严高耸的气质跃然纸面。

这一切都是采用极其娴熟的水彩画技法完成的，大片淡雅晕染的浅黄色浮现出弯曲而弧形的主塔墙面，趁着湿润，几片半开的窗户勾络于上。在其下方则是一排半挑的叠涩拱券，体形轻巧而结实。分为两层的红瓦屋面也是在完全湿润的状况下一次完成，深浅不匀的暗红与深褐揭示出饱经岁月的斑驳沧桑。

更加令人印象深刻的，就是在这张色彩变化不多的水彩画中，盈漾着正午的阳光，而将此映衬出来的则是处在屋檐之下的那片阴影。阴影之中的屋檐内侧与上部阳光之下的弧形塔身形成截然对比，阳光下的主塔挺拔健硕，而阴影中的虚空含蓄凝重。迅疾落下的笔触揭示出梁柱之间的结构关系，水彩色迹之间的相互印染也使得内涵大大丰富。赭石加上深褐，以及透出微泛的淡蓝，使得这块极具分量的阴影丝毫不显呆板之处，相反呈现出多层次的透明以及轻灵。

这张水彩可能与其他画作一样，是在捕得印象后，于短短的三四十分钟内一气呵成。我们可以想见他不可能耗费时间去从事构思酝酿，也不可能详细周全地去分析结构的转承关系，一切都必须依托于迅疾的判断和精确的笔法。于是这类较为随意的普通场景，尽管施以简单色彩，但是通过由心灵运作的画笔、颜料而再现出来，从而显得如此丰富、生动而且耐人寻味。

就如他所言："水彩画的要求是极高的，在阳光下写生，设色之前，预见构图全貌，轻轻勾出铅笔轮廓，先画天空，然后自上而下把阴影部分尽早布置妥善，再着手染建筑材料的淡色及高光并留白。至此，全幅明暗色调基本确立。每染一色都是最后一次，不再重复，以保持颜色的鲜洁，也有时把颜料布在水湿纸面上混合。在任何情况下都避用白粉。"

在一次闲聊中他曾经坦陈，在所有的色彩中最偏爱赭石。我们无从解释一个人对于色彩的偏爱，或许欧洲大多数建筑都由砖石构成，而它们在阳光下呈现的色彩就是各种深浅不一的赭石，就如同他的性格一样，深沉、厚重。

水彩画相对于当时的黑白照片和铅笔速写的一个优势在于，它可以记录下绘制对象的色彩，而且在充足的阳光下写生效果更佳，但是这并不意味着需要采用强烈的颜色。在匆匆旅程的间歇中，绘画色彩绝对不能复杂，而是要简单。由于深受中国文化的浸染，他认为水彩画宜取低调，不强求水彩的"彩"，而求彩外之彩。就如唐代张彦远所云，"运墨而五色具"，或者"用墨写青山红树"。

因此在这本大多数由赭石为主色绘制的画集中，能够打动我们更多的是那些形外之彩。

在一张描绘牛津大学图书馆的水彩画中，带有穹顶的庞然建筑只是采用整体平涂进行体量界定，寥寥数笔湿润的曲线勾勒出建筑轮廓，而那几块稍带高光的方块则反衬出从图书馆内部透射而出的昏暗灯光。这是一个雨中黄昏，英格兰雨天那种特有的氛围呼之欲出。阴雨霏霏、行人寥寥。

再如维也纳的圣史蒂芬主教堂，高大而精美的教堂主塔本身就已经难以描绘，而尖顶上的五彩覆瓦则更加难以表达。但在他的画面中，这一切的处理是如此驾轻就熟，塔身的下半部以一片混沌而融入城市氛围之中，反衬出上半部在阳光照耀下的奕奕神采，跳动的笔触将哥特建筑复杂而精密的细部表现得活灵活现，但所采用的又不是那种刻板的工笔技法，一幅鲜活多彩的场景被近处建筑的暗部托显出来。

同样，这类举重若轻的绘画风格也可以在维罗纳的古罗马竞技场、夏特尔主教堂精美的门廊等画面中都有所展现。

在他的绘画中，大量给我们呈现出的就是哥特教堂的五色玻璃窗，石雕楼塔的玲珑剔透，以及风吹日晒的丹青剥落。

除了这种写实与写意兼具的画作外，我们从他的绘画中也可以看到，随着旅途见闻的积累，他的思想视角以及绘画方式也在发生着多重的转变。除了在整体画作中所呈现出来的那种古典技艺的深厚功底之外，我们也可以看到时新的现代艺术在他身上所即刻产生的反应。

例如在奥地利萨尔茨堡，他的一些绘画索性已经离开水彩，而采用感觉更为浓烈的色纸和彩铅。大约有十几幅绘画直接以深灰色或深褐色的色纸为底，上面施以彩笔和白粉，极其简略而直接地表现出教堂内部那种昏暗而凝重的氛围，或者夜幕下的古城街道的幽暗灯光。这类场景可以令人接着联想到当时被深埋于经济危机之中，处于二战前夜的那种忧郁的欧洲。

如果我们将他的画作与日记对照起来，也可以共享他在旅途中不断出现的惊喜与发现。怀着经典建筑之旅的出发点，在刚到达英伦或法国时，城堡、教堂、宫殿、博物馆是他观看的主要内容和入画重点。但是随后，尤其是当他进入荷兰、德国、瑞士时，高层办公楼、混凝土教堂、玻璃幕墙商场也逐渐成为绘画题材。

伴随着这一变化，他的绘画风格也越来越洒脱而抽象。例如在莱比锡参观的俄国教堂，教堂多棱体的塔顶与天空多变的云彩一同采用几何化的块形进行表达，从而构成了一种奇异的融合，令人恍惚觉得教堂能够向天空延伸到何处；在威尼斯圣马可广场钟塔一画中，天空的云彩索性变成几条平行的弯曲，穿插于其中的凝重塔身则显得那样的梦幻而神秘。然而就在绘就这些先锋之作的同时，刚刚建成的莱比锡战争纪念塔和威尼斯的圣玛丽亚教堂又是那样的庄重典雅。

我们于此很难分辨出他此时性格中的特征，一个后来被称为"老夫子"的严谨学者，也能够尝试做出先锋前卫之举。其实如果结合日记则不难看到，途中所遇一次次的现代展览经常令他眼界大开，而旅程之前的精心准备也预埋了伏笔，使他一开始就对刚刚萌发的现代建筑充满了憧憬之情，如有可能就会不惜绕道，前往一看究竟，并在文字中不吝赞美之词。而原先计划中的罗马、庞贝、西西里也在随后的旅途中悄然消失，此时能够打动他的已经不完全是经典建筑了。

在旅欧日记中，他不仅对于经典建筑、经典绘画如数家珍，而且对于现代建筑的潮流也洞若观火。例如在巴黎去看玻璃穹顶的大皇宫，在布鲁塞尔参观霍夫曼设计的斯托克莱住宅，在法兰克福偶遇格罗皮乌斯的现代建筑展览……同时也令人颇感惊奇的是，他在沿途参观的班贝格圣海因里希教堂、比肯多夫圣三王教堂、乌尔姆天主教城市教堂，这些在主流建筑史上未曾出现过的建筑即使在今天看来，都是如此的令人感动和震撼。

有了如此之经历,可以使我们不难解释,他在回国后的建筑思想会如此激烈地反对因循守旧,他的建筑作品为什么被建筑界誉为求新派。在他的言辞中,不乏那种对于"蟒袍玉带之下,穿毛呢卷筒外裤和皮鞋的文艺复兴的绅士们"的嘲讽,而针对国人对于西方建筑以及现代潮流的一知半解,他的后半生会奉献给现代建筑之研究。

同时在异国他乡所接受的心灵洗涤,也可以用来解释后来他对于故国文化的那份挚爱之情。就是在这份挚爱之情的促动下,他开始了我国近现代的园林研究。也正是在与旅欧见闻的反衬下,面对当时国内的状况,他会"以至于每入名园,低回唏嘘、忘饥永日",深染于"不胜众芳芜秽,美人迟暮之感"。在随后的50余年间,他对于园林的研究才会坚持不断,勤耕不辍。

于是伴随着这本沉甸甸的画集,我们也附加了一册与画集相映的珍贵的旅行日记,以便为读者提供一种全面而综合的视角,去接触并了解他——中国第一代现代建筑师中最杰出的代表之一,去分享他的一次极具震撼力的心灵之旅。

对于他的画作,我们毋庸赘言,它们自己会默默地叙述着各自的内容。这些从不轻易示人的精美卷幅在1979年第一次出版时就曾震撼过我国的建筑界与美术界。

对于他的旅欧日记,整理出版则颇费周折,因为它们是用极其难以辨识的手写体快速记录下来的。这部日记在2006年出版的《童寯文集》第四卷中曾经全文刊登。但由于当时的时间仓促与能力不足,其中不免存有众多的错漏之处。

此次新编版本不仅针对原稿进行了反复的详细校核,而且也对文中涉及的一些地名与人名进行了着重的勘对,并补充了必要的注释。同时为了使这些文字记述更加形象生动,我们也通过各种渠道为日记添加了一些现实场景照片。

尽管如此,在本次版本中仍然不免存有遗误之处,在此敬请读者不吝指正。

童明
2009年8月于上海

目 录

旅欧日记手稿影印	015
旅欧日记	235
Tour of Europe	333
所绘与所摄	393
童寯年谱	417
童寯的职业认知、自我认同及现代性追求　赖德霖	445
读童寯先生画作有感　金允铨	482

AND PARIS

ALLANZA
ESA
OMBE
DS

LUGANO

MENAGGIO
BELLAGIO

COMO

MONZA

MILAN → TO VENICE

→ TO BOLOGNA

↓ TO GENOA

① LAGO MAGGIORE
② " DI LUGANO
③ " " COMO

LOSANNE
— Coming from ~~Switzerland~~ you can stop at Pallanza, Stresa & Borromee Islands Or if you are coming from LUCERNE you can stop at LUGANO & COMO — FROM MILAN you must

旅欧日记手稿影印

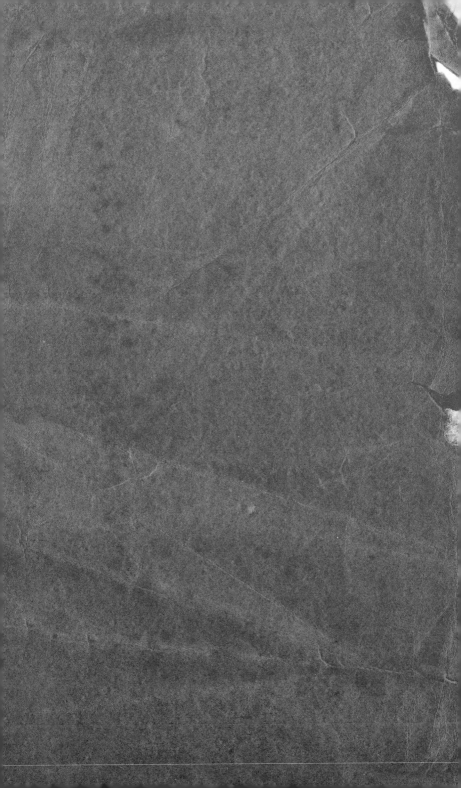

ENGLAND

[1]

- ✓ London
- ✓ Winchester
- ✓ Salisbury
- ✓ Wells
- ✓ Bath
- ✓ Gloucester
- ?{ ~~Hereford~~
- ?{ ~~Worcester~~
- ✓ Broadway
- ✓ ~~Oxford~~
- ? Warwick
- ✓ Stratford on Avon
- ✓ ~~Chester~~
- ✓ Liverpool
- ✓ Edinburgh
- ✓ Durham
- ✓ Lincoln
- ✓ Ely
- ✓ Cambridge
- London — Canterbury.

- ✓ London
- ✓ ~~Canterbury~~
- Ostend
- Malines
- Bruges
- Bruxelles.
- The Hague
- Antwerp
- Rotterdam
- Amsterdam
- Hamburg.
- Bremen
- Copenhagen
- Stockholm
- Berlin

The studio Ltd. 44 Leicester Sq. London W.C.2

GERMANY

- ✓ AMSTERDAM
- BREMEN ?
- HAMBURG   NEW
- LÜNEBURG ?
- LÜBECK   ? TYPICAL
- ✓ BERLIN   WASMUTH VERLAG
- DESSAU   GROPIUS SCHOOL N
- ✓ MAGDEBURG   NEW
- ✓ LEIPZIG   ? NEW · VÖLKERSCHLACHT
-                                     DENKMA
- ✓ DRESDEN   GALLERIE
- NAUMBURG   OLD CHURCH
- ✓ BAMBERG   OLD   1
- ✓ NÜRNBERG
- ✓ WEIMAR   ?
- WARTBURG   ?
- ✓ ROTHENBURG
- ✓ FRANKFURT   NEW
- ✓ STUTTGART   NEW
- ✓ MUNICH   GALLERIE
- ✓ COLONGE [KÖLN]
- ✓ DÜSSELDORF NEW GALLERIE ·
- ✓ HEIDELBERG
- ✓ KOBLENZ
- BADEN-BADEN   HF
- FREIBURG
- COBLEM·STEPHAN.

FRANCE   PARIS   [2]

                              DIJON
—·—·— MAIN LINE   } Bus Stop here
to Bordeaux
   Biarritz   LYON
   Madrid

                                              } change here for
                                                    NIMES   ITALY

           LE PONT DU GARD
                          AVIGNON
              NIMES   TARASCON
                       ARLES   AIX-EN-PROVENCE
                 S⸱T GILLES   CANNES NICE   MONTE CARLO
           AIGUEMORTES
  ASSONNE   MARSEILLE
  RPIGNAN

                    MEDITERRANEAN SEA
AIN

- Stop first at Avignon — there see the palais des Papes and cross the River (Le Rhône) and see "Villeneuve Avignon"
- At Tarascon change trains and go to Nîmes (From there take Busses P.L.M. and go to
  1. Pont du Gard
  2. Arles
  3. St Gilles and Aiguesmortes.
- Carcassonne if you have ti[me] is to be seen as well as Aix en Provence — But they are perhaps out of your i[tinerary]

- Marseille See Cathedral, the Harbour and if you have ½ a day free ta[ke] a boat and go to the small Island in the open sea — called "Le Château d'If" Beautiful a[nd] Romantic place with Arab memories etc. etc. this little trip has been delightful to me ....
- Cannes — Stop there only for few hours

+ Nice: Stop for a couple of days — see la Promenade des Anglais
+ Montecarlo with the Gambling Casino ? ...

Paris –

Museums : – Louvre
- Le Musée Carnavalet
- Le Musée de Cluny
  (see two "Chastity Belts"!)
- Le Petit Palais
- Le Musée du Luxembourg
- Le Musée Rodin
- Le Musée des Invalides
  (Musée de l'Armée et Tombeau de Napoléon)
- École des Beaux-Arts
  (rue Bonaparte 14)
+ Musée et Manifacture des Gobelins
+ Musée Victor Hugo
  (Place des Vosges 6)
+ Musée Grévin (Wax figures)
  (very curious things)

Armenian Theatre, Théâtre Femina.

Buildings. Churches etc.

- ✓ o — Notre Dame (climb the tour - grandious vista)
- ✓ X o — Sainte Chapelle
- o — Palais de Justice et
- + Conciergerie
- ✓ X o — Tour Saint Jacques (outs. only)
- X o — Hôtel de Ville (outs. only)
- ✓ X o — "Saint Séverin" church (near Boul. St. Michel)
- o — Hôtel des Invalides
- ✓ X — Arc de Triomphe
- ✓ (climb on top !!)
- ✓ X — Chambre des Deputés (out's only)
- ✓ o — "Madeleine" church
- ✓ o — "Opera" theatre
- ✓ o — Trocadero (outs. only)
- ✓ o — Tour Eiffel (climb or elevators)
- ✓ o — Pantheon (see underground tombs of great men)
- ✓ — Le Grand Palais &
- o — Le Petit Palais
- ✓ — Le Sacré-Cœur Church (on top of the hill of Montmartre — see it also at night (panorama of Paris!)

nationalities of the world —
- there Kay and I met for
  the first time —
- Ask for "smörbröd" or
  norwegian sandwiches .....

Restaurants — these following Restaurant
are to be avoided because much too
expensive: "Larue", rue Royale
              "Café de Paris", avenue de
                                l'opéra
              "Voisin", rue Cambon
              "Paillard" Chaussée d'Antin
              "Fouquet" Ave. Champs Elys.
              "Foyot", rue de Tournon
- these are excellent:
  ✓ "Prunier", 9 rue Duphot
              famous fish and
              wines
  ✓ "Cazenave", rue Sainte-Anne
  ✓ "Boeuf à la mode" 6, rue de Valois
              (→ one of the oldest Rest. in Paris)
  ✓ "Poccardi" 100 per cent Italian
       food and crowd —
              9, Boulevard des Italiens

  ✗ "Restaurant havenue"
       1, rue du Départ

✗ "La Rotisserie Périgourdine"
   Place St. Michel
  "Le Restaurant on the Roof of
   the "Coupole Café" near
   the Dôme on Boulev. Montpar[nasse]
✗ "Les Vikings" Restaurant
   → rue Vavin
✗ "Le Cheval Pie" Avenue Victor Emm[anuel]
✗ Restaurant "Chiquito"
   → 34, rue du Colisée
   → Décor et clientèle Basque
✗ "La Rotisserie de la Reine Pédoq[ue]"
   → in rue de la Pépinière
   near gare St. Lazare
  "Cazenave" rue Boissy-d'Anglas
✗ "La Grande Chaumière"
   in Boulevard St. Michel Montparnasse
- Other cheaper Restaurants
  all over the city.

• ROUEN
→ to Mont St Michel
ST-GERMAIN
VERSAILLES SEVRES
PARIS
CHANTILLY
• REIM[S]
CHARTRES
• Fontainebleau

BELGIUM.

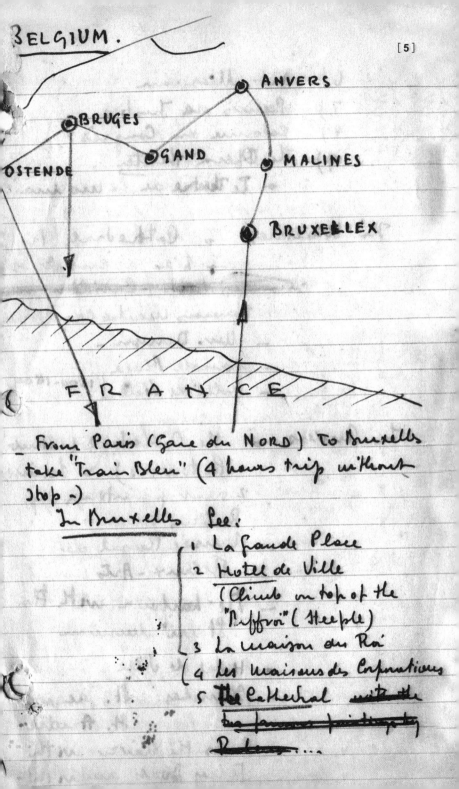

From Paris (Gare du NORD) to Bruxelles take "Train Bleu" (4 hours trip without stop -)

In Bruxelles See:

1. La Grande Place
2. Hôtel de Ville (Climb on top of the "Beffroi" (Steeple))
3. La maison du Roi
4. Les Maisons des Corporations
5. The Cathedral ~~with the~~ ~~its famous paintings by~~ ~~Rubens....~~

6) Art Museum
7) Palais de Justice
8) Colonne du Congrès
9) The Opera Theater
   → Le Theatre de la Monnaie

In Malines → Cathedral (Try
            → hear a concert of
            ~~the bells (Carillon~~
            famous Maître Carillon
   - Mr. Denyn -
   - Grande Place ⎫
   - Hotel de Ville ⎬ (1300-1400

In Anvers → the Cathedral (climb
            the towers) & see in
            2 great paintings by
            Rubens
   - Musée Royal de
     Beaux-Arts
   - The harbour with the
     "Steen" Museum
   - Hotel de Ville
   - Churches ⟨ St. Jacques
              ⟨ St. André
   - Cross the River with
     Ferry Boat and go to

Outside Paris

✓ – "__Versailles__". Take the electric train at the Gare des Invalides. (½ hour fare)

- Visite the __Palais__ of Versailles in the morning and the Parc with the __Grand Trianon__ and the __Petit Trianon__, after lunch in the afternoon.

- (If you are in Paris between May & October don't miss __les grandes eaux de Versailles__ (Playing Fountains in the Park of V. wich take place on the first Sunday of each month and some other special days). –

✓ "__Saint Germain en Laye__" take electric train at the Gare Saint Lazare (30 minutes) Beautiful Park, Terrace dominating Paris and the Seine Valley.

"Fontainebleau" take tra[in]
at the Gare de Lyon
(two hours) or take
special tourist omnibuses.
(see agencies in Place de l'O[péra])

"Chantilly" take a train a[t]
the Gare du Nord (one hou[r])
Half a day is enough for [the]
visite -

"La Malmaison" and Tak[e]
the tramway at the Porte M[aillot]
(from there 1/2 an hour trip)

"Sèvres and Saint-Cloud"
In this little town the[re]
is the famous Porcelain fac[tory]
and museum. (To be visited

"Chartres" Take an early tr[ain]
at the Gare Montparnasse
(1 1/2 hour trip) - Great Cath[edral]

"Reims" (Cathedral and
traumatic war memories
→ Take train at the Gare [de]
l'Est (Three hours trip)
→ the capital of "Champag[ne]"

"Rouen" in Normandy
old, medieval city. Go the[re]
Churches, City Hall etc.
See place where Jeanne d'Ar[c]
was burnt - and Palais de Just[ice]

"Le Mont St Michel" and the trocket [?]
Tours: Orléans, St Malo: Take
a boat trip from St Malo to the Mt
St Michel, visiting Cancale. You can
also arrange a Mont St Michel

"Train a Gare d'Lyon (about 2 h.)
"Les Chateaux de la Loire". A chain
of castles on the banks of the Loire River.
Ask information at the Travel
Agency.

- <u>Sorbonne</u> (rue des Écoles)
  → I lived for two years at the "Grand Hôtel du Globe, 50, rue des Écoles, opposite the Sorbonne and the beautiful "Institut de France" —)
- <u>Odéon</u> - Theatre
    (Classics only)
- <u>Théâtre Français</u> (Drama only)
- <u>Opéra Comique</u> —
✓ - <u>"St. Germain des Prés" Church</u>
  → (Take a drink at the "Café des deux Magots" opposite the Church)
- <u>"St. Julien-le-Pauvre" Church</u>
  → (grandious view of Notre Dame from the little narrow street)
✓ - ✗ <u>"St. Sulpice" Church</u> —
✓ → ✗ <u>"Val de Grâce" Church</u> in rue du Val de Grâce, where Kay and I have lived for several months at the number 8 —
- ✗ <u>"St. Médard" Church</u> —
  → from there walk up the rue Mouffetard on Sunday morning betw. 11 and 12)

Places, Promenades etc.

- ✓ — Place de la Concorde
- ✓ — Jardin des Tuileries
- ✓ — Champs-Élysées
- — Avenue du Bois de Boul[ogne]
  (see it on Sunday morn[ing] and take an old cab with a horse)
- — ~~Bois de Boulogne~~
- x Les Grands Boulevards
- x Les Ponts and les Quais
  (→ Bridges & Banks of the Seine)
- → Walk on the left bank between Notre Dame Ch[urch] and Pont Alexandre)
- Go at night to "Boulevard Montmartre" "Place Pig[alle] and Boulevard Rochechou[art]
- ✓ Jardin du ~~Lux~~embour[g]
- ✓ Parc Monceau
- x — Parc Mont Souris
- x — Cimitière du Père Lacha[ise]
  (→ Fine View – Tombs of Chopin, Molière, De Musset, Balzac, Corot, Sarah Bernhard[t], Delacroix etc.)

- Walk between 6 and 7 p.m. beyond "Notre Dame" Church –
- Left Banks of the Seine
  - Especially Boulevard Montparnasse with the Famous:
    "Café de la Rotonde
    "Café du Dôme
    "La Coupole etc. where artists, Fools and dreamers of the four corners of the World gather – Go there any time but especially at night between 8 o'cl. and 3 o'cl. in the morning)
- "Jardin des Plantes" with beautiful trees and zoological Garden –

Theatres, Casinos, Cafés, Restaurants etc.
  → Read the Newspapers - but
  - don't miss:
    "Le Casino de Paris"
    "Le Palace"
    "Le Moulin Rouge Theatre"
  - Cafés .. "Le Café de la Paix
      in Place de l'Opéra
      → the center of the Globe
    "Le Café and Restaurant
      Viel" on Boulevard de

La Madeleine —
- "Le Café and Restaurant Weber"
  in rue Royale
  → (Perfect french classic food
     Dinner with wine betw.
     1 and 2 $)
- "Le Café Dreher" in Place du
  Châtelet.
  → Excellent music every night
    betw. 8 and 11 ocl.
    Friday night classic music
  - You can have dinner there
    for 1.00 $ during concert.
- "Le Café de la Régence"
  near le Theatre Français
  in Avenue de l'opéra
  → Concert every night. Historic
    and old café, see table where
    Napo[leon] played chess.
  - Many Scandinavian people
    especially girls)
- Many large cafés on the
  Grand Boulevards...
- On Champs-Elysées avenue
  two or three very smart cafés
- On the Left Bank, near
  Café du Dôme, on rue Vavin
- ("Les Vikings" charming and
  crowdy café Norvégien, (many
  Scandinavians, and all the other

Tête de Flandre (lunch with
fresh fish and make a sket[ch]

= Zoological Garden the best
of Europe —

Gand → See:

1) the Church St. Jacques
2) " Cathedral
   (See paintings &
    Van Eyck)
3) Quai aux Herbes
4) Le chateau
      des Fla[ndres]
5) Le chate[au

Bruges → See

1) the Cathedr[al]
   of where there
      Michelange[lo]
2) Hotel Grun[ing]
3) Hôpital S[t
      Musée
4) [?]
5) Be[?]
6) Le [?]
7) Le [?]
8) Le [?]

9) City Hall
10) Coffee House "Vlis..."
where are many memo[ries]
of Rubens and good bie[r]

Ostende — A Summer Resort v[ery]
chic. You will go the[re]
only if it is summ[er]
After 1st. of August th[e]
city is deserted.

...urs.

...e Jaune (yellow)
...Verte (green)

...s
...ie

(...ore the meals)
...th.)

Rossi à l'eau
Martini –
Vermouth Cassis
Cressonnée
Campari Aperitif

"Tipping" in France

Up to 2 frs. give 25%
From 2 to 5 frs.   " 20%
 "   5 " 10 "   " 10%
Never forget to tip in France –
"Le Pourboir" is a Nation

Tipping in Italy –

Tips are officially abol[ished]
pourcentage is alway[s added to]
the bill, for service –
small tip though is [needed]
to make friends...

– Italian "Liquori"
   Liquore St[rega]
   Cordial[e]

– Italian
   × An[isette]
   Ci[nzano]
   Cam[pari]

- Ramazzotti al Seltz (Rather bitter
- Menta al Seltz
- Menta e Anice al Seltz
- Select
- Marsala Florio

"Italian Dishes"

Maccheroni alla Napoletana
Spaghetti   "   "
   "   all' Inglese
Lasagne alla Bolognese
Gnocchi al sugo
...tto alla Milanese
    coi fegatini

        Pavese
        brodo   Salsicce
         "   colle lasagne ...
         alla Milanese
         tartufi alla Bolognese
         ...la Veneziana

            ...mido

                    ...la Verde
                    Bianca
                    e
                    ...ana

P
Parmigiano
Pecorino Vecchio
Emmenthal
Stracchino

Italian Wines
Chianti Ruffino
Nebiolo
Barbera
Grignolino
Colli Romani
Frascati
Soave bianco
Capri
Lacrima Christi
Asti Spumante (like Champagne)
Moscato di Syracuse
Passito Canelli

Italian Specialities

"Cafè Frappè
  (Frosted black Coffee)
"Cafè Expresso (Very strong)
"Zabaglione al Marsala
  (cold or tepid)
  (made with eggs)

Leave N.Y.   May 1st.
England   May 1st to June 1st
           (July in Paris only)
France (Belgium - Holland - Germany -
        Austria, Venice, Switzerland and
        back to Paris)
           June 1st to September 1st
France   from Sept. 1st to Sept. 15th.

Italy   Sept. 15th to December 31th
         Genoa - Milan - Bologna - Florence
         etc.

Greece ; Turkey,
           January 1st to Jan. 15th

Egypt   January 15th to February 15th
                        Bombay
India   Land in Calcutta and cross to
         Bombay - Calcutta
         February 15th to March 1st
China   March 1st to April 1st
                        Home

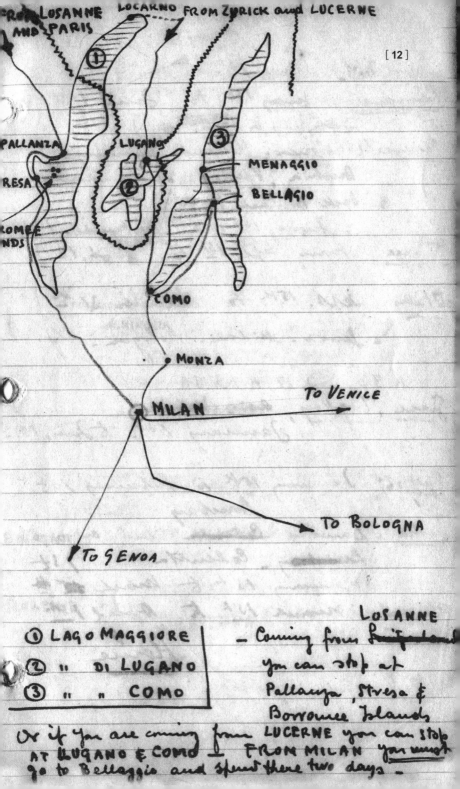

① LAGO MAGGIORE
②   "   DI LUGANO
③   "   " COMO

LOSANNE — Coming from Switzerland you can stop at Pallanza, Stresa & Borromee Islands. Or if you are coming from LUCERNE you can stop at LUGANO & COMO. FROM MILAN you must go to Bellaggio and spend there two days.

[13]

FROM VIENNA

MURANO
MURANO • TORCELLO
VENICE
LIDO
PELLESTRINA
CHIOGGIA

ADRIATIC SEA

BOLOGNA
FLORENCE
RAVENNA

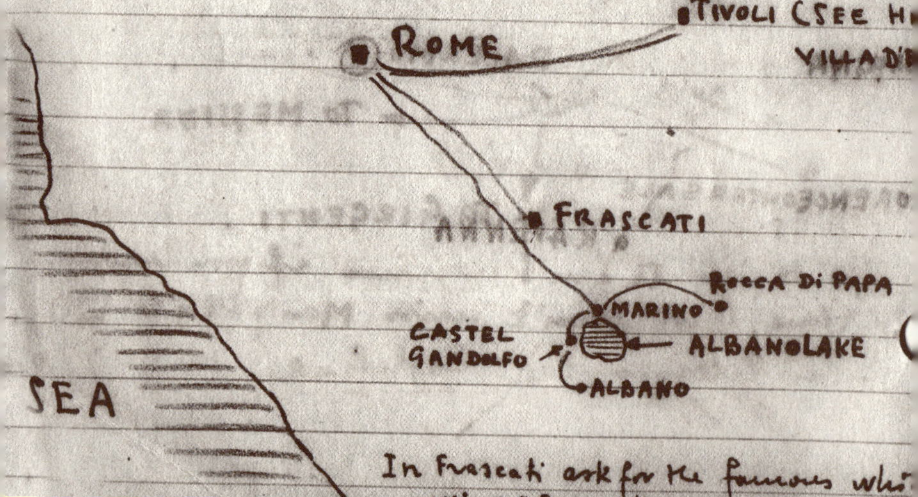

Map 1 (Tuscany/Umbria)

- PISE
- FIESOLE
- FLORENCE
- VALLOMBROSA
- LA VERNA
- AREZZO
- GUBBIO
- SIENA → TO ROME
- TRASIMENO LAKE
- PERUGIA
- ASSISI
- FOLIGNO → TO ROME

SEA

Map 2 (Rome area)

- ROME
- TIVOLI (SEE H... VILLA D'E...)
- FRASCATI
- ROCCA DI PAPA
- MARINO
- CASTEL GANDOLFO
- ALBANO LAKE
- ALBANO

SEA

In Frascati ask for the famous white wine "Frascati" and get drunk. Don't miss any of these places — All wonderful

In Napoli go to visit the popular sector of "Vomero" – Beautiful vista of City, Vesuvio, Golfo, and that classic tree you see in all the pictures of Naples –

[14]

[sketch map showing Naples area with Pozzuoli, Ischia, Sorrento, Capri, Vesuvio, Pompei, Amalfi]

In Napoli take the little railway and climb the Mont Vesuvio –

Take a boat and make this tour:
Sorrento – Capri – Ischia – Pozzuoli, Napoli
In Capri Maxime Gorki is living –

[sketch map showing Mont St. Pellegrino, Palermo, Montereale, From Naples, To Messina, To Girgenti, Tramway]

Go to Monte San Pellegrino if you have time, but don't miss Montereale – In Palermo see Cathedral

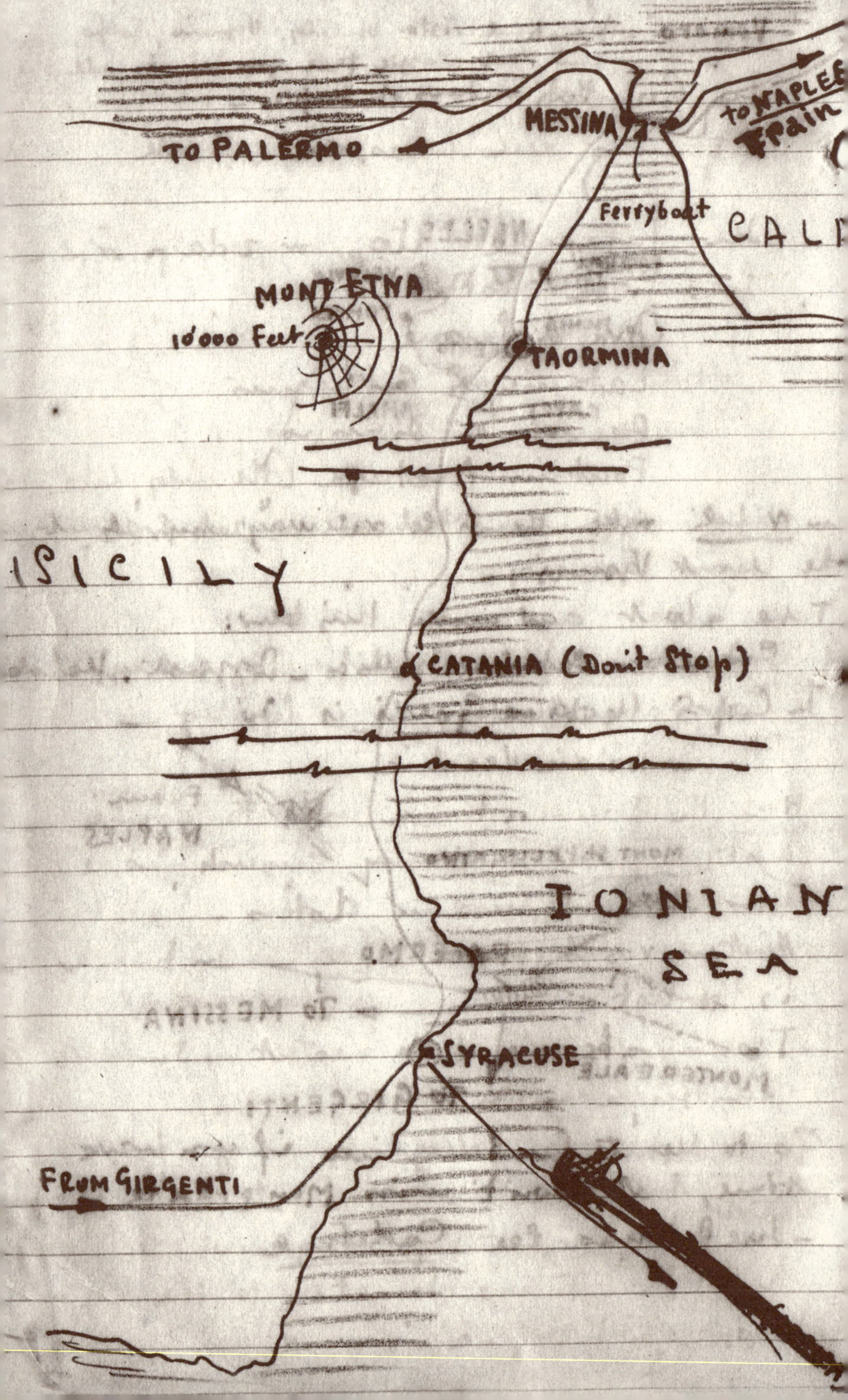

TO PALERMO • MESSINA • to NAPLES Train

Ferryboat

CAL[ABRIA]

MONT ETNA
10,000 Feet

TAORMINA

SICILY

CATANIA (Don't Stop)

IONIAN SEA

SYRACUSE

FROM GIRGENTI

In <u>Girgenti</u> see
  Tempio della Concordia (Greek

In <u>Syracuse</u> stop for 2 days or 3 –
See: Greek theatre
   Ara di Gerone
   Latomia dei Capuccini
   Orecchio di Dionisio
   Fontain Aretusa (the only place
   in Europe where the "papyrus"
   grows)

In <u>Taormina</u> stop for 2 days
See: Greek theatre
   La Badia Vecchia
Here the German Kaiser used to come
before the war – Many English people
now in good modern Hotels –
Winter resort only – In summer
is too hot –
– Taormina has one of the greatest and noblest
   landscape in the world –

When you are in Messina (don't stop
here) take ferryboat, cross the
Strait and go directly to Naples –
The coast of Calabria is poor and
monotonous –

AUSTRIA
KONSTANCE NEAR ~~TO~~ SWITZE
INNSBRUCK
~~SALSBURG~~
HALLEIN ? But nice
~~SCHAFBURG~~
SCHAFBERG
ST. WOLFGANG OLD CHURCH
GESÄUSE (WITH THE SHIP)
FROM MELK – DANUBE DAWN
TO – STEIN – DÜRNSTEIN
THIS PART OF THE
DANUBE IS CALLED
WACHAU –
✓ VIENNA .
SEMMERING ?
BUDAPEST

✓ PRAGUE   NEW FAIR
                BLDG.

BELGIUM
STOCLETHOUS BRUSSEL
BY JOSEF HOFFMANN.

ERNEST PLISCHKE   WIEN III MARXERGASSE 4
         TEL R. 23-7-39

R.S. Morgan et Cie, 14 Place Vendôme
ADPRESS Paris [,17]

L'illustration. 13 Rue Saint Georges Paris
Sacha Guitry — au Théâtre Edouard VII
  comedies —   Yvonne Printemps
  his wife.

— Mr. Ernest Barda
       8, rue du Val de Grâce
              Paris

Moderne Bauformen
    Julius Hoffmann Verlag, Stuttgart

beau coupons Germany Berlin
Wiener Werkstätte, Wien 7,
Döblergasse, 4.

Friedrich Ernst Hübsch verlag
Berlin W 62 maassen St. 3
N.V. Uitgevers-Maatschij "Kosmos"
Amsterdam. (Nieuw-Nederlandsche
Bouwkunst).

Chinesische architekten von
Ernst Boerschmann
Verlag Ernst
Wasmuth   A.G. Berlin.

address

FLORENCE
Pensione Annalena
Via Romana 32

SIENA
MME. EDYTH QUATRESOLES
11 RUE DE MER (MEZZ?)
ST. GERMAIN EN LAYE.
(GARE ST LAZARE)

SIENA
PENSIONE SENESE   PEN 25 L.
VIA CAMOLIA 46   COM 30 L.

ROME
PENSIONE GIULIANO,
VIA PALERMO 36.

PERMITS
FOR POMPEI AND PAESTUM AT NAPLES
VILLAS NEAR ROME AT ROME

PROPERTY OF CHUIN TUNG
34 HO JAN LI, WEST SUBURB
MUKDEN, MANCHURIA
CHINA

[18]

APR. 26	LEFT NEW YORK ON "EUROPA" 12.30 AM.	
27	ATLANTIC OCEAN	
28	"	
29	"	
30	"	" MAN OVERBOARD
MAY 1	LANDING SOUTHAMPTON 3 P.M.	

SOUTHAMPTON — a pleasant town and beautiful country road to Winchester (by Bus). Many pedestrians & cyclists on main road. Houses very picturesque.

WINCHESTER — arrived after 3 and went in to a store. (Cusworth, 16 & 47° High St) where 2 old maids keep business. They let me leave my heavy bag at Gladstone. So went directly to cathedral. First time saw cathedral of such size. Very enthused. Saw Tablet for Jane Austen & an antique black font. The nave etc. is norman. Columns in nave are converted from Norman. Nowhere in the world is quieter than an English cathedral close. Birds sign & grass smell so pleasant by. Made water color of West gate. Saw museum went to see Wolvesey Palace, a Norman keep. It reminds one of the "Old Summer Palace." The stream Itchen quietly flows by.

Had dinner at Goth Begot an old inn. Food not so bad but expensive (6s). Gladstone as heavy as a trunk, and two arms were tired out. Waited long time till 9:50 for train to Salisbury (change at Eastleigh). Arrived at Salisbury at 10:30. Taxi to Old George (2s) and stayed in Rm 14. The George Chamber (17) is a double room where Samuel Pepys used to be. The proprietress is Jane Eyre type. She said there is a room that has plenty of beams but I cured love

a room with just one bean for
G.S.
Sound sleep.

AY 2. — Chambermaid knocked door at
7.30 when I was asleep. After
breakfast went to see Cathedral.
Beautiful interior, colorful
because of black shafts. Good
proportion & homogeneous. Most
beautiful cloister. So peaceful.
and be no sound but birds sing.
Sketched North gate. Saw St.
Thomas church with wood beams
& frescoes. Hall of John Hall
is very fine wood timber front.
Museum closed. Passed St
Anne's gate 3 times. Could
not get into Bishop's Palace.
Saw outside of King's House.
Beautiful gardens & houses
everywhere. Delightful
stream of Avon runs by
the town with arched bridges.
On the road to Sarum one can
see the cathedral at a distance
and the meadows form a
good cushion for the edifice.
* Went to Stonehenge by Taxi

Because the bus company could not find other people going. Costs 16 s. On the way saw Oliver Lodge's house. Not interesting, rather off the road & small.
The Stonehenge looks much smaller than I imagined.
~~Took~~ On way back saw abbey Church (Amesbury), not interesting at all.
Ate lunch & supper (both cold) at same place near St Thomas church.
Took train to Bath at 7:20 arrived 8.40. Stayed at Argyll's opposite station.
Took a stroll on Stall st. Town more Italian Renaiss. than gothic.
More cyclists in England. Half of them are women.
In a small town like this window dressing is quite as good as New York Gimbles. Women are smartly dressed too. Food not so good for its price.

On the mantle piece in my room at Argyll's there is pictures of the P. of W. The duke of York & the duchess and probably an actress

MAY 3. — Breakfast at 8. The best ham & egg (I ever tasted) at the Argyll hotel at Bath. Bus to Wells. Saw Cathedral. Between Bath & Wells nothing on the road is worth looking at. Every house is modern-looking & cheap. Some old houses are not interesting either. English is the best place for gothic. I don't like Bath because it is too classic (Italian) Wells is better — at least the houses around the cathedral are very gothic and picturesque. Saw the dean's, eye the Bishop's eye, the Penniless porch, and Browns gate. The Bishop's palace is not open in the morning of Saturday. I could not stay till 3 P.M. so I had to be satisfied with peeping thru a chink above the gate! The draw-bridge and the moat are just as mediaeval as they ever were. Such a peaceful & beautiful ground, with little children playing, and ducks swimming in water. The Palace ground is strongly fortified with strong walls, with port holes. The Cloister has no open arcades. All the arches are screened with stone tracery. One cypress stands in the middle of the cloister. The Chapel House has a wonderful fan ceiling above the crypt, reached from the cathedral.

The interior of the cathedral is quite horizontal. Saw St. Andrew's cross X under tower. The golden windows too (East End) have such beautiful glass as I ever yet saw. It is a marvelous picture. Wish I could have painted it. Went down to the crypt, saw several stone coffins. It smells earth. Went up through a deep delightful stone stair to Chapel House.

Went up to tower and viewed whole town. Carved my initials & 1930 near the entrance

on lead roof.
door. Also carved initial on wood door. ~~All this~~ top is reached from by a small circular stair case of stone, well lighted with small windows.

The Dining Hall in Vicar's close is very fine, with wonderfully preserved wood work & manuscript. Ceiling is very good, with wood crude tracery & plaster. The pewter pieces were given by ~~Cromwell~~. Cromwell. Saw Chapel House ~~1st + 2~~ at the end of the ~~ct~~ Vicar's Close. Very wonderful wood screen on 1st floor + beautiful ceiling on second floor, reached by a stone staircase worn out in some steps.

The May fair is in Town. Rather noisy near the cathedral. A lively place now. Had lunch near Broad St.

Back to Bath by 4 o'clock. Saw Roman Bath. In the museum there's a model showing the rectangular + circular baths. The great Pump Room has very had Classic style. Had a glass of mineral water. Then bought a ticket (2/5) for a bath in the Queen's. Had a wonderful hot bath in the tub, and after 15 minutes the man came with hot towels + sheet + rap me up first like Emperor Claudius in his toga, then like an Egyptian mummy lying on the bed. Lying for 15 more minutes and then up to get dressed. Sat a while in the cool room.

Before I took the train went through Victoria Park to see the Circus + the Cresent. Both in Renaissance style, but somewhat gothic roofs + chimneys. Almost lost my way back to midland station.

Train for Gloucester. Stayed at midland Royal Hotel. B & B for 8/5. Had ham + eggs for supper.

English tea is abominable yet everybody drinks it, as an institution.

MAY 4 — Breakfast at 8. Saw inside of cathedral at 10. Enormous pink Norman columns in nave. Gothic ceiling. Very finely decorated ceiling in choir. Wonderful window at E end. Sunday service prevented me from going thu the choir & up to the whispering gallery. Also the cloister was closed. Saw procession of clergymen. Some are mere boys clad in red with white collar & a white jacket over it. The top of the tower (supported underneath in crossing by flying arches) has fine tracery like lace. Very ornate in general. Outside S. porch very fine with wooden Norman gates. Some Norman arches are seen outside. Had no idea about cloister until saw photograph.

St. Mary de Lode is not worth seeing.

Several old houses are interesting, like the one in which Bishop Hopper stayed the night before his martyrdom. The new Inn is quite old and I made a good pencil sketch of it, just while it was raining, standing under a store entrance. Made several miles of walking but saw nothing interesting. The plan of the town is like Chinese (Roman), streets & gates are named by the compass. The Royal Hotel is very bad for its price. Food's not good either. 8 s. B.B.

Arrived at B'way by train at 6 P.M.

From the G.W. station to Broadway (The Village) the distance is a mile. And I almost despaired to carry the 50# Gladstone. Had to make many stops before I got to the "Swan" exhausted & perspiring. The "Swan" was filled. So

I had to go to the Lygon-Arms. & what a great pleasant surprise! Such beautiful rooms & everyth'g is clean & so tastefully arranged. It is the best hotel I'd ever saw.

Made a trip through B'way about 2 miles & half long! Saw nothing worth while to photo or to sketch. I think the best is in the Lygon Arms. Had dinner at 7.30 in the great Dining Hall, full of fashionable people. The hall is a master-piece. The hostess in the dining room is a beauty. She reminds me of K's stature only a trifle stouter. She suggested wine and I took cider, very very good, and she poured 'out for me. The dinner is good too, (6/6). Made 2 sketches in Dining Room.

Shown into the Cromwell Room & Charles or

Oak Room (Charles I).
Both are so old and
very charming indeed. Saw
Charles Cromwell sat
in. The Lygon Arms has
a huge back yard for
garage. Had a hot
bath. It is indeed a
pleasure to stay in
such a place, no matter
how much it costs. Because
it is worth it. All my
disgust over long walk
with a heavy bag. and
over the long train of autos
was over, after such
pleasant surprise. The
guide book says many
Americans stay here. I
haven't met one. But
the air here may be American
(The less number of automobiles
& people in street).
There are ones & B'ways
in the woods, and they
are full of Americans!
        Just recalled a
thing I did at Gloucester.

Went to police station to [24] find out whether I needed registration. After 20 minutes they found out if I stay under 2 months I don't have to register. But if over 2 months, it may be necessary.

The man at B'way station smelled liquor. No wonder he took half an hour to find out train schedule for Stratford-on-Avon.

MAY 5 — Did some sketches in the morning. Had breakfast at 9, at the same table as I took my dinner. Left Hotel (bill 1-2-9) Took bus to G.W. station for Stratford on Avon. Arrived at 12 o'clock. Stayed at "White Swan."

Saw Shakespeare's birth place, I was thrilled. Saw Scott's & Carlyle's names on window on 2nd floor (where the poet was born). Took lunch at ~~the~~ Judith Shakespeare's House.

Saw "New place" & a wonderful garden with flowers sent by the King, Queen & the Prince of Wales. Saw old well & foundation of part of old house.

Went to see school in which Shakespeare studied. The beam is like this △. Saw Church of Holy Trinity where Shakespeare was buried near the altar. Then took a long walk to Shottery & had a devil's time in locating Anne Hathaway's cottage. Saw the bed & linen. Also the wood bench by the fire place on which Shakespeare did his courting. Of course Anne's parents sat on either side of the fire. The new memorial building is not up yet. Did not go into the library. Saw Avon.

This is the best place I have yet enjoyed seeing. There are not many things but they are so precious.

Had dinner in the Hotel

and some men dress for meal. Some old Victorian ladies are simply Grotesque.

Saw "Macbeth" tonight and liked the scenery. Lady Macbeth is outshined by her husband. Bed at 12.

The "Red Horse Hotel" is a terrible looking place but Washington Irving stayed there!

MAY 6 — After breakfast tried to take 10 AM Bus to Warwick but there was none. Back to hotel to write. Rainy all day.

Took 11:30 Bus to Warwick. Could not see the town well on account of rain. Just saw the East Gate (on which stands the library) & the outside of the Church of St Mary's. Saw part of the interior of the Castle. Rooms are enormous & beautifully furnished. Many Rubens' & Van Dykes. Walked to Italian Garden, saw a peacock standing in the rain & the Grecian vase in the pavilion.

Feet both soaked.
Could not sketch or take photo.

Went on to Kenilworth, in the bus met a handsome old gentleman who has been in Hanchow. He lives at Kenilworth.

The castle at Kenilworth is in ruins and reminds one much of the old Summer Palace in Peking. As it is rainy there is no splendor falling on the walls. Just took one photo. The great lake as shown on plan (restored) was drained in Cromwell's time. The whole thing must look beautiful in fine weather.

Took "tea" opposite. It is a mile's walk from Kenilworth to the castle. I came back too early & had to sit in the Post Office to wait for bus.

But when I did come

out, still thinking it was early, the bus was already running along. Jumped in all right. Back to that ford on Abonegan. This could have been avoided if I had known, to take a train to
* Oxford right from Warwick. To save time & money —

Had ham & eggs in an inn. First time had coffee, in England. Took 7.45 train to Oxford, arrived at 9.30.

Nothing enrages me more than to carry a 50# baggage for 2 miles & then find the hotel (Mitre) full. Carried the burden still further on & stopped at "East Gate". The place is very gloomy. Rather disappointing.

Feet soaked wet so took a hot bath.

MAY 7 — After breakfast went out seeing different colleges. Saw Dr. Johnson's room first. It is on the 2nd floor near the gate to Pembroke College. A small sitting room with small fire place, and a very little bed room. The upper (3rd) story was added later.

Saw great Tom bell on top of Tower, Christchurch. Most of the colleges have quadrangles have cover'd + lovely. It undoubtedly has the appearance of age. Some students wear gowns, in most cases mere rags. At New College the wall (like Chinese wall) remains, with gate + little meus. Most of the colleges + gothic except Queen's which is classic, and of course the Camere.

Finished sightseeing at 2 P.M. Then made 4 water colors & 4 pencil sketches in the after noon.

Getting myself familiarly with London, hy' an 1898

editor Beadecker.

English food is expensive and not good. The only course they can made well is fish.

MAY 8. Took Train to Windsor after breakfast. Did not arrive till 12. Castle not open but saw some interesting timber horses at the North Terrace, a back of Queens' apartment. also saw interior of Chapel.

Went to Eton, saw old school with old desks & flogging aparato (2 steps). Names carved on all places — panels, desks, even rails?. Saw chapel. In here the uncomfortable & wood benches are called knife boards by the boys. Saw boys in top hats & also in short clothes The dry bobs play cricket, the wet bobs play rowing.

Saw an old house (500 years) called cock pit, at Eton. Took tea there, very good hot rolls with jam. The Queen (Mary) comes there often &

signed her name once (I did not see it) So I signed mine (asked to do so) Went up stairs to see old rooms. Very interesting like Shakespeare's birthplace. There is another one in Canterbury. Behind the house is the pit where people fought cocks till 50 years ago. The floor is paved with pig's knuckles.

Outside the house on the façade there are 2 wood figures corner window. Also on the sidewalk there are those foot lockers made of wood.

Arrived at London Paddington station at 5:30. Took bus to Regent Street but could not get into Regent Palace. Nor could I get into Y.M.C.A. Finally walked to Grafton & got a room B+B 8/s. Took a bath!

saw Tussaud's wax works. But too late to see Chamber of horrors.

Had a very good steak at the hotel.

London is a big place. In those small towns I always walk beyond a place, now in London I never walked far enough to often get near. It is a good place if you take the right bus.

Got films deposited at a Kodak shop on Regent St.

MAY 9 — After breakfast went to the Cook find out about Trans-Siberian Rd. Open & Safe. Went to Regent Street Cones place measured for a black suit £0 8£. Saw outside of St. James Palace, outside of St. Paul, Royal Exchange and Westminster. Tonight again went to Tussaud's place to see Chamber of horrors. But the important

I did today was to see the British Museum, from 1 to 4, and finished seeing it. Bought post cards for Elgin Marbles & some Chinese painting prints. Rather a thrill to see so many precious original things like the oldest paper in the world (Chinese, discovered at Tung huang), autographs of famous men, & sculpture, but not casts. Saw Hyde Park and Epstein's sculpture. Also the artillery monument.

MAY-10. Gray sky but with sunshine in the morning. Then it gradually became cloudy until it started to rain at 5 P.M., till evening. Westminster service at 10. Went to see Parliament. Saw the King's Robing Rm. with carvings (wood) of English artists, and some

dignity is overall. It has the dome & opposite is the fireplace. The Royal Gallery has 2 big paintings, one representing Trafalgar (Nelson's death) & the other Waterloo. I believe it was in this room that King George read his speech before the naval conference.
The House of Lords has beautiful color scheme, — red leathered benches with light streaming through high windows. But the House of Commons looks very drab, plain, & cold. The Lords is about the most colorful room. All these rooms have heroic proportions and very well lighted. Some rooms on account of high windows look very theatrical, with plenty shading & few high lights.
The thing I was interested most in was of course the Poets' corner.

Never suspected Longfellow's bust there. The whole Abbey is just full of busts, tablets and statues. The proportion of the nave is very pleasing because of its great height and length. Beautiful light effect from windows. The cloister has very warm color ceiling & cold tracery facing the court, on account of light. There is another delightful little Italian court yard with fountain, just beyond the cloister. Made a watercolor of the cloister passage.

Saw these two buildings in 2½ hours.

Took a photo of upstairs statue at the Underground head office.

Took bus to Windsor. Entered the Castle at quarter to 3. Saw the state apartments. Most of the rooms are used for the entertainment of state visitors. Every room is beautiful & tasteful beyond. Mere photographs don't give the color effect. Those high ceilings, and tall doors — and every door opens to an enchanting world. The Rubens room & Van Dyke room. For a room has several Holbeins. The arrangement of pictures & furniture is perfect. 3 painters ceiling — same subject (The book of Esther) other rooms have beautiful panelled ceilings. So most of the furniture is French and some rooms are Louis 15. The banquet hall is enormous, and it must be a colorful affair during a state dinner, when serving persons stand in their places as guards. There is

There are too many visitors and one woman just to

show her wonderful sense of touch, felt the blue velvet chair cushion with her glove on.

Went up to the round tower & saw whole Windsor.

Went into the Queen's doll House. But it is entirely unnecessary to go into — merely wasting time.

The best way to see the House of Parliament, Westminster abbey & Windsor is on Saturday like the way I did today.

First time at supper at Lyons today — for 11 P.

Took bus 18 to Holborn to see old houses. In the bus a baby girl "pipied" and the conductor had to stop the car to borrow some sand from the road builder to cover it up. Made a sketch of the old houses. Then went to see old curiosity shop — 14 Portsmouth St.

Walked along Fleet St., in the rain, and there saw the Temple. Also walked around Lincoln's Inn & Park. But never could locate the actual building of Lincoln's Inn.

On my way back to the hotel stopped at a night fair near Euston road — in the slum — and bought 2 oranges for 3 D.

MAY–11. Saw Tower Bridge and outside of London Tower.

The National Gallery contains a good collection of Italian masters. The Dutch Flemish, French School are fairly represented. Spanish is scanty. German not many. British School of course is richly collected. The portrait Gallery is not worth seeing.

The Tate Gallery is very good. The arrangement of sculpture & paintings in one big hall, with tasteful wall paper, is very effective. Usually you see a vista of doors. You

and the plan is such that you would see everything. The largest collection of Turner + Sargeant I ever saw. Downstairs there is an exhibition of Jugoslav art. Bought a photo of a sculpture. Made a sketch of Tower Bridge + Westminster at dusk.

MAY-12. Made a sketch of the "Old Curiosity Shop." Went in to see the shop. Some two busful of tourists came by, stopped for a second and never came down to see the inside. Really there is nothing inside except cheap but expensive souvenirs. The neighboring shop is a tailor's. Saw interior of St. Pauls. In the crypt there are the tombs of Nelson + Wellington. Then went up to the Whispering gallery. Also went up to the very top by circuitous stairs + ladder.

From the Golden hall through a hole on the floor one can see the ground floor of the Chambers with mosaic clearly shown. Of course from the top (over 300 ft) one can see whole London, in a very dreamy character. One has to get permission to sketch from Dean Clupl(?). The cost is 2/6. I made only one sketch of the side aisle.

Went to see the London Tower. The Bloody Tower is where many murders were done. Where Raleigh was imprisoned and married, where Richard III murdered the 2 princes whose bodies were found at the foot of the stone winding stair. Upstairs is their chamber, with window (through which moon beam was said to have streamed in) was blocked. So was the door though which the assassin entered. The walls are full of inscriptions & carvings, all of which are so artistic.

The Beauchamp Tower is a small prison chamber with prisoners' names on walls.

The White Tower is the London Tower proper, now full of armors. The chapel upstairs is a good & simple place, in Norman style. The Jewel Tower has all the crowns & staffs.

They are day drilling army now on the Tower ground.

Had lunch at the Tower waiting room.

Took subway to Hammersmith & then took Train #67 to Hampton Court. The Train gets there in one good hour.

The State apartments are much inferior to

(The a...
ang...

W ri...
cas...
s th...
have...
gard...
exqu... ...e. Th
did no shine much but
it did shine the effect
is very grand. Lost in
the maze for several times
got into the centre & came
out successfully at last.
It helps me to know
the definition — a maze
you can be lost in,
But a labyrinth you
go into & come out again,
without mistake or
difficulty. The wine
cellar & kitchen are not
worth seeing.

Saw Shaw's "Apple Cart"
tonight at Queen's. The
King is not as good as Tom
Powers in New York, nor
Orinthia. But the Prime
Minister is better.

scene, and
I can

has

Pam... ...hope.
-15. Cambridge at 5 p.m. A town
not so picturesque as Oxford.
But the River Cam runs
along the colleges and with
picturesque bridges thrown
across makes an interesting
scenery. What a blessing to
those Cambridge students
who can just lie on the grassy
banks and talk about the
stars!

There are many colleges
at Cambridge, some having the
same name as Oxford. The
plans of the schools are alike
too — the cloister plan —
with a chapel attached.
Most of the colleges are Wren.
There is more Renaissance
than gothic, like Oxford.

Stayed at Garden House Hotel
near the water with a large

garden, facing which
the sitting room stands.
A good dinner too. Have
a small single room,
(and a—) facing a
grassy meadow, with a
murmuring stream.

MAY 16. — Row-boat before breakfast
Saw various colleges after
breakfast and the Museum,
which contains Raphael's 7
cartoons and Augustus John's
portraits of Hardy & Shaw.
  Cambridge is much quieter
than Oxford. and the students
have a better chance of studying
nature — stream & meadow
It's an ideal university-
town.
  Saw several chinese students
there. At early in afternoon, a
  Got to Lin who rather late
went up hill to see the cathed.
But before the train reached
station a fine view (mist-
like a dream castle) of the
cathedral can be obtained.
The cathedral stands on

the hill, which make ~~together~~
it ~~more~~ wonderful.
Stayed at an old and
dirty place. gas light
& hot water bottle in bed.
~~MAY 17.~~ Before ~~breakfast went
out to see the man wall~~
Saw the ~~cathedral, which
has a~~ going to Lincoln stopped at ~~York~~ Ely between 1
& 6. to see the cathedral
the cathedral has a
juny lantern at crossing,
sort of a gothic dome.
The interior is mostly
Norman. Made a sepia
rending of Nave. Nothing else
can be of interest at
Ely.
MAY 17. – A very fine morning. Saw
the Roman Arch, after breakfast
visited the Castle, which
has only a gate and wall
(The other buildings don't
look castle-like.)
The cathedral has nothing
distinguishing. We climbed up
the tower. The close is too

small. Only a narrow road divides the cathedral and the houses. The central tower is being repaired.

Saw the Jewish house and some other local things of little interest. Shop windows even display modern furniture

Arrived at York at 2 P.M. Walked outside the wall till I reached the Castle, which has only the Clifton Tower open.

The cathedral of York is the best of all. The spaces have the wonderful glass and the lofty ceiling (though painted wood). The chapter house has no central column and the glass is beautiful. Climbed up tower again, and carved B.M., K, M, + C.T. at the battlement opening ~~was~~ marked below.

*———— entrance to roof

The "five sisters" window are the best I have seen. The whole church is good. Outside towers are beautiful too.

Roman city walls are there in perfect condition. I walked part of it. Sketched gates. St Mary's Abbey is picturesque. The museum there is not good. Shambles is a very picturesque lane, with butcher shops on each side. It started to rain in the evening. Made a water color in the rain. Made 7 sketches today.

Arrived at Durham at 6 P.M., saw the cathedral on the hill.

No train is going to Edinburgh tomorrow till 11 at night. So I have to go by bus.

MAY 18: Visited the Durham cathedral. Very good towers outside. Most of the windows are Norman. The interior is almost entirely Norman, with massive pillars & barrel vaults. The church is well heated. Did not try to see the Chapter House & Monk's Kitchen.

Saw the old city wall near water gate.

It is very imposing the way the cathedral and the castle stand on the hill.

The castle is closed on Sunday. It is a students' dormitory.

Went to Edinburgh by bus. The castle standing on the hill appeals to anyone's imagination. Some houses on near High Street are 10 or 11 stories high.

Princes street is very imposing.

The monument of Scott, in Gothic, is not good.

MAY-19. The Edinburgh castle looked from distance, is poetic; that is highly imaginative. But after you get up there and look down, there is no dream or romance at all. A man that is worshipped must be worshipped at a distance and there is no hero in any household.

The War Memorial is new. The other towers are of little interest. The whole castle stands on a solid rock, with one side sloping and other three going straight down to lower level.

Nothing is of particular interest at St. Giles and the Parliament. The University is a cold classic structure, with a square court, and looks dirty & old. The Palace is not open. The Scots' memorial is not worth climbing up.

Did much walking but little sketching. Nearly ½ to ½ hip. Took night "Scotsman" back to London.

MAY-20 — Can't buy in evening, too late to see ships.

MAY-21, Went to see cathedral early morning. The outside is good but ordinary, with apse. But the inside is wonderful, especially the ceiling over the crossing, made by fans springing up from pillars, & so cleverly decorated with red & blue sharply used that the whole effect looks very modern in spirit. The glasses are very colorful — every In fact the whole thing has no fault to be found. Nothing unusual in the cloister. The nave is long enough but the choir is equally long, so the cathedral is cut into halves at the choir screen. The plan is almost like 3 crosses +++ counting the chapels at the apsidal end. cf.

Augustine's stone chair stands at the apse.

The west gate is interesting, so are the other gates outside the cathedral. Could have stayed at this place longer to make more sketch. The streets are much less commercial and houses are very picturesque. The Baker's Temperance is cheap & very good.

The boat crossing the channel is small & I was almost seasick. Train from Calais to Paris is fine. The first words I spoke were at the Gard du Nord, asking for baggage.

Paris is just another city but I think the wide avenue of Champs Elysées & other public monuments save it. If it does not have anything else, it should have some beautiful women.

MAY. 22.

MAY 23. Museum Cluny, full of old junk. Did not miss 2 chastity belts.

Museum carnavalet is full of junk, some models of old Paris is interesting.

The most interesting of all is Notre Dame. No English cathedrals can hold candle with it. The very mistic interior with beautiful glass gives you worlds of thrill. Much far the best I ever saw.

Saint chapelle has as rich and wonderful interior, with beautiful glass. It is just a little gem. Gold & red & blue, pieced together by light. ⊕ The first floor is not good.

MAY. 24. Sacré coeur stands high on a hill at Montmartre. It takes labor to climb. Built entirely of white granite. The interior is not wonderful, it is too bright.

It took one hour to get to the top of Tour Eiffel and come down again. The service is slow. But when you do get on top you get a marvelous view of Paris. Everything can be clearly read, especially the garden plots, just like a grand pied de Rome. You see whole Paris like a basket of flowers. The buildings look very fresh & clean, the river Seine gives a green color, with white bridges thrown across so many times.

Tombeau de Napoleon has a beautiful interior, especially at the altar where there are [...] glass windows which [...] in garden [...] onto green marble shaft. Very wonderful. Went down to see Napoleon's tomb.

Rodin museum has a delightful garden (where

the Thinker's) and a chapel.
It has some casts too.
    The Grand Palais has a salon
of 1930 and the exposition of
decorative arts. Very good
modern interiors. Saw salon
of painting & sculpture. Took
Munch for 3 hours.
    The interior of Madeleine is
very misté, as the whole church
is lighted by 3 little
lights from the 3 domes
domed ceiling. The best
classic interior of a
Church I have seen, with
the exception of St Paul
at London.

MAY 25.
    The Louvre has so much
but I have passed thru most
of it and the only pts of interest
are Mona Lisa, Venus de
Milo and the Winged Victory.
    Luxenburg Museum has
Baudelaire's archer.
    Versailles is not a good
place for rainy day, as the

garden has no walks and
trees don't shelter very
much. After seeing the
interior (starting from
gare Invalides trolly)
we walked in the woods
to find Les Trianons. Found
both my feet wet.
very disgusting afternoon.

MAY 26. — Went to see Chartres.
It has beautiful glasses
but the effect is rather
monotone. It does
not have the picturesque
quality & mystic character
of Notre Dame. But every-
body likes Chartres. I
prefer Notre Dame. Saw
the small town by walking.
Only spent 3 hours there.

MAY 29. Saw church St. Etienne
du Mont. It has scrolled
facade and interesting interior
with circular stairs going up
columns, to balcony around
ambulatory (inner) &
across from front also

between choir & nave.
   Pantheon has tombs of Zola, Rousseau, Voltaire in the crypt. On the 1st floor the murals are very good. Mounted to top (dome).
   Rue Mallet Stevens is a new development on the border of Paris. First time saw modern esterии. It has light colors somewhere. Quite interesting.

MAY-28. Up at 6 to catch 7:17 train at gare St Lazare for Rouen. Got to cathedral at 10. The "Butter tower" is very good indeed. But central tower with iron spire is bad. The interior is common as any English cathedral. Saw St. Maclou. Wood-carved doors are beautiful. Also saw St. Ouen, which has a good tower like the "Butter Tower". Both are very good. Saw tower of Joan d'arc.
   Took noon time train from gare de nord to Amiens. Arrived there at 4:30.

saw cathedral at once and
made a sketch of interior.
Also sketched outside. The
cathedral has the most beautiful
facade I ever saw. The
3 door portals have deep
reveal. But inside the
height of ~~church~~ nave which
~~don't~~ deserve a much longer
nave. Made a tour
through an ambulatory &
saw the weeping angel.
Made a tour thru town
in evng. Stayed at "Select"
on Place René Gohlet.
Very reasonable & clean
place.

MAY-29. Took 9 o'clock train to
Reims, got there by 12. Took
lunch and saw cathedral by
1 o'clock. The most wonderful
facade I have ever seen.
It's a gem, Save what
like Amiens but facade
has more color and very
much softened and aged
and broken just the

picturesque enough. The inside
is still being repaired. All the
fine glasses are gone except
central Rose above entrance
on facade side. The choir now
is temporary at the end of nave.
The ambulatory is walled off
for repairs.
  I liked the facade so much
that I went back to it
4 times to look at it, &
worship its beauty. Combine
the interior of Notre Dame
with the exterior of Reims
and you have the best
cathedral in the world.
  Saw new battle monument
very good.
  Reims cathedral has one
advantage I know and that
is, its facade is facing a
fairly wide avenue, where
you can see it from afar.
  Back to Paris evening.
MAY 30. Saw museum Guvien, just
like London wax works.
  Mounted on tower of Notre Dame
in rain. Saw all the grotesque

Looked at the Rose window
inside again. They are
wonderful.

Went to see Theatre Pigalle
tonight. Wonderful interiors.
The facade is (not good)
The inside (Theatre proper)
has a red-black-silver
scheme. Ceiling was white
plaster, slightly painted &
moulded. Red chairs
with silver piped bars.
Balconies all painted wood
painted dark red. The foyer
and Hall are very german.
On the Basement there are
shops & dummy showwindows.
and a modern picture gallery.
In the Vestibule (Ticket place)
there is a model of interior
with seats numbered, so
a patron can see where
he is going to sit.

MAY-31 Went to Gard du Nord took
9.40 train for Bruxelles but
the so-called expressed which
stopped at every place never
got there until 4 o'clock with.

afternoon. The Belgium customs are liberal but they demanded visa and I had none. The gendarme finally asked for 30 F for a piece of paper which is called visa.

Explored Bruxelles a little. Saw Palais du Justice, but did not see the Royal palace which must be hidden in the woods. Tried to find Stocletthaus designed by Josef Hoffman but nobody knew where it is.

Took 5-47 train for Bruges. Ate a banana & 2 cakes for lunch and 3 bananas, one orange and 3 cakes for supper. Hungry at 10 so drank cup of Oxo and ate another cake.

Stayed at Hotel Hubert, 25 F for room. Wonderful.
Walked around the canals. Saw many interesting Houses.
Saw cathedral, ouset of Brick, a very complicated tower. Inside most of stone work is painted. Rather interesting. Many paintings. Some hung right

over gothic moulds or tracery. Another instance of painted stone is the ambulatory of Reims, which is being repaired and still closed to public.

Most of the gables are stepped. Saw several men & women wear wooden shoes. A day without any sketching.

JUNE 1. The Belgians are up early on Sunday. Tramways and autos work before 7. Postman distributes letters at 7 A.M., so are some shops & cafés open. You hear hard soles beat on the pavement.

It kept raining all morning. So sat in a café and made a water color of Bell tower, also 2 pencil sketches of square. Order munich beer but only drank half glass as rain did not stop went on the canal to sketch a bridge & then the Ponte de canal, in front of which is the a steel bridge pivoted at mid stream. Dn Lunched at hotel for 20 F. Good food. ~~Ate~~ ~~~~ 1 o'clock.

Took ~~the~~ train for Bruxelles, arrived there at 9:30. Went by bus to Station Midi to take bagage to Nord. Took 3-42 train to Antwerp, arrived there by 4:30. Stayed at Hotel des Flandres. 50 F for a double room. The town is crowed with visit~~ors~~, as the expositn's on.

Went by trolly to Expositn. Of course everythg's modern, and very good in execusn. It far excells the Philadelphia Sesqui-centennial, both in design and workmanship. And the groud & number of bldgs are much larger than Phila. I arrived there by 6, and all bldgs are closed. So have to go there tomorr. to see inside.

Made a sketch of Hotel de ville and cathedral. ~~&~~ The river is full of steamboats. Just saw one sailg yacht. Did not see any sailg fishg boats at all.

Dinner at hotel is expensive.
40 Fr.

JUNE 2. up at 7 out. Beautiful
morning but could not find any
subject to sketch. Just
walked around. Finally
did the cathedral spire
again. (one last night).
Had 4 cakes + chocolat
for breakfast at 9.30

went to Exposition again
at 10. France Building is open.
Some modern interior and
fashion shows. other buildings
are not worth looking in;
mostly machine products
and wavine. The Flemish
art Building is not yet
open. Walked on the ground
& took photos.

ate 4 cakes + chocolat
again for lunch near
station, after seeing the
american pavilion and
having made a sketch of the
Soviet (very modernistic)
Took 2.10 train for Rotterdam
arrived at ...

Rotterdam is a bigger city than I imagined. city has wide streets but no place is picturesque enough to sketch. Along the canals stand matter-of-fact houses, and no sailing or fishing boats, all steamers (detestable). Finally after walking a long way to look for hotels I chanced to see a windmill standing right in the street! Made a sketch of it and had a large audience. Walked too long & lost my way – By sheer luck found my way back near station. Ate dinner in a restaurant on the boulevard for 2 g. (80¢) then walked to Hotel Europe very good place & cheap b & b for 3.50.g.

Did not see much modern architecture either. Saw a modern theatre & went there to see a movie tonight. The way a story about London crooks. The theatre is nice. ceiling has long parallel lights & curved lights with red & blue dull lights which shine by turns.

JUNE 3. Spent too much time at Rotterdam and saw nothing there. I should have come here (Amsterdam) last night, so as to have whole day here. But instead took train from Rotterdam at 9:30 and got here by 11, stayed at Hotel De Bijenkorf, B & B for 3 guilden. Had lunch in their restaurant & the portions are enormous. Dutch cook makes good soup. Bought 3 modern books here at Kosmos.

Between Rotterdam and Amsterdam there are many modern buildings & windmills. Everywhere one is struck with the flatness of the country. A typical country sight would be:

An avenue of slender trees and a windmill.

Saw real old Dutch towns & villages, with costumed people and narrow streets of 3 feet wide. The places are: from Amsterdam to Tolhus by boat, then steam train to Edam, Volendam, steam boat to Island Marken, again steam boat to Broek (where cheese is made). First time in my life sketched sail-boats at Volendam — a thrill. Men wear ear rings and small boys under 5 are dressed like girls, with the mark of a star on the top of the cap. People wear sabots (wood) and leave them outside the door. Women wear lace caps and generally blue dress with a light colored apron. The scenery is very picturesque.

Saw many new buildings to in south suburb of Amster-

dam, Everyone is good.
Brick work is exquisite.
All wood doors are well
designed. A wooden church
but could not see interior.
Even the post boxes on
the street are modern
in design.
    Bought 2 handkerchiefs
at Marken. In Marken
there is a village of six houses.
    Caught a glimpse of office
life at Amsterdam while
in "Kosmos". There are 2
executives & 3 girls (typists)
They all have lunch in
the office, about 12 o'clock.
    In Amsterdam almost every
house has a pulley over the dormer
for lifting furniture.
JUNE - 4. Took 7.33 train for
Cologne, arrived at 12. Walked
along some busy streets and
made a sketch of the bridge.
Saw Cathedral as soon as I
got off station
JUNE - 5. Went up to Church tower. Saw
some modern exposition remains

across the Rhine.

The cathedral of Cologne is the one finished Gothic church. It is quite high and scale looks forced. There is no high choir screen to hide view. Only one window has old glass, the one directly behind the choir.

The silouette of Cologne along the Rhine at night is something marvelous, though the outline is harsh. Very black silouette with light sky & white band of water below. It is very romantic.

JUNE – 6. Trip to Düsseldorf. It has modern buildings before the war. Saw a tall office building (Wilm Marks House) & went up tower. It has a lobby of brick, with run-up elevator cabs. The tower gives view of city — Rhine Ruhr works.

Went to Exposition, too grand. Saw Prof. Kreis. Planatorium and art

galleries. The Planatorium
was not open today.
Saw the galleries with
recent collections; not
much of interest.
   Düsseldorf is a city
worth seeing, as it has
some of the best modern
buildings in Europe.

JUNE -7. Took photos at old exposition
ground and then went to see
Stadt und Land ausstellungen.
The exposition contains a large
number of photos of modern
architecture in the districts around
Cologne, like Kalkfeld, Bickdorf and Zollstuck; most of
the photo's are very good;
so also is the architecture.
This induces me to go to
Bickendorf and sees most
of the architecture with my
own eyes. Took a large
amount of photos too.
   Took trolley to Kalk
but did not see anything
striking there. Walked
from bridge to universität

and Hindenburg Park. Rode back to see Rathaus.

While at the old exposition grounds this morning went into the copper church. The inside is all steel & glass with wooden pews. The stain glass is good. concrete roof. behind the altar is the crucifixion with Christ in plate copper. The pulpit stands right in front of the crucifixion.

Also saw a wooden church at Birkendorf. The outside is concrete, with pointed ~~arcs~~ arches & a tower. Interior is plaster and red brick bands. Very ~~bright~~. The chancel has a niche with a cross hung on it, while the white wall is flooded ~~with~~ colored light thru stained glass. The effect is wonderful. There are small chapels on each side of the chancel & confessions

booths. At the back is
balcony.
JUNE. 8. Arrived at Bonn from
Cologne at 9. Saw Beethoven
House, museum and attic
where Beethoven was born —
low ceiling (beamed) and
old floor. Museum contains
Beethoven's letters & manuscripts
violins and his ear trumpets
numerous portraits and
busts. One second to
Stratford on Avon in its
inspiring atmosphere. The
courtyard is nice and
has Beethoven's statue
but photos & sketch were
are forbidden.

Saw Bonn University.
and took trolly ride through
Coblenz Strasse. Walked
back on bank of Rhine.
Had lunch and then saw
Münster. The inside is
very colorful & mystic.
Beautiful cloister, where
I made a sketch. also
sketched Beethoven's House

outside.
  Took boat from Bonn to Koblenz. The most beautiful ride I knew. The scenery on the banks is superb, especially when the moon rises and distant spires and castle walls are in dreamy colors. The moon ~~so~~ casts its reflection on water. A sail boat or two. Purple clouds, blue mountains, black trees, orange water. Saw the Seven mountains in detail in the afternoon. Never saw such perfect composition of scenes before. Saw many places when I wish I could ~~sketch~~ stop and sketch.

JUNE 9. Up at 8. Breakfast at 9. Out to see Kaiser Wilhelm's monument, which stands at the corner of the delta where Mosel meets Rhine. There you see different colored water, Mosel being bluish while Rhine is yellow. The monument is very baroque and the details ugly, but it commands such a fine position and it looks beautiful in silouette at night and from the air in day time.

The Kastor Kirche is an ordinary Romanesque bldg. A long walk along Mosel leads to the head of the bridge, where there are some interesting old houses to sketch. Also there stands an old timber house at the intersection of Lohr str. and altor glaken str. The timber has its surface chopped to give texture.

The Schloss is ordinary and the museum (including state apartments) are not worth seeing much.

There is a new modern apartment near the Haupt Bahnhof.

Today is a general holiday and all shops are

closed

Left for Mainz at 9:40 by boat. This ride is even more wonderful than yesterday's, as castle after castle rises above hilltops as you sail on. Everyone is a picturesque masterpiece. It brings you back right to the legendary period.

1st castle to be seen is Marksburg, the most sketchable thing I ever saw.

Then the twin twin castles or "2 Brothers" Sternenberg and Liebenstein; also the "Maus" & Reidenberg.

The Loreley rock is not picturesque but is historically rich.

The "Caub" is the most picturesque house standing on the water.

After the Caub there are many more ruined

castles but not so favorably placed. It is because one has seen the best that one does not care after "Cauli." Then the banks become suddenly flat and you see woods & country homes all along. The picturesque middle ages are no more. The moon, though present, stands far low on horizon and does not hang over any old ruins.
Arrived at Mainz at 8.45. made a trip in town. Saw outside of cathedral.

JUNE 10. Saw cathedral. very simple inside. made a sketch of outside & market, today being market day.

Sketched Holz-pfla tower and then Eisener, a square stone tower (13TH century).

Also sketched St. Quintin.

saw the outside of St. Stephen, the Palace and the Library.

But the best thing is a walk on the bridge, with the moon hanging over the Rhine, the reflection in the water being a long line of golden sparks.

JUNE 11. — Sketches door to Palace and saw Gutenberg Museum, which has photo-stats of pages dating middle of 15 century. Also modern printing in the show room.

Took train to Frankfurt noon time.

Frankfurt is a large town, with suburbs full of modern buildings. Saw Goethe's house. His living room, study and dining room. Took a picture at Goethe's desk.

Saw old market place.

On way to Worbing there
is a large section of
modern buildings.
    Went to Worbing to
hear music (Beethoven's
9th). The chorus consists
of local men + women
simple + intense in nature.
JUNE 12. Made sketches
around old market place.
Every step new
subjects to sketch.
    In Evening walked towards
University.
JUNE 13.
    Saw new Stadium. A large
place in the woods. But the
architecture of the stadium
is very bad.
    Went to see St Boniface
Church at Holbein St.
(car 19). Brick outside
very nice and colorful,
dramatic interior. Made
a sketch of it. The nave
is vaulted, choir has
vaulting higher. It is
concrete but painted blue

in nave & yellow in choir, and crimson steps & altar. Very nice effect indeed.

Went to see Conrad Hannisch school outside town (car 18). Brick bldg with a clock at corner on 2nd story, with white ~~po toto~~ tile ~~as~~ in blocks as numerals, white hands.

Next ~~for~~ is the church on a hill, white concrete exterior. Inside has not good pro~~porti~~this. On the ~~bala~~ balcony stands a spiral staircase painted ~~that~~ looks like Russian constructivist stage setting.

On way back saw grossmarkt halle. Very good modern bldg.

Made a sketch of the ~~stair~~ hall in the court of Römer. Then went ~~to see~~ Frauenfriedenkirche at 79 Zeppelin str. (car 4). Both interior & exterior are good. Outside made of concrete slabs with 3 deep & tall arches in the centre arch is a mosaic relief figure of the Virgin. On each side arch it is mosaic (blue & gold mostly) wall. This Church has 2 chapels that are effective. The stain glasses are very good in throwing light on white stucco walls & solo pieces.

JUNE 14. Went to Frankfurter Kunstverein, an exhibition of modern architecture (mostly factory bldgs) by Walter Gropius.

Saw Kunst Kunstgewerbe museum, it has a good collection. In the Chinese section there is a Han mirror about 4½" diameter, broken through the middle. It is perfectly cleaned, and the first Han mirror I ever saw. There did not seem to be one in the British museum, with all the cleaver ability of the Englishmen to rob us.

There is a small collection of modern art, mostly

commonplace. The room has old wood panels very good color.

Saw Römer, Kaisersaal. Wonderful color. The plan is not a perfect rectangle, the wall facing the square being slant; therefore you have an irregular barrelvault end. But it is hardly noticable be caus the room is big. The floor is polished inlaid wood & is in perfect condition. The whole effect is so colorful like and rich. The rooms Kürfursten zimmer and Bürgersaal are also well kept & colorful. Visitors have to put on felt shoes before they go in.

Saw inside of "Dom". Very colorful & mystic. The glases are bad.

Took car 25 from Schauspielhaus to Hamburg, then to Saalburg, to see the Roman remain. The Kastel was

is entirely a reconstruction.
German restoration looks
hard + awkward. There
is no feeling whatever. Saw
the museum, in which there
are many leather shoes.
 From the Die Saalburg
I went out in search of
Hery berg but got lost in the
woods. Walked for half
an hour and finally came
back to the Saalburg.
again went out from the
mortuary to look for
the round tower called
Fröhlichenmans Kopf.
again could not see
anything after walking for
half an hour. So there
one whole day was wasted.
So saw the Mithraum and
took a drink of the cool
spring water.
 Took tramway back to
Homburg (at 4.) and then
to Frankfurt, but got
off at Dornbush to see
a modern school and

some modern apartments.
Made a sketch there.

Saw opera house in
evening, an exact miniature
of the Paris opera.

JUNE-15.

Saw Städel Museum. Not
much to admire. It has one
Millet and several good
Degas though. One Van Gogh.
and other modern stuff.
Saw museum of sculpture.
It has a Chinese section.
Also china Institut. 中国学院
Could not get in.

Left for Darmstadt.
Saw Marriage Tower. Fine
building and 2 good fountains
also a Russian church.
Went on top of tower.
Darmstadt has some old
houses in slum condition.

Got to Heidelberg in
evening. Took double room
with K.S. with window looking
out at castle.

JUNE-16.

Sketched bridge head in morning

and other subjects. Saw inside of ruined castle in the afternoon, after it became cloudy. The restored part of the castle robs imagination. The whole appearance from afar does not look splendid. The colors too red and the thing has no mass. The only thing that saves it is because it is a ruin. Saw 2 big bear barrels in the cellar.

Took walk on the Philosophers' Walk up to hill across river.

JUNE 17.

Made 7 water colors altogether. Did not see anything new today. But could stay here for a good week and make sketches every day. Delightful little town. Food is more expensive than other places. Developing & printing of films cost money too. 1 reel (6) for 2.50 marks.

JUNE 18. Tue. Took tram at 7:30 to Mannheim. Saw new art gallery modern pre-war (1907) but most of exhibits in there are futuristic, oil, water-colors, and sculpture. Good architecture as well as contents.

Saw Palace, the biggest in Germany, a copy of Versailles. The garden has no plan, just like English park. The Jesuit church has rotten interior.

Mannheim has some ultra modern buildings.

Left for Worms at noon. Saw cathedral & Luther monument. The outside of cathedral has atmosphere of age & charm, like Rheims. But inside is bad, loaded with Baroque sculpture. The Rhein Bridge is good. Made sketch. Saw old wall, St Paulus Kirche, St Andrea, and Jewish synagogue. Worms is

a picturesque little town
that is worth a day's stay.
    Went to Lorsch at 5. P.M.
Saw Romanesque church
(Michael's Kapelle. also
a ruined church behind,
sketched both.
    Worms & Lorsch are
places famous for Nebelunge
saga.

JUNE-19. Overexhaust overexertion
& a little cold made my joints
ache & slept very poorly
last night. Took 2 pills of
quinine sulphate. gave
up breakfast. & tea
    Took morning train to
Würzburg. got there at 1.
    Felt much better at
Würzburg, after sleeping on
the train. Hotel Sonne at
Bahnhof str. is very good.
    Saw church (interior is
bad taste). not very good
in general, just a provincial
church.
    Saw old bridge on main.
very good and simple. made a

sketch.

Würzburg is very Baroque in architecture. All the German architecture I have seen is Baroque.

The Palace from outside is fair. The garden is nothing, a poor imitation of French garden.

Würzburg is not yet frequented by Tourists, except German tourists. It has just as much picturesqueness as Mainz.

JUNE. 20.

Completely recovered. Had breakfast & went across the old Main Bridge. Made a tour below the Castle Marienberg, trying to find entrance. Back to old bridge & sketched it again.

Went up to castle. Made 2 watercolors inside. Did not see inside of houses. Out trying to eat lunch when the guard wanted permit to sketch. Told me to go down near Peterskirche to get it

So I came downhill, stopped in a cafe on my way & eat lunch I bought this morning, 3 boiled eggs, 2 rolls & a bottle of beer. Went near Peter-platz, but wasted one hour there trying to find where to get permit to sketch. A storm was threatening so I came back to hotel to make up parcel post for mail.

Had a lot of difficulty at Post office in trying to get parcel mailed. Finally I had to wrap parcel in oil paper, bought at 13 Kaiserstr. & sealed there. Did not attempt to register. Hope it will get there. It contains all the drawings I made between Bruges and Würzburg & all post cards bought, & photos taken. It's really invaluable, though I put value down as £10 or — Had an enormous omelette fo

dinner, the omelette itself
costing me 40 f, with salad,
beer, and a baggett? for 1.50 m.

JUNE-21, Left Würzburg in morning
and arrived at Rothenburg before
noon. Bought a map of town
and walked through main thoroughfare. Very interesting place and
picturesque beyond imagination.
So many towers, and houses
in conformation with them.

Sketched some of the towers
and Rathaus. Then went
down hill to sketch the old
Tauber bridge.

. Rothenburg is the most
imaginative city I
have yet seen. It's a
combination of medaeval
and modern times. People
seem to still have common
baking oven, for they carry
large pans of pastry on streets.
(It's a small town, half
rural and half city-like -
with 2 main streets.

. Walked towards old way
in evening. It has a bridge

several mills, a church called
St. peter & St. Paul, with a
gateway in front of it.
a picturesque village. Just
before going downhill one saw
the wonderful sunset,
sometimes through green trees.
While going up to Rothenburg
ag ain one heard dogs
barking, crickets singing and
water murmuring. Then on
the Terrace of Bergton, the
silouette looked so light and
unreal like a dream. a
superb sight that.

JUNE 22. Have seen every part of the town
and sketched & water colors. Went
down to Detwang again. to sketch
some houses. This little village has
a black smith shop and a
café. It being Sunday I heard
singing psalms. a woman
came out with a chair to
offer me to sit down, which
I did not.

Went back to Rothenberg to
the market place. waiting for
12 o clock to see the clock. Sure

enough, after the hour struck, the windows on each side of the clock flew open, and 2 full-sized figures, dressed like real, started to move. One drank a big mug of beer and the other seemed to smoke a pipe, for duration of 2 minutes. Then the windows closed.

Went down to see the double Roman Bridge again.

Rothenburg is such a small town and is so easy to get around. The air is delicious.

Left for Nürnberg at 7, but on account of getting on the wrong train did not get there until 11:30 P.M. Got into Hotel and went to bed at quarter to one.

JUNE 23.

Walked thru town between station and Kaiser's thor. Sketched one water-color there. Came down and sketched Henkersteg. Then the weather became cloudy. After lunch on bread & beer went to see Dürer's Haus. Very charming

interior. Museum on 3rd floor
Kitchen on 2nd floor is interest
Saw furniture came down from
Dürer's time.

Did much walking. Nürnbe[rg]
is picturesque but every subject
is painted or illustrated and
you can do nothing new. Things
have become so obvious. Some
of the colored prints & etch[ings]
in shop windows are remarka[ble]

Walked towards the seven rou[nd]
towers weavers' houses in the
evening, on the way saw Hans
Sachs's house ("Meistersinger")
a tinter structure. The 1st
floor must be an alterat[ion]

JUNE, 2 4 Saw nothing new of the tow[n]
today. Rather tired of doing water
colors. So did pencil drawings

Saw Germanic Museum
this afternoon, the room 125 is
the famous "Nürnberg Madona"
in bronze. The museum is a
monastery with several cloisters
and a chapel. The collection
of any interest is tomb tablets
and stone sculpture; the rest

being junk.

JUNE 25. Saw modern church at Bamberg, St. Heinrichskirche, (Dr. Goertz, arch). The outside is of good stone work, with brick at the arch reveals. The inside has a good wood panelled ceiling, the rest being concrete & plaster.

Went to see Priesterseminar way beyond town, concrete exterior, with pleasant court. 9 pilons stand in front of bldg.

Went up hill to die Altenburg. Nothing but a view there. On way back sketched the cathedral from the hill. The cathedral looks hard, though old. It does not have the soft quality of age. The Rathaus is very barogue. So are the "old" & "new" "Residence" The interior of cathedral is good.

The other churches have nothing special, except St Michael's Church, which stands on a hill & has a view. On the whole Bamberg is an ante church after Rothenburg & Nürnberg, it can very well be omitted on the trip.

JUNE 26. Rain almost whole day. Saw Rathaus and Cathedral, Luther cell, and Krämer Brücke.

The Cathedral is the best in Germany, even better looking (from outside) than Cologne. Very perpendicular in style. Also it has a large open space behind and can be viewed from afar. Its approach is nice, — a flight of steps. The inside is filled with Baur monument. The nave & aisles are equally wide — 3 equal parts. or the nave is perhaps even narrower than the side aisles. The glasses are poor. The cloister is rather nice. The choir is screened off, and there is no depth to the church, on account of its square effect produced by the proportion.

St. Severi is close to the Cathedral. Its towers form

a false front, as the roof is detached from them. The roof is of red tile and looks like a big private residence. The color is very rich and silhouette very charming. Did not go inside.

St. Martin's stift is a new church (rebuilt). Luther's cell looks old; it might be a fake, with the burnt Bible. So much for Erfurt.

Weimar is full of 19 century. Walked in garden in the rain, past Goethe's summer house, Shakespeare's monument, and then walked towards Nietsche's house. The museum is on first floor, Nietsche's sister living upstairs. The rooms are newly furnished, with new books, including Spengler's "Decline." Full of portraits and busts. Spengler is a friend of the house and comes often; his portrait hangs on the wall. Nietsche lived here from 1897 to 1900, when he died.

Saw Liszt's house. His bed, study room, portraits; busts

and manuscripts. Liszt as a young man resembles Charles Dickens very much, although in old age he was rather grotesque.

Saw Goethe's house, much bigger and more pretentious than the one at Frankfurt am Maine. The natural history collection is very big and physics laboratory looks much up to date. I believe it has be enlarged every year. His bed room looks humble, with only one little window to the garden. The arm chair by his bed is the one in which he died.

Schiller's house is not as palatial as Goethe's. It has many busts and portraits. Also it contains the poet's bed chamber, with writing desk.

The archives contain letters and books. Goethe's hand written are there; also so many letters written to & from Goethe, Schiller, the Carlyles, Byron's letters to Goethe. Beethoven's letter to Goethe. Goethe's diary, and his works in different languages.

Saw the outside of the theatre, Palace, and Frau Von Stein's house.

Took train for Leipzig at 6.24. arrived at 7.40.

JUNE 27 – Saw outside of new theatre. Not good. The museum looks imposing. The university too. There are two new skyscrapers (about 10 stories high) sprung up at the square.

The Auerbach's Keller, scene of Goethe's "Faust", is now a wine restaurant and is very much touched up. The philosopher's furnace now is lighted by electricity, like a stage setting. Everything look fake. But there are several Goethe handwritings, framed & hung on the wall.

St Thomas is the Church in which Bach sang in the Choir. The inside has nothing to look at, we sat on the pew & read Baedecker.

The Rathaus is new. The old one stands at the market, a colorful tower it has. Near the Church of St. John there is a modern building which houses the Graeci Museum. The Museum has a good collection of modernistic & old art, mostly Kraft work.

Went to outskirts of the town (Car 32 from station) to see Deutsches Bücherei. There is also a modern Russian Church nearby, built in 1913, with a curious dome, which is well built up inside. The bronze hand work of religious art is good. The exposition ground has modern buildings. The clinic of the university is modern and is also near

by.
    Ran through whole town to get a bath.
    Heard good concert at the Conservatory, by students, between 6 & 8.

JUNE-29. Saw museum at augustus platz. It contains some popular paintings and a good collection of Max Klinger's works. Klinger sometimes used colored marble in different two pigment in figures. His Beethoven is there. His paintings has new idea of composition, too. The current exhibition of paintings and sculpture is very good.
    Saw Ausstellungsgelände again. This time went in to see juri exhibit, of which I was not interested. Want to sketch the Völkerschlacht Denkmal, etc but did not go up. Sketched Russian church and saw the new market, which has two domes.
    The new theatre has the same appearance as the

New York Metropolitan and the Philadelphia Academy, only it has a smaller capacity.

JUNE 29 — Thomas Church has a good choir. Most of the boys are under ten. Organ is good and the orchestra plays with it.

Have seen enough of Leipzig and am sick of it.

The Zoo has about twenty lions + a number of peacocks. It has some modern architecture for the elephants + the bears. The planetarium is modern but is cheap & is closed.

JUNE 30 — Got to Magdeburg about 10 in the morning. Saw cathedral, not very interesting, the facade is all right but it is a very false front, the central gable stands way above the roof over nave. Also the 2 towers don't have anything behind.

The Exhibition ground is very interesting. Saw the inside of the Stadthaus, an auditorium for concert. The organ has screen

is made of vertical pins covered
with blue velvet trimmed with
red. The interior is lined with
horizontal bands of wood. The
windows are made of ribbed
glass and are heavy. The
arrangement of light fixtures
is very interesting. Color scheme
very effective. The best
modern interior I ever saw.

Saw market, and Rathaus, not
much to like.

Arrived at Potsdam about
5. P.M. Started for Sanssouci
garden, walked till I saw the
windmill.

Made a sketch of the new
Palace.

JULY 1 — Made a sketch of the windmill,
walked towards the Ruinenburg,
an artificial work of imitation of
Roman grandeur, but very
terrible when looked at close.
Loafed in garden for a while then
took trolley to Klinker Brücke.
Saw gothic castle at Babelsberg at a distance.

Tried for 2 hours to find

the Einstein Tower and finally when I got there the old lady at the gate would not let me in. One must have introduction from a certain professor. I was so eager to see the thing that I walked around the property of the observatory far enough to catch a glimpse of the top. The photograph usually shows the tower as being dark. It looks white & clean in reality.

Started for Berlin at 5, got there half an hour later. Stayed near Friedrich str. station. Hotel Victoria.

July 2. Did not see any thing till 5, going about to get way through Russia (am. Ex. Cook, at Legation).

Saw zoo at 7 & Planetarium at 8. The equipment of the planetarium is wonderful. A projection of sky map, with all the stars on it, looks like real.

July 3. Saw National Gallery, which does not contain much. Saw old & new Rathaus, rotten architecture especially the old one.

In the afternoon walked along Kürfürsten damm & saw Universum film theatre.

July 4. Saw old & new museum, plenty of Greek Roman & Egyptian collections. Mostly sculpture. In evening went to Universum film Theatre. The outside has very good lines & movement. The theatre proper has red color scheme, people get in from side aisle doors, no central aisle. My foyer has blue color scheme.

July 5. Saw Pergamon, "PERGAMON MUSEUM" superb and unique beyond words. The museum is not yet ready; but we got in through the American institute. The pergamon altar is housed under glass roof. The relief is in purely "GIGANTOMACHIA" fragmentary state and no restoration made. The

[margin: fragment from Priene, Mesopotamia, sic.]

architecture of the temple above
is a restoration, with
original fragments shown
clearly. Better than the way
it is done in the British Museum, where the fools try
to plaster the relief and make
it more whole, thereby destroying imagination. Besides
Pergamon altar there is
a Romanesque like door
at Sia. also fragments
from Milet. The proportions
of the antiques are perfect.

Saw Kaiser Friedrich museum.
It has a good collection of
Dutch. Also many Rubens
and a few Hals & Van Dykes.
But the treasures are those
Italian paintings & sculpture,
Raiscance masters like
Della Robia (over 50 piece)
, Donatello, Sansavino,
etc. also one Da vinci and
2 Michaelangels. One
Raphael's madona is also
here. It has 5 Raphaels
altogether.

[64]

Saw Crown Prince Museum. It has modernistic paintings & sculpture on the top floor. Superbs thp. Cezzanne, Degas, Henri Matisse, Kandinsky. Some are very radically modern.

~~JUNE~~.

JULY 6. Saw flying field at Tempel-hof. Then took train for Breslau. Saw Rathaus at Breslau. Very charming + odd. Made sketch.

JULY 7. Saw almost every church in town (not inside) including the cathedral. They are all made of red brick and are rather picturesque. The cathedral is especially colorful.

Saw the modern group called Jahrhunderthalle, a great auditorium with stepped dome of glass. Very effective inside. All of concrete & glass. Don't know how the acoustics works.

JULY 8. Saw Clemens Maria Hofhaner Kirche, south west of town. The outside is conservative, only the top of the tower has modern note. All the arches are eliptical. But the inside is nice & colorful, although there are no side aisles. ~~On the~~ The Church is on second floor, as you go up the stairs there are colored terra cotta reliefs set in wall which look interesting. The note of decoration is red, very much like a theatre.

Saw Stadium, which consists of tennis courts, field & swimming pool. ~~too~~

Went all the way to ~~Dawitz~~ on trolley (15) to see Kaiser Wilhelm Gedächtnis turm, which appears good in photograph. But in reality the color is horrible. A cheap kind of red brick & gray stone tower. So I just made a pencil sketch. On way back went into a cemetery to see a new crematorium, very good.

Germans are after all people of sound habit. ~~Bo~~ Women ~~especially~~ take gigantic strides in walking ~~they~~ and are fond of carrying things on their back. Men put a lot of junk on their bicycles &

almost convert ~~them~~ motorcycle to automobiles.

Germans are fond of carrying their own lunch everywhere, sandwich and pastry, men and women alike.

July 9. In the morning at Breslau in the station saw a chimney sweep with a silk top hat on, a double institution that ought to be abolished.

Saw Picture Gallery at Dresden. Very good collection. Saw Raphael's Sistine Madonna, Andrea del Sarto's Holy Night, Titian's Tribute money. Raphael's Madonna has good composition & drapery but the color is drab.

Dresden is a good Baroque city, as it is the cradle of Rococo art.

The modern section of the Picture Gallery has some radical paintings. Warsily Kandinsky uses geometric forms (globes etc).

Lyonel Feininger passes planes through objects.

Paul Klee uses Egyptian forms in line drawings and sometimes the pattern looks like children's drawings.

Ernst Ludwig Kirchner paints not radically in forms but uses color green and purple on people's faces.

There is not much traffic in Germany but they are particular about lights and usually a police stands and controls the light signal. Also there is no demand for hurry but th every town (war mainly) has an automat, which sells more beer and wine than sandwiches.

JULY. 10. Saw Porcellain museum, which has a good collection of Chinese things.

Saw Industrial art museum, which has one 宣和鎮畫之 磨, 文徵明 and 劉石庵 題字

JULY. 11. Saw Sculpture gallery, which has some original Greek masters like Praxiteles. Saw Academy exhibit, price for entrance 1 mark. But it does not have much good stuff in it.

In the picture gallery there

seem to be copies passing as originals.
There are 2 Rubens' Drunken
Hercules in the same room. One
must be a copy. Another Rubens
looks like a copy too. The only
genuine ones are Raphael's Sistine,
Giorgione's Sleeping Venus and
Correggio's Holy Night.

In front of the Johanneum there
are two sculptured boys, one of
which is a Chinese. Took a photo of
it.

JULY 12. Saw Hygiene Exhibit. The
exposition is so arranged that
to me it is more of an architectural
exhibit than hygien. There are
so many photographs of buildings
(homes, factories, hospital) and models
too. Several crematoriums are
shown in photo.

One model shows a town
of circular plan. Blocks are divided
in concentric circles, and streets
radiate from centre, dividing
the city into 8 sectors. This, they
claim, perhaps, solve the problem
of facing the sun more equally all
round, as they call it "the

"Gesunden Grosstadt" (Recovering or "Convalescence city")

The Russians put up a big show and their idea about it is very radical. On the balcony there are albums of photographs + informations. The whole ceiling is covered (pasted on) with placards of propaganda.

The Japanese have a section also. The architecture is imitating German to the last detail. You cannot tell the difference.

The Hygiene Museum is very good in architecture + contents. On the 1st floor back there is a chapel-like with ambulatory, a statue in the center. Statue that has celoloid body + organisms inside, every part lighted by turns and corresponding names given on panels on table. The salon on top floor has a good color scheme (blue) and is in good proportion.

In the Russian Hygiene Exhibit the poster says "visit Russia. It takes 6 weeks to get a Visa and you can't have camera or books when traveling. The Russians must have good sense of humor.

JULY 13. In Prag at Noon. Saw Mozart house in west suburb of town. It has a garden, rather un Kempt. There is nothing particularly interesting about the house, except during 1787-1791, he lived there as guest of Duschea.

There is a foto ground for stadium, which is yet to be built.

Near Karl's Bridge there are many points of interest, like the Rathaus. and bridge towers. Very sketch- able like Wurzburg.

Prag is rather gray in color. In a garden the red flowers look exceedingly red because the surroundings are so drab. The modern buildings lack refinement. The YWCA is rather good.

Bohemian life is rather cheap to live. Food seems

to be less expensive than Germany.

Saw Beggars Opera at New German Theater. The music is half jazz — good jazz at that. I suspect this version is a corrupted one. Standing place costs only 4 Krone (1 Ke = 12½ pf or 3¢).

JULY. 14. Sketching whole day.

The Bohemians are less sophisticated. People don't dress much. But some girls are amply beautiful.

Bohemian cooking is wonderful. It has the flavor of Chinese dishes. The meat balls in soup is just like Chinese. Also the gravy.

The old town of Prague is as picturesque as any good German city.

Spengler's address at Munich is Wiedenmayerstr. 2.

JULY 15. The street cars and automobiles keep to the left. Pedestrians are also supposed to keep to the left. But some people do not seem to know what to do. Some insist on keeping to the left even if you keep to the right.

The National or museum has nothing to see, full of botanic and physiological collections. Art treasures there are few, or none.

Went up to the Burg in late afternoon, and saw cathedral St. Veit. The 2 towers look like Cologne, one smaller. The inside is quite good. The nave proper is very sober. The choir and chancel has some Baroque sculpture. Some glasses are passably fine. Everything seems to be in good taste. The whole interior is open, without screen of any kind. This is probably the best Gothic one in the Bohemia.

The Burg commands a sword view of the city.

Almost lost my umbrella, forgot to take it after finishing

a sketch. In about 3 or 5 minutes recalled & ran back for it. It y still stood there.

Got into a Bohemian restaurant in the evening. The wine is cheap & good. Food is cheap but not wonderful. Pastry is very bad. After everything the waiter took away the wine glass and nodded, I nodded too. So he brought another glass of wine. I refused but he said I ordered it. I did not take it anyway.

There are plenty of beggars. Women beggars usually have babies with them.

Need another day to finish sketching & sightseeing. 2 days are really too short for Prague.

The city hall has tricky clock like in Rothenburg, there are many figures passing behind the windows. The astronomical instruments are also supposed to work

The Bohemians are up early. Shops ran at 8. architects advertise with photos of works at entrance door.

but did not see them.
JULY. 16 – arrived at Vienna from Prague at 11.14.

Stephan dom has good Gothic exterior, towers similar to Cologne. In strong sunlight the effect of the tower is charming, the upper part being a white shaft with black dots and lines and the lower part is dark gray with cream-colored patterns.

Saw the outside of Kunsthistorich Museum, neue Burg, and garden. Rode trolly to Schonbrunner and Schloss Park, modelled after Versailles and similar to Sanssouci (really not) garden, on a smaller scale.

Vienna cooking is just as good as Bohemian, and very cheap. Besides Prag Vienne is a place to live cheaply.

Went to Marxergasse and found No 7 with difficulty, for it is on the other side of the bridge. Rang the bell and a Man came out

He rang for the janitor, an old man. I persuaded him to show me where Ernst Plischke was. He climbed up and I followed, 5 or 6 stories right to the top flr. The stairs had no lights. Then finally he opened a series of what looked like closet doors and knocked at the first. Plischke came out without shirt and a bare foot, which had a hurt toe. So he hopped on one foot. He He said the work was busy but not much prospect nor (perhaps reward). The studio drafting room is just like any one in America, dirty & disordered. All the drawings are modernistic of course. He showed me photos of his work. They look good. Then we talked about sights in Vienna. He came down with me and to the bridge. I did not know how he felt but I felt some pathos about what once we had been. There is a strange feeling when you meet some one again at a different place after a while.

On the route between ~~Eggen~~ Prague and Vienna the scenery is good, with rolling hills, black trees (cedar & pine) well grouped, and fleety clouds. At Eggenburg (Austria) there stands a church (nice color, red roof & white stucco walls) with ruined fortifications. It's quite picturesque.

July 17. Went to Kunsthistorisches Museum. It has some good things but cannot compare with other big European museums. There are many Rubens, Van Dykes, Rembrandt & Titians. But I suspect some are copies. One Raphael may be a copy too. It's Madonna with Child & St John. A small picture. There are many small objects of art, and many armors.

Modern ~~Museum~~ Gallery is very good. There are not many pieces (paintings & sculpture) but what is there is good. There are

In the moderne galleries every room has a different color scheme. The general arrangement is tasteful.

4 or 5 by Gustav Klimt. His costumes are original (black silver and gold) and compositions are wonderful. The sculpture is not good in general but some is quite praiseworthy.

The modern gallery is in the Orangerie, and on the other axis of the Belvedere is the 19 century museum, which is very poor and does not have a single thing of note except one or two Renoirs. The Salvator Rosa's are terrible.

There is an exhibition on Karlsplatz on bookbinding & home art. It's quite worth while, with all the ~~Viennese for~~ Viennese craftsmanship on display. Part of the exhibition is also devoted to architecture.

Saw Haydn Museum. The house has only 2 chambers on view, the inner one full of portraits and busts, the outer one has a piano & furniture. The old drawing shows the house as having thatched roof, alone in the countryside. Now the street is only a slum.

Saw interior of Stephansdom, which has some of the mystic quality of Notre Dame. The glasses are not good but they do well in a dark church. This church and the St Veit at Prague use low gothic arches very effectively at the main entrance in the interior.

Walked all the way to the D. umhe. Could not see its color (probably green) on account of the dark night.

A Viennese woned take the trouble to help you to find the way even to the extent of dogging you.

JULY 18.

After breakfast went to Heiligenstadt on stadtbahn

to see modern apartments. They are good; found out from the milk shop about Beethoven houses. Got there and saw two houses near each other where Beethoven lived. But both are private. The one at Pfarrplatz has a nice courti. It is when one stands beyond the threshold that imagination plays free. Made a rather good sketch of the white-stuccoed exterior.

Saw Schubert house on way back. It also has a nice court, but the gate is facing a busy street, instead of being like Beethoven houses which are rather secluded.

Ate near Schubert house, in a restaurant where the mother cooks (she looks dreadful) and daughter waits on table, while the son serves wine and beer. The cooking is very good and I ate a big dessert, besides a glass of beer.

Crossed the Danube under an impending storm in the afternoon. It is like Beethoven's music. Sturm und Drang. The Danube is light green in color. The water looks shallow now but the dykes are very far from the main bed.

JULY 19. Went to see Secession Museum. There is something good there, not much radical stuff.

Went to District III to see modern apartments, where if one pass from one court to another and to streets. Very well planned and good architecture also.

Walked in Stadt Park. Saw Court of the Burghof.

Saw Rathaus at close range in the evening. Then went to Wurzbach St. to see modern apartment. There are nice tile fountains

in arcaded courts.
JULY 20. Arrived at Salzburg at noon train. Went up to see Mozart's little house (which was moved from Vienna) on the hill. It is just a wood cabin, filled with impossible prints.

Sketched the castle. The castle looks very English. It has a good composition from the river. Saw most of the landmarks.

Salzburg is such a small town it is easy to get around.

Beautiful landscape between Vienna and Salzburg. Rocky hills and distant mountains (snow clad), with black trees grouped very architecturally. Houses begin to assume the Tirolian character, with hard looking boarded roofs, eaves overhanging on all sides.

JULY, 21 – Saw König See and took motor boat to Bartholomä and

Obersee. There is nothing to see at Obersee. But Bartholomä has a nice little building with restaurant. Fine sketching subject. Mountains are beautiful, with thin waterfalls and glassy lake. At one place the man on board blew the bugle and the echo was distinct as the original, only a little fainter. Made a sketch at Bartholomä and a pencil at Königsee. Very beautiful scenery on the way and mountain air is delicious. The water looks cold. I had sweater on.

Went up to the castle, the most picturesque composed and there are so many sketchable spots. Better than English castle in composition and picturesqueness but details are bad (Baroque). On the whole it is the best in Europe. The mere fact that it stands in the town on top of hill is dramatic. Two good terraces are taken by restaurants. Those who dine there can enjoy the best scenery one can ever wish. It is superb. Distant mountains with beautiful outline, strange clouds and fields and houses. Who would not have appetite!

Could not have time to see Mozart's houses. Nor the Festival house. But went to Marionette theatre tonight. The first marionettes I ever saw and the best. The first one is "Bastien and Bastienne" which is a merry comic opera. But the second one is "Wolfgang and Der Selcher Meister", which illustrates Mozart as a little boy being dopy'ing the new music teacher, who did not even know what minuet was. So he left. Mozart is very sweetly played and the others are cleverly done too. It is rarely better than some of the stage plays.

Spengler 26 Widenmayer str.
Munich.   [74]

July 22. Up early (5:30) for Munich train,
arrived at 8. Found room near station
and looked around town. Saw Prinzregent
Theatre where Wagner's operas are
given. The lowest price there is 15 m.
At the Residenz Theatre, where Mozart's
operas are given. In one of the poster-
photographs I saw a scene of
plays named Li-Tai-Pe, where I
inquired it was given 2 years
ago. First time drank Munich
beer — Löwenbräu, very good
so rich and does not make you
thirsty. Saw Spfly Spengler's house, top floor.
Took train for Oberammergau at 2,
arrived at 6. Stayed at house no.
119 Haupt Str. Maria Klammer
the landlady, is an excellent cook.
The room has an 8-foot ceiling
and 4 windows, very nicely
furnished. It has a narrow windy
stair to the 1st floor, you you go
through the barn to the vestibule.
It is a super white stucco
house with blue blinds. The
dining room has plan-planks for
ceiling, probably the underside
of floor above.

The whole congregation are American except myself. One woman from Washington D.C. had a long argument with the landlady in German. I thought she was German too so I called her a damned nuisance. She turned around and looked at me. I knew then she knew it. So I determined to be ugly, and not to talk to anybody. Two young girls from America sat at the end of table and probably have rich parents the way they talk. Silly heads both. R.S. tried to entertain them.

The meal is excellent but it seems to be out of place, in a little village like this to have table manners and politeness. It kills the fun. Women make one feels uneasy to start with. I never was nervous with women in America. But they made me here nervous. Because they are not interesting and carefree.

What one notices as soon as one came out of the station

also the horse-carriages and men with beard and long hair. The children and boys also grow their hair long. Some say they do it 3 years before the event of Passion Play. But they make the village look very picturesque indeed. The houses are very alpine, with overhangs eves on all sides, white stuccoed usually, or brown.

The place is full of Americans. Some dumb English people are also there. They of course are out of place. Even the Germans themselves look out of place in that matter, if they do not live at Oberammergau.

This is the only occasion perhaps I come in direct contact with American tourists. They are so ignorant that to speak to them means wasting breath. It is a kind of blessing to sleep in this little quiet village, anticipating one of the greatest events that only happens at long intervals.

July-23, The weather today is very clement, cloudy in the morning and sunshine in the afternoon, while the rain in the evening is too late to spoil anything.

Had very satisfactory breakfast, with plenty of rolls and fresh butter, jam, and mountain honey. The coffee also tastes good.

The Passion Play starts at 8 AM. in the theatre, which has hidden orchestra and open stage. I sat too low in front but I believe those up behind can see the distant mountains.

All the tableaux vivants are good, music, costume, acting, can be said leaving nothing to be desired. The music is given only when there is prologue. It's simple and pure and as great as any great opera music.

Judas acts very well

although a little too forcibly. But on the whole he knows what he ought to do. On the other hand Christ is rather uncouth, peasant-like and none too gentle. He does not even have a carefree face, which is very rough. His voice is too strong, and movements and gestures are not up to the standard.

Mary is quite good, anyway she does not have much acting to do. She is a beautiful woman.

The play starts from Christ entering Jerusalem to the Ascension or Transfiguration. It takes 8 hours schedule two actually it starts at 8 A.M, ends at 5.45 P.M., with intermission at noon time between 11.30 and 2 P.M.

Ate a good lunch of chicken and a marvelous nachtisch, like melted cream made of eggs and bananas. Excellent indeed.

In the afternoon the sun shines and serves as a

light source for the stage. The effect is very good. Some of the characters stand in shade and some in light. It is really stage lighting at its best.

The whole performance makes the Bible alive. I think for a long time hereafter when I see a crucifix or anything that has to do with Christianity I will be reminded of the Passion Play. It really makes you live the life of and I think it is true especially with the villagers.

The Germans are fond of using flowers in a long row to make them count as ornament.

JULY 24. Back to Munich in early morning. It rains whole day at Munich. Saw Bavarian museum, full of junk. Then went to see old Pinakothek, which has many Rubens, Van Dyke, Rembrandts, 2 Raphael-madonnas, and some very good Titians. I never yet saw so many Murilios. There are also some Goyas. Dürer's 4 apostles are also there, together with other good works by him. His own portrait I have seen in almost every museum and don't know which is copy or which is not.

Went to Prince Regent Theatre in the eveng to hear Wagner's "Flying Dutchman", (15 marks for cheapest seat) which starts at 7, and ends at 10. The setting is excellent, music is simpler and singing very much better than any I heard at Metropolitan. It is the best Wagner I enjoyed besides Lohengrin.

JULY 25 - Went to see Nyphemberg Palace, just a group of Baroque buldgs with Park. Not worth a trip at all. It is not far from Munich. Trolly takes 15 minutes from station.

The hospital near the Palace is modern and is not bad.

Saw exhibits at Glass Palace in the afternoon. The collection is good in quality and quantity. It is to my mind even better than the Salon at Grand Palais in Paris. Some of the watercolors are inspiring too. It is a show of painting and sculpture, with lithographs and prints and etchings. It is quite worth seeing.

Saw new Pinakothek. It is entirely impossible, not only in quality but there is very scanty painting indeed.

Saw State gallery, which is wonderful in its French collection. The other rooms are all right but the French room has Van Gogh's self portrait. Cezanne's self portrait. Van Gogh's still life (sun flowers) and landscape. Cezanne's landscape and landscape. Also there is one Pissaro,

One Matisse, 2 Gauguins, and 2 Renoirs. One Manet. The museum in this respect is worth a trip.

Went to Theatre Museum. It does not have much, But a unique thing. Photographs, models, and prints, of dancing and drama. Also masks and costumes.

Saw Deutsche Museum on the island. It is purely scientific. I just walked through all the parts that are open and came out.

Saw Austellung Park building. Modern, with colored terra cotta figures lined on the path.

JULY 26. Did not see any museum today. But sketched 5, the Rathaus old + new, the tower of Austellung bldg., and a terra cotta figure there. Also a street scene.

Heard Beethoven's Moonlight Sonata, and Serenade

tonight, in the courtyard of the Residenz. It is excellently done. In between the program some wind instruments were played on the tower, with lights flooded on the painted roof, and the musicians are just discernable. The effect is very theatrical. Candles are used in most of the lamps and in window sills in the Entrance Court. It looks like middle ages.

Oswald Spengler must be easy to see, as R.S. sent up a letter of self-introduction and got an interview. Spengler is described as a man about 50, bald headed but with handsome or sharp-featured face. He had a kind of smoking jacket on and soft slippers. His rooms are comfortably furnished with long rows of books and old pictures. Spengler must be playing on the Piano, which he has, and his "Decline" shows his knowledge of music. He live on the main floor with a maid + a housekeeper apparently.

Spengler does not like Richard Strauss nor modern jazz. He thinks Liszt especially Wagner, was the last great musician. Modern architecture to him is not yet likable agreeable. In the Tribune tower competition he likes the building built and prize (Saarinen). The German competition drawings he does not think much at all.

I rather would not see him. What after all can an interview do? If he is too great we would not understand him. If he's not great at all we better wait till he comes to see us. A man has no business to intrude on another just for the sake of curiosity.

July 27. arrived at Augsburg from Munich in the morning, at 8.30. Went to cathedral at once.

during service, with organ music and chorus. very beautiful. Baedeker mentions a bronze candelabrum of the middle ages, but there are 4 or 5. No one knows which is. The interior is rather nice, not much Baroque. The South bronze door is good.

On the South side of the Cathedral there is a group with excavated remains (Roman?) Baedeker does not mention it. probably very recent. To me it looks like a Roman Bath.

The Rathaus is very poor. So is the Perlach Thurm. Went to S[t]. Johan. St. looking for Holbein's house, but saw an old house and Vogl Thurm + sketched both. There was a fair going on, and circus for children. Several boys led me through Fuggerei but no one knew where Holbein's house is. Instead one boy called out a Frauen

The boy must have thought I was looking for a countryman. There were 4 or 5 Chinese merchants (vagabonds). They talk aloud and play mah-jong on the beer table. Fortunately the place is full of people who eat with their knives (even a woman did that). They are a disgusting lot anyway. So I never saw Holbein's home.

Arrived at Ulm at 2:30. Ulm is an old town on the Danube. Saw the cathedral. It looks like an American skyscraper in silhouette. The inside is quite plain and nice, with double aisle on each side. Took trolly to go across Danube & see a modern church (Kath. Stadtpfarrkirche). The outside is a modern version of Romanesque. The inside is very wonderful (almost cubistic). By Prof Dominikus Böhm. There is not much color but the light and shade plays on white plaster is very effective. There are several chapels and each is different. The one fault perhaps is the low ceiling.

Sketched the watch-tower on the Danube. The Danube has redish green color.

I imagine the train passed through the Black Forest region. But the forest is not different from others in South Germany.

Arrived at Stuttgart at 7.15. The new main station is beautiful. I never saw such a good thing, probably the best station in existence.

Saw the Palace at night and some of the modern buildings. The Old market has many old houses. The Rathaus is too new to be good.

JULY. 28. Rainy morning. Saw Schocken Dept. Store. The best department store (ar-

chitecturally of course) I
have ever seen. It has
combination of brick horizontal
lines and stucco. The use of
shop name in huge light
blue letters is effective.
 Opposite Schocken
is a ⬛⬛ tall buedig (about
15 st⬛⬛ (News paper press)
The ⬛⬛est in Germany
and perhaps in Europe. Made
sketches of both.
 Left Stuttgart at noon
time. for Friedrichshaven,
which is on Lake Constance
Took boat (St. Gallen) to
cross the lake to Romanshorn.
 Constance has green water
glassy. Felt a thrill to
see the distant alps for
the first time. The weather
is cloudy, but one can see
distant mountains in sun-
shine. Some mountains are
hidden by clouds. of others
only the peaks are visible.
It is very much like Chinese
painting, which always pro-

duces the greatest effect with the most simple means.

Had to wait at Romanshorn for the train to Zurich. So went to an old church (which I saw from the lake) and made a sketch of it. Romanshorn is a small town. So is Friedrichshafen. The Zeppelin hanger is visible across from the lake.

Train left Romanshorn at 6.24, arrived at Zurich at 8.05.

Went into a gay place tonight by mistake. It is a restaurant with "Konzert." On the platform women dressed in fancy costumes in lace caps to play instruments. Men dressed in blacks, with tight coat and ample trousers. Colored fine lace around neck and chest. One has to pay 30 centimes to for the concert.

Bier- und Konzerthalle „Wolf", Zürich 1
Inhaber: Emil Schlatter

Konzert-Billet No. 27635

Aufbewahren und beim Verlangen vorweisen
— Nicht übertragbar —

Wenden!

As I could not get a room at Hotel Limmathof, I left my luggage there and came to this place. After I got the room I said I was going for baggage. It did not take long to get it. The hotel keeper was suspicious and demanded payment. He asked if I came from another hotel.

Had all kinds of weather this day. Swiss landscape in a cloudy day is like Chinese painting.

July 29. Up very early. Out to see the Zurich See. All Swiss lakes appear to be the same.

Saw Lindenhof- Site of old Roman Palace, now an elevated

grounds with trees and benches. No remains of any kind.

Saw Statue of Pestalozzi. Sketched covered wooden bridge and old museum.

The Bankof Strasse of Zurich is the main street and on both sides early in the morning there are lines with stalls for fruits. It is a market street.

Lucern is on the Vierwaldstätter See, which is more beautiful than Zurich see. Made sketch of covered bridge on the Reuss. Then went to see the famous Lion of Lucern. Also saw Glacier Park. The only museum of its kind in the world, and marvelous things. Worth while to see, especially the palm impressions on stone. Glacier mills and round stones. One is set at work by water fall.

Went up to Gütsch tower but the view is very ordinary.

[83]

Arrived at Bale at 5.30 p.m. Right outside the station there is the market hall, modern but not very good. Got to Spalen by mistake. But from a shop (post card place) near there found out the the location of the modern Antonius Kirche. Walked to there at once. The tower (concrete) is the best I saw. Inside is also very sober and non theatrical. But the proportion does not seem right. The section of it is a barrel vault over nave and flat ceiling over aisles. All ceiling is treated with

| CONFESSION CHAPEL BOOTHS |

square panels sunk in concrete. The stained glass windows are modernistic and have figures besides cubistic designs. The choir is on the balcony facing the chancel. The pulpit is made of copper and has

a flat hood over it. This church is very worth seeing. I believe the new building now under construction is Sunday School.
Saw Rathaus, which has a fresh pink color and richly decorated roof. St. Martin is close by and its tower is good from certain angle. The Cathedral is of red stone and is rather nice to look at.

Stayed at Basel only for 2 hours, and yet saw many things although did not make any sketch.

Took train for Bern. A nice evening with crescent moon.

Too dark to see Bern tonight. While in the train saw pictures of Chillon, near Montreux, just on way between Lausanne and Milan. So determined to stop at Montreux.

Did not have time for dinner

So bought 2 bananas and 3 pieces of pastry to eat on the train

July – 30. Up and out to see Käfigturm, the Münster, which looks new, (gothic). and Rathause, which has no tower but a stairs of stone with shelters stairs outside. Very unusual.

Bern is famous for its numerous fountains. But Zurich has just as many. One good thing about Bern is its covered sidewalks or arcades on all principal streets. It's an old thing but modern architects are drawing it for the hip metropolises of tomorrow. The Bernese alps are not clear from terraces on account of clouds. also could not see the "Alpine glow" which must be seen on clear evening.

Saw an accident. a truck was turning street corner

and hit a motorcyclist.
I don't know what became
of the victim. But he seemed
to hold his own, an old
man too.

~~Arrived at Lyon~~ The
Rhine has a light yellowish
green color and has
swift current.
Arrived at Lausanne
at 2:00 P.M.
Up to Bern people speak
german, from Bern on
they talk french. Railway
language change accordingly.

Saw Rathaus, very
insignificant, with
painted cornice.

But the ~~mus~~ cathedral
restored by Violett du
Duc is the best gothic
in Switzerland and
is better than any church
in Germany. The tower
is dwarf and has a
spire. But the main
portal is excellent.
The interior is marvelous

for its simplicity. The Rose
window recalls Chartres and
Saint Chapelle. There are
few glasses, but they are all
splendid. The details as
well as proportions are
superb. Because of its being
a little squat it's better
than any forced height
(false Ⓒ because it is
misleading) to give sense
of height, by narrow
(width) it is wide
so one has sense of space.

Saw chateau. Excellent
because it is a good combination
of brick and stone. Nice
mellow pink brick.
it is low and massive.

/\   /\
[..] Brick [..]
  ‾‾‾‾‾‾
    Stone.

Went up to the Signal
for view, But it Ⓑ is no
better than the view from
the train. another view

As soon as I got there went to see the Chateau of Chillon. In the evening light it looks splendid, and grows bigger as you approach it. Must go there tomorrow morning. Made sketch and took photos. It is in the twilight just like the "Island of Death." Very imaginative. The air is delicious. I was swim in water and frequently some submerged.

I like to hear Dutch. At Bern people speak both German & Dutch. But at Lausanne & Montreux they only speak Dutch, which charms my ears. One sees more beautiful women too. The food is more Frenchy, in Soui Anyway.

July 31. Saw inside of Chillon. Views from the windows are superb, even from the prison cell. There are Torture chambers, @ Justice' room, Dining Hall, Knights hall etc. No medievalism about it is very unique. In Bonivard's cell I looked for Byron's name. Could not find it on the Column. But there is a modern tablet (1924) on the wall opposite to that column. The Dent du Midi was hidden in clouds all morning, the top is clear in the eving, but main body is cloudy. Also saw Snow capped Shafts behind.

Aug - 1. Took train in morning to Martigny, there took bus to Great St. Bernard.

the train before arriving at
Martigny passed St. Maurice.
The church probably took five.
The bus had a good driver.
We arrived at great St.
Bernard at 12:30. Passed
many villages. The houses
have truly the rugged
character of the mountains.
also the inhabitants have
hard and worn faces (dry
looking). At Bourg St. Pierre.
there is a hotel where upstairs
Napoleon had breakfast.
It has a good carved wood
ceiling. The church looks
very aged and the tower
has stone spire. good character
On the wall of the church (?) and
stands a Roman milestone.
after passing Bourg St. Pierre
we saw what I thought was
Mont Blanc. It looked
extremely grand. waterfalls
snow-capped mountains.
The road winds itself
up toward the top. And
as you look back it reach

like a snake.

The bus almost had an accident. Another truck came. Both stopped just on time to avoid collision. Beyond is the deep ravine!

The sky is very clear and the air cool. But when the bus stops in the village the sun is fierce.

The party consists of 3 Americans (husband & wife with daughter) 2 French or Swiss (man & wife) and myself. The American one counts the height of mountains.

St. Bernard, when you reach it, is a disappointment. The best part of the ride is before you reach it, when the mountains rise one after another.

The St. Bernard Hospice is very common place looking (commercial looking too). It has an old chapel and all the rooms are numbered like hotel. The dining room is on the first floor. The priest eats with the guests. The Hotel du St. Bernard is opposite and is connected with a bridge. The food is fine. Wine is the best I have drunk. The cooking is excellent except the beef, which no wonder, they call à la l'anglaise. The white wine is called Étoile and is so rich and fragrant, besides some porch.

The famous St. Bernard dogs (I only saw three (behind the Hospice) They look like a cross between a bull dog and wolf. Crossed the Italian border. Photograph forbidden.

It is very mild up there. The lake is not frozen, though some snow never melts.

One has to use a good deal of imagination to see St. Bernard in summer time. As writing

snow there can be no danger;
and the dogs are taking a
rest.

On the return trip I felt
tired and took several winks.

The train for Milan was
one half hour late. Crossed
the Simplon Pass at 6 o'clock
It took about 22 minutes
to cross the 3 major ones,
And the other short tunnels
together with Simpeon took
about one hour.

On the North Side of
the Alps the sky was blue.
On the Italian Side it was
cloudy, though the crescent
moon once a while shone
through the clouds.

It is a thrill to see
Italian villages the
first time. They are
all charming things.

At Stresa a middle
aged French woman welcomed
a couple of young people at
the station. Not only their
French charmed my ears

but also their manner and grace and some beauty.

AUG-2. Saw S. Fedele the first thing. Outside is very charming. The brick work reminds one of modern Germantwork, with bands horizontally run sunk & raised. The facade is splendidly proportioned (Renaissance stone).

Saw Museum of La Scala, the inside of the opera house (which look so small) and the stage. The ceiling is high enough to distinguish itself from the mediocre opera house at Phila & New York, and Prague. The general color scheme is dark red. The facade is fine. Leonardo's statue stands in the square.

The Cathedral does not look as well as the photograph. But the interior is extremely fine; like Notre Dame and much bigger.

The windows are good, and they are placed to advantage on account of the dark interior of the church. The High nave, and double aisle. The whole thing is very simple looking indeed.

Saw city — front view and roof. Atmosphere not clear and the alps are not distinct.

Saw the coffin of St. Charles. It is made of silver. The whole chapel ceiling is silver ornamented. The coffin has glass crystal windows so you can look in and see the scull, with clothes intact. An ornament in the coffin by Cellini. The skull is dark brown, hand covered with white gloves and rings.

Palazzo Ambrosiana has collection of Renaissance paintings, like of Leonardo's drawings and some paintings. Raphael's cartoon of the

School of Athens
   Piazza Mercanti has
~~a restored Room~~ Palazzo
della Ragione, ~~rest~~ part of which is
Roman remains. This is the centre
of old Milan.
   Biblioteca Ambrosiana
has a picture gallery, the
most important thing being
Raphael's cartoon ~~for~~
the School of Athens. Leonardo
has a cabinet too, with
albums & all kinds of
his drawings. Also there
are some small paintings
attributed to Leonardo.
   San Satiro has a choir
in perspective (sculptured)
Baedeker says it is
painted. But the modelling
is of stone. It is very ingenious
(on account of narrow street
~~beyond~~ beyond it is impossible
to have a choir.
   Santa Maria Presso
San Celso has a good
atrium, the first atrium
I have yet seen in Italy

of a church.

San Lorenzo is the most ancient church of Milan; it is Romanesque, and has good color up inside. Outside is the row of Roman columns with architrave of brick and stone. The columns are corinthian and are weather worn.

San Ambrogio has an atrium also. Romanesque. And according to tradition Augustine was baptized here.

The most charming church, no doubt, is Santa Maria della Grazie. The dome is after Bramante's design. The chief thing there is Leonardo's Last Supper, in the monk's dining room of the Dominican Monastery. The whole picture was restored and the door opening which appears in some of the prints is blocked up and painted over, with trace left to be seen. A wonderful thing it must have been to look at when new! How

it is damaged to such an extent that it is more like a cartoon. Christ's face is barely visible. The composition is somehow grand and original. The 12 disciples are grouped 3 and 3. The colors are very simple. The lunettes are also painted by da Vinci.

The church has a very nice portal. The inside looks old. That's all I can remember.

I must confess the seeing of the Last Supper did not give me any thrill. It looks like an old friend; and seeing it merely means identification.

The castello looks grand. The Lombardic tower has an original composition and character. It reminds me of the Cremelin(?) at Moscow. The round tower at the corner reminds me of the towers at Nüremberg, only those in Milan have stone rustication and

look better. The buildings surrounding the castle are
very good and civic, some of
which are in Florentine
style.
   Saw outside of Palazzo di
Brera and Pal. Crespi.
Di Brera has a fine court
and good picture gallery,
which I am going to see
tomorrow.
   I have finished seeing all
the things outlined by Baedeker.
The inside of museums
at DiBrera and Castello
remain to be seen tomorrow.
Made my one sketch of
the cor? cloister of Santa
Grazie.
16, 3. In the morning went to
the Castle, saw museum.
The best thing there is the
ceiling by Leonardo. It is
the most original thing one
can imagine. The cross
ceiling, penetrated by
arches, is treated as a
covered bower of green trees

leaves, with shields of blue and gold at four sides, and brown branches coming down to the cornice. It is very rich, and simple and restful to the eye. The wall is covered with red silk, and dark brown wood panels on seats. The floor is again a wonderful design of black & white marble in the most interesting pattern. The whole conception is almost modern.

There is a collection of China (Ming and Kang Hsi) and some Jap. art.

The Museum at Du Brera is very good, and rivals with Dresden and Munich. It has Raphael's "Nuptials of the Virgin". The Titians I did not see.

Took train for Como from Station Nord at 1.02, arrived at 2.02. From there took boat (Milano) to Bellagio (arrived at 4.30. But in 5 minutes took

(Savoia)
return boat back to Como)

From Como to on the first half
hour is very dull, with uninteresting
houses on both banks. But as soon
as one gets to Nesso the houses
suddenly look nicer and they
pile up so picturesquely, with
an old hunch-backed bridge
and a big waterfall. Next
good place is perhaps ~~Lenaggio~~,
where on the hotel wall the trees
or vines are as trained as to
climb in trunk and rest in
leaves.

But before that, ~~there is~~
~~afor~~ Argegno, where there
is a charming old Romanesque
tower and a horrible new

grey Romanesque church.

Bellagio is nothing but a pile of big villas, in block form. It is not picturesque. The church of San Giovanni I could not have time to see or sketch, but I saw it from the distance on boat. It is gray stone, maybe sketchable.

All those lake towns and villages are good to look at from the water, but when you get inside it looses its charm.

Stayed at Bellagio only for 10 minutes and took next boat back. On the return trip the west side of the lake is already in shade.

On the train from Martigny to Milan, on the Italian frontier, there was a customs officer who looked like B. Moioli. In a restaurant yesterday noon

I saw another person who looked more like him, even to the gesture and way of eating.

In Giubiasco the panel doors are often like this ⟶

But in northern Italy the door panels are often horizontal, recalling the stone joints.

Aug 4 - left Milan 9.32, arrived at Certosa 9.50, took th

In the train an old woman put 9 pieces of large baggage overhead, the others having nothing to occupy the space.

Two French women are traveling to the Certosa and on presenting their tickets to the conductor who got so excited that the women thought they took the wrong train. But they only had to pay extra for express train.

At the station of Certosa a driver has his rail-horse carriage waiting for the

(These pages were written while
I was half drunk, head swimming anyway)
monastery. But, on seeing me
walking along the track without
taking his car, he pointed me the
wrong direction, which I followed
and walked a complete circle
around the ~~east~~ wall.

The central gem is the
Chapel with tower. Such
perfect inlaid marble work
on the facade, of different
colors. The facade is white
marble and the rear apse
is red ~~brick~~ brick. The
combination is most charming.
The tower builds up very well
also. The interior of ~~the~~ church
looks grand. Every chapel is
a gem, with a ~~fine~~ altar
~~and of~~ fine inlaid marble.
The choir is a little Baroque.
The cloister (~~grand~~ of the fountain
is ~~good~~ grand. So is the
Grande chiostro, which
is surrounded with the
monks' cells. ~~The~~ Each
monk has their own room on
the 1st floor, with a fire
place and a good convenience,

~~and~~ (dumb waiter turned). The
~~cut~~

The Fontana and guide and check of articles require no fee, to my wondering.

This no doubt is the finest Early Renaissance work in Lombardy.

Nearby is a Restaurant, where one dines in the open, sheltered ~~with~~ by tree and vines. No place is more cool and peaceful. The hostess is charming and speaks French. The wine is excellent and puts me ~~into that~~ forgetful condition from which all the thirsty souls are reluctant to return. The ~~food~~ is equally good. And two monks beside me are having as good an appetite as any earthly creature.

Took train (1:15) to Genova. On the way first passed Pavia. Its excellent dome and bell tower stand out with the covered bridge (the arches are different in width). It is a little gem again and the Italians are as incapable of doing it now as any other race at all this.

I forgot to mention the fact when one enter's the court towards the chapel on the right wall or the windows are painted also the doorway has painted order in stucco.

arrived at Genova 5:20 (took train from Certosa at 1:15) The weather is cloudy; and the whole town does not seem to be interesting, except the old winding narrow streets with tall houses on each side, bannered with clothes just washed. All the Palazzos and churches Baedicker praised are nothing at all. The best part of the town is along the harbor, where houses of ten stories high pile

up most picturesque, like
a miniature New York, only more
artistically.

The harbor is far different
from what I imagined. I expected
sail-boats (at least some) but
there are nothing but steamships.

Had dinner "on the quai", under
a big arch — spaghetti. wine, beef
and fruit for 8 Lire.

Stayed at Hotel Bellevue,
on the hill near station, for
15 L.

Aug 5. Up very early (#5:45) Caught
train for Pisa at 5.25, and
arrived at 9.15. Went towards
the river. Sketched Torre Torre
Guelfa. Saw San Paolo, which
has a fine facade resembling
the Duomo. There's a
stair going down near the
church to the river bank,
where the smell of human
deposits is unbearable and
my sketch was made right
there.

Santa Maria della
Spina has a curious gothic

facade of bi-part composition;
and is the smallest church I
ever saw.
    Saw the University, a very
classical facade. San Frediano
has ancient columns inside.
Palazzo agustini is in
venetian style. Santa
caterina has fine glass inside.
The feeling of proportion is
almost modernistic. Horizontal
blue bands, too, suggest modernism. The ceiling of dark
wood painted (blue pattern) is
fine.
    Saw the Leaning Tower, en-
tirely of white marble, so are
the Cathedral and Baptistery.
Therefore in the sun the white
stone reflects light and
too dazzles your eye. Went
on top of the tower and took
a photo of myself.
    The cathedral is very
good, although the dome from
outside looks funny. Horizontal
blue marble bands were precious.
The mosaic by Cimabue over

the altar (gold background) is so bold that it looks very modern, especially the treatment of Christ's face.

The Baptistery has the finest dome one can imagine. The outside looks superb. The inside is again so bold and simple that any modernistic architect would be inclined to do. The gem there is Niccolo Pisano's pulpit. The workmanship of marble is superb.

Did not have any breakfast so had lunch at Pisa, near the Cathedral.

The Campo Santo has frescoes and tomb stones.

The monuments at Pisa are such as to suggest the vigor and simplicity of an age which just realized its greatness, without yet any sophistication.

Took train for Florence at 1.30, arriving at 3.30. Stayed at Pension Matillin 13 Via dell Alora.

Saw outside of Pal. Pitti.
Also saw Santa Maria della
Carmine and San Spirito.
Sketched Ponte Vecchio, the
best bridge I yet saw.

AUG. 6. Went to the Cathedral first,
saw inside, rather bare but
very monumental. The glass
windows in the drum are
the best, sparkling and full
of mystic quality. The choir
is under the dome, which is
quite novel, and good.
  Inspected the doors of
the Baptistery. They are very
simple in modelling and
that is why they are good,
just enough and not too
much for Baroque Baroque.
The inside of the Baptistery
is just like Pantheon at
Rome, very simple, and
impressive. Did not go
up the Campanile, but
saw Donatello's "Zuccone"
way up in the sky.
  The cathedral Museum
has Luca della Robia's

Sing is Gallery and Donatello. These are perhaps the only outstanding collection there.

Palazzo Vecchio has a tower (high) that looks like a castle and swallow-tailed battlements (Ghibelline). Very impressive.

The rooms upstairs seldom have square (~~regular~~) or rectangular shapes. They are just haphazard four-sided rooms ~~with~~. This amazingly frankness recalls the irregular streets by which the palace is bound. The interiors are better than most the palace that is open.

Saw bronze slab (in the Piazza della Signoria) about Savonarola's being burnt to death on the statue there.

Loggia dei Lanzi, a copy of which is in Munich, far surpasses that in beauty. The number of sculptures there is amazing; and mostly masterpieces. It is ~~an~~ a little open-air ~~museum~~.

Saw Uffizi gallery. It is on top of a U-shaped colonnade, and has an important collection but not as good as Pitti; though here they have a combination of painting and sculpture. ~~It has Raphael's~~

The National Museum has more Donatellos than any other place. Also there is Michael Angelo's Drunken Bacchus. His unfinished Brutus is also here. The della Robbias are also numerous.

Spedale degli Innocenti has medallions by Andrea della Robbia, with blue ground.

Santissima Annunziata has numerous frescoes. ~~by Fra Angelico~~

Palazzo Medici is not worth seeing at all. The apartments are very poor in taste & the museum is not any good either.

Monastery of San Marco has many frescoes in the cloister and the cells upstairs. Some of the cells were once occupied by Savonarola.

Gallery of the Accademia di Belle arti has Michaelangelo "David", and 5 unfinished Prigione group, very much like the finished work of Rodin. David has nothing particular except it is big and vigorous.

San Lorenzo has an unfinished façade. Saw the Medici chapel, the whole thing being marble of different colors inside. Of sorts Baroque. The marble floor (mosaic) begun at 1888, is now only half done, with 3 people working on it.

The New Sacristy was built by Michaelangelo and contains his famous Medici tombs. One for Giuliano and the other Lorenzo or

"Il pensieroso".

Palazzo Strozi has fine iron work and unfinished cornice.

Palazzo Pitti is the most impressive and grand building in Florence, with its monumental garden. The picture gallery contains Raphael's Madonna della Sedia (also his Granduca), and also numerous portraits of Pope & ladies by him.

Fiesole is about 25 minutes ride from the Duomo. As one approaches the hill the view of Florence looks very grand, with the Dome and Campanile in the mist, and cypresses stand up like sentinels, black green against silver gray of the olive leaves.

AUG. 7. Went up the Dome in the morning. The fresco in the ceiling can be seen in detail. The inner dome follows the cor top of the the outer dome. The details of marble of the lantern is very fine. From there the view of whole Florence is superb. It is quite different from the view obtained at London from the dome of St. Paul. There one saw smoke and ugly drab buildings. Here the houses and churches and cypress trees blossom before your eye.

Or San Michele has a very flowery Gothic (S.P. story). The niches are filled with statues (outside). The interior is not wonderful

Santa Croce has Michaelangelo's Tomb. The murals by Giotto in the chapels are good.

Casa Buonarotti has fine interiors and the museum is all right, though not much.

Saw frescoes at San Marco. Savonarola once lived here or

the 1st floor, which is divided into cells.

Santa Maria Novella has unequal bays in side. Saw the frescoes in the Spanish chapel.

Aug 8. Rain in Venice.

Saw inside of San Marco. The first impression of it is grand, with so much color and such richei-fonetti. It is the best church I have seen.

The mosaics (nicely examined from the gallery) is grand. The atmosphere is excellent as a church. The floor is very old and has hills and valleys.

Saw inside of Doges Palace. Very good interior. The Prison reminds one of Chillon. Only this is on a bigger scale. Walked inside the Bridge of sighs.

The academy of fine arts has collection of Titian. But it otherwise is full of junk. Titian's assumption of the Virgin, said to be here, I could not find. But there are many Titians.

Aug. 9 — Glorious weather in the afternoon, and at night the perfect moon over the Adriatic.

In the morning it was still cloudy. But made several sketches of sailing boats.

Walked over the Rialto, a wide bridge with 3 open passages and 2 rows of inclined covered arcades in between. It's a beautiful thing.

Went to where Marco Polo used to live. A court with a square tower (much altered) which is the sole remain of his house. The tower has a old doorway of carved stone. Beyond is the Marco Polo Bridge, not different from any other.

Walked all the way to the Public Park, the extreme end of the island. Made 7 sketches.

Aug. 10. Another glorious day. Went to see Colleoni's statue.

San Giovanni e Paolo)
is somewhat like San Marco
in exterior. The inside is
nothing.
    Went to Marco Polo's court
again, found with difficulty
through maze of streets.
This time found a house
marked with tablet, saying
the site to be Marco's house.
The house is too new
to be original, which was
burnt down in 16 century.
    Walked through most
of the streets in the afternoon
and after all even in
Venice most of the streets are
alike.
    Heard music in Piazza
San Marco. very common.
    In the morning I climbed
up the Campanile. One sees
the whole island and the
mainland. made 6 sketch.
AUG-11. Went to Lido in the
morning. very common place.
The bathing is the main thing.
    Saw international art

[101]

exhibit in Public Park, paintgs. representing France, Germany, Czechoslovakia, Russia, U.S.A. Belgium, England, and Italy; which last has a large collection of futuristic paintgs and some goldsmith work along modern lines. All the other countries send in very scanty and had examples.

The Exposition buildings are mostly modernistic, in very poor taste.

Bathed for 1/2 hour on the Lido beach in late afternoon. May go there tomorrow again.

Made six sketches.

On way back from San Marco to station, just close to San Georgio Maggiore, the moon shone on the water and the dome & campanile of San Georgio stood in silouette, the male and female sing (extremely good) was was heard from the either the gondolas or small boats. The whole trip looked so much like a dream, and very romantic.

Aug. 12 – Walked a long way in the morning, made 2 pencil sketches. Took a gondola ride on the Grand Canal, seeing Palazzo Vendramin. The stone slab has Wagner's profile and some Baroque ornament, then carried the following words:

F.T. Cadorin F.

IN QUESTO PALAGIO
L'ULTIMO SPIRO DE RICHARD WAGNER
ODONO LE ANIME
PERPETUARSI COME LA MAREA
CHE LAMBE I MARMI
        G.AB D'ANNUNZIO
✠ XIII FEBBRAIO
MDCCCLXXXIII
IN MEMORIAM.
MCMX

went to Lido to bathe again, there being hardly any sunshine.

(Made) water colors at Piazza San Marco.

While taking dinner at the usual place, a man and a woman played music — among Ramona. The woman reminded me so much of 白鹿鳥蛋它行.

Aug-13. took train for Verona at 7. arrived at 9.

Porta Nuova is very good in proportion. Porta Palio, which Jolita praised, does not look as good as Nuova.

San Zeno Maggiore is the best Romanesque church I ever saw. The wood ceiling over the Nave (14 c) is grand, made of carved wood ribs forming little square panels, on which faint paintings can be seen. The effect is very modernistic.

The font supported by an inverted capital is also in modernistic form. The whole aspect of the interior is good. And the choir is original in treatment, with marble rail on which stand Christ and his disciples. The little windows with orange light through them, look effective. The outside Romanesque portal is very charming and colorful, besides being graceful. The whole proportion of the facade is fine. The doors are covered with separate bronze plates of sculpture in the most archaic manner.

Porta Bosari has lost its entableture. There are two arches on the street and above them 3 rows of windows or open arcades. The view from the bank looking towards the fortress, across the old bridge (Ponte Pietra) is very fine, with beautiful piles of houses. The thing reminds one of Würzburg.

The cathedral has nothing particularly good,

the ceiling is painted blue with gold stars, and the general aspect is Baroque. The new addition (looks new) of the campanile is very poor.

The garden of Palazzo Guisti is good, with steep slope treated with niches & probably cascades, with cypresses lining on both sides. Very imposing. Visitors not admitted.

Saw supposed house of Juliet's Parents. (13 c.) with Balcony very high (on 3rd story). The other balcony was removed with brackets remaining. The court yard is square with long rows of railed balconies. The place is being remodelled.

Then saw Juliet's tomb an open stone coffin with admission tickets collected in it. It lies in the little loggia of Romanesque arcades. It looks too well trained to be true. All fictitious anyway. Shakespeare's statue bust stands on the backwall

Saw the group of buildings
around Piazza Dante. Loggia
(Palazzo del Consiglio) is
gracefully proportioned.

The arena is still in good
shape (Roman) and has practically
no order. It is being used as
a regular theatre now.
(The modern setting destroys
the looks here and. papery
in such a solid structure.

Also saw the Roman theatre
apparently closed to visitors.
But one can see things the
railing.

On the wall of Juliet's
Tomb are 2 stone tablets
with these words:

①

  Sacro aede
Seraphico Patri addicta
 Turris cognomento a Palea
nitrosi pulveris cadis
  abunde referta
  ovo fulgusito
 incendi vi subitari
  in lapidum fragmina aructa

Foede Tritas illisit Terrae
CIƆ IƆ C XXIV

② Easdam Praeses
Co Aloysius Turrianus
Basilica urbus Stipeet Piorum
~~Bas~~ in Havcce Augustam speciem
Ex Redivvus Excitavit
Sebastiano Ciconea a consilis
Hieronymo Capontanio Ah Aedy
CIƆ IƆ C XXV

In San Marco, Venice, on the
pillars the marble slabs are
laid vertically with fastur joints
at the corners.

~~Aug~~ Took 9.25 p.m. train for Innsbruck.
AUG 14. — Arrived at Innsbruck at
4 o'clock in the morning, without much
sleep the whole night. Took a
nap in the 3rd class waiting room
when at 6 the station guard
came and chased me out.
Took breakfast at a
place near the centre of the
town, walked up to the
mountain half way, made
a sketch and came down to

lunch.

Weather in the morning is fine. Towards noon it becomes cloudy.

Have no more desire to sketch.

Mailed 2 guide books to Snyder

Aug 15. No more sight seeing from now on. The things I shall see at Berlin (if any) and Poland and Russia will be recalled later on, as I must part with this book from tomorrow till I reach home. A sad feeling came over me in the evening. One cannot get sick of life or anything in Southern Italy. But in the north what with the rain it is very miserable, alone and to have no desire to do anything.

One delightful thing is to see Austrian and German modern architecture again.

JUG 16

JUG 17. Saw Charlottenburg garden from outside. Full of trees —
Took train for Russia.

UG 18. Passed Warsaw. Poland is very drab. The only color is on the scarf of a woman. The architecture is strangely Russian and German. Roads are bad.

Reached Niegoreloje at 4.00 P.M. Between Russia & Poland there is a wood gate, which marks the boundary. On both sides stand soldiers. And the formality requires the train to stop on both sides of the gate.

The customs are not very nasty. They did not care for my watch. Nor did they bother with books. They did look after writings. Money (American) must be registered. And when one changes American notes for Russian Roubles registration is necessary.

~~Aug 19.~~ Reached I was assigned to a sleeping compartment where there had been 3 women. (Whom later I found the missionaries to China, 2 American & one Chinese). I never thought of the embarrassing situation and was impatiently waiting them to clean things from my berth. But after I came out from the dining car the elder woman told me they had moved me to another place. I was thankful and at the same time reproached myself for being so absent-minded about the whole thing.

Aug 19. Reached Moscow 11 A.M. John Willis at station to meet m We stayed in the station (Alexander for a long time, probably waiting for that drunk girl who lost her baggage check. (The girl is daughter of a man in the same firm with Willis. Finally Willis took me to his apartment. There took a shower (cold) and had a steak dinner prepared by his wife.

We set forth to the Kremlin accompanied by another man Bulgarian by birth, now an American, and working in the same firm. He speaks Russian and knows Moscow pretty well.

Kremlin is very wonderful, with its many towers and gates and walls. It's also colorful. The Red Square is being repaved; and when it is finished it is going to be the most impressive thing in the world. Lenin's Tomb is enclosed as it is being rebuilt in black and red granite in the old design. We were late in applying for entrance to the Kremlin.

St. Basil is a curious church. It has 10 units and each unit goes up to be a tower. The plan cannot be read from the actual building, which seems to be full of dark alleys and small spaces. The work is cheap and details are rotten. But the exterior ensemble is

perfectly beautiful. People
don't show any reverence. They
have their hats on! and
one can touch anything at
all. In one chapel there did
sit a old women forbidding
visitors to touch an old
lamp

Just to show how little
the Russians know about
Physics they put a glass
bar on the arch (which
is going to crack worse) with
both ends in plaster of
Paris! Sure enough
the plaster cracks leaving
the glass unbroken.

Plan of St. Basil

The dust in moscow is the
worst in Europe. and also the
gutter into which I fell.
I actually saw people lie
comfortably in the gutter too
The Russians think nothing of
change. Anyone can change

over night — Streets, names, museums, and buildings. If the street is curved on account of the projection of a certain building, the projection can be torn down, no matter it belongs to what building.

They buy the best of machines. One wonders where they got the money. — By export. The whole population is industrial minded. That is their religion. No advertisements, no salesmen, But one sees good posters advocating industrialism.

Passed Tolstoy's house, now museum; but had no time to go in. The Contess Tolstoy is a bourgeois but they let her live for the museum.

The Housing problem in Moscow is acute. The city can only take care of one million but now there are 3 millions. They have 5-day week. Every day one-fifth of the population are on holiday. People have little manners. They line up for everything — for tobacco, food, and even for dying. There are so few hospitals to take care of the sick. On the 7th I telegramed Willis, 17th and the telegram arrived on the 19th, one hour after I arrived at his apartment.

When we reached the modern French art museum (by inquiry) it was nearly 4 o'clock. No people are willing to work full time, much less overtime. So the custodians refuse entrance. By argument we won't win. So we just ascended the stairs by vulgar insistence. The women there spoke French. And calling them medames pleased them. I spent 15 minutes there but I would wish 15 days. The treasures of the whole world are here. Whole rooms of Cézanne, Van Gogh, Renoir, Matisse, Picasso, Gauguin. Nowhere else in the world can

One see so many ~~good~~ masterpiece in one museum.

Saw church of Christ the Savior, built to commemorate the siege of Napoleon on Moscow. It is of white marble outside. Very simple. We ascended the top and had a good panorama of Moscow. There is some good inlaid marble work in the interior.

Took Trans Siberian train from the Siberian station, at 6.45. P.M.

I asked some food from Willis's wife. ~~She~~ but forgot the loaf of bread. She ran after us after we left for the street car to station and that half a loaf did do some good service.

Shared a compartment with a young Russian communist, handsome and intelligent. He knows about all the big names of Russian literature. He gave me some candy and I him an orange.

VG 20
VG 21. The Russian went down

at Viatka.

The common address in Russia is citizen and citizeness. My watch stopped and the clock at the station showed different time on both sides. The station clock is Moscow time.

People in Siberia apparently stop washing their faces, much less their shirts.

AUG 22. The peasant women sell things at the station. But they are so silent and look so drunk. They stand there saying nothing; and of course nobody buys anything. In that silence there must be concealed an immense suffering. Anyhow they are better than before, as there is no one to whip them.

AUG 23: Cloudy, hilly country.

AUG 24. Passed Irkutsk, saw barracks. And then Lake Baikal. Fine scenery and not yet exploited by steam ship or hotel. Mountains

now.
/25 Passed Chita, 7 P.M.
06   up early to see dawn.
0626, ~~reached~~ ~~7.15 A.M.~~
Saw barbed wires and trenches
Reached Manchouli at 7.15. A.M.
went into town and found
war ruins.
    As I found out later baggage
should be checked to Manchouli
or attend to baggage examination
at Manchouli. As mine was
held at Manchouli for 2
days by the customs.
627, Harbin 8.30. A.M.

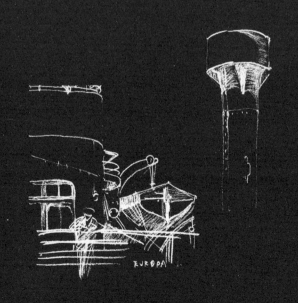

旅 欧 日 记

旅欧日记由童明根据童寯先生手稿译出。由于原手稿部分有所残破,并且字迹难以辨识,在翻译过程中已多方面进行了查证与核实,但难免仍会存有遗漏和错误之处,敬请读者谅解。同时为了方便读者阅读,本译稿对于文中一些重要地名、人名、建筑、物品等增加了译注,也配置了相应的索引照片,供读者参考。

图 1 温彻斯特大教堂 Winchester Cathedral
图 2 温彻斯特大教堂 Winchester Cathedral
图 3 渥西宫 Wolvesey Palace
图 4 索尔兹伯里大教堂 Salisbury Cathedral

4月26日　中午12:30乘"欧罗巴"号从纽约启程。
4月27日　在大西洋中。
4月28日　在大西洋中。
4月29日　在大西洋中。
4月30日　在大西洋中,人们拥上甲板。

5月1日　下午3点于南安普顿上岸。

　　南安普顿,一座宁静小镇,美丽的乡村公路通往温彻斯特(乘汽车)。大路上有很多行人和自行车。风景甚佳。

　　3点钟后抵达温彻斯特,走进一爿由几位老妇经营的商店(库斯沃斯,高盛街164–170号)。她们让我留下沉甸甸的格莱斯顿行李箱[1],得以径直前往大教堂[2](图1,图2)。第一次看见如此宏大之

---

[1] 格莱斯顿式旅行提包,由中部对开的旅行包,也称架子包。
[2] 温彻斯特大教堂(Winchester Cathedral),英格兰最大的教堂之一,位于汉普郡(Hampshire)的温彻斯特(Winchester),也是全欧洲拥有最长中殿的教堂,长约160米。教堂内供奉着圣三一、圣彼得、圣保罗及圣斯威辛,它亦是温彻斯特的主教座堂及温彻斯特主教辖区的中心。

教堂，非常激动。研读了简·奥斯汀[3]的碑文，所采用的是一种古老的黑体字。教堂十字交汇处采用的是诺曼风格。教堂正殿的立柱也是由诺曼风格演化而来。英国大教堂的内院[4]是世界上最幽静之处，鸟语草香，宜人惬意。画了一张西门的水彩画。参观了博物馆。参观了渥西宫[5]（图3），这是一处诺曼遗址，令人回想起旧时圆明园。溪水静静流过。

在"上帝之赐"吃的晚餐，这是一家老饭店，饭菜尚好但有点贵（6先令）。格莱斯顿行李箱死沉如同一只推车，两支胳膊已经累垮。等待许久，直到9:30才搭上前往索尔兹伯里的火车（在东罗夫站换车）。10:30抵达索尔兹伯里，乘出租车前往老乔治旅馆（2先令），住14号房间。乔治房（17号）是一间双人间，塞缪尔·佩皮斯[6]曾经在那儿住过。女主人名叫简·埃戈·泰。她说某一间房中有许多屋梁，但我花了6先令才住上一个只有一道梁的房间。

睡得很死。

5月2日　7:30客房服务员敲门，而我还在睡觉。早餐后前往参观大教堂[7]（图4）。室内很漂亮。由于黑色门柱的缘故，色彩很好，比例也很好，并且很巴洛克。回廊庭院则是最漂亮的，如此宁静，除了鸟语叽叽啾

图5　圣·托马斯教堂
St. Thomas Church

图6　圣·托马斯教堂内景
Interior of St. Thomas Church

图7　约翰厅　Hall of John Hall

---

3 简·奥斯汀（Jane Austen, 1775—1817年），英国著名小说家，代表作品有《理智与情感》、《傲慢与偏见》等。她逝后被安葬于温彻斯特大教堂。
4 教堂内院一般指附属于教堂的一些其他辅助性建筑，如教区办公室、学校、小礼拜室、主教以及牧师的住屋等场所。
5 渥西宫（Wolvesey Palace），中世纪温彻斯特大主教的住宅，最后一次盛大活动是1554年玛丽女王的婚礼。现在基本上已经成为残垣断壁，石头墙上长满青草，成为发思古之幽情的地方。
6 塞缪尔·佩皮斯（Samuel Pepys, 1633—1703年），17世纪英国作家和政治家，著有《佩皮斯日记》，其日记包括有对伦敦大火（1665年）和大瘟疫（1666年）等事件的详细描述，成为17世纪最丰富的生活文献。佩皮斯曾任英国皇家海军部长，是英国现代海军的缔造者，他也曾任英国皇家学会会长，以会长的名义批准了牛顿巨著《自然哲学之数学原理》的初版印刷。
7 索尔兹伯里大教堂（Salisbury Cathedral）建造于1220年—1265年，它拥有全英国最高的尖塔、最壮观的回廊，是早期英国哥特式建筑的主要代表。

图8.1 圣安妮门 St. Anne's Gate
图8.2 圣安妮门 St. Anne's Gate
图9 石环阵 Stonehenge
图10 阿姆斯伯里修道院教堂 Amesbury, Abbey Church

啾没有别的声音。画了一张北门的速写，参观了带有木梁和壁画的圣·托马斯教堂（图5，图6），约翰厅（图7）有着非常漂亮的木构门面。博物馆关门。三次路过圣安妮门[8]（图8.1，图8.2），没能进入主教府邸，只是在外面看了看王宫。到处都是漂亮的房屋和花园，埃文河[9]欢快的流水穿过带有一座座拱桥的小镇。在向南前行的路上，很远就可以看见大教堂，因此花了16先令。顺道参观了奥利佛·洛奇[10]的故居，没什么特别之处，离路相当远并且很小。石环阵（图9）远比想象的要小。在返回途中参观了修道院教堂（阿姆斯伯里）（图10），十分无趣。

中饭和晚饭（有点冷）都是在靠近圣·托马斯教堂附近的同一个地方吃的。清晨7:20乘火车前往巴斯，8:40到达，停靠在阿盖尔旅店对面的车站，逛了史托街。这座城市更加偏向意大利文艺复兴风格而不是哥特风格。

在英格兰骑自行车的人更多，一半都是妇女。这是一座小镇，就像索尔兹伯里，橱窗的装饰与纽约的金贝尔[11]差不多。妇女们的衣着也很得体，饭食则与价格不相符合。

---

8 圣安妮门（St. Anne's Gate），建于1330年左右，是进入索尔兹伯里主教堂的入口之一，也是英格兰最大的内街。
9 埃文河，发源于英格兰洛斯特郡南格劳塞斯特的奇平索德伯里，长120公里，流经马姆斯伯里（Malmesbury）、奇彭纳姆（Chippenham）、梅尔克舍姆（Melksham）、埃文河畔布拉德福德（Bradford on Avon）、巴斯、凯恩舍姆（Keynsham），在布里斯托尔埃文茅斯的河口与塞文河汇合，注入爱尔兰海。
10 奥利佛·洛奇（Oliver Joseph Lodge, 1851—1940年），英国物理学家，先后在伦敦大学和利物浦大学任教。洛奇在法国 E. 布冉利的检波器的基础上研制成功金属粉末检波器。1894年，他将金属粉末检波器、继电器、电铃、打字机等连接起来，组成了一台接收机，曾接收到55米远处的摩尔斯电码。洛奇的实验影响很大，A.C.波波夫、G.马可尼的无线电通信研究都是在这些成果的基础上完成的。
11 金贝尔（Gimbels），纽约的一家零售商店，由贺拉斯·塞克斯（Horace Saks）与伯纳德·金贝尔（Bernard Gimbel）于20世纪早期在纽约34街分别经营。

图 11 威尔士大教堂 Wells Cathedral

图 12 贫困者门廊 The Penniless Porch
图 13 布朗之门 Brown's Gate
图 14 主教府邸 Bishop's Palace
图 15 维卡胡同 Vicars Close

在阿盖尔旅店房间里的壁炉台上,有一幅威尔士亲王[12]的画像,约克公爵[13]及夫人[14]很可能是一副演员的装扮。

5月3日 8点钟吃早餐,这是我在巴斯的这家阿盖尔旅店吃到的最好的火腿与鸡蛋。乘汽车前往威尔士,参观了在巴斯和威尔士之间的大教堂[15](图11),沿途没有什么值得一看的东西。每座房屋看上去都显得时髦而且廉价。一些老房屋也没有什么意思。英格兰是哥特风格的最佳之处。我不喜欢巴斯,因为它太传统了(意大利)。威尔士更好一些,至少大教堂周围的房屋是非常哥特的,并且很漂亮。参观了教长之眼[16]与主教之眼[17],贫困者门廊(图12),以及布朗之

---

12 原文 P. of W., 应该为 Prince of Wales, 即威尔士亲王。当时的威尔士亲王是爱德华王子,他于1936年1月授位于乔治五世,成为英国国王爱德华八世。但是由于他坚持要与美国离婚妇女威利斯·辛普森结婚,迫于压力不得不放弃王位,将王位传给其兄弟阿尔伯特王子,随后隐居于温莎城堡,成为著名的温莎公爵。

13 也称阿尔伯特王子,1936年接替其兄长爱德华八世成为英国国王,即领导英国参加第二次世界大战的乔治六世。

14 约克公爵夫人名为伊丽莎白·博维-里昂(Elizabeth Bowes-Lyon, 1900—2002年),她于1923年与阿尔伯特王子也就是约克公爵相遇并结婚,当今英国女王伊丽莎白二世以及玛格丽特公主即其女儿。

15 威尔士大教堂(Wells Cathedral),位于英格兰索莫塞特郡威尔士市,建于1175年至1490年,是巴斯与威尔士主教所在地。

16 教长之眼(Dean's eye),是布朗之门的别称。

17 主教之眼(Bishop's eye),是贫困者门廊的别称,也是通往主教府邸的主要大门。

门[18]（图13）。主教府邸（图14）在星期六上午不开放，而我最多只能待到下午3点钟，因此只能满足于透过门缝瞄上一眼。绘画角度及其氛围一如既往都是中世纪的。多么安宁而美丽的地方！群童嬉戏，浮鸭翩翩。宫殿的背景由于一道带有射击孔的长墙而大大增强。回廊庭院的拱廊并非开敞，所有的拱券都带有石饰格。一株柏树矗立于回廊庭院当中。小礼拜堂处在可由教堂通达的地宫上方，它拥有一个非常不错的吊顶。

教堂的室内空间相当扁平。参观了钟塔下方的圣安德鲁十字[19]。金色窗户（东端）镶有我未曾见过的漂亮玻璃，这是一幅壮美的画面，真希望能把它画下来。向下进入地宫，参观了几个石棺，气味很糟糕。向上穿过一段令人愉快的石阶进入礼拜堂。

爬上钟塔，观赏整座小镇。在入口大门的铅皮屋顶上，刻下我名字的开头字母和1930年。在木门上也刻上了名字的开头字母。有一个圆形小石梯直通塔顶，塔顶透过小窗得以良好采光。

在维卡胡同[20]（图15）中的食堂相当不错，内有精美的木作和手绘，天棚非常漂亮，带有木质花边以及石膏花饰。那些锡具曾经为克伦威尔[21]所拥有。参观在维卡胡同尽端的礼拜堂，一楼有非常漂亮的木屏风，二楼则有漂亮的天棚，可由几级伸在外面的石阶通达。

上流住宅区在城内。大教堂周围相当喧闹，现在这是一个生气勃勃的地方。在布鲁德街附近吃了午餐。

4点钟回到巴斯，参观了罗马浴场[22]（图16）。在博物馆内有一个模型，展示着方形和圆形的浴池，巨型泵房采用的是很糟糕的传统式样。喝了一杯矿泉水，然后买票（4先令）在苏利斯浴室洗澡。在浴缸中洗了一次痛快的热水澡。15分钟后，有人进来用热毛

---

18 布朗之门（Brown's Gate），建造时间约在14世纪。它与大教堂周围其他大门都是在贝肯顿（Bekynton）神父在任期间建造的。
19 圣安德鲁十字（St. Andrews Cross），也称英式十字，形状如X。
20 维卡胡同（Vicars Close），也称牧师内街，是英格兰最古老的街道之一。
21 奥利弗·克伦威尔（Oliver Cromwell，1599—1658年），英国资产阶级革命时期的主要军事、政治领导人，宗教领袖。17世纪英国资产阶级革命中，资产阶级新贵族集团的代表人物、独立派的首领，从1653年开始掌权并进行独裁统治。他执政期间鼓励重商主义，使经济得到发展。宗教方面，他虽然给予英国人民部分宗教自由，但也把清教徒戒律强加在所有人身上。
22 罗马浴场（Roman Bath），巴斯最早由凯尔特人在此发现温泉。在罗马人入侵与占领时期，这里在长达300年期间逐渐被建造成为一个洗浴中心。罗马浴场目前由四部分组成，圣泉、罗马神庙、罗马浴室以及博物馆。

巾、布单将我包裹起来。开始时就像穿着宽袍的罗马皇帝克劳迪乌斯[23],接着就像埃及木乃伊躺在床上。15分钟后,起来穿好衣服,在冷却室中坐了一会儿。

在乘火车之前,穿过维多利亚公园去看圆形广场和新月大楼[24](图17),两者都是文艺复兴风格,但是屋顶和烟囱则带有一点哥特风格。在回米德兰火车站的途中几乎迷了路。

乘火车前往格劳塞斯特,住在米德兰皇家旅馆,B&B[25]的价格为8先令。晚饭吃了火腿和鸡蛋。

仍然不喜欢喝英国茶,作为一种规矩,它令人感到厌烦。

5月4日 8点钟吃早饭,10点参观了大教堂[26]内部(图18),正殿内有粉红色的诺曼风格巨型立柱以及哥特式屋顶。在唱诗席上方的装饰性天棚非常漂亮。在东端的窗户也很棒。由于星期天有活动,我们不能进入唱诗席,也不能进入私语廊,回廊庭院也关门了。看到牧师行伍,有些还只是孩子,穿着带白领的红衣服,外面再罩上一件白夹克。钟塔的顶端(从底部的交叉部位得到飞券的支撑)有五个窗饰,就像一条花边。从外面看装饰性很强。南门廊带有诺曼风格的木质

图16 罗马浴场 Roman Bath
图17 圆形广场与皇家新月大楼 The Circus & Royal Crescent
图18 格劳塞斯特大教堂 Gloucester Cathedral
图19 洛德圣玛丽教堂 St. Mary de Lode Church

23 克劳迪乌斯(Claudius Nero Germanicus,公元前10年—公元54年),公元41—54年间为罗马皇帝。长袍代表罗马公民身份,其渊源来自希腊文化传统。
24 18世纪,建筑设计师约翰·伍德(John Wood)按照乔治式风格设计了新巴斯市,并设计了圆形广场(The Circus),其子小约翰·伍德(John Wood the Younger)则设计了皇家新月大楼(Royal Crescent)(1767—1774年),该楼由30座住宅所组成。
25 B&B,英文Bed and Breakfast简写,意思是向客人提供早餐和床,大多表现为家庭式的客栈。英国早期的B&B全是家庭私营,独门独户做生意,将家里的一个或两个客房出租。
26 格劳塞斯特大教堂(Gloucester Cathedral),又称圣彼得与圣三一大教堂,建于681年,坐落于格洛斯特城北侧,临近河边。

大门，因而显得非常漂亮。一些诺曼风格的拱券在外面就能看见。看了照片后才弄明白回廊庭院是怎么回事。

洛德圣玛丽[27]（教堂）（图19）不值得一看。

几座老建筑十分有趣，例如霍普主教[28]在殉道前一晚曾经住过的那一个。"新酒店"倒是显得非常老旧，此时正好下雨，我站在一个石门廊下，为它画了一幅很好的铅笔素描。走了若干英里的路，但是没有看见什么有意思的东西。小镇的平面有些像中国的（罗马），街道和大门则按照罗盘来命名。皇家客栈宾馆价格昂贵，食物却很糟糕。B&B客房价格8先令。

乘火车于傍晚6点钟抵达百老汇。

从G.W.火车站[29]前往百老汇（村庄）的距离有1英里，我差一点因为携带一只50号的格莱斯顿旅行箱而被累垮。在抵达"天鹅"旅馆前就已经气喘吁吁、筋疲力尽。"天鹅"旅馆已经住满。因此只能前往莱贡阿姆斯旅店[30]，这真是令人喜出望外！这么漂亮的房间，干净而又整洁，品位十足。这是我所见过最好的一家旅店。

沿着百老汇大街行走大约2英里半。没看见什么值得拍照或者速写的东西。我认为最好的就是在莱贡阿姆斯旅店。7点半在大餐厅吃晚餐。挤满了穿着时髦的人。大厅则是一所绝处，餐厅的女招待真是一位美人，她让我觉得K的雕像[31]只是一个不值一提的小矮胖。她建议我喝红酒，而我选择了苹果酒，味道真的真的很好。她为我倒上了酒。晚餐也非常可口（6先令）。在餐厅画了两幅速写。

参观了克伦威尔室，以及查理室或者橡树间（查理一世）[32]。

两间房都非常阴冷，但确实迷人。看到了克伦威尔曾经坐过的椅子。莱贡阿姆斯有一个很大的后院用于停车场。洗了一个热水

---

27 洛德圣玛丽（St. Mary de Lode Church），地处格劳塞斯特大教堂附近，是城市中最古老的教区教堂。"lode"一词来自古英语，意思是渡口或者河道。
28 约翰·霍普（John Hooper, 1500—1555年），曾任格劳塞斯特与沃塞斯特的主教。
29 G.W.火车站，指在托丁顿（Toddington）的格劳塞斯特与沃尔维奇线路火车站（Gloucestershire & Warwickshire Steam Railway Station）。
30 在百老汇市中心的一家传统小旅店。
31 可能指克伦威尔。
32 查理一世（Charles I, 1600—1649年），詹姆士一世的次子，英格兰苏格兰与爱尔兰国王，英国历史上唯一一位被公开处死的国王。查理一世于1625年继位，与国会之间存有深刻矛盾。从而也加剧了皇室与资产阶级的矛盾，造成国会和国王彻底决裂。在经历1642年第一次内战与1647年第二次内战后，国会军在克伦威尔的指挥下粉碎了苏格兰王军。随后，国会与军队共同组织了特别法庭审判查理一世，1649年1月27日，法庭判处查理一世死刑。它标志着英国封建专制的结束，资产阶级共和国时代的开始。据传说查理一世被行刑后，其无头鬼魂在Chavenage House中游荡。

澡，住在这里确实令人愉快，无论需要花费多少钱，因为它物有所值。令我难忍不堪的就是在这些惊喜之余，还要带上一只沉重的行囊长途跋涉，以及没完没了的火车和汽车。旅行手册说有很多美国人住在这儿，我却没有碰上一个。但是这里的氛围也许是美国的（在大街上的汽车及行人数量）。

全世界只有两条百老汇大街，都挤满了美国人，正好想起我在格劳塞斯特需要做的一件事情。

前往警察局看看是否需要注册。20分钟后他们发现，如果没有超过两个月，我就不需要注册，但是如果超过2个月，就必须注册。

在百老汇大街车站的那个人酒气熏天，花了半个多小时才找到前往埃文河畔斯塔德福德的火车时刻表。

5月5日 早晨画了一些速写，9点钟在吃晚饭的同一张桌子上吃早饭。离开旅馆（账单1-2-7）。乘公共汽车到G.W.车站，前往埃文河畔斯塔德福德。12点钟到达，住在"白天鹅"旅馆。

参观莎士比亚出生地，我被震撼了。在二楼诗人的诞生处，看到窗户上司各特夫妇和卡莱尔夫妇[33]的名字。在朱迪斯·莎士比亚故居[34]吃了午餐。

参观"新地方"，这是一个由国王邓肯[35]与威尔士王子所赠送的开满鲜花的美丽花园。参观老井以及部分老房子的基础。

前往参观莎士比亚曾经学习过的学校，梁架就像汉字中的"金"。参观了圣三一教堂（图20），莎士比亚被安葬在靠近圣坛的地方。步行了很远前往肖特里[36]，花费很长时间才找到安妮·哈瑟维[37]的故居。看到了最好的床，亚麻做的。还有莎士比亚曾经坐在上面进行求婚的、靠近火炉边的木凳椅。当然，安妮的父母坐在火炉的两侧。新的纪念馆尚未建造起来，没有走到图书馆里面，参观了埃文河。

这是我所喜欢参观的最佳之处。这里没有太多的东西，但是它们珍贵无比。在旅馆吃的晚餐。

---

33 沃尔特·司各特爵士（Sir Walter Scott，1771—1832年），英国19世纪著名历史小说家和诗人。托马斯·卡莱尔(Thomas Carlyle,1795—1881年)，苏格兰讽刺作家、历史学家。
34 威廉·莎士比亚的女儿。
35 指苏格兰国王邓肯一世，他是莎士比亚戏剧《麦克白》中麦克白将军的表兄。麦克白是一位很有野心的英雄，他在夫人的怂恿下谋杀邓肯，做了国王。
36 肖特里（Shottery）是一个小村庄，距离埃文河畔斯塔德福德西侧1英里。肖特里是莎士比亚的妻子安妮·哈瑟维的家乡。
37 安妮·哈瑟维（Anne Hathaway, 1556—1623年），莎士比亚的妻子。

图20 圣三一教堂
Church of Holy Trinity

图21 圣玛丽教堂
The Church of St. Mary's

图22 肯尼沃斯的城堡
Kenilworth Castle

图23 东门宾馆 East Gate Hotel

一些衣着正经的男士前来用餐,而一些老派的维多利亚淑女就是令人感到古怪。

今晚观看了《麦克白》[38],并且喜欢里面的场景。

饰演麦克白夫人的演员见绌于其夫君。12点钟上床睡觉。

"红屋旅馆"是一个看上去很糟糕的地方,但是华盛顿喜欢住在那儿。

5月6日 早餐后,尽力去赶早晨10点钟的汽车前往沃尔维奇,但是没有汽车。回到旅馆写了些东西。下了一整天的雨。

乘坐11:30的汽车前往沃尔维奇,由于下雨,看不太清楚城镇。只看到了东门(其上矗立着图书馆)以及圣玛丽教堂(图21)的外观。参观了城堡的部分室内。有无数个房间,装饰华美。有许多伦勃朗和凡·戴克的作品。步行前往意大利花园,看见一只孔雀伫立雨中,还有在凉亭中精美的希腊花瓶。外套都湿透了。

既不能作画也无法拍照。

前往肯尼沃斯[39]。在汽车上遇见一位俊朗的老者,他去过杭州。他住在肯尼沃斯。

肯尼沃斯的城堡(图22)已成废墟,并且很让人想起北京的老圆明园。由于经常下雨,墙面已经失去光泽。只拍了一张照片。在图纸上看到的湖面(复建的)在克伦威尔时期就已经干涸。天气晴朗时,这一切必定非常美丽。

不喜欢喝"茶"。从肯尼沃斯到城堡需要走1英里,我回来太早了,只得坐在邮局里等汽车。当我出来时,以为时间仍然尚早,但是汽车正在准备开走。还好跳了

---

38 《麦克白》(Macbeth),莎士比亚的四大悲剧之一。
39 肯尼沃斯(Kenilworth),位于沃尔维奇郡中部的一座小镇。

上去。又回到了埃文河畔斯塔德福特。如果知道可以直接从沃尔维奇乘火车前往牛津，我就可以不用回来，既省时间又省钱。

在一家小饭店吃的火腿与鸡蛋，第一次在英国喝到咖啡。乘坐7:45火车前往牛津，9:30到达。

扛着一件50号的行囊，行走2英里才找到一家旅店，却发现它已经住满，没有什么比这更恼人的了。扛着行囊一直向前走到"东门"[40]（图23），这个地方十分晦暗。非常失望。

脚湿了，洗了一个热水澡。

5月7日 早餐后出去参观各个学院。首先参观约翰逊博士[41]的房间，它在2楼，靠近彭布罗克学院[42]（图24）的大门。一间带有小壁炉的小会客厅，以及一间非常小的卧室。上面一层（3楼）是后加的。

参观了大钟塔。站在基督教堂[43]的塔顶（图25），学院大部分由四方建筑构成，显得既阴寒又冷清。它无疑拥有历史感的外表。一些学生穿着学袍，很多情况仅仅就是一块布。在新学院，院墙仍然保留着（有点像中国的长城），有大门和铭牌。大多数学院都是哥特风格的，除了皇后学院[44]（图26），它是古典风格的。当然还有卡迈拉[45]（图27）。

下午2点钟参观完毕。随后画了2张水彩画和4张铅笔速写。

通过一本1898年版的贝德克旅行指南[46]，我熟悉了伦敦。

英国的饭菜较贵并且不太好吃，他们唯一做得还可以的是鱼。

5月8日 早餐后乘火车前往温莎，直到12点钟才到达。城堡不开

---

40 东门（East Gate），是一家宾馆的名称。
41 塞缪尔·约翰逊（Samuel Johnson, 1709—1784 年），常被称为约翰逊博士（Dr. Johnson），英国历史上最有名的文人之一，文评家、诗人、散文家。在18世纪时，法国和意大利已有许多字典，但在英国却没有相应的字典，从而被视为一种国耻。1746 年，塞缪尔·约翰逊花费9年时间独力编出《约翰逊字典》。
42 彭布罗克学院（Pembroke College），彭布罗克为英格兰一郡名称，学院成立于 1624 年，以彭布罗克郡三世伯爵命名，该学院位于牛津市中心，塞缪尔·约翰逊曾在此工作。
43 基督教堂（Christ Church）所在的基督教堂学院是牛津大学最大学院之一，该学院曾经培养出13位英国首相，电影"哈里·波特"曾在该学院取景。
44 皇后学院（Queens' College），由菲利普皇后的牧师罗伯特·艾格莱斯菲尔德以皇后的名义成立于 1341 年。
45 全称为拉德克利夫圆厅（Radcliffe Camera）。Camera 原意是库房或房间。现在是牛津大学图书馆的主楼。
46 贝德克是一家专门针对世界游行的德国出版公司，由卡尔·贝德克（Karl Baedeker）于1827年创办。该公司出版的旅行指南包含由最好的旅行专家所撰写的有关建筑、纪念物、景点等重要信息的介绍。

图 24 彭布罗克学院 Pembroke College 图 25 基督教堂 Christ Church
图 26 牛津皇后学院 Queens' College 图 27 牛津大学图书馆 Radcliffe Camera
图 28 北部公寓 North Terrace

放,但是参观了一些有意思的木结构房屋、北部公寓[47](图28)以及皇后公寓的背面,同时也参观了礼拜堂的室内。

前往伊顿[48],参观了老学院,其中有老课桌和笞打台(2步),所有地方都刻有姓名——板牌上、课桌上,甚至栏杆上。参观了礼拜堂,在里面,很不舒适的木凳被孩子们称为刀架。看见戴高帽的男孩,还有穿运动服的。不沾水的孩子在玩滚圈,沾水的孩子则在游泳。

---

[47] 北部公寓(North Terrace),温莎城堡北面的公寓。
[48] 伊顿公学(Eton College),英国私立男校,坐落在温莎小镇,是英国最有名的男校之一,由亨利四世于1440年创办,与皇后钟爱的温莎宫隔泰晤士河相望。

在伊顿看见一幢名叫公鸡的老房子（500年）。在那里喝了茶，还有抹了果酱的热卷。皇后（玛丽）经常去那里，有一次签下她的名字（我没看到）。因此我签下了更多的名字（别人要求这样去做）。上楼去参观一些老房间，非常有趣，就像莎士比亚的诞生地。在坎特伯雷还有另外一座老房屋，屋后有一个斗鸡场，50年前人们还在那里斗鸡。地面上铺着猪蹄骨。

在建筑外部的正立面上有两个木头人像。角窗，在人行道上还有那种木制的矮柜。

5:30抵达伦敦的帕丁顿火车站，乘汽车前往摄政街，但是不能进入王宫。同样也不能留宿于基督教青年会[49]，最后前往格拉夫顿，并获得一间B&B，花了8先令，洗了一个澡。

参观了杜莎夫人蜡像馆[50]。但是由于太晚而没能看到恐怖屋[51]。

在旅馆享用了一顿非常不错的牛排。

伦敦是个大城市。在那些小镇中，我总是步行走完全程，眼下在伦敦，再也不能依靠步行了。如果能乘对汽车，伦敦就是一个好地方。

在摄政街的一家柯达店冲印了胶卷。

5月9日 早餐后前往西伯利亚大街，试探着寻路，发现它开放并且安全。前往摄政街的街角，定制了一套黑色西服，花了8英镑。在外面参观了圣詹姆斯宫[52]（图29），还有圣保罗大教堂、皇家交接仪式和西敏寺。今晚又去了杜莎夫人蜡像馆，参观了恐怖屋。然而重要的是，我今天去了大英博物馆，从1点到4点钟，参观了所有的内容。在额尔金大理石展厅[53]买了几张明信片，以及一些中国画的饰针。看到如此之多的珍贵原物，感到有些震撼，例如世界上最早的纸（在敦煌发现的中国纸），名人手稿以及雕像，都是免费的。参观了海德公园以及爱泼斯坦[54]的塑雕，还有炮兵纪念碑。

---

49 YMCA全称是Young Men's Christian Association，即基督教青年会，是美国最大的非营利社区服务组织，并在世界上120个国家设有分会。
50 杜莎夫人蜡像馆，杜莎夫人是一位生活在巴黎的法国人，她先是在法国的凡尔赛做尝试，1802年杜莎夫人带着她的蜡像收藏品来到英国伦敦，成立第一家"杜莎夫人"蜡像馆。
51 恐怖屋是蜡像馆的一个主要展厅。
52 圣詹姆斯宫是伦敦最早的一座宫殿，坐落于蓓尔梅尔街，圣詹姆斯公园的北面。
53 额尔金大理石（Elgin Marbles）指英国不列颠博物馆所藏古希腊大理石雕刻。它是由第七代额尔金伯爵汤玛斯·布鲁斯在其任职奥斯曼帝国大使时，于1801—1803年，将希腊"帕提农神庙"大理石雕塑运回苏格兰。现大部分存于大英博物馆。
54 爱泼斯坦（Sir Jacob Epstein, 1880—1959年），雕塑家，出生在美国，主要的工作活动在英国，是一位先锋的现代主义雕塑家。

图29 圣詹姆斯宫 St. James Palace
图30 更衣室 Robing Room
图31 诗人角 Poets' Corner
图32 朗菲娄 Longfellow

5月10日 早晨天色灰蒙，但还有阳光。随后天气变得多云，下午5点开始下雨，直到傍晚。

西敏寺10点钟开放。前往参观议会大厦，参观了国王的更衣室（图30），墙上挂着描绘英国历史的木雕，还有一些绘画。更衣室里有一个王座，对面是壁炉。皇家画廊中有2条长幅绘画，一张描绘特拉法戈[55]（纳尔逊战死）[56]，另一张描绘滑铁卢。我相信就在这间房间里，乔治国王在海军会议上发表演讲。

上议院的色彩配置非常漂亮——红色皮凳加上从高窗射入的光线。但是下议院则显得较为沉闷、平淡而且阴冷。上议院大概是最为色彩斑斓的厅堂，所有这些厅堂都具有宏伟的比例，并且照明非常良好。一些房间由于高窗而显得非常剧场化，带有大量的投影和少量的高光。

令我最感兴趣的地方当然就是诗人角[57]（图31），朗菲娄[58]的半身雕像（图32）让我留连忘返，整个回院里充满了半身塑像、碑刻和雕像。中庭由于它巨大的高度和长度，其比例显得非常和谐，缤纷的光线透过窗户形成特殊效果。由于这种光线效果，回院的天棚显示出浓厚的暖色调，而面对庭院的窗饰则显示为冷色调。回院

---

[55] 指特拉法戈海战 (The Battle of Trafalgar)，这是1805年10月21日在西班牙特拉法加角外海发生的英国皇家海军与法国、西班牙联军之间的一场著名海战，是拿破仑战役 (1803—1815年) 中的一部分。该海战以英国胜利告终，并成为19世纪海战的经典。
[56] 纳尔逊勋爵海军上将为特拉法戈海战英国皇家海军的总指挥，他在战斗中阵亡。
[57] 诗人角 (Poets' Corner) 处于西敏寺教堂 (Westminster Abbey) 十字形内堂的南翼中殿之东南角，内有许多文学伟人的纪念碑与纪念文物，如莎士比亚、狄更斯等人，也有许多纪念文物在此展出。
[58] 朗菲娄 (Henry Wadsworth Longfellow, 1807—1882年)，美国教育家与诗人，其作品有《保罗·莱沃尔的旅行》(*Paul Revere's Ride*)、《希亚瓦萨之歌》(*The Song of Hiawatha*)、《福音》(*Evangeline*) 等。他也是翻译但丁《神曲》的第一位美国人，是被称为"炉边诗人"的组员之一。

外还有一个令人愉悦的、带有喷泉的意大利小庭院。画了一张回院走廊的水彩画。

花了不到2个半小时参观了这两座建筑。

在地下室商店里拍了一张爱波斯坦雕塑的照片。

乘汽车前往温莎。2点3刻进入城堡。参观了国宾馆，大多数厅室供全国各地游客娱乐之用。每个房间的布置都很漂亮且有品位，仅从照片不能反映色彩效果。这里有高耸的天棚和很高的房间，每扇门都通往一个有意思的地方，如鲁本斯展厅和凡·戴克展厅。在某个展厅中有几幅霍尔拜因的画。画作和家具的摆设十分精美。有3个绘画顶棚，描绘的是同样主题（以斯帖记[59]）。其他一些展厅拥有漂亮的镶饰顶棚。大部分家具是法式的，一些展厅则是路易十五风格的。宴会厅非常宏大，当举办国宴时，服务人员站立两旁进行伺卫，它必定是一个五彩缤纷的场面。

参观者太多，一些女士去那里仅仅是为了戴上手套，去感受蓝色天鹅绒坐垫的美妙感觉。

登上圆塔，整个大温莎全貌尽收眼底。

走进皇后玩偶屋[60]（图33）。但是完全没有必要进去，费钱也费时间。

参观议会大厦、西敏寺以及温莎的最佳方式是在星期六，就如我今天所做的。

今天头一次在里昂饭店吃晚餐，花了11便士。

乘坐18路汽车前往荷尔朋[61]去参观老建筑。在车上，一个婴儿"尿尿"，售票员只能停车，从修路工人那里借来一些沙土将它盖上。画了一张老房子的速写。然后前往参观普茨茅斯街14号的古玩店。在雨中沿着胡特街行走，然后参观了市寺教堂[62]（图34），也走到了林肯饭店和公园。但是没能找到林肯饭店的确切建筑。

在回旅馆的途中，在靠近东大道（贫民窟）的一家夜市停留一会儿，花3美元买了2只橙子。

---

59 以斯帖记（The Book of Esther），旧约中的一卷，讲述以斯帖如何拯救她的人民免遭大屠杀。
60 玛丽皇后喜欢各种模型，她在贵族公寓中建造了一间巨大的玩偶屋（Queen Mary's Dolls' House），由埃德温·勒琴斯设计。
61 荷尔朋（Holborn），位于伦敦中心区的一个区域，同时也是该区域一条主要道路的名称。
62 市寺教堂（The City Temple），坐落于伦敦市中心荷尔朋大道南端，大约始建于1640年，是当时新教改革的产物。今天的市寺教堂重建于1874年，是一个集教堂、会议中心为一体的场所。

图 33 玛丽皇后玩偶屋 Queen Mary's Dolls' House
图 34 市寺教堂 The City Temple
图 35 伦敦塔 London Tower
图 36 血腥塔 Bloody Tower

5月11日 参观了伦敦塔桥,以及伦敦塔的外围。

国家美术馆有很多意大利大师的作品,荷兰、法兰德斯[63]、法国画派的作品也有很多,西班牙的则很少,德国的不是很多。英国画派当然是最为丰富的。肖像画廊不值一看。

泰特美术馆很棒,雕像以及画作被陈列在一座大厅内,加上有品位的壁纸,很有效果。通常你可以看到由许多道门所构成的一种情景,并且由于这种布局,你能看到所有的东西。这里的特纳和萨金特藏品的规模是我所见最大的。楼下有一个南斯拉夫艺术展。买了一张一座雕塑的照片。在黑暗中画了大桥[64]与西敏寺的速写。

5月12日 画了一张"老古玩店"的速写,本想到里面看一看,但两辆坐满游客的汽车驶过,因此停顿了几秒钟,还是决定不进去。事实上,里面除了贫质而且昂贵的纪念品之外,没有什么东西。紧邻着的是一家裁缝店。

参观了圣保罗大教堂的室内。地宫里有纳尔逊和威灵顿[65]的墓室。然后向上进入私语廊。接着向上经过圆梯和直梯,到达最顶端。从金殿透过一个地板上的孔洞,人们可以清楚地看到带有马赛克地板的房间,人们当然也可以从顶层(大约300英尺高)看到

---

63 法兰德斯(Flemish),为西欧的一个历史地名,泛指古代尼德兰南部地区,大体上包括现在的比利时、卢森堡以及法国东北的部分地区。法兰德斯画派的黄金时期在17世纪,鲁本斯和凡·戴克都是法兰德斯画家中的重要人物。

64 指西敏寺大桥。

65 威灵顿公爵(Arthur Wellesley Wellington, 1769—1852年),英国第25、27任首相,陆军元帅。被公认为是19世纪上半叶最具影响力的军事、政治人物。威灵顿公爵出生于爱尔兰都柏林的一个贵族家庭,毕业于法国昂热军事学校,最初以少尉军阶加入英国陆军,并凭借在印度若干战争中的出色表现而获连番擢升。1815年威灵顿公爵统帅欧洲联军在滑铁卢战役中击败拿破仑,并成为了英国陆军元帅。

笼罩着一层梦幻色彩的整个伦敦。如果要速写必须从卢格院长那里获得许可！这让我花了2英镑，我只画了一张侧廊的速写。

前往参观伦敦塔[66]（图35），这座血腥之塔[67]（图36）曾经发生过许多杀戮。这里是拉雷[68]入狱并且结婚的地方，也是理查三世[69]谋害两位王子[70]的地方，人们在石头旋转楼梯的底部发现了他们的尸体。楼上是他们的卧室，窗户被钉死了（据说月光会由此弥漫而入），这就是谋杀者的潜入之门。

墙壁上布满了碑铭和石刻，所有这些都显得非常艺术化。

博尚塔[71]（图37）是一座小型狱室，墙面上刻着狱囚的名字。

白塔[72]（图38）是伦敦塔的前身，现在堆满了武器。楼上的小教堂是一个优雅简洁的地方，采用的是诺曼风格。乔维尔塔[73]（图39）内保存着所有的王冠和权杖。

他们现在是在地面上操演仪仗队。

图37 博尚塔 Beauchamp Tower
图38 白塔 White Tower
图39 乔维尔塔 Jewel Tower

---

66 伦敦塔占地7.2公顷，是一组历经900多年兴废的城堡群，自1140年起，它成为历代英王的主要住地之一。伦敦塔本来是用来防卫和控制伦敦的一座城堡，塔群中最古老的建筑是位于城堡中心的诺曼底塔楼，它也是英格兰最早的石制建筑。在将近千年的岁月中，伦敦塔的作用在不断变化，它既是保卫或控制全城的城堡，也是举行会议或签订协约的王宫；它是关押最危险的敌人的国家监狱，也曾经是全英国唯一的造币场所；它既是储藏武器的军械库、珍藏王室饰品和珠宝的宝库，也是保存国王在威斯敏斯特法庭大量记录的档案馆，今天已成为伦敦一个重要的观光区。
67 血腥塔（Bloody Tower）被国王用来专门囚禁政治要犯及国王的死敌，是一座死牢。被关进这座塔里的人大多数处死。
68 沃尔特·拉雷爵士（Sir Walter Raleigh, 1552—1618年），冒险家、诗人、历史学家、情人、勇士、政客，一生跌宕起伏、丰富多彩，曾经推进英国在非洲的殖民进程。
69 理查三世（Richard III, 1452—1485年），英格兰国王，1483年到1485年在位，他是爱德华四世之弟，格洛斯特公爵，同时也是约克王朝的最后一任国王。理查曾短暂的以护国公的身份替爱德华五世摄政，但他在将爱德华五世与第一任约克公爵送进伦敦塔后夺权成功，并于1483年7月6号被加冕为英格兰王。理查三世在历史上战死于波斯沃平原战役。
70 在莎士比亚戏剧《理查三世》中，理查三世为了登上王位，将爱德华四世的两位幼子囚禁于伦敦塔，并在伦敦塔中把他们杀害。
71 博尚塔（Beauchamp Tower）专门关押高级犯人的地方，亨利六世与理查二世都曾经在此坐牢。
72 白塔（White Tower）是整个伦敦塔建筑群中历史最悠久的建筑，建于1086年，完成于1100年。顶楼曾经是历代皇室居住的地方。白塔因为1240年时用石灰水洗擦后变得透白而得名。
73 乔维尔塔（Jewel Tower）是伦敦西敏寺中世纪的皇家宫殿所仅存的两个部分之一，另外一个就是西敏寺大厅。

在伦敦塔的等候厅吃了午餐。

乘地铁前往汉默史密斯[74],然后乘7路火车前往汉普顿庭[75],火车正好1个小时后到达那儿。

这里的国宾馆比温莎的要差很多……(缺)在迷宫里迷失了好几次才进入到中心,并最终成功地走出来,它让我理解了迷宫的定义:maze可以让人迷失于其中,而labyrinth则可以让人毫无困难、准确无误地进入并走出。酒窖和厨房不值得一看。

今晚在莱斯姆剧院观看了"苹果车"[76]的演出。饰演国王的演员不如纽约的汤姆·鲍尔斯,演奥林塔的也不行,但是演首相的却要好很多。(缺)

……下午5点钟抵达剑桥,这座小镇不如牛津那么漂亮。但是河流可以流经各个学院,许多美丽如画的桥梁跨越其上,形成了一道有趣的风景。剑桥的学生是多么的幸福啊,他们可以躺在河岸的草坡上,谈论着天上的星星。

在剑桥有很多学院,有一些与牛津有着相同的名称。这些学院的平面也很相似。回廊内院平面,一座小礼拜堂连接其上,大多数学院都由雷恩[77]设计。这里与牛津一样更多采用文艺复兴风格,而不是哥特风格。

住在一家临水的花园旅店,在其中有一座大型花园,客厅正当其面。又是一顿丰盛的晚餐。住在一个单人小间,面前则是一块带有潺潺小溪的草坪。

5月16日 早餐前划了一会儿船。餐后参观了许多学院,还参观了美术馆,该美术馆拥有7幅拉斐尔的草稿,以及奥古斯都斯·约翰[78]为哈丁和萧伯纳所作的肖像。

剑桥比牛津更为安静,而且学生有更好的机会去学习自然——溪流、草地。这是一座理想的大学城。

在那里看到几个中国学生。下午前往埃利,到达林肯时已经相

---

74 汉默史密斯(Hammersmith),泰晤士河北岸的一个伦敦自治区。
75 汉普顿庭(Hampton Court),常常也称作汉普顿庭宫(Hampton Court Palace),是伦敦北部的一处皇家别墅。
76 《苹果车》为萧伯纳的一部政治讽刺剧作品,写作于1929年,以英国议会制为抨击对象,剖析了资产阶级民主为金融寡头所操纵的真相。
77 克里斯托弗·雷恩爵士(Sir Christopher Wren,1632—1723年),英国天文学家、建筑师。伦敦的圣保罗大教堂就是他的代表作。
78 奥古斯都斯·约翰(Augustus Edwin John,1878—1961年),威尔士画家,制图能手。在1910年左右,他一度是英国后印象派的主要拥护者。

当晚了。爬上山去参观大教堂[79]（图40）。但是在火车进站前，就可以获得一个观看大教堂的良好视角（朦胧得就像一座梦幻城堡）。大教堂矗立于山顶，这使它更加美丽。住在一个老旧而且不太干净的地方，煤气灯，床上有热水瓶。

在前往林肯之前，1点钟到6点钟之间停留于埃利。前去参观大教堂[80]（图41），大教堂在十字交汇处有一个有趣的采光塔，它有点像哥特式的尖顶。室内更多是诺曼风格的。画了一张中庭的深褐色渲染，在埃利没有其他有意思的东西。

5月17日 一个非常晴朗的早晨。早餐后参观了林肯城堡，看到了罗马风格的拱门，城堡目前只剩下一扇门和一段墙（其他一些桥梁不太像是城堡类型的）。

大教堂没有什么特别之处。我爬上了钟塔。教堂内院太小，一条狭窄小道将大教堂和住区分隔开来。大教堂的钟塔已经整修过。

参观犹太住区以及其他一些没有什么意思的当地东西。商店橱窗甚至展示着现代家具。

下午2点钟抵达约克，在城墙外一直步行，直到城堡，只有崖塔（图42）在开放。

约克大教堂[81]（图43）是目前所见最好的。宽敞的中庭，精美的玻璃窗，以及高

图40 林肯大教堂 Lincoln Cathedral
图41 埃利大教堂 Ely Cathedral
图42 崖塔 Clifton Tower
图43 约克大教堂 Cathedral of York

---

[79] 林肯大教堂（Lincoln Cathedral），建于1192—1280年。林肯大教堂的平面带有比较典型的英国特征，在教堂的南侧有回廊和议事堂，而且教堂的圣堂部位采用了矩形平面。教堂的西立面源自以前存在的罗马风建筑，经过加宽以后形成现在的门厅式格局，在增建了两座钟塔以后，具有了哥特式建筑的一些特征。
[80] 埃利大教堂（Ely Cathedral），位于英格兰剑桥郡埃利市，是埃利主教所在地，由西蒙主教始建于1082—1094年。
[81] 约克大教堂（Cathedral of York），又称圣彼得大教堂，是欧洲现存最大的中世纪时期的教堂，也是世界上设计和建筑艺术最精湛的教堂之一。现存教堂于1220年开始兴建，1470年完工。教堂内拥有世界面积最大、以单扇窗镶嵌的中世纪彩绘玻璃和世界最古老的侧廊。

图44 "五姐妹"窗 "Five Sisters" Window
图45 圣玛丽修道院 St. Mary's Abbey
图46 杜兰大教堂 Durham Cathedral

耸的天棚（虽然木板是油漆过的），教士居室没有中央立柱，玻璃非常漂亮。又一次登上钟塔，并且在下面露出来的基座上刻上BM, K.M. & C.T.。

"五姐妹"窗[82]（图44）是我所见最好的。整座教堂很漂亮，外面的群塔也很漂亮。

城墙维护得很好。我在上面走了一段，画了城门的速写。圣玛丽修道院（图45）风景如画：那里的美术馆不太好。肉铺街是一条非常漂亮的巷弄，两旁分列着肉店。傍晚开始下雨，在雨中画了一幅水彩画。今天画了7幅画。

晚上10点钟到达杜兰，看见山上的大教堂。明天晚上11点钟以前没有火车去爱丁堡，所以只能乘汽车。

5月18日 参观杜兰大教堂[83]（图46），非常漂亮的钟塔，外面大部分的窗户是诺曼风格的。室内几乎完全采用诺曼风格，带有巨大

---

[82] "五姐妹"窗（"five sisters" window），是约克大教堂历史最悠久的玻璃窗，也是英国最大的灰色调单色玻璃。
[83] 杜兰大教堂（Durham Cathedral），位于杜伦郡首府杜伦市，始建于1093年，诺曼风格。

图 47 圣吉尔斯礼拜堂 St. Giles Kirk
图 48 议会大楼 Parliament
图 49 坎特伯雷大教堂 Canterbury Cathedral

的柱子和筒拱。教堂的供暖非常好,没有去看牧师的居室和厨房。

参观水门旁边的老城墙。

教堂和城堡矗立在山顶上的样子非常壮观。

城堡在星期天关闭,这是一个学生宿舍。

乘车前往爱丁堡。城堡矗立于山顶的样子令人浮想联翩,一些靠近高盛街附近的住房有10到11层楼高。

王子大街十分壮美,苏格兰纪念碑是哥特式的,不是太好。

5月19日 远远看去,爱丁堡的城堡是极具想象力的。但是等你到达那里并且向下俯视时,就完全没有梦幻和浪漫了。一个受到崇拜的人必须远距离地接受崇拜,在家里是没有英雄的。

战争纪念碑是崭新的,其他一些钟塔也没有什么意思。整座城堡矗立在一块坚石上,一侧是斜坡,其他三面则是峭壁。

在圣·吉尔斯[84](图47)和议会大楼[85](图48)没有什么特别有意思的东西。爱丁堡大学是一座带有方形庭院的传统建筑,看上去肮脏而且陈旧。宫殿没有开放,苏格兰纪念碑不值得爬上去。

---

[84] 圣吉尔斯礼拜堂(St. Giles Kirk),是爱丁堡最高等级的教堂,位于爱丁堡皇家大道上,大教堂原建于1120年,后遭大火烧毁,于1385年重建。是苏格兰长老会的发源地。
[85] 议会大楼(Parliament),在圣·吉尔斯礼拜堂的背面。

图 50 圣奥古斯丁修道院
St. Augustine's Abbey

图 51 克吕尼博物馆
Museum Cluny

图 52 圣礼拜堂
Saint Chapelle

走了很多路,但是很少作画。城市太大了。乘坐"夜归苏格兰人"列车回到伦敦。

5月20日 夜色中的坎特伯雷,太晚而看不到什么东西。

5月21日 一大清早前去参观大教堂[86](图49),带有半圆形拱顶的外观看上去虽好但却普通。里面倒是棒极了,尤其是十字交会部上方的屋顶,它由从立柱上升起的四个弧顶所构成,非常清晰地饰以红、蓝两色,非常简洁,整个效果看上去在气质上非常得现代。玻璃窗色彩缤纷。事实上,所有这一切都显得完美无缺。回廊庭院没有值得一提的东西。

中庭非常的长,而唱诗席也同样很长,因此大教堂在唱诗屏处被分为两半。平面几乎就像3个十字,小礼拜堂处在拱端。圣奥古斯丁修道院[87](图50),在半圆形拱顶附近有一个石椅。

西大门很有意思,大教堂外面的其他一些大门也同样如此。如果可以在这里待更长的时间,就能画更多的速写了。街道缺乏商业氛围,而房屋却非常漂亮。

面包房的无酒精饮料非常便宜,也非常好喝。

横渡海峡的船只较小,我几乎都快晕船了。从加莱到巴黎的火车很好。我第一次说法语是在火车北站,查问行李。

巴黎只不过又是一座城市,但是我认为宽阔的香榭丽舍大街和其他公共纪念物拯救

---

[86] 坎特伯雷大教堂(Canterbury Cathedral),位于肯特郡坎特伯雷市,是英国最古老、最著名的基督教建筑之一,它是英国圣公会首席主教坎特伯雷大主教的主教座堂。现存教堂始建于1070年,后来又经历了几次续建和扩建,才形成现今规模。

[87] 圣奥古斯丁修道院(St. Augustine's Abbey),圣奥古斯丁是坎特伯雷大教堂缔造者。公元6世纪初,圣奥古斯丁不远万里,渡过海峡从罗马来到英格兰布道,就住在这座修道院里。

了它。即便没有别的东西,巴黎也应当还有一些漂亮的女人。

5月22日

5月23日　克吕尼博物馆[88](图51)里充斥着陈旧的老货。没有错过两条贞操带。

加纳瓦泰博物馆[89]也堆满了垃圾,一些老巴黎的模型比较有意思。

最有意思的是巴黎圣母院。没有一座英国大教堂可以与之相媲美。带有漂亮玻璃窗的异常神秘的内部空间将你带入一种颤动的世界,这是我所见过最好的。

圣礼拜堂[90](图52)拥有一个富丽而壮观的、带有漂亮玻璃窗的室内。它就像一颗小宝石,金色、红色、蓝色通过光线而交织在一起。一楼并不太好。

5月24日　圣心大教堂[91](图53)高高矗立于蒙马特山上,得花点力气才能爬上去。它完全由白色花岗岩建成。室内并不十分漂亮。它太亮了。

花了一个小时才爬到埃菲尔塔顶,然后又爬下来。过程很缓慢,但是当你爬到塔顶时,就获得了观赏巴黎的绝佳视野,任何东西都可以看得很清楚,尤其是花园园地,就像罗马大奖赛[92]的作品。你看到整个巴黎就像一只花篮,塞纳河赋予它以绿色,白色桥梁来来回回跨越其上。

---

[88] 克吕尼博物馆(Museum Cluny),也称中世纪博物馆,内容皆是中世纪重要的画作及工艺、雕刻品,其中有最著名的"少女与独角兽"(La Dame a la Licorne)一画。全馆共有2层楼,收藏品包括中世纪彩绘手稿、挂毯、贵重金属、陶器等,最重要的还是占大部分比例的宗教圣物,如十字架、圣杯、祭坛金饰等。博物馆外的建筑遗迹就是2000年前的罗马公共浴池,因遭破坏而残破不堪。

[89] 加纳瓦泰博物馆(Museum Carnavalet),一座描述巴黎历史的博物馆。

[90] 圣礼拜堂(Saint Chapelle),位于西提岛上的巴黎高等法院内,是一座精彩的哥特式建筑。圣礼拜堂由路易九世国王建造,用来典藏他从君士坦丁堡购得的圣物(耶稣荆冠和十字架碎片等等)。整座教堂细长挑高,分上下两座礼拜堂,由建筑师皮耶·德·蒙托尔(Pierre de Montrouil)设计,于1248年间花费33个月完成。

[91] 圣心大教堂(Sacre Coeur),位于巴黎北市区蒙马特山顶,其造型独特、视野绝佳。圣心大教堂由建筑师保罗·阿巴迪(Paul Abadie)设计,建筑风格采用罗马和拜占庭的混合式,教堂通体白色,又称白教堂。中间是一个大圆顶,四周围绕4个小圆顶,教堂后面还有1个高84米的钟楼,教堂前的平台是除了埃菲尔铁塔以外俯瞰巴黎的第二制高点。建造圣心大教堂的最初动机是1870年普法战争,法国人在签下丧权辱国的凡尔赛条约后,不断自我反省,其中有许多基督徒抱着赎罪的心,公开募捐建造一座献给上帝的殿堂,并于1876年在蒙马特山上动工兴建,1910年正式完成。

[92] 罗马大奖(Grand Prix de Rome)由路易十四于1666年设置,用来促使具有天赋的艺术学生通过在罗马学习古典艺术来完成学业。罗马大奖每年通过竞赛由法国政府颁发给在巴黎美术学院及其他院校的15～30岁的艺术学生,范围包括绘画、雕塑、建筑、雕刻以及音乐。

图 53 圣心大教堂 Sacre Coeur
图 54.1 大皇宫 Grand Palais
图 54.2 大皇宫 Grand Palais
图 55 玛德琳教堂
L'Église de la Madeleine
图 56 布德尔的弓箭手
Bourdelle's Archer

  拿破仑陵墓的室内非常的漂亮，尤其是在圣坛周围，那里有棕褐色的玻璃窗，将金色光线投射在绿色大理石棺椁上。向下俯瞰拿破仑灵柩真是很棒。

  罗丹美术馆有一座令人愉悦的花园（思想家在那里）和一座礼拜堂，它同样也有一座城堡。

  大皇宫[93]（图54.1，图54.2）曾经举办过1930年的沙龙和装饰艺术展览，非常棒。现代风格的室内，参观了绘画、雕塑的沙龙，花了3个多小时。

  玛德琳教堂[94]（图55）的室内非常神秘，因为整座教堂的光源来自于穹窿顶棚的3盏小灯。这是除了伦敦的圣保罗教堂以外，我

---

93 大皇宫（Grand Palais），现为巴黎大皇宫美术馆，位于香榭丽舍大道，是为了举办1900年世界博览会所兴建，由建筑师德格拉那及卢伟两人共同建造，正面长240米、高43米。
94 玛德琳教堂（L'Église de la Madeleine），大约建于1764年，古典希腊式风格。

所见到的最经典的教堂室内。

5月25日 卢浮宫有这么多展品,我参观了大部分的展品,唯一感兴趣的就是蒙娜丽莎、维纳斯和胜利女神。

卢森堡美术馆里面有布德尔的弓箭手[95](图56)。

图57 大特里亚农宫 Les Trianons

雨天中的凡尔赛并不是一个好地方,因为花园里不能行走,树木也遮不了雨。参观了室内之后(从残疾人车站开始),我们走在树林中去寻找特里亚农[96](图57)。两个都找到了,脚都湿透了,非常晦气的下午。

5月26日 前往参观夏特尔大教堂[97](图58)。它有漂亮的玻璃窗,但是效果却相当单调。它并不具有如画的品质,以及巴黎圣母院那种神秘的气质。但是所有人都喜欢夏特尔。我更喜欢巴黎圣母院。步行参观了小镇,在那儿只花了3个小时。

5月27日 参观了圣艾提安杜蒙教堂[98](图59),它带有涡卷装饰的立面以及很有意思的室内:圆形楼梯盘柱而上,将人带到游廊

---

[95] 布德尔(Emile Antoine Bourdelle, 1869—1929年),法国现实主义雕塑家,曾经是雕塑大师罗丹的学生和助手,布德尔研究并汲取了古代东方和哥特时期的雕塑的特点,其作品把英雄式的魄力和夸张起伏的表面,与古希腊罗马艺术的平滑而富于装饰性的简洁相结合,给20世纪初的雕刻注入了新的活力。"弓箭手",也称为"拉弓的赫拉克勒斯",是布德尔一生中最重要的作品之一。

[96] 大特里亚农宫是路易十四为自己和情妇建造的行宫。小特里亚农宫则是路易十五受大特里亚农宫的启发,为他的情妇蓬巴杜夫人(Pompadour)建造。其建筑风格典雅别致,与众不同,是新古典主义的杰作。

[97] 夏特尔大教堂(Charters Cathedral),位于法国巴黎西南约70公里处的夏特尔市。据传圣母玛利亚曾在此显灵,并保存了圣母的颅骨,夏特尔因此成为西欧重要的朝圣地之一。夏特尔主教座堂最初以巴西利卡式兴建,公元8世纪到12世纪,夏特尔教堂数次遭火灾。1020年9月7日的大火后,在福尔贝(Fulbert)主教的领导下,采用有木屋顶的仿罗马式主教座堂在原址重建,取代原有的巴西利卡式建筑。夏特尔主教座堂高155米,最大玫瑰窗直径13.4米。是第一座完全成熟的哥特式主教座堂,成为法国哥特式建筑高峰时期的代表作,其建筑结构及平面配置成了以后各主教座堂模仿的蓝本。教堂西面的两座尖塔有着明显的差异,因为南塔于1145—1170年建成,是晚期罗曼式建筑向哥特式建筑过渡的风格,较为朴素;而北面的一座建成于1507年,有更多的雕刻,并更纤细,是典型的哥特式建筑风格。

[98] 圣艾提安杜蒙教堂(Église St. Etienne du Mont),位于先贤祠旁边的一座小教堂,兴建于15世纪。

图58 夏特尔大教堂 Charters Cathedral　　图59 圣艾提安杜蒙教堂 Église St. Etienne du Mont
图60 先贤祠 Pantheon　　图61 奶油塔 Butter Tower

（内部）旁边的平台之上，平台于正面横跨于唱诗席和中庭之间。

先贤祠[99]（图60）的地宫里有左拉、罗素、伏尔泰的墓室。在一楼的壁画非常漂亮，一直延伸到穹顶。

马莱-斯蒂文斯街是在巴黎外围的一项新开发，第一次看到现代化的外景。它在某些地方有着鲜亮的色彩，非常有意思。

5月28日　6点钟起床去赶圣拉扎尔车站的火车，前往鲁昂。10点钟到达大教堂。"奶油塔"[100]（图61）确实非常好。但是带有铁筋

---

[99] 先贤祠（Pantheon），位于法国巴黎拉丁广场，最初是法王路易十五兴建的圣日内维耶大教堂，历经数次变迁以后现在成为法国最著名的文化名人安葬地。先贤祠是新古典主义建筑的早期典范，其正面仿照罗马万神殿（Pantheon in Rome），拱顶采用布拉曼特风格。
[100] 奶油塔（Butter Tower），完成于1506年，是鲁昂大教堂的一重要组成部分。当时南方的牛油生产商为了将奶油售往北方地区，向教会支付大量金额来疏通贸易禁令，而教会则利用这笔资金在鲁昂大教堂增建了这座哥特风格的塔楼，并被称为奶油塔。

图62 圣马克隆教堂 St. Maclon 图63 圣沃昂教堂 St. Ouen
图64 让·阿克塔 Tower of Joan d' Arc 图65 亚眠大教堂 Amiens Cathedral

的中央塔却很糟糕。室内与英国的大教堂一样普通。参观了圣马克隆[101]教堂（图62），木雕门非常漂亮。也参观了圣沃昂教堂[102]（图63），它有一座类似"奶油塔"的钟塔。两者都非常漂亮，参观了让·阿克塔[103]（图64）。

乘坐中午的火车从北门前往亚眠，4:30到达那里。立即参观了大教堂[104]（图65），画了一张室内的速写。也画了教堂的外观。大教堂立面是我所见过最漂亮的。三个门廊带有深深的侧框。但是在室内，中庭的高度以及宽度需要一个更长的中庭。逛了一圈游廊，

---

101 圣马克隆教堂（St. Maclon），建造于1437—1521年，法国著名晚期哥特风格建筑之一，雕刻及装饰极为丰富。
102 圣沃昂教堂（St. Ouen），也就是鲁昂大教堂的具体称谓，建造于14—16世纪，哥特风格。
103 让·阿克塔（Tower of Joan d' Arc），也称圣女贞德塔，是鲁昂建于12世纪城堡所保存下来的最后一座建筑物。贞德在接受审判的过程中被监禁于鲁昂的这座高塔中，后来这座塔便被称为圣女贞德塔。
104 亚眠大教堂（Amiens Cathedral）。亚眠大教堂是法国最大的教堂，位于皮卡第地区中心，索姆省亚眠市，在巴黎以北100公里，是哥特式建筑顶峰时期的代表作。亚眠大教堂始建于1152年，由于在1218年遭受雷击而摧毁，1220年开始重建。南部塔楼（高62米）建成于1366年，而北部的塔楼（高67米）则在1406年建成。

参观了"哭泣的天使"[105]。晚上逛了一圈小镇,住在兰内·戈布莱[106]广场(图66)的一家旅店,它价格公道而整洁干净。

5月29日 乘坐9点钟的火车前往兰斯,12点钟抵达。1点钟吃过午饭并参观大教堂[107](图67),这是我所见过最壮美的立面。它是一颗宝石,虽然有点像亚眠大教堂,但是立面却更具色彩,而且更加柔美,更为古老,看上去足以入画。室内也在进行维修,除了正立面入口上方的玫瑰窗,所有五块玻璃窗都一样。唱诗席目前被临时放置在中庭的尽端,回廊已经被围护起来进行维修。

我非常喜欢这个立面,因此我来来回回看了4次,去欣赏它的美丽。如果把巴黎圣母院的室内与兰斯教堂的外观叠加在一起,你将会看到世界上最美丽的教堂。参观了新的战争纪念碑,非常漂亮。

我认为兰斯大教堂一个令人称道的地方在于,它的正立面面对着一条相当宽阔的林荫道,从那儿你可以很远就看到教堂。

晚上回到巴黎。

5月30日 参观了格莱温蜡像馆,其中的蜡像作品就如同伦敦的蜡像。雨中前往圣母院的塔楼,参观了所有的怪诞之物,又一次观看了室内的玫瑰窗,它们如此美丽。

今晚参观皮加勒剧院[108](图68),精彩的室内,正立面不太好看。室内(剧院

图66 兰内·戈布莱广场 Place René Goblet
图67 兰斯大教堂 Reims Cathedral
图68 皮加勒剧院 Theatre Pigalle
图69 最高法院 Palais de Justice

---

105 哭泣的天使(Weeping Angel),亚眠大教堂内一著名雕塑,在圣坛后一棺墓上。
106 兰内·戈布莱(René Goblet, 1828—1905年),法国政治家,1886—1887年曾任法国总理。
107 兰斯大教堂(Reims Cathedral)坐落于巴黎北部兰斯市,为纪念圣雷米主教为克罗维受洗,兰斯大教堂从1211年开始建造,1241年落成。兰斯大教堂和巴黎圣母院同属哥特式教堂建筑,但其雄浑的建筑形态和建筑尺度都在巴黎圣母院之上。大教堂既是兰斯的标志性建筑,也是法国最美丽壮观的教堂之一。
108 皮加勒剧院(Theatre Pigalle),位于巴黎蒙马特地区,建于1929年,其内部按照最新舞台技术进行设计,外表按照当时最风行的art-deco风格设计。

本身）采用一种红-黑-银的配色，天花是白色塑料，略微进行了涂彩和塑形。红色坐椅带有银色管状的扶手，所有的包厢饰木被漆成暗红色，休息厅和大厅带有很浓的德国味。在底层有商店和餐厅，橱窗和现代绘画画廊。在前厅（售票处）有一个座位标号的室内模型，观众由此可以看到他要坐的座位。

5月31日 前往北站，乘9:40火车前往布鲁塞尔。这种所谓的特快列车，其实几乎每站都停，直到下午4点钟才到达。比利时的海关只是名义上的，但是他们要求签证，而我没有。最后警官要了30法郎，以获得这张叫做签证的纸。

在布鲁塞尔逛了一会儿。参观了最高法院（图69），但没有看到皇宫，它必定藏在树丛中。试图寻找由约瑟夫·霍夫曼[109]设计的斯托克莱住宅[110]（图70），但是没有人知道它在哪里。

乘坐5-47火车前往布鲁日，以一只香蕉加两块蛋糕作为午餐，3只香蕉，1只橙子和3块蛋糕作为晚餐，10点钟就开始饿了，所以喝了一杯OXO[111]，又吃了一块蛋糕。

住在赫伯特旅馆，25法郎一间房，太好了。

在运河边走了一会儿，看见很多有趣的房屋，参观了砖砌的教堂，一座非常复杂的钟塔。在室内，大多数石作被漆上油漆，非常有意思。许多画就挂在哥特风格的饰边和窗花上。另一个运用彩色石头的案例则是兰斯大教堂的回廊，它正在进行维修，没有对公众开放。

大多数山墙都是阶梯状的，一些男人和女人穿着木鞋。这一天没有画任何速写。

6月1日 比利时人在星期天起得很早，电车和汽车7点钟之前就开始有了。邮递员7点钟送信，因此所有商店和咖啡店都已经开门。你可以听见硬底鞋敲打在铺地上。

早晨一直在下雨，因此坐在咖啡馆里，画了一张钟塔的水彩

---

109 约瑟夫·霍夫曼（Josef Hoffmann，1870—1956年），奥地利最杰出的建筑师之一，维也纳分离派的核心人物，于1903年组建了维也纳版的工艺美术运动工作室，名为"维也纳工作同盟"。
110 斯托克莱住宅（Stoclet House），位于比利时首都布鲁塞尔郊区，建于1905年至1911年，是装饰艺术风格建筑的代表作。斯托克莱住宅系银行家兼艺术收藏家阿道尔夫·托克雷特（Adolphe Stoclet）于1905年委托维也纳分离派运动的主要建筑师约瑟夫·霍夫曼设计。住宅和花园于1911年完工，严格的几何特征成为新艺术派的一个转折点，预示着建筑业中装饰派艺术和现代主义运动的到来。斯托克莱住宅是维也纳分离派运动的最精湛和同质性建筑之一，具有科罗曼·莫塞尔（Koloman Moser）和古斯塔夫·克里姆特（Gustav Klimt）作品的特征。
111 OXO是一种较为烈性的酒。

图 70 斯托克莱住宅　Stoclet House
图 71 布鲁塞尔市政厅　Bruxcelles Hotel de Ville
图 72 布鲁塞尔大教堂　Bruxcelles Cathedral
图 73 帕拉丁美术馆　Museum Plantin

画，还有2张广场的铅笔速写。叫了一杯慕尼黑啤酒，但是只喝了半杯。由于雨下个不停，走到运河边去画一座桥，然后是运河的吊桥，在它前面是一座支撑于中梁的铁桥。在旅馆花了20法郎吃的午餐，吃得很好。

乘1点钟火车前往布鲁塞尔，2:30到达，乘汽车到中央车站，去取在北站的行李。乘3-42次列车前往安特卫普，4:30到达，住在亨得斯旅馆，50法郎一间房，由于有展览会，城里挤满了游客。

路过博览会场[112]，当然所有东西都是木制的，并且制作非常精美。无论在设计还是做工上，博览会都远远超过了费城的一百五十周年博览会。建筑的数量远远大于费城。我于6点钟到达那儿，所有的建筑都已关门，因此只能明天再去那里，去参观室内。

画了一张市政厅[113]（图71）和大教堂[114]（图72）的速写，河内

---

112 安特卫普于1930年举办了殖民地、海事及法兰德斯艺术国际博览会（Exposition International Coloniale, Maritime et d'Art Flammand）。
113 布鲁塞尔市政厅（Bruxcelles Hotel de Ville）是一座典型的弗兰德哥特式建筑，造型宏伟，空灵高耸。市政厅大楼始建于1402年，它上面的厅塔高约91米，塔顶塑有一尊高5米的布鲁塞尔城的守护神圣米歇尔的雕像。
114 布鲁塞尔大教堂（Bruxcelles Cathedral），也称圣米歇尔大教堂，1220年由St. Michael和Ste Gudule赞助建造，哥特风格，采用双塔式建筑，门口有雄伟的三智者和教徒的塑像。

挤满了蒸汽船，只看到一艘帆船，没有看见一艘航行的渔船。

阿米那罗旅馆很贵，40法郎。

6月2日　7点钟起床，出门。美丽的早晨，但找不到任何值得一画的东西，只是转了一圈。最终又画了大教堂的螺旋塔。（最后一晚），9:30吃早餐，4块蛋糕和巧克力。

10点钟又去了博览会场，法国馆开放了，其中有一些现代风格的室内和时尚展览。其他展馆不值得进去一看，大多数是机器制品，还有航海制品。法兰德斯艺术馆还没有开放，在会场里转了一圈，拍了些照片。

参观帕拉丁美术馆[115]（图73），并且画了一张庭院的速写（非常糟糕的速写），在车站附近又以4块蛋糕和巧克力作为午餐。乘坐21次列车前往鹿特丹，4点钟到达。

鹿特丹是一座比我想象要大的城市。它有宽阔的街道，但是没有地方足够美丽可以入画。沿运河是许多农舍，没有航船或者渔船，所有都是蒸汽的（令人讨厌）。为了找旅馆走了很长的一段路，最后碰巧看见一座风车就矗立在前面。给它画了一张速写，并引来一大堆的围观者。走得太远而迷了路。完全凭运气才找到回车站的路。在大街旁的一家餐厅吃的晚餐，花了2盾（80克朗），然后步行回到欧罗巴旅馆，旅馆非常好，而且套房才3.5盾。

后来没有看到很多现代建筑，参观了一座现代剧院，今晚随后前去看一场电影（顺便提一下，是一部关于伦敦无赖的剧情）。剧院很棒，天棚有很长的平行光带，可以依次由红、蓝色光进行照明。

6月3日　在鹿特丹花了太多的时间，没看到什么东西。我应当于昨晚就来到这里（阿姆斯特丹），就可以在这里待上一整天。但是9:30从鹿特丹乘上火车，11点才到这里。住在比恩霍夫旅馆，套房是3个荷兰盾。在旅馆吃了午餐，份额的量很大。荷兰厨师的汤做得不错，在科斯默斯[116]买了三本现代书。

在鹿特丹和阿姆斯特丹之间有许多现代建筑和风车。随处可见的平坦乡村给人留下深刻的印象，这就是典型的乡村景观：一条由细长树木所构成的林荫道加上一座风车。

---

115 帕拉丁美术馆（Museum Plantin）是以比利时著名印刷师——帕拉丁(Plantin)命名的博物馆，这里拥有34个展览室以及一个由帕拉丁建造的印刷室。
116 科斯默斯(Kosmos) 为一荷兰出版社名称。

参观了真正的荷兰老镇和村庄，身着传统服装的人们和仅有3英尺宽的窄巷。这些地方有：乘船从阿姆斯特丹到图尔布斯，然后乘火车去艾登、沃伦丹姆，乘汽船到伊斯塔德马肯，然后再坐船到布鲁克（做奶酪的地方）。平生头一次画了航船（沃伦丹姆的船），很激动。男人们戴着耳环，5岁以下的小男孩穿得像女孩。在帽顶上别有徽标。

人们穿着传统木鞋（木制）并把它们放在门外。妇女们戴着有花边的帽子，并且通常穿着蓝色服装，配以浅色围裙。风景如此优美。

在阿姆斯特丹南郊参观了很多现代建筑，个个都很棒，砖作很精细。所有的木门都设计得很好。有一座现代教堂，但没法参观室内。甚至街头的邮箱设计得都很现代。

在集市上买了两块手帕。在集市当中，有一个6幢房屋的村庄。在科斯默斯看了一眼在阿姆斯特丹的办公室生活。有2名职员和3名姑娘（通常如此），他们都在办公室里吃午餐，大约12点钟。

在阿姆斯特丹，几乎所有房屋在老虎窗上方都装有吊轮，用来提升家具。

6月4日 乘7:33火车去科隆，12点钟到达。逛了一些商业街，画了一张大桥的速写。一出火车站，就看见了大教堂。

6月5日 爬上大教堂的钟塔。在史迹陈列馆参观了罗马古迹。走过莱茵河。

科隆大教堂[117]（图74）是一座建成的哥特教堂。它很高，尺度逼人。没有采用很高的唱诗屏封来收拢视线。只有一个窗户带有老玻璃，也就是正好处在唱诗席后面的那一个。

科隆沿莱茵河畔的夜色剪影非常壮丽，尽管轮廓有点粗糙。

非常黑的剪影加上单桨小船，还有下面白色的水滩，真是浪漫极了。

6月6日 前往杜塞尔多夫。在战前它有一座现代桥梁。参观了一座很高的办公建筑（WM马克大楼），爬到楼顶。它有一个砖砌的大厅，其中有运行的电梯轿厢。从楼顶可以看到城市全景。很精致的砖作。

---

[117] 德国科隆大教堂（Cathedral of Cologne），欧洲北部最大的教堂，建于1248—1880年，它以法国兰斯主教堂和亚眠主教堂为范本，是德国第一座完全按照法国哥特盛期样式建造的教堂。

前往展览中心。参观了克瑞斯教授的天文馆[118]（图75）和艺术画廊。天文馆今天不开放。观赏了画廊的近期藏品，没有什么意思。

杜塞尔多夫是一座值得一访的城市，因为它有几座欧洲最好的现代建筑。

6月7日 拍摄了几张老展览中心的照片，然后参观了"朗根地区城市与土地"展览。展览中有大量关于科隆周边地区的现代建筑的照片，如卡尔克费尔德、比肯多夫和佐尔斯克，大多数照片都很棒，当然建筑也很棒。这诱惑我前往比肯多夫并亲眼参观大多数这些建筑，也拍摄了大量照片。

乘电车前往卡尔克，但是在那里并没有看到什么特别的东西。从大桥步行前往大学和兴登堡公园。乘车回头参观市政厅。

今天早晨在老会展中心时，走进了铜皮教堂，其内部完全都是由钢、玻璃加上木制长椅构成。楼梯玻璃很棒，混凝土屋顶，在神坛后面是十字架和在铜板上的基督。布道圣坛就在十字架的前面。

同时也参观了比肯多夫的现代教堂[119]（图76），其外表是混凝土的，带有尖券，还有一座钟塔。室内是石灰加上红砖，非常明快。教堂内有一壁龛，十字架就悬于当中，白色墙面布满了透过有色玻璃投下的彩色光斑，效果非常美妙。在教堂的两侧都有小礼拜堂，还有忏悔室，后面是阳台。

6月8日 9点钟从科隆抵达波恩。参观了贝多芬故居（图77）、博物馆和贝多芬诞生的阁楼。低矮的顶棚（有梁）和老旧的楼板。博物馆里有很多贝多芬的信件和手稿、小提琴以及他的助听器，还有大量的肖像和胸像。其氛围仅次于埃文河畔斯塔德福德。庭院很美，安放着贝多芬的塑像，但是不能拍照也不能写生。

参观了波恩大学，乘电车穿过科布伦茨大街。步行走回莱茵河岸。午餐后参观了修道院。内部色彩绚丽并且略显神秘。美丽的回廊庭院，我在那儿画了一张速写。当然也在外面画了贝多芬故居。

乘船从波恩到科布伦茨，这是我所知道的最美航程。两岸风光无与伦比，尤其是当月色升起，远方的尖塔和城堡围墙被笼罩于梦幻般的色彩之中时。月亮在水中投下倩影，一艘航船或者两

---

118 杜塞尔多夫天文馆（Planetarium），由威廉·克瑞斯（Wilhelm Kreis）教授设计，建于1926年，坐落于莱茵河上卡塞尔大桥（Oberkassel）边，该建筑原先作为天文馆，后被改造为音乐厅。
119 教堂确切名称为 Kirche St. Dreikönigen，圣三王教堂。

朵紫色云彩，蓝色山脊，黑色丛林，橙色水光。下午细致参观了七岭山[120]，以前从来没有见过如此完美融合的景色。有这么多的地方令我想停下来作画。

6月9日 8点钟起床，9点钟吃早餐，外出参观威廉一世纪念塔[121]（图78）。它矗立在摩泽尔河与莱茵河交汇的三角洲的一端。你可以在那里看见不同颜色的河水。摩泽尔河是蓝色的，莱茵河是黄色的。纪念碑非常巴洛克，细部很丑陋。但是它占据了这么好的位置，所以它在夜晚的剪影或白天很远看上去很美。

卡斯托尔教堂[122]（图79）是一座普通的罗马风建筑。走了很长一段路才走到桥头，在那里有一些可以入画的、很有意思的老房子，在卢伍街与奥特·格莱伯街的交会处也矗立

图74 科隆大教堂 Cathedral of Cologne
图75 杜塞尔多夫天文馆 Planetarium
图76 圣三王教堂 Kirche St. Dreikönigen
图77 贝多芬故居 Beethoven House
图78 威廉一世纪念塔 Kaiser Wilhelms Monument
图79 卡斯托尔教堂 Kastor Kirche

---

120 此山因格林著名童话《白雪公主》而闻名遐迩，这七岭山就是七个小矮人居住的山岭，他们各居一个山头。

121 威廉一世纪念塔（Kaiser Wilhelms Monument），1888年，威廉一世去世以后，为了感谢他为德国统一所做出的努力，帝国决定为其建造一座纪念碑。当时德国各地都期望这座纪念碑能落户在自己的城市。1891年，年轻的皇帝威廉二世（Wilhelm II.）将地点选在了科布伦茨，并且就在莱茵河和摩泽尔河的交汇处。建造塑像所需的100万金马克全部由募捐得。纪念碑始建于1893年，完成于1897年。

122 卡斯托尔教堂（Kastor Kirche），始建于836年，现存建筑建于12世纪末。公元843年分割法兰克帝国的凡尔登条约(Vertrag von Verdun)在此签订。

着一座古老的木构房。木结构的表面被砍劈过，形成了纹理。

宫殿[123]（图80）很普通，博物馆也不值得一看（包括国宾馆）。

在火车总站附近有一座新的现代公寓。

今天是公共假日，所有商店都要关门。

2:40乘船前往美因茨。这次航行甚至比昨天的还要好，因为伴随着航程，城堡一个接着一个在山顶呈现，它们每一个都是风景如画的杰作，将你直接带回到光辉岁月。

第一个要参观的城堡是马克斯堡[124]（图81），这是我所见过的最可入画的一座城堡。

在那里，双堡或者"兄弟堡"：斯特伦堡和里本施坦[125]（图82），还有"老鼠城堡"[126]（图83）以及莱辛施坦堡[127]（图84）。

图80 科布伦茨宫殿 Koblenz Schloss
图81 马克斯堡 Marksburg
图82 斯特伦堡和里本施坦堡 Sterenberg and Liebenstein
图83 老鼠城堡 Castlemaus
图84 莱辛施坦堡 Reichenburg

123 科布伦茨宫殿（Koblenz Schloss），也称选帝侯宫(Kurfürstliches Schloss)，是选帝侯和大主教的行宫，巴洛克风格，现在成为罗马－德意志中央博物馆（Römisch- Germanisches Zentralmuseum)的展馆。
124 马克斯堡（Marksburg），奠基于1173年，哥特风格。马克斯堡是这一地区众多的古堡中唯一一座从未遭受过战火和天灾人祸毁坏的古堡，也是今日德国保存最完好、内容最丰富的中世纪历史博物馆。
125 斯特伦堡和里本施坦堡（Sterenberg and Liebenstein），因这两座城堡相向而立，因此也称为兄弟城堡。
126 罗马元帅德路威斯在公元前8世纪修建的关税塔。在公元10世纪时，美因茨主教在这里储藏了大量的粮食，引来了大批老鼠啃噬，饥民将这位主教大人禁锢在堡中，也成了老鼠的美餐，因而得名。
127 莱辛施坦堡（Reichenburg）这里应当为莱茵岩城堡，它是莱茵河两岸最大的城堡遗迹，13世纪时卡策奈伦伯格侯爵为确保圣高阿的关税征收而建。1479年黑森－卡塞尔侯爵接手城堡并进行了大规模扩建，使城堡成为一个富丽堂皇的文艺复兴式的宫殿。1692年的普法茨遗产继承战争中，该城堡成功地抵住了28000名法军的围攻。现城堡遗迹只保留了原貌的三分之一。

罗蕾莱岩[128]（图85）并不入画，但是历史丰富。

"考伯"[129]（图86）在河面上是最漂亮的建筑。

在"考伯"之后还有更多的废墟城堡，但是位置并不太好。这是因为一旦人们看到最好的"考伯"之后，就不太关注在它之后的东西了。随后河岸突然变得平缓，你可以一直沿途看见树林和乡村住宅，再也没有风景如画的中世纪建筑了。月亮虽然出来，但远远低悬于地平线上，没有落在任何废墟上。

8:45分到达美因茨，在镇里逛了一圈。在外面参观了大教堂。

6月10日 参观了大教堂[130]（图87），内部非常简洁。画了一张教堂外观以及市场的速写，今天是集市日。画了一张圣塔的写生，然后是艾森特姆[131]（图88），这是一座方形石塔（13世纪）。

还画了圣康坦教堂（图89）。

在外面参观了圣·斯蒂芬教堂[132]（图

图85 罗蕾莱岩 Loreley Rock
图86 考伯 Kaub
图87 美因茨大教堂 Mainz Cathedral
图88 艾森特姆 Eisenturm

---

128 罗蕾莱岩（Loreley Rock）。罗蕾莱为一女妖名，传说美女被魔咒所困，被迫用其美貌和动人歌喉吸引莱茵河上的船夫，他们行船至罗蕾莱岩时，听其歌声，不觉仰头观望，便忘乎所以，船便会触礁而沉。此岩高132米，宽90米，位于莱茵河东岸。
129 考伯（Kaub）是莱茵兰-法耳茨州的一座位于莱茵河中游右岸的城市，考伯拥有莱茵河流域最大的葡萄园，山上有古城堡。
130 美因茨大教堂（Mainz Cathedral）与科隆大教堂、特里尔大教堂同被认为是德国的三大教堂。该教堂于975年开始动工建造，至今已有1000多年历史，建筑风格是罗马式与哥特式的结合。建筑取材于附近一带的红砂岩，大教堂内收藏了许多意义重大的历史文化珍宝。
131 艾森特姆（Eisenturm），在数个世纪里美因茨都是被城墙包围的。沿城墙布置有多个防御塔楼，有一些的基础建造于罗马时期。艾森特姆是这些塔楼的其中一座，建造于13世纪，但是看上去却具有现代特征。
132 圣斯蒂芬教堂（St. Stephen's Church），始建于公元990年，现存建筑建于1267—1340年，是美因茨最重要的教堂之一，也是上莱茵地区最早的哥特风格教堂。该教堂在二战期间遭受轰炸，后于1968—1971年修复。

90)和王宫,还有图书馆。

但是最美的事情是在桥上步行一段,月亮挂在莱茵河上,于水中投下倒影,形成长长的金色涟漪。

6月11日 给通往王宫的大门画了一幅写生,参观了古滕堡博物馆[133](图91),那里有远至15世纪中叶的纸质文件的影像,在展室里也有现代印刷品。

中午乘火车前往法兰克福。

法兰克福是一座大城市,郊区充满了现代建筑。参观了歌德故居[134](图92),他的出生房间、书房和餐室。拍摄了一张歌德书桌的照片。

在前往霍姆堡的途中参观了老市场,那里有大量的现代建筑。

前往霍姆堡去听音乐会(贝多芬第九交响曲)。乐队由当地人组成。气质简洁而强烈。

6月12日 在市场周围画了很多速写,每走一步就有新的可画主题。

傍晚步行前往大学。

6月13日 参观了新体育馆,它在树林中显得体量巨大,但是建筑本身却很糟糕。

前往参观在霍尔拜因街(19世纪)的圣

图 89 圣康坦教堂 St. Quintin
图 90 圣斯蒂芬教堂 St. Stephen's Church
图 91 古滕堡博物馆 Gutenburg Museum
图 92 歌德故居 Goethe's House

---

133 古滕堡博物馆(Gutenburg Museum),以美因茨的金属工艺师约翰·古滕堡为名,他发明了活版印刷术。古滕堡一心追求最完美的手艺,但晚景萧条。然而在他死后,他的发明的伟大价值和对社会的巨大贡献终于被人们所认识。在该博物馆中,有古滕堡用活版自行印刷的《圣经》,堪称世界最古老的活版印刷《圣经》。

134 歌德故居(Goethe's House)。约翰·沃尔夫冈·冯·歌德于1749年出生于美因河畔法兰克福。歌德出生的房屋位于格罗撒·希尔施格拉本(Großer Hirschgraben)街。

图 93 圣伯尼费斯教堂 St. Boniface Church
图 94 法兰克福市政厅 Römer
图 95 法恩弗里登教堂 Frauen-Friedenskirch

伯尼费斯教堂（图93）。外面的砖砌得很美，室内则色彩丰富。画了一幅该教堂的速写。中庭采用拱顶，唱诗席则是更高的拱顶。中庭被涂成蓝色，唱诗席采用黄色，踏步和圣坛采用深红色，效果确实非常好。

前往参观在城外的坎纳德·哈米什学校（18世纪），这是一座2层楼的砖砌建筑。墙角有一只钟，在黑块中嵌入白色面砖作为数字。

不远处有一座教堂矗立于山顶，外观是混凝土的。内部比例不太好。在平台上有一个别致的楼梯，它的油漆方式看上去很像俄国构成主义的舞台布景。

在回来路上参观了市场大厅，这是一座很棒的现代建筑。

画了一张在罗马广场中的市政厅[135]（图94）。然后前往参观齐柏林街99号的法恩弗里登教堂[136]（图95）（4世纪）。内部与外部都很棒，外部由水泥条板构成，带有3个很深的高拱券。在拱券中央有一幅描绘圣母的马赛克浮雕像。在拱券的两侧是马赛克墙（大多数是蓝色和金色）。教堂内有两个小礼拜堂，很有效果。锈蚀玻

---

[135] 法兰克福市政厅（Römer）。Römer 为德语中 Roman 的写法，是法兰克福最重要的标志性建筑之一，它作为法兰克福市政厅已达 600 余年。
[136] 法恩弗里登教堂（Frauen-Friedenskirche），意思为圣母和平大教堂。

璃很棒，它将光线投射在白色泥灰墙面和柱面上。

6月14日 前往法兰克福手工艺馆（图96），这里有一个沃尔特·格罗皮乌斯的现代建筑展（大多数是工业建筑）。参观工艺制造博物馆（图97），里面有丰富的藏品。在中国展区，有一面汉代的镜子，直径约4.5英尺，从中间断裂。它非常漂亮，这是我所见过的第一面汉镜。似乎没有必要前去或者待在英国馆中，英国人所有的智慧就是用来掠夺我们。

有一小部分的现代艺术，都是大路货。某个展厅里有老木板，非常好的色彩。

参观了市政厅中的皇帝大厅（图98），漂亮的色彩。平面并不是一个完整的矩形，面对广场的墙面有点斜，于是就形成了一个不规则的筒拱端面。但是人们很难察觉，因为厅室很长。楼板是镶嵌打磨的，木头的状况也很好。整个效果如此色彩斑斓、丰富多彩。议员厅和市民厅（图99）也维护良好，色彩绚丽。参观者在进入前必须脱鞋。

参观了法兰克福大教堂的室内，色彩丰富并且神秘。玻璃窗却很糟糕。

乘坐25路车从话剧院到霍姆堡，然后前往萨尔堡去参观罗马古迹，整座城堡是重建的。德国人的复建看上去粗糙而且笨拙，没有任何感觉。参观博物馆，里面有很多皮制鞋。

从萨尔堡出发去寻找赫兹堡，但是在树林中迷了路。走了半个小时后才最终回到萨尔堡。然后又从殡仪馆出发去寻找一座名叫夫豪·赫奇曼考夫（此地名因辨识不清，有待考证）的圆形小镇，步行半个多小时后没看到任何东西，因此整整浪费了一个小时。前去参观米特罗姆，喝了一

图96 法兰克福手工艺馆
Frankfurt Kunstverein
图97 法兰克福工艺制造博物馆
Kunstgewerbe Museum
图98 法兰克福市政厅，皇帝大厅
Römer, Kaisersaal
图99 市民厅 Bürgersaal

些冷泉水。

乘火车回到霍姆堡（4点钟），然后再去法兰克福。在大教堂下车，回去参观一所现代学校和一些现代公寓，在那里画了一张素描。

傍晚参观了歌剧院，这真是巴黎歌剧院的一个缩样。

6月15日 参观了施坦德美术馆[137]（图100），虽然里面有一张米勒画作、几张上好的德加画作、一张凡·高画作以及其他现代画家的作品，但是没有什么内容。美术馆还有一个中国展区以及中国学院，但是不能进去。

前往达姆施塔德。参观了婚礼塔，漂亮的建筑和两个漂亮的喷泉，还有一座俄国教堂。爬到塔顶，达姆施塔德有一些老房子处于贫民窟状态。

傍晚前往海德堡，与R.S.[138]一起住双人间，房间里有窗，可以向外眺望城堡。

6月16日 早晨画了桥头堡，还有其他一些主题。下午参观废墟城堡的内部。随后天气转多云。城堡的修复部分令人浮想联翩。整个外观远远看去并不壮美。颜色太红，内容并不厚重。唯一值得一提的就是它是一处遗迹。在地下室看见两个大啤酒缸。

沿着哲学家的道路爬山涉水。

6月17日 总共画了7幅水彩画。今天没有看到什么新鲜东西，但是可以在这里足足待上一个星期，并且每天画画。明快的小塔，食物比其他地方要贵很多。冲印照片也很花钱，1卷合2.5马克。

6月18日 晴天，7:30乘火车前往曼海姆，参观战前（1907年）新艺术现代美术馆。但是大多数展品是未来主义的，油画、水彩画以及雕塑。好建筑加上好内容。

参观了王宫，这是德国最大的王宫，是凡尔赛宫的一个翻版。花园没有平面，就像英国的公园。耶稣教堂的室内腐坏了。

曼海姆有一些棒极了的现代建筑。

中午前往沃姆斯，参观大教堂和路德纪念碑，大教堂的外观带有岁月的痕迹和迷人的氛围，就像莱茵河，但是内部却糟糕透顶，就像巴洛克的雕塑。莱茵河大桥很漂亮，画了一张速写。参观了旧

---

137 施坦德美术馆（Städel Museum）是德国最重要、最著名的艺术博物馆之一。它是法兰克福博物馆区所有博物馆中最精彩和最重要的一个，是参观法兰克福的必游之地。
138 可能是童寯在宾夕法尼亚大学的同学 Rowland Snyder.

城墙、圣保罗教堂（图101）、圣安德拉教堂和犹太会堂（图102）。沃姆斯是一座风景如画的小镇，值得停留一天。

下午5点前往洛希。参观罗马风教堂（圣米歇尔礼拜堂）（图103），还有一座处于后面的教堂遗址，画了两者的速写。

沃姆斯和洛希以尼伯龙根传说[139]而闻名。

6月19日 疲劳至极，一丝寒意就令我的关节感到疼痛，因此昨晚睡得不好。吃了两片喹啉药片，起来吃早饭。

乘坐晨车前往维尔茨堡，1点钟到达那里。

火车上睡了一觉之后，在维尔茨堡就感觉好多了。同样住在火车站附近，街道非常不错。

参观了教堂（内部品位很差），总体上不太好，这只是一座地区教堂。

参观了美因河上的旧桥，非常漂亮而且简洁。画了一张速写。

维尔茨堡的建筑非常巴洛克，我所见过的所有德国建筑都是巴洛克的。

从外表上看，王宫很一般，花园不值一提，是法式花园的拙劣翻版。

除了德国游客之外，维尔茨堡的游客并不多，它与美因茨同样风景如画。

6月20日 彻底恢复过来。吃过早餐，跨过老主桥，在马瑞恩堡（图104）的城堡下面逛了一圈，试图找到入口。回到老桥并且又画了一张速写。爬上城堡，在里面画了2张水彩画，看不到建筑室内。当门卫要求出示写生许可证时，我正想着出去吃午餐。他告

图100 施坦德美术馆 Städel Museum
图101 圣保罗教堂 St. Paulus Kirche
图102 犹太会堂 Jewish Synagogue
图103 圣米歇尔礼拜堂 Michael's Kapelle
图104 马瑞恩堡 Marienburg

---

[139] 尼伯龙根传说（Nibelungen Saga）是德国的民间史诗，产生于13世纪，说的是公元5世纪的故事。Saga 意为北欧神话的英雄传奇。

诉我向下在彼得教堂（图105）附近可以获得许可证。因此我下了楼，在沿途的一家咖啡店里吃早晨买的午餐，3个水煮蛋、2个肉卷和1瓶啤酒。走到彼得广场附近，在那儿却浪费1个小时去寻找发放写生许可证的地方。一场暴雨即将来临，所以回到旅馆去准备一个邮寄包裹。

在邮局试图将包裹邮寄出时，遇到了很多麻烦，最后不得不在凯萨街13号买了油纸并用它将包裹包起来，密封好。没有想去登记。希望它能寄到那儿。里面是我画的所有画，从布鲁日到维尔茨堡的，以及所有买的明信片和拍的照片，真是无价之宝，尽管我在上面填写了价值不到10马克。

晚饭吃了一大份煎鸡蛋，仅是煎鸡蛋就花了40盾，再加上色拉、啤酒和八字形饼干[140]，共计1.5马克。

6月21日 清晨离开维尔茨堡，中午前抵达罗滕堡。买了一张城市地图，步行穿过主要集市区。这是一个非常有意思的地方，景色超乎想象。有这么多的塔楼，房屋与它们协调相处。

画了一些塔楼和市政厅的速写，然后下山去画老陶伯河桥（图106）。

罗滕堡是我所见的最具想象力的城市。它是中世纪和现代社会的一种融合，人们似乎仍然在使用公共烤炉，因为他们在街上扛着巨大的糕饼平底锅。这是一座小镇，一半乡村一半城市，只有两条主要街道。

晚上步行前往代特旺[141]。它有一座几英里长的大桥，一座教堂名叫"圣彼得与圣保

图105 彼得教堂 Peters Kirche
图106 老陶伯河桥 Old Tauber Bridge
图107 刽子手桥 Henkersteg
图108 丢勒故居 Dürer's House

---

[140] 德式碱面包结，一种脆饼干，有紧致咸香的外皮，松软充满弹性的里层，富有质感和嚼劲的传统德国风味，搭配啤酒最佳。
[141] 罗滕堡郊外一村庄名称。

罗",正立面有一个门廊。这真是一个风景如画的村庄。就在下山之前,人们可以看见壮美的日落,有时需要穿过绿色丛林。当爬上罗滕堡时,又可以听到犬吠,头饰叮当,流水潺潺。有一片叫做伯格特[142]的台地,轮廓看上去如此轻盈而且虚幻,就像是一场梦。这场景太棒了。

6月22日 已经参观完小镇的每一个地方,画了4张水彩画。又一次前往代特旺,去写生一些房屋。这座小村庄有一间铁匠铺和一间咖啡馆,我听见有人在很响亮地唱圣歌,一位妇人拿出一把椅子让我坐,但我没有坐下。

回到罗滕堡前往集市,等12点钟去看敲钟。当时钟敲响后,大钟两侧的窗户必定打开,一个真人大小的人像,穿着像真的一样,开始做动作。一个人喝了一大杯啤酒,另一个似乎在吸一只烟斗,表演持续了2分钟,随后窗户关上。

又一次前去参观罗马双桥。

罗滕堡是如此一座小镇,所以很容易到处走遍。空气非常新鲜。

7点钟出发前往纽伦堡,但是由于错过了一班车,直到晚上11:30才到达那里。走进旅馆,12点3刻上床睡觉。

6月23日 从车站到凯撒门步行穿过小镇。在那儿画了一张水彩速写,接着又画了刽子手桥(图107)。午餐吃的是面包和啤酒,随后天气变得多云。前往参观丢勒故居(图108),非常漂亮的室内。博物馆在3楼,厨房在2楼,这很有意思。一些家具是丢勒时期遗留下来的。

走了很多路。纽伦堡风景如画,但是每个主题都被画过,或者被说明过,你做不出新的事情。景色随处可见,一些在商店橱窗中的镂空印刷品也值得一看。

走向纺织工街的第七街,住宅都被笼罩于夜色中。顺路参观汉斯·萨克斯(著名歌唱家)[143]的故居,这是一座木构建筑,一层楼必定是改造过的。

6月24日 今天在城里没有看到什么新东西。比较厌倦画水彩,

---

142 意思为城堡大门。
143 汉斯·萨克斯(Hans Sachs)是一名鞋匠,也是一名工匠歌手,作为16世纪中叶德国纽伦堡的一位真实的历史人物,他被著名音乐家理察·瓦格纳写进经典歌剧《纽伦堡的名歌手》(Die Meistersinger von Nürnberg),成为剧中的主角之一。

于是画了一些铅笔画。

下午参观日耳曼博物馆（图109），第125室是著名的青铜雕像"纽伦堡的玛多纳"[144]（图110）。该博物馆是一座带有几间内庭和一座小礼拜堂的修道院，藏品中比较有意思的是墓碑和石雕，其余都是垃圾。

6月25日 在班贝格参观了现代教堂，圣海因里希教堂（图111.1，图111.2）（建筑师为高蒂博士）。外观是精美的石作，在拱券侧框有一些砖作。室内有很好的木板天棚，其余部分则是混凝土和涂料。

在出城时，前去参观了神学院（图112），混凝土的外观，有一个很舒服的内庭，建筑前面有一根柱子。

爬上山前往阿尔滕堡[145]（图113），那里一无所有，回来时仅在山上画了一张大教堂[146]（图114）的速写。大教堂看上去很坚硬，尽管已经老旧了，它没有被岁月所锈蚀。市政厅非常巴洛克，新老王宫也是

图109　日耳曼博物馆　Germanic Museum
图110　纽伦堡的马多纳　Nürnberg Madonna
图111.1　圣海因里希教堂　St. Heinrichskirche
图111.2　圣海因里希教堂　St. Heinrichskirche

---

144 纽伦堡的马多纳（Nürnberg Madonna），作于16世纪，传说可能为丢勒作品。
145 阿尔滕堡（Die Altenberg），位于班贝格城北一座山丘上的城堡，始建于1109年。
146 班贝格大教堂（Bamberg Cathedral），也称为班贝格圣彼得与圣乔治大教堂（Bamberger Dom St. Peter und St. Georg），于1012年完成兴建，但曾经烧毁了两次。现存教堂重建于1237年，有四座高塔，为罗马风格与哥特风格，班贝格历史上最重要的几个历史人物沉睡于其中。

如此。大教堂的内部很漂亮。

除了圣米歇尔教堂[147]（图115）外，其他一些教堂没有什么特别之处。它坐落于山顶上，拥有很好的视野。总而言之，班贝格是在罗滕堡和维尔茨堡之后的首选，它很容易在旅程中被忽略掉。

6月26日 几乎下了整整一天的雨。参观了市政厅和大教堂，路德的斗室，还有克莱默桥（图116）。

大教堂是德国最好的，外表看上去（从远处）甚至比科隆的还要好，风格上垂直高耸。它在后面也有一个很大的开敞空间，并且从远处就可以看到。它的行进路线很棒，踏步有一种飞动之感。内部则充满了巴洛克风格的纪念物，中庭与边廊等宽，几乎三等分，或者中庭甚至比边廊还要窄。玻璃窗很糟糕，回廊庭院则相当的好。唱诗席被屏封起来，相对于教堂也缺乏进深，因为这是由比例所带来的方正效果。

圣泽威利教堂[148]（图117）离主教堂很近，它的钟塔构成了一个假立面，因为屋顶与它们分离开来，屋顶铺设红瓦，看上去就像一座大型私人住宅，色彩非常丰富，轮廓非常美丽。没有进去。

圣马丁修道院是一座新教堂（重建），路德斗室看上去很旧，它也许是一个假的，还有被烧过的圣经。这些就是关于爱尔福特的。

魏玛完全是19世纪的，雨中漫步于花园中，参观了歌德的夏季故居、莎士比亚的纪念碑，然后前往尼采故居。陈列室在一楼，

图112 班贝格神学院
Priesterseminar

图113 班贝格老城堡
Die Altenberg

图114 班贝格大教堂
Bamberg Cathedrale

图115 圣米歇尔教堂
St. Michael's Church

---

147 圣米歇尔教堂（St. Michael's Church），建造于12世纪，罗马风格，坐落于班贝格郊外一山丘上，可以俯瞰整个城市。
148 圣泽威利教堂（St. Severi Church），坐落于爱尔福特旁边，始建于1121年，哥特风格。

图 116 克莱默桥 Krämer Brüke
图 117 圣泽威利教堂 St. Severi Church
图 118 奥尔马赫酒馆 Auerbachs Keller

尼采的妹妹住在楼上,房间刚刚整修过,还有一些新书,包括斯宾格勒的《衰落》[149],挂满了肖像,还有胸像。斯宾格勒是房东的一位朋友,经常光顾这里,他的肖像被挂在墙上。尼采从1897年到1900年住在这儿,直到去世。

参观李斯特故居,他的睡床、书房、肖像、胸像以及手稿。李斯特年轻时很像查尔斯·狄更斯,晚年时看上去则有些古怪。

参观了歌德故居,比美因河畔法兰克福的故居要大,而且更加壮观。有关自然历史的藏品非常多,物理实验室看上去很新。我相信这里每年都在进行扩张。他的卧室看上去比较简陋,只有一扇面对花园的小窗。他去世于床边的坐椅上。

席勒故居没有歌德故居宽敞。里面有很多的胸像和肖像,还有诗人带有书桌的卧室。

文档包括信件和书籍,歌德的《浮士德》写作于此,还有许多写于歌德、席勒等人之间的信函,卡莱尔[150]、拜伦[151]写给歌德的信函,贝多芬写给歌德的信函,歌德以多种语言写作的日记和著作。

参观了剧院广场的外景,并参观了冯·施坦因[152]的故居。

6:24乘火车前往莱比锡,7:50到达。

6月27日 参观新歌剧院的外景,不是太

---

149 斯宾格勒的两卷本著作《西方的衰落》(*Der Untergang des Abendlandes*),第一卷发表于1918年,后于1922年修改后再次发表,第二卷发表于1923年。

150 卡莱尔(Thomas Carlyle,1795—1881年),苏格兰文学家。卡莱尔为一石匠之子,早年敏慧过人;当其肄业爱丁堡大学之时,即已开始写作,表显他的文学天才,不久即驰誉文坛。卡莱尔不仅著述丰富,而且文笔流畅,深刻感人,思想独到,故能自成一家。著有《法国革命》、《腓特烈大帝传》、《帝勒尔传》、《英雄与英雄崇拜》、《过去与现在》等书。

151 乔治·戈登·拜伦(George Gordon Byron,1788—1824年),英国19世纪初期伟大的浪漫主义诗人。其代表作品有《恰尔德·哈罗德游记》、《唐璜》等。

152 冯·施坦因(Charlotte Albertine Ernestine von Stein,1776—1789年),歌德最著名的情人。

图 119 圣托马斯教堂 St. Thomas Church　　图 120 格拉西博物馆 Grassi Museum
图 121 德意志图书馆 Deutsches Bucherei　　图 122 俄罗斯教堂 Russian Church

好,博物馆看上去令人印象深刻,大学也是如此,有两座新摩天楼(约10层楼高)在广场上拔地而起。

奥尔马赫酒馆[153](图118)是歌德"浮士德"的原型地,现在是一个非常火爆的葡萄酒餐厅,哲学家的火炉现在由电力来照亮,就像一个舞台布景。所有东西看上去都像是假的,但是有几份歌德的手稿,裱好挂在墙上。

巴赫[154]就是在圣托马斯[155](图119)这座教堂的唱诗席上唱歌。室内没有什么可看的。我坐在座席上阅读贝德克旅行指南。

市政厅是全新的,老市政厅则在市场当中,它有一座多彩的塔楼。在靠近圣约翰教堂的地方有一座现代建筑,也就是格拉西博物

---

153 奥尔马赫酒馆(Auerbachs Keller)是莱比锡最著名的餐馆,因《浮士德》作品中的一幕场景而闻名。
154 约翰·塞巴斯蒂安·巴赫(Johann Sebastian Bach,1685—1750年),巴洛克时期的德国作曲家,杰出的管风琴、小提琴、大键琴演奏家。
155 圣托马斯教堂(St. Thomas Church),建于1500年,晚期哥特风格。巴赫自1723年开始,直至1750年逝世时的27年间都在此教堂工作。

图 123 博览会场
　　　　Austeilung Gelände
图 124 民族会战纪念碑
　　　　Völkerschlacht Denkmal
图 125 马格德堡大教堂
　　　　Cathedral of Magdeburg

馆[156]（图120）。该美术馆有很多现代和传统艺术的收藏品，大多数是手工艺作品。

前往莱比锡郊外（从火车站乘32路车）去参观德意志图书馆[157]（图121）。附近还有一座现代风格的俄罗斯教堂[158]（图122），它建于1913年，带有一个盔顶穹窿，室内也建造得不错。宗教艺术的青铜手工艺很漂亮，展览中心有一些现代建筑，大学的诊所采用现代风格而且距离很近。

穿过整座城市去洗一个澡。

6点~8点之间，在音乐学院听了一场优美的交响乐，由学生演出。

6月28日 参观了奥古斯都广场上的博物馆，那里拥有一些著名的画作和很多马克斯·克林格尔[159]的藏品。克林格尔有时采用彩色大理石在不同的画像中进行创作。他的贝多芬就在这里。他的画作也带有构图的新思想。现在的绘画和雕塑展览非常棒。

又参观了博览会场（图123）。这次参观从展品开始看起，对此我并不感兴趣。前去画民族会战纪念碑[160]（图124），但是没有上去。画了俄国教堂并参观了新市场，它有两个穹顶。

新剧院与纽约的大都会[161]以及费城的音

---

[156] 格拉西博物馆（Grassi Museum）为乐器博物馆，由3个博物馆组成，收藏了大约5000件展品，它们来自16至20世纪的欧洲及欧洲以外的地区，还有一间圣像收藏馆和历史上录音媒体的收藏馆，其中收藏了约3500个用于自动演奏钢琴的乐谱卷和大量录音。
[157] 德意志图书馆（Deutsches Bucherei），建于1913年，收藏自那时以来的全部德文书籍，现藏书超过800万册。
[158] 俄罗斯教堂（Russian Church），也称为圣阿列克苏斯纪念堂（Memorial Church of St. Alexius），由波克罗夫斯基（W. A. Pokrowski）于1912—1913年设计。
[159] 马克斯·克林格尔（Max Klinger，1857—1920年），德国象征主义画家和雕塑家。克林格尔出生于莱比锡，最欣赏戈雅和门采尔的蚀刻版画，因而自学成为一名出色的蚀刻版画家。他最著名的作品是一个系列蚀刻版画"关于寻找一个手套的释义"，是源自他在一个溜冰场寻找手套的梦境，他图解了弗洛伊德对于恋物的研究结果，其中"手套"成为他追求浪漫理想的象征。
[160] 民族会战纪念碑（Völkerschlacht Denkmal），纪念1813年10月16日至19日在莱比锡城南为对抗拿破仑入侵德意志而发生的莱比锡战役。纪念碑高91米，为目前欧洲现存最大纪念碑。
[161] 指纽约大都会歌剧院（Metropolitan Opera in New York）。

图126 遗迹山 Ruinenberg　　图127 格列尼克大桥 Glienicker Brücke　　图128 爱因斯坦塔 Einstein Tower

乐学院有着相似的外观，但是容量要小。

6月29日　托马斯教堂有一个非常好的唱诗席，大多数男孩都不满十岁。乐器很好，乐队用它演奏。

在莱比锡看得够多了，有些厌烦了。

动物园有大约20只熊，还有一些孔雀。里面有一些现代建筑，用于大象和熊。天文馆是现代风格的，但是比较便宜，而且关闭了。

6月30日　早晨10点左右前往马格德堡。参观了大教堂[162]（图125），比较乏味。立面还可以，但是它是一个非常虚假的正立面，中央山墙矗立在中庭顶棚的上方，两座钟塔也没有任何东西在后面。

博览会很有意思。参观了市政厅的室内，这是用于交响乐的观众厅。乐器屏风是由覆以蓝色天鹅绒加上红色竖向格栅所构成。室内由水平的木件进行建造，窗户由浮雕玻璃所组成，并且很沉重。灯光的托架很有意味。色彩配置很有效果，这是我所见过最好的现代室内。

参观了市场和市政厅，不是太喜欢。

下午5点左右到达波茨坦。从塞茜琳花园[163]开始，一直走到看

---

[162] 马格德堡大教堂（Cathedral of Magdeburg），正式名称为圣卡特里娜与莫里斯大教堂（Cathedral of Saints Catherine and Maurice），是德国最早的哥特教堂之一，两座主塔高约100米。
[163] 无忧宫取名自法文的 Sanssouci（无忧），意指国王可在宫中无忧无虑、逍遥自在。因坐落在沙丘之上，故又有沙丘上的宫殿之称。无忧宫由著名建筑师诺比尔斯多夫（Knobelsdorff）设计，外观模仿法国凡尔赛宫，并加入腓特烈个人的爱好，是18世纪德国建筑洛可可式艺术的精华，也是腓特烈大帝留给后人印象深刻的建筑。

见风车。

为市政厅画了一张速写。

7月1日 画了一张风车的速写。步行前往遗迹山（图126），这是一个模仿罗马宏伟气势的假货，近距离观看时很糟糕。在花园里逛了一会儿。然后乘电车前往格列尼克大桥[164]（图127）。在远处观看了巴贝尔斯贝格[165]的哥特城堡。

花了一个小时去寻找爱因斯坦塔[166]（图128），最终当我到达那里时，门口的老妇不让我进去。我非常急迫地想看上一眼，因此围着观察站的周边走了很远，才看到它的顶部。爱因斯坦塔在照片上通常是黑色的，但是在现场看上去却是白色的，而且很洁净。

5点钟出发去柏林，半个小时后到达，住在弗雷德里希车站附近的维多利亚旅馆。

7月2日 5点钟之前没有参观任何东西，四处寻找穿过俄国区（一个展览和公使馆）的通道。

7点钟参观动物园，8点钟参观天文馆。天文馆的设施棒极了。有一个天空图像的投影，所有的星星都在上面，看上去很像真的。

7月3日 参观了国家美术馆，里面没有什么太多内容。参观了新老市政厅，都是腐朽的建筑，尤其是老的。

下午沿着选帝侯大街[167]行走，参观了环球影院。

7月4日 参观新老博物馆，里面有大量的希腊、罗马、埃及的藏品，大多数是雕塑。晚上前往环球影院。外观是非常优美的线条和构图。剧院恰当地进行了红色配色，人们从侧边门进入，没有中央走道。休息厅是蓝色的。

7月5日 参观了佩加蒙（佩加蒙博物馆）[168]（图129），高雅而独特，难以言表。博物馆尚未开放，但是我们通过美国机构得以进入。佩加蒙神坛[169]被罩于现代玻璃顶之中。浮雕（巨人与诸神之

---

164 格列尼克大桥（Glienicker Brücke），横跨Havel河，连接波茨坦（Potsdam）与柏林（Berlin）。大桥于1907年完工。
165 巴贝尔斯贝格（Potsdam-Babelsberg），是波茨坦最大的城市街区，以山丘Babelsberg而名。
166 爱因斯坦塔（Einstein Tower），由德国建筑师孟德尔松（Eric Mendelsohn，1889—1953年）于1919年至1921年设计，是表现主义重要的代表作品。
167 选帝侯大街（Kurfuerstendamm），柏林最著名的购物街。
168 佩加蒙博物馆（Pergamon Museum）位于柏林的博物馆岛（Museum Island），1930年才正式开放参观。该博物馆由德国建筑师阿尔弗雷德·梅瑟尔（Alfred Messel）与路德维希·霍夫曼（Ludwig Hoffmann）设计。
169 指在佩加蒙博物馆中的宙斯祭坛，全长120米，祭坛上雕刻了各种浮雕。该浮雕原先坐落在希腊佩加蒙城内。

战）[170]（图130）处于一种完全破损的状态，而且没有进行任何修补。上面的神庙建筑是重建的，残片原物显示得很清楚。这比在英国博物馆中所做的要好，在那里，人们愚蠢地试图将浮雕黏合到一起，使之更加完整，于是就破坏了想象。除了佩加蒙神坛之外，还有一个来自锡安山[171]的罗马风大门，还有来自米勒[172]的残片。古迹的比例很完美。

参观了弗雷德里希大帝博物馆[173]（图131），里面有很好的荷兰收藏品。同样还有许多伦勃朗、哈斯[174]以及凡·戴克的作品。但是那些意大利的绘画和雕塑则是这里的珍宝。文艺复兴大师如德拉·罗比亚[175]（50多件）、多纳泰罗、桑萨维罗[176]等等，还有1件达·芬奇和2件米开朗基罗的作品。一幅拉斐尔的玛多纳也在这里，总共有5件拉斐尔的作品。

图129 佩加蒙博物馆
Pergamon Museum
图130 巨人之战浮雕
Gigantomachia
图131 弗雷德里希大帝博物馆
Kaiser Friedrich Museum

参观了太子博物馆[177]，在顶层它拥有现代主义的绘画和雕塑。棒极了。塞尚、德加、亨利·马蒂斯、康定斯基，其中有一些极其的现代。

---

170 巨人之战（Gigantomachia），指希腊神话中巨人对天神的搏斗，基迦巨人都是暴力和战斗的化身，他们与奥林比亚众神对抗，这次的战争被称为巨人战役。巨人之战处在宙斯祭坛中，是围绕基座一周的浮雕饰带。全部浮雕由115块大型大理石组成，描绘了神话中大地女神的儿子巨人们因为反抗奥林比亚众神与神之间的形象，战斗激烈凶猛，群像之间密切穿插，强调了运动中的频繁扭曲，以及面部的细腻感情变化。
171 锡安山是耶路撒冷老城南部一座山的名称。
172 米勒（Milet）是土耳其距伊兹密尔市东80公里的一座城市，通常被称为米利都（Miletus），土耳其语为Milet。
173 弗雷德里希大帝博物馆（Kaiser Friedrich Museum）。柏林博物馆岛第四大建筑，由建筑师恩斯特·冯·伊内设计，1904年建成，以德皇弗雷德里希三世命名，二战后1956年改为博德博物馆（Bode-Museum）。
174 哈斯（Frans Hals，1580—1666年），荷兰黄金时期著名画家，擅长肖像画。哈斯以其松散画笔技法闻名，对荷兰艺术产生重大影响，并带动了17世纪的组群肖像绘画的发展。
175 德拉·罗比亚（Luca della Robbia，1400—1482年），佛罗伦萨雕刻家，以雕刻阳台上的装饰图案而出名。
176 桑萨维罗（Sansovino，1486—1570年）意大利文艺复兴时期手法主义雕塑家。
177 指弗雷德里希·威廉四世（Friedrich Wilhelm IV），是他提议建造了柏林的博物馆岛。

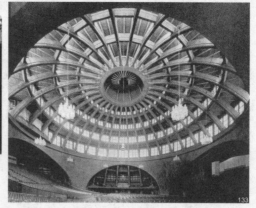

图 132 布雷斯劳主教堂
Breslau Cathedral
图 133 百年纪念堂
Jahrhunderthalle

7月6日 在坦佩霍夫机场[178]看见了跑道,然后乘火车前往布雷斯劳。参观了布雷斯劳的市政厅,色彩非常明快而偏红色,画了速写。

7月7日 参观了城内几乎所有的教堂(没有进去),包括布雷斯劳主教堂[179](图132),它们全都用红砖建成,并且相当漂亮,大教堂尤其色彩斑斓。

参观了一个名叫百年纪念堂[180](图133)的现代建筑群,这是一个带有梯状玻璃穹顶的大报告厅,室内效果强烈。到处充满了混凝土和玻璃。不知道音响效果如何解决。

7月8日 参观了克莱门斯·玛利亚·霍夫鲍尔教堂[181],它处在城市的西南。外观较为保守,只有钟塔顶部带有现代节点,所有拱券都是椭圆形的。尽管没有侧道,但是室内很漂亮,而且五彩缤纷。教堂处在二楼,当你上楼时,有一群彩陶的浮雕嵌于墙中,看上去很有意思,装饰的基调是红色的,非常像一所剧院。

参观了体育场,它由网球场、田径场和游泳池所组成。

---

178 坦佩霍夫机场坐落于柏林坦佩霍夫舍讷堡区内,曾是柏林三个主要机场之一。
179 布雷斯劳主教堂(Breslau Cathedral)。布雷斯劳今属波兰,名为弗罗茨瓦夫(Wroclaw)。教堂始建于10世纪,现存建造重建于1951年,是一座带有新哥特风格的哥特式教堂。
180 百年纪念堂(Jahrhunderthalle),由建筑师马克斯·伯格(Max Berg)设计,建于1911—1913年。该会堂是钢筋混凝土建筑史上的一个里程碑,是当时弗罗茨瓦夫的市政厅。百年纪念堂是一个多功能娱乐场所,其结构为中心对称式,呈现出对称的四叶片形状,中心是开阔的圆形空间(直径65米,高42米),可容纳6000多人。会堂上方是由钢和玻璃构成的灯笼式穹顶,窗户由进口硬木制成,墙面则由印有木质模板条痕的混凝土构成,并在局部覆盖一层由水泥和一般木材或软木混合而成的绝缘层,以改善音响效果。
181 圣克莱门斯·霍夫鲍尔教堂(Saint Clement Hofbauer)。克莱门斯·玛利亚·霍夫鲍尔(Clemens Maria Hofbauer,1751—1820年)是维也纳的一位宗教隐士和资助人。

乘电车（15路）前往奥斯维茨去参观威廉皇帝纪念塔（图134），它在照片上看上去很好。但是在现场的颜色却很糟糕，这是一种廉价的红砖和灰色石块的塔楼，因此我只画了一张铅笔速写。在回来的路上走进一个墓地，去参观一个新建的殡仪馆，非常棒。

总体上德国人具备良好的习惯，尤其是妇女走路时，穿着宽大裤子，并喜欢在背上带东西，而男人则将很多东西放在自行车上，或者几乎将摩托车当作汽车。

德国人喜欢随身携带自己的午餐，三明治和糕饼，男人女人差不多。

7月9日 早晨在布雷斯劳火车站看见一个戴着丝绸高帽的烟囱清扫工，这是一种应当废除的双重制度。

在德累斯顿参观了绘画美术馆，很棒的收藏品。看到了拉斐尔的《西斯廷圣母》，安德烈亚·德尔·萨托的《圣夜》[182]，提香的《贡币》（图135）。拉斐尔的玛多纳的构图和服饰都很好，只是色彩有些暗淡。

德累斯顿是一座漂亮的巴洛克城市，因为它是洛可可艺术的摇篮。

画廊的现代部分有一些先锋派的绘画作品，瓦西里·康定斯基[183]采用几何形式（球形等）。

利奥尼·费宁格[184]将平面穿过物体。

保罗·克利[185]在线描中，有时也在样式

图134 威廉皇帝纪念塔
Kaiser-Wilhelm-Gedächtnisturm

图135 提香《贡币》
Tribute Money, Titian

---

182 作者应为柯雷乔（Antonio Allegri da Correggio, 1489—1534年），他是意大利文艺复兴盛期帕尔马画派（Parma School）的主要画家之一。
183 瓦西里·康定斯基（Wassily Wassilyevich Kandinsky, 1866—1944年），俄国画家、理论家。他于1922年至1933年间任教于包豪斯（Bauhaus）。
184 利奥尼·费宁格（Lyonel Feininger, 1871—1956年），德国血统的美国画家。20世纪20年代初期，费宁格曾在包豪斯接受艺术工匠方面的培训，随后又在魏玛继续学习建筑学。结束学业后，他曾在汉堡、巴黎和斯德哥尔摩等地工作。
185 保罗·克利（Paul Klee, 1879—1940年），德国籍的瑞士画家，他与康定斯基是朋友，也曾在包豪斯任教。

上采用埃及形式，看上去就像儿童画。

恩斯特·路德维希·凯尔希纳[186]的绘画在形式上不算激进，但是他在人们的脸部采用绿色和紫色。

德国的交通不算繁忙，但是德国人特别遵守信号灯，通常只有一名警察站在那里控制交通信号。另外也没有必要匆忙，但是每座城镇（甚至村庄）都有一个自动售货机，出售比三明治更多的啤酒和红酒。

7月10日　参观了瓷器博物馆，那里有很多中国藏品。

参观了工业艺术博物馆，里面有宣和御笔之鹰，文徵明和刘石庵的题字。

7月11日　参观了雕塑画廊，其中有一些希腊大师，如普拉克西特利斯[187]的原作。参观了学院展览，门票1马克，但是里面没有太多的内容。

在画廊中，复印品似乎比原作还要多，在同一个展室中有2幅鲁本斯的《醉酒的海克力斯》（图136）。其中一幅必定是复制品。另一幅鲁本斯的绘画也像是复制品。唯一的真迹是拉斐尔的《西斯廷》（图137），乔尔乔内的《沉睡的维纳斯》（图

图136　《醉酒的海克力斯》　Drunken Hercules
图137　《西斯廷圣母》　Sistine Madonna
图138　《沉睡的维纳斯》　Sleeping Venus
图139　《圣夜》　Holy Night

186　恩斯特·路德维希·凯尔希纳（Ernst Ludwig Kirchner，1880—1938年），德国艺术家。凯尔希纳是著名的艺术家协会"桥社"的创建人中年纪最大的，他积极地继承和发展了当时的以及古典的艺术。与他性格内向的朋友海格尔和施米特·鲁特勒夫相反，他性格外向。在慕尼黑他曾从师青春艺术派元老之一赫尔曼·奥柏里斯特，同时学习丢勒的木刻。20世纪30年代他接受了毕加索立体主义绘画的某些特点。而正是这种灵活性和他对超凡事物的感觉赋予了他最杰出的才能。

187　普拉克西特利斯（Praxiteles，公元前4世纪中叶）希腊最有创造性的艺术家之一，雅典雕刻家，以其大理石雕像闻名。其作品将神话人物纳入平凡的日常生活加以抒情描写，风格柔和细腻，确立了当时希腊雕塑的特征。其著名作品现仅存大理石雕像《赫尔墨斯》。

138）和柯雷乔的《圣夜》（图139）。

在约翰诺伊姆[188]（图140）前面有两尊男孩塑像，其中一个是中国人。拍了一张照片。

7月12日 参观了卫生展览。展览布置得更像是一个建筑展览而不是卫生展览。有如此之多的建筑照片（住宅、工厂、医院），还有模型。一些殡仪馆也以照片展出。

有一个模型展示了一座采用圆形平面的现实城市，街区被划分为向心圆形，街道从中心放射出来，将城市分割成扇区。这可能会解决使所有地区都同样能够朝阳的问题，正如他们所谓的Gesunder Grosstadt（恢复或者康复城市）。

俄国人四处进行现场表演，传播他们的思想，非常激进。在展室里有照片簿和信息簿。整个天棚被覆盖以海报或者宣传资料。

日本人也有一个展区。他们建筑的每一个地方都在模仿着德国人，令你无法区分。

卫生博物馆在建筑及其内容上都很出色。在一层楼的后面有一个带有步廊的小礼拜堂，一尊塑像矗立于当中。塑像拥有赛璐珞的身体和内部器官。每个部位依次被照亮，相应名称显示于桌面的铭牌上。顶层沙龙的配色很棒（蓝色），而且比例很好。

在俄国的卫生展览上，海报上写着"欢迎到俄国来"。签证需要6个星期，而且旅行时不得携带照相机或者图书。俄国人必定很幽默。

7月13日 中午抵达布拉格。参观了坐落于城市西郊的莫扎特故居，它带有一座花园，相当零乱，故居没有什么令人感兴趣的东西，除了在1787—1791年期间，莫扎特作为杜谢克[189]的客人曾经居住在这里。

有一片用于体育馆的场地，但是没有建造。

靠近卡尔大桥[190]（图141）附近有许多有意思的地方，如市政厅和桥头堡，就像维尔茨堡，很入画。

布拉格的色彩相当的灰暗。在一座花园里，红花看上去格外鲜

---

188 约翰诺伊姆（Johanneum）是一座建于1856年的文艺复兴风格建筑，萨克森州（Sachsen）的选帝侯在这里停放马车。自1877年起，该建筑就开始举办展览。
189 杜谢克（Frantiek Xaver Duschek, 1731—1799年），捷克音乐家。 1777年，莫扎特于萨尔斯堡结识杜谢克夫妇，导致1787年莫扎特前往布拉格，出席歌剧《唐·乔凡尼》在布拉格的首演，并住在杜谢克在布拉格郊外的家中。
190 卡尔大桥（Karl's Bridge），也称查理大桥（Charles Bridge），以国王查理四世为名，建于14世纪。

图140 约翰诺伊姆 Johanneum
图142 圣维塔教堂 St. Vitus Cathedral
图141 卡尔大桥 Karl's Bridge
图143 施蒂芬大教堂 Stephan Dom

红，因为背景是如此的晦暗，现代建筑缺乏修饰。基督教青年会旅社相当不错。

波希米亚的生活费用相当便宜，食品似乎比德国的要便宜。

在一座新的德国剧院看了《乞丐歌剧》[191]，音乐带有点爵士味儿，很好的爵士。我怀疑演奏者有些堕落。站票只需4克朗。

7月14日 一整天作画。

在波希米亚，人们想得较少，穿着也不多，但是一些姑娘特别漂亮。

波希米亚的饮食很棒，它有点中国餐饮的风味。汤中的肉圆就像是中国的，还有肉汁。

布拉格老城与任何一座德国漂亮的城市同样风景如画。

（斯宾格勒在慕尼黑的地址是魏登梅尔街2号。）

7月15日 街车和汽车是靠左行驶。步行者也被要求靠左行走。但

---

[191]《乞丐歌剧》（Beggar's Opera）约翰·盖伊（John Gay）创作于1728年，是一出叙事歌剧（ballad opera）。

是有些人似乎不知所措。如果你靠在右侧，有些人仍然坚持靠左。

自然博物馆没有什么东西值得一看，全都是植物和生理学的展品，几乎没有艺术品。

下午偏晚的时候前往城堡，并且参观了圣维塔教堂[192]（图142）。两座钟塔看上去就像科隆大教堂，只是略小一些。室内却十分壮观。中庭的比例非常适宜。唱诗席和圣坛有一些巴洛克雕塑。一些玻璃窗还可以。所有的东西似乎品位还不错。整个室内开敞，没有任何屏封，这也许是在波希米亚最好的哥特建筑。

城堡拥有全城最好的景色。

差一点弄丢雨伞，在画完一张速写后忘拿了。大约35分钟后，想起来并奔回去，伞还在那儿。

晚上去了一家波希米亚餐厅，红酒便宜而且好喝。饭菜虽然便宜却不够好，面点非常差。吃完所有的东西后，侍者拿走红酒瓶并朝我点点头，我也点点头。于是他又拿来一瓶红酒，我没有要，但他说我点了，无论如何我也没要它。

有许多乞丐。女乞丐通常带着婴儿。还需要一天时间去完成速写和参观。2天对于布拉格而言有些太短了。

市政厅有一座如同罗滕堡那样精巧的钟。在窗后有许多人像在转动，可能是由天文仪器来运行的，但是没有看到它们。

波希米亚人起得很早，商店于8点钟开门。

在入口处有附上作品照片的建筑师广告。

7月16日 下午1点钟从布拉格到维也纳。

施蒂芬大教堂[193]（图143）拥有漂亮的哥特风格外观，钟塔与科隆教堂很像。在强烈的阳光下，钟塔的效果很迷人，上半部是一座带有黑点和线条的白色框架，塔身部则是带有淡黄色的深灰色。

参观了靠近城堡和花园的艺术史博物馆[194]（图144）。乘电车前往舒熊布朗宫[195]和王宫公园，它模仿着凡尔赛宫，并且类似于塞

---

192 圣维塔教堂（St. Vitus Cathedral），中欧最早的哥特式教堂，圣约翰的遗体保存于此。
193 施蒂芬大教堂（Stephan Dom），兴建于12世纪，至今已经800多年，是维也纳的宗教中心，历代皇帝的葬礼都在这里举行，也是全世界第二高的哥德式尖塔教堂，仅次于德国的科隆大教堂。
194 艺术史博物馆（Kunsthistorische Museum），坐落在维也纳环城大街旁边，与霍夫堡皇宫相对。19世纪下半叶，维也纳老城墙被拆除之后，博物馆于1871—1891年建造，是世界第四大艺术博物馆。
195 也称美泉宫，坐落于维也纳西南部，巴洛克风格。美泉宫曾是神圣罗马帝国、奥地利帝国、奥匈帝国和哈布斯堡王朝家族的皇宫，是哈布斯堡王朝的夏季行宫，也是维也纳最漂亮的宫殿，茜茜公主曾在此居住。

图144 艺术史博物馆 Kunsthistorische Museum
图145 艾根堡宫殿 Schloss Eggenburg
图146 草地上的圣母 Madonna in the Meadow
图147 美景宫 Belvedere Palaces
图148 卡尔广场 Karlsplatz
图149 海顿博物馆 Haydn Museum

茜琳花园（不完全是），但尺度较小。

维也纳的饮食与波希米亚同样的好，但是十分便宜。除了布拉格之外，维也纳也是一个生活便宜的地方。

前往马克塞小巷，花了很大力气才找到1号，因为它处在桥的另一侧。摁了门铃后一个人出来。他摁了看门人的门铃，出来一位老者。我费劲地让他告诉我恩斯特·皮奇克在哪里，他爬上楼去，我跟着。爬了5~6层后，就在顶层。楼梯没有光线，一系列看似密室的门最终出现在眼前，于是在上面敲了几下。皮奇克走出来，没穿衬衣，赤着脚，有一个脚趾受了伤。因此他在地板上跳着走，他说工作很忙，但没什么前途（或许也没什么回报）。绘图室与任何一家美国的绘图室差不多，脏乱而无序。当然所有的绘图都是现代风格的。他向我展示了他的作品照片，看上去很棒。随后我们讨论了在维也纳的参观。他与我一起下楼，去了大桥。我不知道他感觉怎样，但是我对于曾经听说过的事情感到一丝同情。每当相隔一段时间在他乡遇到故人时，就会有一种奇怪的感觉。

在从布拉格到维也纳的沿途中，风景很漂亮，绵延的群山，黑色的森林（西洋杉与松树），成团流动的浮云。在艾根堡[196]（图145）（奥地利）有一座教堂（色彩宜人，红屋顶和白草墙），非常破败的城堡，看上去非常入画。

7月17日 前往美术史博物馆，一些藏品非常好，但是不能与其他大型欧洲博物馆相比。其中有很多鲁本斯、凡·戴克、伦勃朗和提香的作品。但是我怀疑有一些是

---

[196] 艾根堡宫殿（Schloss Eggenburg），位于格拉兹西部3公里，建造于1635年，由意大利建筑师设计的文艺复兴风格建筑。

复制品。一张拉斐尔的作品也许是复制品,《玛多纳、孩童和圣约翰》[197](图146),这是一幅小画。还有很多艺术品,以及许多盔甲。

现代画廊很棒,里面没有多少作品(绘画与雕塑),但其中的东西还是不错的。有4~5件是古斯塔夫·克里姆特[198]的作品。他的服饰很原创(黑色、银色和金色),构图也很美妙。雕塑总体而言不是太好,但是有一些非常值得称道。(在现代美术馆中,每间展室都有不同的配色,总体布局很有品位。)

现代美术馆坐落于橘园内,在美景宫[199](图147)的另一条轴线上是19世纪的美术馆,该美术馆很贫乏,除了一两件雷诺阿的作品外,没有什么值得一提的东西。萨尔瓦多·洛萨[200]的作品糟透了。

在卡尔广场[201](图148)有一个关于图书建筑和住宅艺术的展览,很值得一看。其中有全套的维也纳手工艺的展览,一部分是关于建筑的。

参观海顿博物馆[202](图149),住宅只有两个房间可供参观,里面的一间充满了肖像和胸像,外面的一间有一架钢琴和家具。老画面显示沿着乡村有稻草屋顶的住宅。现在整条街只是一座贫民窟。

参观施蒂芬大教堂的室内,它有着与巴黎圣母院同样神秘的品质。玻璃窗不是太好,但是它们在一座黑暗教堂中还可以。这座教堂和布拉格的圣维塔教堂在室内的入口处很有效地采用了哥特式低拱券。

步行前往多瑙河,由于天色已黑,看不清它的颜色(也许是绿色的)。

一个维也纳人可以不厌其烦地为你指路,直到你失去耐心。

---

197 也称《草地上的圣母》(Madonna in the Meadow),作于1505年。
198 古斯塔夫·克里姆特(Gustav Klimt, 1862—1918年),奥地利表现主义画家,也是新艺术运动的主要画家,奥地利"分离派"的创始者和主要成员,克里姆特的画面具有强烈的装饰色彩,人体扭曲变形,色彩和谐,达到一种略带颓废和矫揉造作的美感,绘画风格带有浓郁的伤感情调。
199 美景宫(Belvedere Palaces)是尤金王子(1663—1736年)的夏宫,故又名太子宫,建于1714—1725年,为哈布斯王室宫廷之一。
200 萨尔瓦多·洛萨(Salvator Rosa, 1615—1667年),17世纪意大利的著名画家、诗人。
201 卡尔广场(Karlsplatz)是维也纳的重要广场,位于第一区和第四区边界,是该市重要的交通枢纽,广场正中为卡尔教堂。
202 海顿博物馆(Haydn Museum),位于维也纳六区,海顿曾在此居住12年直至去世。

7月18日 早餐后乘轻轨前往海雷根城[203]去参观现代公寓[204](图150),它们很棒。从牛奶站打听到贝多芬故居,到那里看到两个贝多芬曾居住过的,并且彼此相邻的住宅,但它们都是私人的。其中在教区广场上的住宅带有一个漂亮庭院,只有当你站在门槛上的时候,想象力才能释放出来。画了一幅不错的速写,是关于白色粉墙外观的。

回来的路上参观了舒伯特故居。它也有一个不错的庭院,但是大门面对着一条热闹的大街,而不是像贝多芬故居那样相当的封闭。

在舒伯特故居附近吃饭,餐厅由妈妈做饭(她看上去有点可怕),女儿在桌旁端盘子,儿子则负责红酒和啤酒。烹饪手艺很棒,除了一杯啤酒外,我还吃了一份甜点。

下午在一场暴风雨来临之前穿过多瑙河,这就像贝多芬的音乐,狂飙突进[205]。多瑙河的颜色是浅绿色的,目前水面较浅,堤岸与主河床相距甚远。

7月19日 前往参观分离主义美术馆,那里有一些好东西,没有太多激进的内容。

前往三号街区参观现代公寓。在那里,你可以从一个庭院穿行到另一个庭院,一直到达路边。规划得很好,建筑也很棒。

在城市公园里漫步。参观了布格霍夫庭院[206](图151),傍晚时分近距离地参观了市政厅,然后前往沃兹巴赫街去参观现代公寓。在带有顶棚的庭院里有很好的喷泉。

7月20日 中午时分到达萨尔兹堡,前往参观山顶上的莫扎特小屋(它从维也纳搬过来)。这只是一间木头小屋,塞满了多得不可思

---

203 海雷根城(Heiligenstadt),德文翻译过来是"圣城"的意思,以紧邻著名的"维也纳森林"(Wienerwald)闻名,贝多芬在此写下《圣城遗书》(一译海雷根施塔德遗书)(Heiligenstdter Testament)。

204 卡尔·马克思大院(karl-Marx-Hof)。20世纪初,维也纳市政府为了缩小贫富差别,把维也纳建成一个社会福利化的都市,积极推进公共住房建设。从1919年到1934年社会民主党执政期间,为了改善维也纳中下阶层人民的居住条件,在维也纳市建造了6万套住房。其中最为典型的就是卡尔·马克思大院。这座大院长达1公里,共有1400套住房。

205 狂飙突进(Sturm und Drang),是18世纪60年代初至80年代末在德国文学和音乐领域兴起的一场运动,该运动强调个人的主观性,尤其强调对于极端情绪的自由表达,以应对启蒙运动和相应的美学运动的启迪。哲学家哈曼、文学家歌德、席勒,音乐剧贝多芬、莫扎特等都是该运动的代表性人物。

206 布格霍夫庭院(Court of Burghof)即Innerer Burghof(Inner Castle Court),位于维也纳一区的霍夫堡皇宫,为皇室宫殿所包围,左侧为瑞士卫队楼(Schweizertrakt),右侧为约瑟夫广场(Josefsplatz)。

图 150 卡尔·马克思大院 Karl-Marx-Hof　图 151 布格霍夫庭院 Court of Burghof　图 152 巴托洛玛 Bartholomae

议的东西。

画了城堡的速写。城堡看上去很有英国味，它从河边看去形态很美。参观了大多数的景点。

萨尔兹堡真是一座小镇，很容易将它逛遍。

在维也纳和萨尔兹堡之间的风景很美，绵延的山丘和远方的群山（雪峰）带有非常建筑化的树丛，房屋可能是蒂沃利[207]风格的，木板屋顶较难看，屋檐在四边都挑出。

7月21日　参观了科维奇湖[208]，乘摩托艇前往巴托洛玛[209]（图152）和奥伯湖[210]。在奥伯湖没有什么好看的东西，但是巴托洛玛有一幢很好的带有餐厅的小房子，这是最佳的绘画主题。群山很优美，其中有稀薄的水幕和镜面的湖水。某个地方有人在船上吹号，其回声就像原声那样清晰，只有一点点的衰减。在巴托洛玛画了一张速写，在科维奇湖画了一张铅笔画，沿途风光极其美丽，山中的空气也十分新鲜。湖水看上去很冷，于是我将毛衣穿上。

爬上城堡，它所构成的风景绝佳，而且有这么多的入画题材。在造型和风景方面比英国的城堡还要美，但是细部却很糟糕（巴洛克）。总体而言欧洲是最好的。处在一个山顶小镇中真是令人难

207　蒂沃利（Tivoli）是意大利拉齐奥区的一个古镇，离罗马30公里，曾是罗马皇帝和贵族建造别墅园林避暑的首选地。以埃斯特别墅（Villa d'Este）和哈德良别墅（Villa Adriana）闻名。
208　科维奇湖(Königsee)，也称帝王湖或国王湖，位于德奥边界，是德国四大名湖（波登湖、蒂蒂湖、国王湖、基姆湖）之一。
209　巴托洛玛（Bartholomae），指圣巴多罗买礼拜堂（德语：St. Bartholomä），始建于12世纪，国王湖的标志。礼拜堂边的同名狩猎屋是12世纪与礼拜堂一同建造的，后来成为一家小餐厅。
210　国王湖一共由三个湖泊 Königssee，Obersee，Hintersee 组成。

忘。两个很棒的台地被用作餐厅。在那里吃饭的人们欣赏着可以想象到的最佳景色。真是太美了！远山显露出美丽的轮廓，奇异的云彩、田野、房舍，有谁会不喜欢呢？

没有时间去参观莫扎特故居，也没能去参观节日大厅[211]（图153）。但是今晚去了木偶剧院[212]。这是我第一次看木偶剧，而且是最好的。第一场是《牧羊人与牧羊女》[213]，这只是一出喜剧，但第二场则是《沃尔夫岗与如此教师》，内容讲述的是孩童时期的莫扎特如何戏弄新来的音乐教师，他从不知道时间是什么，因此离开了。莫扎特欢快地演奏着，其他人也十分聪明地跟从着。这确实比一些舞台剧要好。

斯宾格勒，魏登梅尔大街26号，慕尼黑。

7月22日 一大早起床（5:30）去赶前往慕尼黑的火车，8点钟到达，在车站附近住下来，并在城市中逛了一圈。参观了王子皇家剧院，那儿正在上演瓦格纳的歌剧。最低票价15马克。当时在皇家剧院正在上演莫扎特歌剧。在一张海报照片上，我看到一个名叫"李太白"的系列演出，而我认为它在两年前就已经演出。头一次喝慕尼黑啤酒，罗瓦啤酒，非常温和而醇厚，并不使你感到口渴。参观了在顶楼的斯宾格勒故居。

2点钟乘火车前往奥伯阿玛高[214]（图154），6点钟到达。住在豪普特街119号的一家民居，房东名叫玛利亚·克拉梅，她是

图153 节日大厅 Festival Hall
图154 奥伯阿玛高 Oberammergau

---

211 节日屋（Festival House），指节日大厅（Festival Hall），沃尔夫·迪特里希（Wolf Dietrich）设计，建于1607年，这里现在是萨尔兹堡主要的音乐中心。
212 萨尔兹堡木偶剧院（Salzburg Marionette Theatre），成立于1913年，是世界上历史最为悠久的木偶剧院之一，起初的木偶剧是由现场的演出和音乐所构成，萨尔兹堡木偶剧院曾经为儿童上演了大量的歌剧、芭蕾、音乐剧。
213《牧羊人与牧羊女》是莫扎特12岁时写的第一部歌剧。
214 奥伯阿玛高（Oberammergau），即上阿默高，是位于德国南部黑森林地区阿尔卑斯山脚下的小城镇，以耶稣受难剧和房屋外墙的壁画闻名，壁画多以格林童话和宗教故事为题。

一名好厨师。房间有8英尺的顶棚和4扇窗户,装修得很漂亮。它有一道狭窄弯曲的楼梯通往一楼,你需要穿过房屋到达门廊。这是一座带有蓝色遮阳布的白色泥灰建筑。餐厅采用平板作为天花。很可能就是楼上地板的底部。

除我之外还有一大群美国人。一名妇女来自华盛顿特区,她与德国的主妇高谈阔论,我想她也是德国人,因此我称她为"该死的家伙"。她转过身来看我,我想她听得懂,因此决定装得很生气,并且不再与任何人说话。两名来自美国的年轻女孩坐在桌子的端头,从她们的谈话可以看出父母可能很有钱。两个白痴,R.S.试图取悦她们。

晚餐很好,但似乎放错了地方,在这样一座小山村里,很有餐桌氛围和礼节,但是毫无乐趣。这些女人让人感到不自在。在美国,女人从未让我感到紧张,但是她们在这里令我不安。因为她们毫无品位,并且肆无忌惮。

一走出车站,立即引起注意的就是马车以及留着胡须和长发的男人。儿童和男孩也留着长发。人们告诉我他们在受难剧[215]活动三年之前就这样去做了。但是他们确实使得村庄看上去非常漂亮。马匹是地道的阿尔卑斯品种,两侧总是带有装饰,通常是灰白色的,或者是棕色的。

这个地方到处都是美国人,除了一些装聋作哑的英国人。他们当然不是本地人。即使德国人自己,如果他们不住在奥伯阿玛高,在这方面看上去也不是本地人。

这也许是我与美国游客唯一的一次直接接触。他们如此傲慢,与他们交谈就意味着浪费口舌。睡在这样一座安宁的小村庄真是一种幸福。希望这只是一次难得一遇的不快事件。

7月23日 今天的天气在早晨非常温暖而多云,到下午则阳光普照,夜晚的雨由于姗姗来迟而没影响到什么。

吃了一顿非常满意的早餐,有很多肉卷和新鲜黄油、果酱,还有山区蜂蜜。咖啡也很好喝。

受难剧于早晨8点钟开始。在一座带有隐蔽乐池和开敞舞台的剧院里举行。我坐在前排,但是太矮了,我相信坐在后排高起的观众可以看见远处的群山。

---

215 耶稣苦难剧(Passion Play)是一种宗教剧,以德国南部巴伐利亚地区(Bavaria)奥伯阿玛高村(Oberammergau)所演出的最著名。

所有现场舞台造型生动而且漂亮，音乐、服饰、表演，可以说好得不能再好了。只有在序幕时才有音乐响起。音乐简洁而纯粹，堪比于任何大剧院中的音乐。

犹大表演得尤其好。尽管有一些过头，但是总体而言他知道该做什么。基督则有点笨拙，像个农民，而且一点也不优雅。他的表情从来没有轻松过，显得非常僵硬，声音也太重了，动作和姿态不够标准。

玛丽演得很好，她的表演一直不是很多。她是一位漂亮的女人。

剧情从基督进入耶路撒冷升天或者变身开始，按计划它将演出8个小时，实际上它从早晨8点开始，下午5:45结束，中午时分在11:30至2:00之间，有一次幕间休息。

吃了一顿丰盛的午餐，鸡肉与很棒的餐后甜点，好像用鸡蛋和香蕉调成的奶昔，确实不错。

下午阳光普照，它被用作舞台的照明，效果非常的好。一些演员站在阴影之中，一些站在阳光之下。这的确是最好的舞台灯光。

整个演出演活了《圣经》，这让我留连了很长时间，后来每当看到十字架以及其他涉及基督教的事情，我就会想到受难剧。这确实使你生活得年轻，而且我认为这对于村民犹其如此。

德国人热衷于采用一长串花束来装饰他们的院子。

7月24日 一大清早回到慕尼黑。慕尼黑下了一整天的雨。参观巴伐利亚博物馆，里面堆满了垃圾。然后去参观老美术馆[216]（图155），那里有许多鲁本斯、凡·戴克、伦勃朗的作品，2张拉斐尔的玛多纳，还有一些很棒的提香的作品。我从来没见过这么多牟利罗[217]的作品，还有一些戈雅的，丢勒的四教徒[218]（图156）也在那儿，还有其他一些丢勒的优秀作品。他自己的肖像我已经几乎在每个美术馆都看到过，不知道哪一张是复制的，哪一张是真实的。

---

216 老美术馆（Old Pinakothek），慕尼黑老美术馆位于慕尼黑市中心偏北的一处绿地，是世界上最古老的艺术博物馆之一，拥有大量文艺复兴时期至18世纪的欧洲古典绘画。它不仅拥有以丢勒为代表的德国文艺复兴时期的众多大师之作，而且收藏了意大利文艺复兴、17世纪荷兰、佛兰德斯绘画的大量精品。

217 牟利罗（Bartolome Esteban Murillo，1617—1682年），17世纪西班牙最受欢迎的巴洛克宗教画家，以其理想化的有时是过分讲究的风格而驰名。

218 四教徒（Four Apostles），阿尔布莱希特·丢勒（Albrecht Dürer）作品，1526年。左面一块画的是约翰和彼得，右面一块画的是保罗与马可。

晚上前往王子皇家剧院（图157）去听瓦格纳的《漂泊的荷兰人》[219]（最便宜的座位是15马克），7点钟开始，10点钟结束。舞台布景很漂亮，音乐较简洁，而且演唱比我在大都会听过的所有曲目都要好。这是我所听过的除了《罗恩格林》[220]之外最好的瓦格纳作品。

7月25日 前往参观宁芬堡宫[221]（图158），这是一群带有公园的巴洛克建筑，完全不值得一访。它距慕尼黑不算太远，从火车站坐电车需要15分钟。

王宫附近的医院是现代风格的，相当不错。

下午在玻璃宫参观展览，展品在数量和质量上都不错，在我看来甚至比巴黎大皇宫里面的沙龙还要好。一些水彩画也令人称绝。这是一个绘画与雕塑的展览，还有版画以及印刷品，还有蚀刻画。很值得一看。

参观新王宫。真是难以置信，不仅质量较差，一些绘画还存有严重的缺陷。

参观国家美术馆，其中的法国藏品很棒。其他一些展室还可以，但是法国展室有凡·高的自画像、塞尚的自画像、凡·高的静物（一些花卉和风景）、塞尚的风景。同时还有1张皮萨罗的，1张马蒂斯的，2张高更的，以及2张雷诺阿的，1张马奈的。在这

图155 老美术馆 Old Pinakothek
图156 四教徒 Four Apostles
图157 王子皇家剧院 Prince Regent Theatre
图158 宁芬堡宫 Nymphenburg Palace

---

219 漂泊的荷兰人（Fliegender Holländer），英文为"The Flying Dutchman"，也译作"彷徨的荷兰人"、"飞行的荷兰人"、"环球航行的荷兰人"，这是流传在欧洲民间的一则古老传说，述说一群触怒了神而被诅咒的水手，必须永远在海上漂泊，七年才可以靠岸一次，这也是幽灵船故事最原始的版本。1839年德国的作曲家瓦格纳在前往巴黎发展的海上航行途中曾遇到暴风雨，这段意外的经历，成为日后写作歌剧《漂泊的荷兰人》的灵感来源。1843年，《漂泊的荷兰人》举行了首次公演，其音乐曲风相当前卫。
220 《罗恩格林》（Lohengrin）是德国作曲家瓦格纳创作的一部三幕浪漫歌剧，1850年由李斯特指挥在魏玛首演，该剧代表着浪漫主义歌剧的最高峰，并且也是瓦格纳本人创作中最重要的转折点。
221 宁芬堡宫（Nymphenburg Palace），位于慕尼黑西郊，是一座巴洛克式宫殿，建于1675年。

方面，该美术馆值得一去。

前往剧院博物馆，里面没有很多展品，但是有一件奇特的东西，照片模型以及舞蹈和剧情的印刷品，还有面具和服装。

参观在岛上的德意志博物馆，纯粹是科学性的。我只是步行穿过所有开放的区域，随后出来。

参观奥斯特隆公园（图159）的建筑，是现代风格的，带有排成一列的赤陶塑像。

7月26日 今天没有参观任何博物馆，但是画了5张速写，包括新老市政厅，奥斯特隆建筑的塔楼，以及其中的陶土塑像。还画了一幅街景。

今晚在王宫庭院聆听了贝多芬的月亮奏鸣曲和小夜曲。演奏得很棒。在两场演出之间，有人在塔楼上演奏了一些风琴乐器，月亮洒满在尖顶上，而音乐家们则依稀可辨，其效果是非常剧场化的。大多数灯具都采用蜡烛。有的在窗台上，有的在入口庭院中，看上去就像回到了中世纪。

奥斯瓦尔德·斯宾格勒必定很容易拜见的，因为R.S.递上一封自荐信就与之见了一面。他将斯宾格勒描述为一位50多岁的人，秃顶，但是有一张英俊而棱角分明的面孔。他穿着一件烟灰色的夹克，以及一双软拖鞋。他的房间非常舒适地饰以长排的书籍和老照片。斯宾格勒一定会在他的钢琴上演奏曲目。他的《西方世界的衰落》显示了他在音乐方面的知识。他居住在主要楼层中，显然有一名女佣和一名清洁工。

斯宾格勒并不喜欢理查德·斯特劳斯或者现代爵士乐。他认为李斯特，尤其是瓦格纳是最后一位大音乐家。现代建筑于他而言尚不能接受。在芝加哥论坛报塔楼[222]（图160）的方案竞赛中，他喜欢最终建成的建筑，以及二等奖方案（萨里宁的）。而德国的竞赛图纸他看都不看一眼。

我宁愿不去见他。这种会面又能怎样？如果他太伟大，我们将不能理解他。如果他一点也不伟大，最好等他来见我们。一个人没

---

[222] 芝加哥论坛报塔楼（Tribune），位于芝加哥密西根路北部的一座哥特式36层建筑，是美国三大报社之一芝加哥论坛公司总部大楼。1922年，为了纪念《芝加哥论坛报》成立75周年，全世界各国264个创作团体来竞争"世界上最完美的建筑设计"，最后由纽约的建筑师约翰·米德·豪威尔（John Mead Howell）和雷蒙德·胡德（Raymond M. Hood)的联合作品获胜，其他许多著名现代建筑师，如阿道夫·路斯、沃尔特·格罗皮乌斯等也参加了此次设计竞赛，使之成为现代建筑史中一件著名的事件。

有必要仅仅因为好奇而去打扰另外一个人。

7月27日　早晨8:30分从慕尼黑到达奥格斯堡，立即前往大教堂。教堂在开放时会有管乐器和唱诗表演，非常美妙。贝德克旅行指南提到了"一个"中世纪的蜡烛支架[223]。但是那里有4~5个，没有人知道哪一个是的。室内相当漂亮，巴洛克风格并不过分，南侧的大门也很漂亮。

在教堂南侧有一片场地，其中有挖掘现场（罗马？），贝德克没有提及，很可能是最近发掘的，在我看来就像一个罗马浴室。

市政厅很破，佩拉赫塔[224]（图161）同样如此。前往雅各布街去寻找霍尔拜因故居。但是看到一处老房子和鸟塔，画了两者的速写。有一个正在举办的展览会，还有孩子们的马戏团。几个孩子领我穿过富格区[225]，但是没有人知道霍尔拜因的故居在哪里，另一名男孩则叫了一声"中国人"。

那个男孩一定认为我是在寻找一名乡下人。那里有4~5个中国商人（游荡的），他们大声说话，并在啤酒桌上玩麻将。幸运的是那个地方到处都是人。他们用刀吃饭（甚至一名妇女也是如此），无论如何他们是一群令人厌恶的人，因此我再也没能看到霍尔拜因故居。

2:30到达乌尔姆，乌尔姆是一个坐落在多瑙河上的老镇。参观了大教堂[226]（图162），它在轮廓上看上去就像美国的摩天楼，室内非常简洁而且不错，在两侧有

图159 奥斯特隆公园　Ausstellung Park
图160 芝加哥论坛报塔楼　Tribune
图161 佩拉赫塔　Perlachturm
图162 乌尔姆大教堂　Ulm Minster

---

223 一种枝状大烛台。
224 佩拉赫塔高78米，宏伟壮观，建于12世纪，再于1618年改建为今日模样。
225 富格区（Fuggerei）是富格尔家族于1521年捐赠给奥格斯堡（Augsburg）市贫困市民的居住区。
226 乌尔姆大教堂（Ulm Minster），整个乌尔姆城市布局的中心，始建于1377年，哥特式建筑，砖石结构，主塔高161.6米。

图 163.1 天主教城市教堂
　　　　Kath Stadtpfarrkirche
图 163.2 天主教城市教堂
　　　　Kath Stadtpfarrkirche
图 164　肖肯百货商店
　　　　Schocken Department Store

双重走道。乘电车穿过多瑙河去看一座现代教堂（天主教城市教堂）[227]。其外观是罗马风的一个现代版本（图163.1）。室内则非常漂亮（几乎是立体主义的）（图163.2），由多米尼库斯·波姆教授[228]设计。没有太多的颜色，但是投射在整个墙面上的光线和阴影很有效果。有几个小礼拜堂，每一个都有所不同，唯一的缺陷也许就是低矮的天花。

在多瑙河畔画了水塔，多瑙河带有一种红绿色的色彩。

我想象着火车穿过黑森林地区，但是森林与其他德国南方地区的森林没有什么区别。

7:15抵达斯图加特。新火车站很漂亮。我从未看到过这么一件好东西，也许是已建成的最好的车站。

晚上参观了王宫以及一些现代建筑，老市场有许多老房子，市政厅由于太新而不是太好。

7月28日　早晨下雨。参观了肖肯百货商店[229]（图164）。这是我所见过最好的百货商店（当然指建筑学方面）。其墙面由水平线

---

227 天主教城市教堂（Kath Stadtpfarrkirche），应当指圣约安·巴普蒂斯教堂（Kirche St. Johann Baptist），位于乌尔姆新城。1922—1926年建造。
228 多米尼库斯·波姆（Dominikus Böhm, 1880—1955年）德国著名教堂建筑师，他在20世纪20年代对教堂建筑进行的空间改革，影响了此后德国与美国教堂建筑的风格。
229 肖肯百货公司由西蒙与塞尔曼·肖肯建立，坐落于斯图加特的肖肯百货公司大楼建于1926年，由最著名表现主义建筑师埃里克·门德尔松（Erich Mendelsohn, 1887—1953年）设计。

条的砖砌与泥灰组合而成，采用大型灯箱来显示商店名称，效果非常好。

肖肯的对面是一座高层建筑（大约15层）（报社），这在德国，也许在欧洲是最高的。画了两者的速写。

中午时分离开斯图加特，前往弗雷德里希港，这是在康斯坦斯湖畔的一座城市，乘船（圣加仑）跨湖前往罗曼肖恩。

康斯坦斯有着绿色镜面的湖水，头一次看到远方的阿尔卑斯山，有点激动。天气有些多云，但是可以看到在阳光下的远方群山。一些山体被云层遮掩住，其他一些只有山峰显露出来。这幅场景非常像中国画，它总是用简单的寥寥数笔，产生出最大的效果。

不得不在罗曼肖恩等火车前往苏黎世。因此前往一座老教堂（我从湖边看到了它），在它前面画了一张速写。罗曼肖恩是一座小镇，弗雷德里希港也是一座小镇。从湖畔可以看到依稀可辨的飞船吊架。

6:24乘火车离开罗曼肖恩，8:05到达苏黎世。

今晚误入了一个同性恋地区，这是一个有"演出"的餐厅。女人穿着艳丽，戴着花边帽在舞台上演奏乐曲。男人穿着黑色紧身外衣和肥宽裤，脖子和胸前挂着五颜六色的饰带，人们只需付30分就能听音乐会。

由于我在利曼霍夫饭店订不到房间，于是将行李留在那里，前往别的地方。当我有了房间之后，就说我要取行李。很快就拿到了行李，旅店保管员有点怀疑并要求付费，他问我是否从另外一家旅店而来。

今天遇上了各种各样的天气，多云天气中的瑞士风景就像中国画。

7月29日 一大早起床，出去看苏黎世湖，所有瑞士的湖泊看上去都差不多。

参观林登霍夫山丘[230]，这是罗马旧王宫的遗址，现在是一个布满树木和坐凳的高地，没有任何古迹。

参观佩斯特拉齐[231]的雕像。画了一幅有顶的木桥和老博物馆。

苏黎世的车站大街是主要街道，而且清晨在其两旁排列着水果

---

230 林登霍夫山丘（Lindenhof），罗马帝国时期重要的关卡，有城墙遗址，是欣赏老城区最佳的位置。
231 佩斯特拉齐（Pestalozzi，1746—1827年），提倡实物教学法的瑞士教育学家。

图165 圣安东教堂 Antonius Kirche
图166 巴塞尔市政厅 Rathaus Basel
图167 圣马丁教堂 St. Martins Church
图168 西庸城堡 Chillon

摊。这是一条市场街。

卢瑟恩处在琉森湖畔[232],它比苏黎世湖还要漂亮。画了一张卢兹河廊桥的速写。然后前往参观著名的卢瑟恩狮子。还参观了冰河公园,这是世界上唯一的此类博物馆,里面棒极了的东西,很值得一看,尤其是印在石头上的掌印。冰川壶穴和圆石,其中一个由流水推动运转。

爬上葛特西塔[233],但是景色却很普通。

下午5:30抵达巴塞尔。在火车站外面就有市场大厅,虽属现代风格但不是很好。误打误撞走到了斯帕棱城门[234],但是在一家商店(明信片上的地方)的附近找到了现代的圣安东教堂[235](图165),立即步行前往那里。钟塔(混凝土的)是我所见过最好的。室内也非常肃穆,富有戏剧性效果。但是比例看上去不够协调。它的剖面是中庭上的尖券和走廊上的平顶。所有的天棚都处理成嵌入混凝土的方格。锈蚀玻璃窗是现代风格的,除了立体主义的设计外,还有人像在上面。唱诗席在面向圣坛的包厢上。讲坛用黄铜制成,有一块平板覆于其中。这座教堂非常值得一访,我相信目前正在建造的新建筑就是周日学堂。

参观市政厅[236](图166),它带有鲜艳的粉红色,而且由于装饰屋顶而显得丰富。圣马丁教堂[237](图167)靠得很近,从某个

---

232 也可称四森林州湖。
233 葛特西塔(Gutsch Tower)。葛特西为卢瑟恩的一处山地城堡,可以俯瞰全城。
234 斯帕棱城门(Spalen Tor)是1400年防御工事中现存的三座城门之一,气势恢宏。
235 圣安东教堂(Antonius Kirche),现代教堂,混凝土建筑,建于1925—1927年,由卡尔·莫塞尔教授设计(Prof. Karl Moser)。
236 巴塞尔市政厅(Rathaus Basel),位于中莱茵桥头,面对市集广场,是1504年所建的晚期哥德式建筑。
237 圣马丁教堂(St. Martins Church),11—14世纪建筑,是巴塞尔最老的教堂。

角度来看，它的钟塔非常漂亮。大教堂采用红石建成，看上去相当漂亮。

在巴塞尔只停留2个小时，尽管没有画任何东西，但是已经参观了很多地方。

乘火车前往伯尔尼，这是有着一轮弯月的美好夜晚。

今晚由于太黑而不能参观伯尔尼。靠近蒙特卢时，在火车上看到了西庸城堡[238]（图168）的照片。它就处在从洛桑到米兰的途中，因此决定在蒙特卢停一下。

没有时间吃晚饭，因此买了2只香蕉和3块饼在火车上吃。

7月30日 起床前往参观监狱塔[239]，行政院，它看上去很新（哥特风格），还有市政厅，它没有钟塔，但是设在户外的、带顶棚的石阶梯显得很特别。

伯尔尼因其无数的喷泉而闻名。但是在苏黎世也有很多。伯尔尼一个好的方面就是它在所有主要大街上都有带顶的人行道和拱廊，这是一项传统事物，但是现代建筑师所梦想的未来大都市都会拥有它。

由于云雾，从平台上看不太清楚伯尔尼的阿尔卑斯山，因此也看不到"阿尔卑斯神光"[240]，它必须在晴朗的夜晚才能看到。

看到一场车祸，一辆卡车正在街角转弯，撞上了一辆摩托车。我不知道是什么原因，但是受伤者似乎还可以，是一位老人。

莱茵河带有明快的黄绿色，奔流向前。

下午2:00到达洛桑。

图 169 伯尔尼大教堂
　　　Bernese Cathedral
图 170 夏特尔大教堂圣礼拜堂
　　　Chartres Cathedral

---

238 西庸城堡（Chillon）位于蒙特卢莱茵河畔，始建于11世纪，因拜伦的诗《西庸的囚徒》而闻名。
239 监狱塔（Käfigturm）是伯尔尼的第二座塔，也是西部的第二个城门。该塔建于1256年到1344年，1641年到1643年期间成为监狱，此后直到1897年，该塔一直被用作监狱。
240 阿尔卑斯神光（Alpine Glow），日落时的一种景象，淡红色的光投射在雪山上，也称为高山辉现象。

一直到伯尔尼前，人们都在讲德语。然而一到伯尔尼，他们开始讲法语，火车上的语言也随之改变。

参观市政厅，由于彩绘过的飞檐而特别显眼。

由维勒奥·勒·迪克[241]所整修的大教堂[242]（图169）在瑞士是最好的哥特建筑，并且比在德国的任何一座教堂都要好，钟塔较为低矮，并且有一道脊。但是主要的门廊却很棒。

室内由于简洁而显得壮丽，玫瑰窗使人想起夏特尔大教堂的圣礼拜堂[243]（图170）。玻璃很少，但是它们都很灿烂。细部和比例都很棒，由于它有一点儿粗短，它比任何气势逼人的高拔的设计都要好（由于它通过紧缩宽度以体现高度来进行误导，因而是虚假的），它是宽敞的，使人感受到空间。

参观城堡。棒极了，因为它将砖块与石头很好地组合到一起。精细柔和的红砖。

它低矮而且庞大。

登上信号台去观景，但是景色不如在火车上看到的好。另一种景色来自于蒙布浓公园（图171）。参观了威廉·泰尔的雕像[244]。

下山去看莱茵湖，比所有其他的瑞士湖泊要好，帆船、天鹅还有阳光点缀着湖面。画了一张帆船的速写。

乘火车前往蒙特卢。我一到那儿，就乘着夜色前往参观西庸城堡，它看上去很壮丽，当你接近它时，就变得越来越大。明天早晨一定要去那儿。画了一些速写并拍了一些照片。它在今晚必定就像"死亡之岛"，很令人浮想联翩。空气很清新，天鹅在水中游泳，时常会潜下湖面。

我喜欢听法语。在伯尔尼，人们既说德语也说法语。但是在洛

---

241 尤根尼·维奥列·勒·迪克（Eugène Emmanuel Viollet-le-Duc，1814—1879 年），法国建筑师与理论家，主张恢复中世纪建筑，强调建筑中的一致性，昭示了即将出现的现代建筑精神。
242 伯尔尼大教堂（Bernese Cathedral），始建于 1421 年，历时 4 个世纪完成，以浮雕和彩画玻璃著名。
243 夏特尔大教堂圣礼拜堂（Chartres Cathedral）位于法国巴黎西南约 70 公里处的夏特尔市，最大玫瑰窗直径 13.4 米。
244 威廉·泰尔（William Tell），瑞士建国传说中的英雄，原为乌里州的农民。14 世纪时，哈布斯堡王朝在当地实行暴政，新任总督葛斯勒在中央广场竖立柱子，在柱顶挂着奥地利皇家帽子，并规定居民经过时必须向帽子敬礼。泰尔因没有向帽子敬礼而被捕，葛斯勒要泰尔射中放在泰尔儿子头上的苹果才释放他们，否则两人都会被罚，结果泰尔成功射中苹果。第二箭瞄准葛斯勒总督，泰尔射偏了。当时泰尔回答："如果我射中儿子，那么第二箭会射中总督心脏。"总督大怒，将泰尔父子囚禁起来。后来在人民起义中，泰尔于混乱中逃出来，并在一次行动中用十字弓杀死葛斯勒。

桑和蒙特卢,他们只讲法语,这使我的耳朵感到很舒服。也可以看到更多的漂亮女人。饭食在某种程度上也更加法国化了。

7月31日 参观西庸城堡的内部,即使在监狱的狱室里,从窗户看到的景色都是棒极了。监狱带有行刑室、审判厅、食堂、骑士厅等等。有关的中世纪故事非常奇特。在伯尼瓦德[245]室,我寻找拜伦[246]的名字(图172),在柱子上没有能够找到。但是在墙上有一个现代的碑刻(1924年),正对着那根柱子。

密迪齿峰[247]整个上午都躲在云层里,晚上它的顶部开始明朗,但是主体仍然笼罩于云雾之中。同时也看到了后面闪光的雪峰。

8月1日 早晨乘火车前往马蒂尼[248],在那里乘汽车前往大圣伯纳德[249]。

火车在到达马蒂尼之前路过圣莫里斯修道院[250](图173)。教堂看上去大概还可以。汽车配了一位好司机。我们于12:30到达大圣伯纳德,路过许多村庄。村舍完全带有山区的崎岖特征。居民的面孔也显得僵硬而憔悴(干枯的表情)。在圣皮埃尔堡[251]有一家旅馆,拿破仑曾在楼上吃过早餐,它有

图171 蒙布浓公园
　　　Promenade de Montbenon
图172 拜伦刻名 Byron Engnaving
图173 圣莫里斯修道院
　　　St. Maurice's Abbey

---

245 弗朗索瓦·伯尼瓦德(François Bonivard)日内瓦的独立主义者,1530年至1536年间曾被囚禁在此。
246 1816年英国诗人拜伦(Byron)参观此座城堡地牢后,于石柱上签了大名,并由感而发地写下《西庸的囚徒》。
247 "密迪齿峰",意思为最高峰上的齿形山,海拔3757米。
248 马蒂尼(Martigny)是该地区的法语区首府,隶属瑞士的瓦莱州(Valais)。马蒂尼位于由瑞士通往意大利和法国的交叉口处。有一条道路途经大圣伯纳德山口(Great St. Bernard Pass)连接了该城镇与意大利的奥斯塔城(Aosta);另外还有一条道路途经Forclaz山口可以到达法国的夏木尼镇(Chamonix)。
249 大圣伯纳德为阿尔卑斯山区一地名,11世纪奥斯塔的副主教为了营救游客,在此处建造了救济院(Hospice),当时的救助犬的名字就取自山谷的英文名圣伯纳德(St. Bernard)。
250 圣莫里斯修道院(St. Maurice's Abbey)位于圣莫里斯(St. Maurice),是辛普伦山口(Simplon Pass)一处风景如画的地方。该修道院的建造历经了15个世纪。
251 圣皮埃尔堡(Bourg St. Pierre),是往意大利边境的瑞士终点站,距离山隘20公里。是一个海拔1632米的静谧小镇。

一个非常精美雕饰的木吊顶,教堂看上去历史感很强,钟塔带有石脊,气质很好。在教堂庭院的墙壁上矗立着一块罗马磨石。在过了圣皮埃尔堡之后,我们看到了我所以为的勃朗峰[252]。它看上去特别巨大,是一座带有瀑布与雪峰的山脉。道路蜿蜒向上,直到顶峰,当你回头看时,它就像一条蛇。

汽车差一点出事故。另一辆卡车开过来,两辆车及时刹车避免了相撞。外面就是深渊。

天空格外晴朗,空气也很凉爽。但是当汽车停在村中时,阳光就变得毒辣了。

旅客中包括3名美国人(夫妇及其女儿),2名法国或瑞士人(丈夫和妻子),还有我自己。美国人只会去算计群山的高度。

当你到达圣伯纳德时会失望的。旅行中最好的一段就是在你到达之前,山峰一座接着一座地冒出来。

圣伯纳德救济院[253](图174)看上去平庸而且寻常(也是商业性的外观),它带有一个很差的小礼拜堂,所有的房间像旅馆那样都有编号。餐厅在一楼,牧师与客人在一起吃饭。圣伯纳德旅馆就在对面,并且与一座桥梁相连接。饭菜不错,酒也很好,我喝了一些。饭菜看上去都不错,除了牛排,毫无疑问,他们称之为英式的。白酒是埃托勒[254],除了一些酒劲,它是如此醇厚而芳香。

我只看到三只著名的圣伯纳德狗(在救济院后面),它们看上去就像是牛头犬与狼之间的杂交。

跨过意大利边境,不能拍照。

那里较为温暖,湖面没有结冰,尽管一些积雪从不融化。

必须使用很多想象力才能透过夏天的圣伯纳德看到冬天的雪景,这里没有任何危险,狗也休息了很长时间。

在回来的路上,我感到疲倦,并打了几个盹。

开往米兰的火车晚点1个半小时,8点钟才过辛普朗山口[255]。花了2分钟过了3个主要隧道,而另一个短隧道加上辛普勒花了将近1

---

[252] 勃朗峰(Mont Blanc(法),Monte Bianco(意),意为白色之山),是阿尔卑斯山的最高峰,位于法国的上萨瓦省和意大利的瓦莱达奥斯塔的交界处。
[253] 圣伯纳德救济院(St.Bernard Hospice)是一处为在瑞士的旅行者提供住宿的招待所,位于海拔2469米的大圣伯纳德之路途中。其南边数百米处就是意大利边境。
[254] 埃托勒(L'Etoile)是法国朱罗区(Jura)的法定葡萄酒产地(AOC)之一,主要生产白葡萄酒。
[255] 辛普朗山口(Simplon Pass),亦译辛普伦山口。瑞士南部本宁阿尔卑斯山脉(Pennine Alps)与勒蓬廷阿尔卑斯山脉(Lepontine Alps)之间的山口。

个小时。

在阿尔卑斯山北侧,天空是蓝色的,而在意大利一侧,天空多云,尽管一轮弯月不时地透出云层。

第一次看到意大利村庄时,一阵激动,它们都是迷人的东西。

在斯特雷萨[256],一位中年法国妇女在火车站迎接一对年轻人,不仅他们的法语让我听得很舒服,而且他们优雅的礼仪和美丽也很打动我。

8月2日 在户外参观的第一项内容就是圣费德勒教堂[257](图175),非常迷人。砖作让人想起某个现代的德国砖作,带有水平延伸的、凹进或凸出的条带,立面的比例十分漂亮(文艺复兴式样)。

参观斯卡拉歌剧院[258](图176),还有剧院的室内(看上去如此之小)以及舞台。天棚如此之高使之有别于在费城、纽约、莱比锡和布拉格的中世纪剧院。总体色调采用暗红色,正立面很漂亮。莱昂纳多的雕像矗立在广场上,米兰大教堂[259](图177)看上去不如照片上的好看,但是室内却出奇的好,就像巴黎圣母院,而且更大。

窗户也不错,选位也很好,考虑了教堂幽暗的室内。高耸的中庭以及双侧走廊,整体看上去很简洁。

从钟塔和屋顶上俯瞰城市。空气不是很清澈,阿尔卑斯山也不是很明朗。

图174 圣伯纳德救济院
    Great St. Bernard Hospice
图175 圣费德勒教堂 St. Fedele
图176 斯卡拉歌剧院
    La Scala Opera House
图177 米兰大教堂 Milan Cathedral
图178 圣查理灵柩
    St. Charles Borromeo

---

256 斯特雷萨(Stresa)是位于意大利米兰西北约80公里的小镇。
257 圣费德勒教堂(St. Fedele),耶稣教堂,建于1559年,位于米兰市中心,靠近玛利诺广场,与斯卡拉歌剧院相邻。
258 斯卡拉歌剧院(La Scala Opera House)是世界上最著名的歌剧院之一,是世界名演员心驰神往之地,有"歌剧的麦加"之称。
259 米兰大教堂(Milan Cathedral)历经5个世纪完工。它的正殿穹窿高达45米,是已经完工的哥特式教堂中最高的。

参观了圣查理[260]的灵柩（图178），它由纯银制成。整个礼拜堂的吊顶是银色装饰的。灵柩带有水晶窗户，因此你可以看到内部，见到原封不动穿着衣服的遗骸。灵柩的装饰是由切利尼[261]制作的，遗骸呈深褐色，手上戴着白色手套和戒指。

安布罗夏纳府邸[262]有文艺复兴绘画的藏品，例如莱昂纳多的制图以及一些绘画、拉斐尔的雅典学院的草图。

在莫坎提广场[263]（图179）有拉吉尼宫[264]（图180），它的一部分是罗马遗迹，这是老米兰的市中心。

安布罗夏纳图书馆[265]（图181.1，图181.2）有一个画廊，最重要的内容就是拉斐尔的"雅典学院"的草图。莱昂纳多也有一间密室，里面有各种线描的画册，同时还有一些莱昂纳多的小绘画。

圣萨蒂罗教堂[266]（图182.1，图182.2）有一个带透视的唱诗席（通过雕塑制作

图 179 莫坎提广场 Piazza Mercanti
图 180 拉吉尼宫 Palazzo della Ragione
图 181.1 安布罗夏纳图书馆 Biblioteca Ambrosiana
图 181.2 安布罗夏纳图书馆 Biblioteca Ambrosiana
图 182.1 圣萨蒂罗教堂内景 San Satiro

260 圣查理（St. Charles Borromeo, 1538—1584 年）是意大利圣贤，同时也是罗马天主教教廷的一位红衣主教。他的主要工作时间经历了反宗教改革时期，他对天主教教会改革产生了重要的影响，其中包括为牧师提供教育的神学院的建立。
261 切利尼（Benvenuto Cellini, 1500—1571 年），意大利文艺复兴时期的雕塑家、金银工艺师、作家。
262 安布罗夏纳府邸（Palazzo Ambrosiana），即安布罗夏纳图书馆（Biblioteca Ambrosiana）。由米兰大主教费代里科·博罗梅利奥红衣主教（1564—1631 年）创建，始建于 1603 年，1609 年对公众开放，是欧洲第二座公共图书馆。
263 距离米兰大教堂广场不远的莫坎提广场（Piazza Mercanti），原意为商人广场，仍然维持着中世纪米兰的风格。该广场原本为正方形，共有六扇大门，分别通往不同的 13 世纪时期的城市。
264 拉吉尼宫（Palazzo della Ragione），始建于 1228 年，在数百年期间曾作为市政府和商业中心。
265 安布罗夏纳图书馆（Biblioteca Ambrosiana）是米兰的一所具有悠久历史的图书馆，它包含了安布罗夏纳画廊（Pinacoteca Ambrosiana）。
266 圣萨蒂罗教堂（San Satiro）据说是由布拉孟特（Bramante）设计。教堂的唱诗席因为外面的街道太窄而不得不缩短，但是布拉孟特干脆采用一幅透视画面取而代之。这是艺术史上首次对错视法（trompe l'oeil）的运用。

而成），贝德克旅行指南介绍它是画上去的。但是模板则由石头制成。它显得如此原真（由于狭窄的通道），肯定不能在上面举行唱诗活动。

圣萨蒂罗的圣玛利亚[267]有一个漂亮的门廊，这是我在一座教堂前面看到的第一个门廊。

圣洛仑佐教堂[268]是米兰最古老的教堂，其风格属于罗马风，内部色彩很漂亮。外面是一排罗马列柱，属砖石结构建筑。柱子采用科林斯式，而且有点风化了。

圣安伯乔教堂[269]（图183）也有一个门廊，罗马风，据说奥古斯丁就在这里接受洗礼[270]。

毫无疑问，最美丽的教堂是圣玛丽亚感恩教堂[271]（图184），它的穹顶仿照了布拉孟特的设计。

这里的重头戏是莱昂纳多的《最后的晚餐》（图185），它处在多明尼克修道院的牧师餐厅中。整幅画面被修复过，门处在打开状态，而在一些印刷品中它是关着的，并且被涂上颜色，留有看得出来的痕迹。当它在崭新的时候必定是一件伟大作品。由于已经受损到如此程度，它看上去就像是一幅草稿，基督的脸很难看清，构图非常宏伟而且

图182.2 圣萨蒂罗教堂 San Satiro
图183 圣安布罗乔教堂 San Ambrogio
图184 玛丽亚感恩修道院 Santa Maria delle Grazie
图185 最后的晚餐 Last Supper

---

267 圣萨蒂罗的圣玛利亚（Santa Maria Presso San Satiro）是一组建于15世纪的宏大建筑群，有10世纪的钟楼，还有布拉孟特一件相当特殊的早期作品。
268 圣洛仑佐教堂（San Lorenzo）由伯鲁莱列斯基（Brunelleschi）接受美第奇家族的委托于1419年对其进行改造设计。但是伯鲁莱列斯基在世时并没有完成全部的设计。美第奇劳伦廷图书室（Laurentian Library）和新圣器室（New Sacristy）后来由米开朗基罗设计完成。
269 圣安布罗乔教堂（San Ambrogio），圣安布罗乔是米兰的守护神，该教堂是米兰最古老的教堂之一，于379年开始修建。现存建筑基本体现为10世纪罗马风格。
270 奥古斯丁（Augustine）在圣安布罗乔教会（Chiesa San Ambrogio）接受了圣安布罗赛（Saint Ambrose）为他进行的洗礼。
271 玛丽亚感恩修道院(Santa Maria delle Grazie)和教堂，由米兰公爵斯福扎下令始建于1469年，完成于1490年，建筑师为索拉里（Guiniforte Solari），于1463年开始修建。达·芬奇创作的巨画《最后的晚餐》就画在这座教堂旁的修道院餐厅。

新颖。12个门徒被分为3人一组,色彩非常简洁。半圆壁[272]也是由达·芬奇绘制的。

教堂有一个非常漂亮的入口大门,内部看上去很陈旧,这是我所记得的全部。

必须坦言,观看《最后的晚餐》并没有引起我任何的激动,它看上去就像一位老朋友,而且观看它仅仅意味着去门辨识。

城堡[273](图186)看上去很宏伟,伦巴第塔有着一种特殊的构图和气质,它让人想起莫斯科克里姆林宫(?)的某座塔,角落中的圆形城堡让我想起纽伦堡的塔楼,只有那些在米兰的塔楼才用糙面石,而且看上去更美。城堡周围的建筑非常漂亮并且更具有城市味,它们中有一些是佛罗伦萨风格的。

参观了布雷拉府邸[274](图187)和克雷斯皮府邸的外景。布雷拉府邸带有一个漂亮的庭院和一个很棒的画廊,明天我将会去参观。

我已经参观完贝德克旅行指南列出的所有内容,只有布雷拉和卡斯泰罗美术馆的内部留待明天去参观。只画了一张感恩圣母大教堂的回廊庭院的速写。

8月3日 早晨前往城堡参观美术馆,那里最好的东西就是莱昂纳多所绘制的天棚[275](图188),这是人们可以想到的最原创的

图186 斯佛尔扎城堡
Castello Sforzesco

图187 布雷拉府邸
Palazzo di Brera

图188 达·芬奇所绘制的天棚
Ceiling Painting by Da Vinci

---

272 一般的印刷品中都不会出现《最后的晚餐》画面上方的三个半圆壁(Lunettes)。半圆壁中的三幅画是献给达·芬奇的资助人斯弗查公爵(Duke Lodovico Sforza)的。中间一幅表示公爵和他的妻子的武装力量,两侧的则是代表他们的两个儿子。
273 斯佛尔扎城堡(Castello Sforzesco),曾是米兰公爵居住的城堡。许多建筑师,如布鲁内莱斯基、伯拉蒙特、克莱蒙纳、达·芬奇等都参与了这座城堡的建设。
274 布雷拉府邸(Palazzo di Brera)。整座建筑呈四方形庭院,共两层,均有柱廊。1572年,耶稣会接管后开始在建筑师里基尼(Francesco Maria Richini)领导下大规模改建(1627—1628年)。1773年,耶稣会被解散时,这里保持了天文台和耶稣会建立的图书馆。1776年,布雷拉美术馆正式成立,新古典建筑师皮尔马里尼(Piermarini)领导扩建了这个博物馆。它是世界上最重要的美术馆之一,展出意大利文艺复兴时期以及巴洛克时期的绘画作品,重点是15—18世纪的伦巴第(Lombardy)和威尼斯(Venice)画家的作品,其他还包括20世纪现代艺术作品。
275 米兰斯福扎城堡中有一间"无轴厅"是由达·芬奇装饰,大厅每边长15米,全部房间的墙上为一整幅壁画:众多的树木交错成一个大藤架。天花板上至今仍可依稀可见由他绘制的茂盛的槭树。

内容。被拱券所打断的吊顶被处理成为一种倒扣的绿色圆顶,四边饰以蓝色和金色的屏风,棕色树枝则蜿蜒而下到达檐口。它非常丰富而且简洁,给人以平和的视觉效果。墙面被覆以红色丝绸,座位采用深棕色木板。而地板又是一种精彩设计,由黑白大理石按照最有趣的纹理所构成。整个概念几乎是现代的。

其中有一组中国的收藏品(明代和康熙年间),还有一些日本艺术品。

布雷拉的美术馆非常好,可以与德累斯顿和慕尼黑的美术馆相媲美,里面有拉斐尔的《圣母的婚礼》[276](图189),而提香的画作我没有看到。

1:02从北站乘火车到科莫[277],2:02到达。从那儿乘船(米兰)到贝拉焦(4:30到达)。但是5分钟后乘回船(萨维亚)返回科莫。

图189 圣母的婚礼
　　　The Nuptials of the Virgin
图190 奈索 Nesso
图191 阿尔杰诺 Argegno

从科莫开始起的第一个钟头非常无聊,两岸的建筑没有什么意思,但是一旦等你到了奈索[278](图190),建筑突然变得很好看,并且它们如此美妙地组合在一起,还有一座拱桥和一个大型瀑布。下一个好地方也许就是伦诺[279],在那里旅馆的墙面上,树木和藤蔓被修剪成如此这般:枝干向上延伸,而叶子则停滞下来。

但是在此之前还有阿尔杰诺[280](图191),在那里有一座很漂亮的老罗马风格的钟塔和一座吓人的灰色新罗马风格的

---

276 圣母的婚礼(The Nuptials of the Virgin)绘制于1504年。整幅画以透视法构图,精巧绝伦,位于灭点中心的圆形神庙更是展现了拉斐尔的建筑天才。
277 科莫(Como)位于米兰以北约45公里,科莫湖西南角南岸。
278 奈索(Nesso)是伦巴第大区(Lombardy)科莫省的一个自治区,位于科莫东北约13公里处。
279 伦诺(Leno)是伦巴第大区布雷西亚省(Brescia)的一个小镇。
280 阿尔杰诺(Argegno)是伦巴第大区科莫省的一个自治区,位于科莫以北约15公里处。

教堂。

贝拉焦[281]（图192）除了是一堆以街区为组织的、有人居住的别墅外，就一无是处。它并不好看，我没有时间去参观或者描绘圣吉奥瓦尼教堂[282]（图193），但是在船上从远处观看了它。它由灰色石头构成，或许可以入画。

从水面看去，所有那些湖边塔楼和村庄都很好看。但是当你进入之后，它们就失去了魅力。

在贝拉焦只停留了10分钟，随后乘坐另一艘船返回。在回来的路上，湖的西侧已经被笼罩于黑暗之中了。

从马蒂尼乘火车前往米兰时，在意大利边境有一名海关官员，他看上去就像B.米翁。在昨天中午的一家餐厅里，我看到另一个更像他的人，甚至手势和吃饭的姿式都很像。

在德国，木板门就像这样开启。

但是在意大利北部，门板经常是水平方向的，令人想起石头铰链。

8月4日　9:22 离开米兰，9:50到达塞托萨[283]（图194）。

在火车上，一名老妇将9件大行李放在头顶上，其他人则没有需要占地方的行李。

两名法国妇女正在前往塞托萨，并向查票员出示自己的车票。查票员表现得如此激烈，以至于她们认为自己坐错了车，但是她们只需为特快列车支付差额费用。

图 192　贝拉焦　Bellagio
图 193　圣吉奥瓦尼教堂　San Giovanni
图 194　塞托萨　Certosa di Pavia
图 195　小礼拜堂　Chiostro Piccolo

---

281 贝拉焦（Bellagio）是伦巴第大区（Lombardy）科莫省的一个自治区，它位于科莫湖南边的两个分支中间的半岛上，可以北望阿尔卑斯山。
282 圣吉奥瓦尼教堂（San Giovanni）。吉奥瓦尼是距离贝拉焦2公里左右的一个小渔村。
283 塞托萨（Certosa di Pavia）是一个修道院社区，位于伦巴第大区，距离帕维亚约8公里，建造于1396—1495年。

在塞托萨车站，有一名司机让他的有轨马车等待修道士（这几页我是在半醉之中写的，头晕脑胀），但是当他看到我们沿着轨道走出来而没有乘他的马车，就给我指了错误的方向，我听信了他，沿着城墙兜了一整圈。

最大的宝贝就是带有钟塔的小礼拜堂（图195），立面由如此完美、色彩斑斓的大理石镶嵌而成，正立面采用白色大理石，后部正中采用红砖。这种组合是最迷人的。钟塔建造得也非常完美。教堂室内看上去很宏伟，每一个小礼拜室都是一颗宝石，其中都有一个镶嵌着精美的内地大理石的精美圣坛。唱诗席略带巴洛克风格，带喷泉的回廊庭院非常壮丽，大回廊庭院也是如此，它由僧侣的居室所环绕，每位僧侣在一楼都有3个房间，带有一座火炉，并有一个聚餐点（哑巴侍者转过身来）。

正如我所料，入口、向导和检查物品都不收费。

这毫无疑问是伦巴第优秀的早期文艺复兴作品。

附近有一家餐厅，人们在露天用餐，上面覆盖着树木和藤蔓，极其别致而宁静。老板娘很漂亮，而且说法语。葡萄酒口味上佳，使我进入酩酊状态，魂不附体。饭菜同样也很可口，我旁边的两个僧侣与其他的世间生物一样有着好胃口。

乘火车（1:15）去热那亚，沿途第一站经过帕维亚，美丽的穹顶和钟塔矗立在廊桥边（桥拱带有不同的宽度）。这又是一颗小宝石。如同其他种族一样，意大利人再也做不出来了。

我忘提了，当人们进入庭院前往右墙的礼拜堂时，那些窗户也是绘制过的。门道采用白灰涂刷过。

5:20到达热那亚（1:15从卡托萨乘火车而来），天气有些多云，整座城镇看上去没有太大意思，除了古老蜿蜒的街巷之外。高房子分列两侧，上面飘扬着刚洗过的衣服。所有贝德克旅行指南称赞过的府邸和教堂都没有什么意思。镇上最好的地方就是港口沿线，那里的房子有10层楼高。最多从美学角度来说，就像一个微型的纽约，只不过更加人工化。

海港与我所想象的远不相同，我期待着至少有一些航船，但是那里除了一些蒸汽船外，一无所有。

在码头吃的晚餐，在一条长长的拱券下，葡萄酒、牛排和水果，8里拉。

住在火车站附近山上的贝尔维尤旅馆，花了15里拉。

8月5日　起得很早（4:45），赶5:25火车前往比萨，9:15到达。

前往河边，画了魁尔法塔（图196），参观了圣保罗教堂[284]（图197），它有一个模仿大教堂的立面，在教堂旁边有一个台阶走下去到达河边。在那里，垃圾味道令人难以忍受，而我就在那儿画的速写。

斯皮拉圣母教堂[285]（图198）拥有一个奇怪的哥特立面，带有高耸的构图，这是我所见过的最小的教堂。

参观比萨大学[286]（图199），一个非常古典的立面。圣·弗雷迪亚诺教堂[287]（图200）在内部拥有古老的立柱。奥古斯丁府邸采用威尼斯风格，圣卡特里纳教堂[288]（图201）在内部有很漂亮的玻璃窗，比例给人的感觉几乎是现代的，也是水平的蓝色线条。漆成黑木的天棚（蓝色花纹）很漂亮。

参观了比萨斜塔[289]（图202），全部采用白色大理石，大教堂和洗礼堂也是白色大理石。于是在阳光下，白色石头反射着光线，并刺灼着你的眼睛。爬上塔顶，给自己拍了一张照片。

大教堂非常漂亮，虽然从外面看穹顶有

图 196　魁尔法塔　Torre Guelfa
图 197　圣保罗教堂　San Paolo a Ripa d'Arno
图 198　斯皮拉圣母教堂　Santa Maria della Spina
图 199　比萨大学　University of Pisa
图 200　圣·弗雷迪亚诺教堂　San Frediano

284　圣保罗教堂（San Paolo a Ripa d'Arno）是意大利塔斯干地区（Tuscany）最好的中世纪罗曼风格（Romanesque）教堂之一。它在当地也被称作老教堂（Duomo Vecchio）。
285　斯皮拉圣母教堂（Santa Maria della Spina）是一座哥特式的小教堂，建于1230年。1333年因收藏了基督在十字架上所戴的荆棘而改名为荆棘圣母教堂。1871年曾因阿诺河水上涨而垫高重建。
286　比萨大学（University of Pisa）是意大利最著名的大学之一，创立于1343年。
287　圣·弗雷迪亚诺教堂（San Frediano）的立面采用罗曼风格，具有典型的比萨地区的中世纪建筑特征。
288　圣卡特里纳教堂（Santa Caterina）的立面采用白色和灰色的大理石。上部是哥特式的两层廊柱，中间有一个玫瑰花窗。
289　比萨斜塔（Leaning Tower），建于1173年，在比萨大教堂及洗礼堂建成后，按原建筑规划需再建一座钟楼。钟楼建成后，塔身向南倾斜，尽管塔顶中心线偏离垂直中心线2.1米，但该塔却屹立不倒，成为世界建筑史上一奇迹。

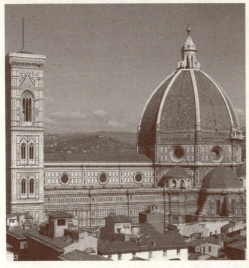

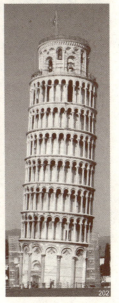

图 201 圣卡特里纳教堂 Santa Caterina
图 202 比萨斜塔 Leaning Tower
图 203 圣母百花大教堂 Santa Maria del Fiore Duomo

些滑稽,到处采用的是水平蓝色大理石线脚。由契马布埃[290]在圣坛上方所做的马赛克(金色衬底)如此大胆,以至于它看上去非常时髦,特别是对基督脸部的处理。

洗礼堂拥有人们可以想到的最完美的穹顶,外表看上去棒极了。内部同样又是如此大胆和简洁,任何现代建筑师都会这样去做。那里的重要节点就是尼古拉·皮萨诺[291]所设计的讲坛,大理石的做工非常精美。

没有吃早餐,因此在靠近比萨大教堂的地方吃的午餐。

---

290 契马布埃(Giovanni Cimabue, 1240—?1302 年),通常被认为是乔托的老师,又称作意大利绘画之父。
291 尼古拉·皮萨诺(Nicola Pisano, 约 1220—1278/1284 年),意大利雕刻家。1255 年,他受委托建造比萨洗礼堂(Baptistry)内的讲道坛,并于 1260 年完成。

圣堂[292]里有浮雕和陵墓。

比萨的纪念建筑如此这般，为的是提示一个时代的精神和简洁，以呈现其伟大之处，而不需要任何复杂的东西。

1:30乘火车前往佛罗伦萨，3:30到达，住在阿洛罗街13号马蒂利尼旅店。

参观了皮蒂宫[293]的外景，同时也参观了卡尔米内圣母教堂[294]和圣灵教堂[295]。画了维奇奥桥[296]，这是我所见过最漂亮的桥。

8月6日 首先前往大教堂[297]（图203），参观了内部，相当平庸，但是纪念性很强。穹顶上的玻璃窗是最好的，光辉灿烂但也充满了神秘色彩。穹顶下面的唱诗席也很新颖，非常漂亮。

图204 佛罗伦萨洗礼堂 Florence Baptistry
图205 天堂之门 Gates of Paradise

292 也称纳骨室，在大教堂和洗礼堂北侧，建于1277年，建筑本身呈回字形，有一个被壁画环绕的长条状中庭，其中共有600座墓碑。

293 皮蒂宫（Palazzo Pitti）原先是与美弟奇家族竞争的富商皮蒂（Luca Pitti）延请菲利普·伯鲁莱列斯基（Brunelleschi）设计，未完工其家族即已没落。随后被克西莫一世（Cosimo I）收购并续建，增建了波波里花园（Giardino di Boboli），使之成为一座华丽宫殿。皮蒂宫一直到19世纪中期都是托斯卡纳大公的府邸。

294 卡尔米内圣母教堂（Santa Maria del Carmine），建于13世纪，内部的布兰卡齐礼拜堂（Capella di Brancacci）内有画家马萨乔和马佐利诺绘制的壁画。

295 圣灵教堂（Church of San Spirito）的室内被认为是文艺复兴建筑的杰作之一。该处原先的建筑在13世纪毁于火灾，1435年伯鲁莱列斯基被委托重建教堂。教堂的穹顶由伯鲁莱列斯基设计，他在剩下的其他工程完成前他就去世了。

296 维奇奥桥（Ponte Veccio）。维奇奥桥是架在阿诺河上佛罗伦萨最古老的桥。桥两侧全是黄金雕刻工艺品店和珠宝店，所以又被称为金桥。据说这条时髦的步行街两旁在13世纪时全是皮革店和肉店，臭气冲天，费尔迪南一世讨厌宫殿的附近有这么臭的市场，所以在1593年下令拆去了市场，建起了与宫殿相称的珠宝店。上面一层是巴扎利设计的，曾是乌费齐宫与皮蒂宫之间的通道。

297 圣母百花大教堂（Santa Maria del Fiore Duomo），位于意大利佛罗伦萨城中，是天主教佛罗伦萨总教区的主教座堂，也是天主教宗座圣殿。教堂建筑群由主教座堂、钟塔与洗礼堂构成。主教座堂于1296年奠基，1347年秋天爆发黑死病迫使工程中断。1367年由全民投票决定在教堂中殿十字交叉点上建造直径43.7米，高52米的八角形圆顶，由精通罗马古建筑的工匠菲利普·伯鲁莱列斯基任总建筑师。在建造拱顶时，没有采用当时流行的"拱鹰架"圆拱木架，而是采用了新颖的"鱼刺式"的建造方式，从下往上逐次砌成。主教座堂于1436年3月25日，举行献堂典礼。

仔细观察了洗礼堂[298]（图204）的大门[299]（图205），在模式上非常简洁，这就是它们为什么如此漂亮的原因，就是恰到好处而不成为巴洛克。洗礼堂的内部就像罗马的万神庙，非常简洁，并且气势恢宏。没有爬上钟塔，但是参观了多纳泰罗的"愚者"[300]，一直升到空中。

大教堂的博物馆有卢卡·德拉·罗比亚的作品。

前往美术馆，参观多纳泰罗的作品，这也许是那里唯一的杰作。

维奇奥宫[301]有钟塔（很高），看上去就像一座城堡和燕尾形的堡垒，令人印象深刻。

楼上的房间很少采用正方形或者矩形，它们只是随机的并且构成了侧室。这种令人惊讶的坦率，使人想起不规则街道，宫殿由此得以界定。室内比任何一座开放的宫殿要好。

参观了青铜板台（在西格诺里广场），据说萨沃纳罗拉就在那儿被烧死在柴堆上[302]。

罗基西·迪·兰兹博物馆[303]远比它在慕尼黑的复制品要漂亮。这里雕塑作品的数量是惊人的，而且大多数是杰作。这是一座有些露天的美术馆。

参观了乌菲齐画廊，它处在一个U形柱廊建筑的顶层，藏品极

---

298 佛罗伦萨洗礼堂（Florence Baptistry），全名为圣若望洗礼堂（Baptistero di San Giovanni），是佛罗伦萨的一座宗教建筑，拥有次级圣殿的地位。洗礼堂是佛罗伦萨现存最古老的建筑之一，建于1059年到1128年，采用了罗曼式建筑风格。洗礼堂以其在艺术上很重要的洛伦佐·吉贝尔蒂（Lorenzo Ghiberti）的三组刻有浮雕的青铜大门而著称。这些门由于非常美丽，而被米开朗基罗称为"天堂之门"，被称为开启了文艺复兴。圣若望洗礼堂呈八角形，坐落在主教座堂广场，与圣母百花大教堂和乔托钟楼相对。
299 佛罗伦萨洗礼堂的东门被米开朗基罗称为天堂之门（Gates of Paradise）。
300 多纳泰罗（Donatello，1386—1466年），意大利早期文艺复兴美术家，也是15世纪最杰出的雕塑家，多纳泰罗于1423—1425年，创作了著名的雕塑哈巴谷（Habacuc，俗称Zuccone），意思为大南瓜、大傻瓜。
301 维奇奥（Vecchio）在意大利语中是"旧"的意思，维奇奥宫即为旧宫，全宫以石块砌成，粗犷厚实有如城堡，并拥有城垛、炮口等防御工事。至今仍然用作佛罗伦萨的市政厅。
302 萨沃纳罗拉（Girolamo Savonarola，1452—1498年），意大利天主教神父。15世纪末，天主教改革者从1494年到1498在佛罗伦萨推动了一场未成功的宗教和道德改革。萨沃纳罗拉在讲道时抨击教皇和教会的腐败，揭露佛罗伦萨美第奇家族的残暴统治，反对富人骄奢淫逸，主张重整社会道德，提倡虔诚修行生活。1494年，萨沃纳罗拉成为城市平民起义的精神领袖，领导平民赶走美第奇家族，恢复佛罗伦萨共和国。1498年4月，教皇和美第奇家族利用饥荒，煽动群众攻打圣马可修道院。共和国失败，萨沃纳罗拉被加以裂教及异端狂想分子的罪名，在佛罗伦萨闹市中被火刑处死。
303 罗基西·迪·兰兹博物馆（Loggia dei Lanzi），在领主广场（Piazza del Duomo）的右前方有一个长廊，称为佣兵凉廊（Loggia dei Lanzi），建于1382年，据说曾有兵营在此宿营，而称之为"佣兵凉廊"。

其重要，但是不如皮蒂宫的好，尽管这里既有绘画也有雕塑。

国立美术馆比其他地方有更多的多纳泰罗的作品，还有米开朗基罗的《沉醉的酒神》[304]，他未完成的建筑也在这里。安德烈·德拉·罗比亚[305]的作品也很多。

孤儿院[306]有安德烈·德拉·罗比亚的带有蓝色背景的莫多利奥斯。

天使报喜教堂[307]有无数的壁画。

美第奇府邸[308]完全不值得一看，公寓的品质很差，美术馆也不是很好。

圣马可修道院[309]在回廊庭院中有许多浮雕，在楼上有许多房间，其中一些房间曾经由萨沃纳罗拉居住过。

美术学院[310]的画廊有米开朗基罗的《大卫》，以及未完成的一组垂死的奴隶，非常像罗丹完成了的作品。除了很大并且有力，大卫没什么特别的。

圣洛伦佐教堂[311]（图206.1）有一个未

图 206.1 圣洛伦佐教堂内景
Basilica di San Lorenzo
图 206.2 圣洛伦佐教堂外观
Basilica di San Lorenzo

---

304 沉醉的酒神（Drunken Bacchus），作于 1497 年，开始由米开朗基罗为一雕塑花园所作。
305 安德烈·德拉·罗比亚（Andrea della Robbia, 1435—1525 年），意大利雕刻家，代表作品有佛罗伦萨育婴堂敞廊拱间壁上的 14 块圆形浮雕（约 1463 年）。
306 孤儿院（Ospedale degli Innocenti），文艺复兴时期代表性建筑，由伯鲁莱列斯基设计门廊。
307 天使报喜教堂（Santissima Annunziate）。罗马天主教堂，始建于 1250 年，由教堂牧师作天使报喜内部壁画而建，但牧师因缺乏信心而使工程搁浅。1469 年建筑师阿尔贝蒂接手完成教堂设计，并于 1481 年建成。
308 美第奇-里卡迪府邸（Palazzo Medici-Riccardi），在圣洛伦佐教堂的斜对面，最初由美第奇家族于 1444 年建造，此后美第奇家族在此居住了 80 多年时间。后来被里卡迪家族所夺取，后者进行了扩建并加上了华丽的巴洛克风格内部装饰。整个王宫为典型的佛罗伦萨文艺复兴式。这里后来成了佛罗伦萨的皮蒂宫及斯特罗兹宫的建筑参考。该立面由名建筑师阿尔贝蒂于 1458 年设计。
309 圣马可修道院（Monastery of San Marco），修建于 13 世纪，并于 1437 年在原来的基础上得到扩建。受柯西莫·艾尔·维奇奥的邀请，多米尼加的修道士们从附近的费索移居至此，米开朗基罗负责完成建筑设计。装饰简洁的回廊和禅房为日后佛罗伦萨画家和多米尼加修道士费拉·安吉列科在此创作一系列伟大的壁画提供了良好的基础。
310 佛罗伦萨美术学院（Accademia di Belle Arti），1785 年在奥地利国王皮特罗·列奥帕多（Pietro Leopardo）的倡导下成立。当时的专业有雕塑、绘画、建筑、版画和裸体素描。教学是沿用古典主义绘画的教学方法，称之为"写实主义大师聚集的皇家美术学院"。
311 圣洛伦佐教堂（Basilica di San Lorenzo）是美第奇家族历代的礼拜堂，由 3 个时代、建筑样式都不同的空间组成：伯鲁莱列斯基建造的旧圣器室、米开朗基罗建造的新圣器室、17 世纪的君主礼拜堂。

完成的立面（图206.2）。参观了美第奇小礼拜堂[312]（图207），全部由大理石建成，内部有着不同的色彩。它是巴洛克风格的，大理石地板（马赛克）开始于1888年，现在只完成了一半，有3个工人在工作。

新的圣器收藏室[313]由米开朗基罗建造，其中包含他著名的美第奇墓室（图208），一个是吉拉诺，另一个是洛伦佐，《沉思者》[314]。

斯特罗兹宫[315]有很精美的铁制部件，以及未完成的檐口。

皮蒂宫[316]及其纪念性花园是佛罗伦萨最令人印象深刻、最宏伟的建筑。画廊收藏了拉斐尔的《椅中圣母》（还有他的《圣子图》），还有许多由他创作的教皇和淑女的肖像。

费欧索雷[317]距离大教堂[318]大约25分钟的车程，当人们接近山顶的时候，佛罗伦萨的景色看上去非常宏伟，中间夹杂着穹顶和钟塔。柏树站立于两旁，就像是哨兵，墨绿色衬在银灰色的橄榄叶上。

8月7日 早晨爬上穹顶，可以非常清楚地看到天棚上的浮雕。内侧穹顶跟随着外侧穹顶的轮廓。穹窿顶塔的大理石细部非常精

图207 美第奇小礼拜堂 Medici Chapel
图208 美第奇墓室 Medici Tombs

---

312 美第奇小礼拜堂（Medici Chapel）是美第奇家族成员的墓地。由米开朗基罗负责建筑设计和内部雕塑工程，以纪念家族4位先祖。礼拜堂的雕塑包括著名的朱利亚诺、洛伦佐雕像和象征着沉思、活力的昼、夜、晨、暮的雕像。礼拜堂内分为三个区域：墓穴、八角形的君主礼拜堂和新圣器收藏室。
313 旧圣器收藏室由伯鲁莱列斯基建造。
314 沉思者（il Penseroso），米开朗基罗为洛伦佐·美第奇所作，这尊作品因公爵姿态的凝重和沉思，而被称作"沉思者"，再现了他生活中作为一名设计师和思想家的特征。
315 斯特罗兹宫（Palazzo Strozzi），文艺复兴时期建造的著名宫殿，于1489年开始为斯特罗兹家族建造，耗时8年，建筑师为贝奈德托·达·迈亚诺（Benedetto da Maiano）。
316 皮蒂宫（Palazzo Pitt），佛罗伦萨文艺复兴时期的经典宫殿。佛罗伦萨的商人皮蒂完成了宫殿的建造，因此而得名。1539年，皮蒂宫被当时住在维奥奥宫的美第奇家族的科西莫一世购买，这个宫殿由美第奇家族购买，并作为托斯卡纳大公的主要住所。建筑师为伯鲁莱列斯基。
317 费欧索雷（Fiesole）位于佛罗伦斯市郊，是一个小城。
318 指圣母百花大教堂。

美，从那里看出去，整个佛罗伦萨的景色美极了。这非常不同于在伦敦从圣保罗穹顶所获得的景色，在那里，人们只能看到烟雾和丑陋平庸的建筑。在这里，房屋、教堂以及柏树在你眼前次第展开。

圣米歇尔教堂[319]有一个非常富丽堂皇的哥特风格的一层楼，壁龛里放满了雕像（户外），室内则不够精彩。

圣克罗斯教堂[320]（图209）有米开朗基罗的墓室。由乔托在小礼拜堂创作的壁画很漂亮。

波那洛蒂宅邸[321]有精美的室内，美术馆也还可以，尽管藏品不是太多。

新圣母教堂[322]内部的分隔不太均等。参观了在西班牙小教堂中的浮雕。

8月8日 威尼斯，下雨。

参观了圣马可大教堂[323]的室内，第一印象它很庞大，色彩如此之斑斓，轮廓如此之丰富，这是我所见过最漂亮的教堂。

内部的马赛克很宏伟（从回廊看过去），氛围与教堂同样的好。地板非常陈旧，可以看到山丘与河谷。

图209 圣克罗斯教堂 Santa Croce
图210 总督府 Doge Palace
图211 叹息桥 Bridge of Sighs

---

319 圣米歇尔教堂（San Michel），瓦萨里设计，教堂正面为哥特式建筑，正门装饰华丽，有圣经和各神话故事题材融合。
320 圣克罗斯教堂（Santa Croce），也称圣十字教堂，由瓦萨里设计，是米开朗基罗、伽利略、但丁等显赫名人的长眠之地。
321 波那洛蒂宅邸（Casa Buonarroti），曾被米开朗基罗购买，但其本人从未在那里居住过。
322 新圣母教堂(Santa Maria Novella)是多明尼哥派的教堂，紧邻着中央车站前广场。该教堂是为了布道而建造，于1278年开工，1458年完成。设计师为两位道明会修道士，西斯多·费奥伦蒂诺（Sisto Fiorentino）和里斯多罗·坎皮（Ristoro da Campi），莱昂·巴蒂斯塔·阿尔伯蒂则设计了黑白相间的大理石的教堂正立面的上部。
323 圣马可大教堂矗立于威尼斯市中心的圣马可广场上。始建于公元829年，重建于1043—1071年，它曾是中世纪欧洲最大的教堂，是威尼斯建筑艺术的经典之作。教堂建筑循拜占庭风格，呈希腊十字形，上覆5座半球形圆顶，为融拜占庭式、哥特式、伊斯兰式、文艺复兴式各种流派于一体的综合艺术杰作。

参观了总督府[324]（图210）的室内，非常棒的室内，它的禁闭室让我想起了西庸城堡，只是在尺度上这个更大一些。在叹息桥[325]（图211）的里面走了一圈。

美术学院收藏有提香的作品，但是其余的都是垃圾。据说提香的《圣母升天图》[326]（图212）就在这儿，我没找到。但是这里有很多提香的作品。

8月9日 下午的天气非常晴朗。夜晚时分，一轮满月挂在亚德里亚海上。

早晨天气仍然多云，但是画了几幅航船的速写。

走在里亚托桥[327]（图213）上，这是一座带有3个开敞通道，中间夹着两排倾斜覆顶拱廊的宽桥。它非常漂亮。

前往马可波罗曾经居住过的地方，这是一座带有方塔的庭院（变动很大），这是他家仅存的东西。庭院有一条拱石做成的旧门廊，除此之外就是马可波罗桥，没有什么与众不同之处。

沿途走到公园，这是威尼斯岛的尽端。

图212 圣母升天图 Assumption of the Virgin
图213 里亚托桥 Rialto
图214 圣·乔瓦尼·保罗教堂 San Giovanni e Paolo

---

324 总督府（Doge Palace），始建于公元9世纪，历经数次重建，于文艺复兴时期完工。正立面建于公元1309年至1424年，由乔瓦尼（Giovanni）与巴托罗梅·波翁（Bartolomeo Buon）设计。
325 叹息桥（Bridge of Sighs），建于1603年，因桥上死囚的叹息声而得名。叹息桥两端连结着威尼斯共和国总督府和威尼斯监狱，是古代由法院向监狱押送死囚的必经之路。叹息桥造型属于早期巴洛克式风格，桥呈房屋状，上部穹隆覆盖，封闭得很严实，只有向运河一侧有两个小窗，当犯人在总督府接受审判之后，重罪犯被带到地牢中，在经过这座密不透气的桥时，只能透过小窗看见蓝天，从此失去了自由，不自主地发出叹息之声。
326 圣母升天图（Assumption of the Virgin）画于1516年至1518年间，现藏于威尼斯的圣母之光教堂（Santa Maria Gloriosa dei Frari），是意大利最大幅的祭坛画。
327 里亚托桥（Rialto），建于1180年，它又名商业桥，原为一座木桥，1580—1592年改建为石桥，是威尼斯的象征。桥长48米，宽22米，离水面7米高，桥上中部建有亭阁，两侧店铺林立，销售各种纪念品和特产。

画了7张速写。

8月10日 又是愉快的一天。前往参观科勒奥尼[328]塑像，附近的教堂（圣·乔瓦尼·保罗）[329]（图214）在外表上有点像圣马可大教堂，室内没有什么可看的。

又去了一次马可波罗的庭院，穿过迷宫般的街巷，很艰难地找到它。这次找到一所由石碑所标识的房屋，上面写着这块基地就是马可的故居。这个故居太新了，肯定不是原先的，它应当是16世纪建造的。

下午走过大部分街巷，总而言之，即使在威尼斯，大多数街巷都很相似。

在圣马可广场听音乐，非常一般。

早晨我爬上了钟塔[330]（图215），可以看到整个威尼斯岛和大陆。画了6张速写。

8月11日 早晨前往利都岛[331]，这是一个极其普通的地方。洗浴是其主要内容。

在公园观看了国际艺术展，有来自法国、德国、捷克斯洛伐克、俄罗斯、美国、比利时、英格兰和意大利的绘画，意大利作品中包含了大量的未来主义绘画以及现代生活中的一些金饰作品，所有其他国家则提交了非常平庸而且糟糕的作品。

展览建筑是最现代化的，品质十分低劣。

傍晚在利都海滩洗了半个小时的澡，明天还可以再来一次。

画了6张速写。

在从圣马可广场返回车站的路上，就在

图215 圣马可广场钟塔 Campanile di San Marco
图216 文德拉明·卡拉基宫 Palazzo Vendramin-Calergi
图217 波塔诺瓦 Porta Nuova
图218 帕里奥城门 Porta Palio
图219 圣泽诺大教堂 Basilica di San Zeno

---

328 巴托洛米奥·科勒奥尼（Bartolomeo Colleoni，1395—1475年），意大利历史上最受尊敬的军阀兼任威尼斯共和国的统帅和威尼斯军队的司令官。韦罗基奥为他设计了在圣乔凡尼广场上的青铜雕像。

329 圣·乔瓦尼·保罗教堂（San Giovanni e Paolo）。威尼斯最大教堂之一，原始教堂不详，于1333年拆除重建，现存教堂建于1430年，采用意大利哥特风格。

330 圣马可广场钟塔（Campanile di San Marco）是圣马可广场最高的建筑，修建于15世纪，大约有100米高，塔顶为浅绿色，主体则是砖红色。塔顶上站立着一个圣马可神像的金色雕塑。

331 利都岛（Lido）是威尼斯的一个11公里长的沙洲，以海滩和电影节闻名。

靠近圣乔治教堂[332]的地方，月光映射在水面上，圣乔治教堂的穹顶和钟塔矗立在剪影中，男声和女声的歌声（极其美妙）从贡多拉和小船上飘过来，整个世界似乎如此梦幻，非常浪漫。

8月12日　早晨步行了很远的距离，画了2张铅笔速写，在大运河上乘坐了一次贡多拉，参观了文德拉明府邸[333]（图216）。石碑上刻有瓦格纳的侧面像，以及一些巴洛克装饰，并刻有以下一段文字：

F.T. Cadorin F

在这里，

灵魂听到了里卡多·瓦格纳的呼吸

怦然有如涛声

在大理石下面[334]

加夫列拉·邓南遮

1883年2月13日

留念

1910

又一次前往利都岛去洗海水浴，几乎没有任何阳光。

在圣马可广场画了3张水彩画。

在老地方吃的晚餐，一对男女演奏音乐，主要是些意大利浪漫情歌。那位妇人很容易让我想起白居易的琵琶行。

8月13日　乘火车前往维罗纳，9点钟到达。

波塔诺瓦[335]（图217）的比例很好看。歌德曾经赞美过的帕里奥城门[336]（图218），它并不如波塔诺瓦好看。

圣泽诺大教堂[337]（图219）是我所见过最好的罗马风教堂，中庭上方的木吊顶（14C.）非常宏伟，由弯曲的木肋所构成，并由小方木块所加强。在上面依稀可辨一些绘画，其效果非常现代。

由一个倒转头像所支撑的洗礼盆也采用了现代形式，室内的整体效果很棒，唱诗席在处理上也很有创意，大理石的栏杆上站立着

332　圣乔治教堂（San Giorgio Maggiore），建于1610年，位于圣乔治·马焦雷岛（San Giorgio Maggiore）上，由意大利文艺复兴时期的著名建筑师帕拉迪奥（Andrea Palladio）设计。

333　文德拉明·卡拉基宫（Palazzo Vendramin-Calergi），16世纪早期文艺复兴式的代表作。文德拉明宫在15世纪的时候曾经是威尼斯贵族的住宅。

334　英译稿为：In this palace / the souls hear / the last breath of Richard Wagner / perpetuating itself like the tide / which washes the marble beneath

335　波塔诺瓦（Porta Nuova），意思为新门，位于从火车站前往维罗纳古城的途中。

336　帕里奥城门（Porta Palio），建于公元16世纪，位于维罗纳古罗马竞技场附近。

337　圣泽诺大教堂（Basilica di San Zeno）是维罗纳最著名的教堂，可能是因为在莎士比亚的戏剧中，这里的教堂地下室是罗密欧与朱丽叶结婚的地方。

基督和他的信徒，橙色的光线从小窗中透射进来，效果非常强烈，外面的罗马风格的大门不仅优雅端庄，而且非常漂亮，色彩斑斓。整个立面的比例很好。大门采用最为古色古香的方式，覆以分隔的青铜雕塑板。

伯萨里城门[338]（图220）缺失了它的台口，在街道上方有两个拱券，在它们上方有3行窗户，或者开敞的拱廊。

从河岸穿过皮亚塔老桥[339]（图221），去观看城堡的景色，它带有美丽的民居群落，非常漂亮，这令人想起维尔茨堡。

大教堂[340]（图222）没有什么特别之处，天棚被漆成蓝色，并饰以金色星星，总体效果是巴洛克的。新增加的钟塔（看上去很新）非常难看。

古斯提府邸[341]（图223）的花园很漂亮，它有着很陡的坡度，带有壁龛，也许是流水，两侧种植成行柏树，令人印象深刻。参观者不得进入。

参观据说是朱丽叶父母的故居（13C.），它带有很高的阳台（三层楼高）。另一个阳台被拆除了，留下了支架。庭院是方形的，带有一长串拦起来的台地。这个地方被重新整修过。

图220 伯萨里城门 Porta Borsari
图221 皮亚塔老桥 Ponte Pietra
图222 维罗纳大教堂 Verona Cathedral
图223 古斯提府邸 Palazzo e Giardino Giusti

---

338 伯萨里城门（Porta Borsari），古罗马时代维罗纳的城门之一，建于西元3世纪原本城墙的一部分。
339 皮亚塔老桥（Ponte Pietra），维罗纳的"石桥"，维罗纳人亦惯称为"旧桥"（Ponte Pietra）是一座罗马时期遗留下来的石桥。
340 维罗纳大教堂（Verona Cathedral）始建于1139年，因文艺复兴后期的大画家提香的"Assumption"而出名。
341 古斯提府邸（Palazzo e Giardino Giusti）。贾蒂诺·古斯提是维罗纳公爵，他于1570年设计古斯提府邸，是意大利最好的文艺复兴时代花园之一。曾接待过莫扎特、歌德等无数名人。

随后参观了朱丽叶的陵墓,一个开敞的石棺,里面堆积着门票,被放置在罗马风格拱廊中的小凉廊中。它看上去过于完美而不像是真的。总之,所有都是虚构的。莎士比亚的胸像被放置在背景墙上。

参观但丁广场[342](图224)周围的建筑群,拉罗基亚(双层敞廊府邸)[343](图225)的比例很优雅。

图224 但丁广场 Piazza Dante
图225 双层敞廊府邸 Loggia del Consiglio

竞技场的形状仍然完好(罗马),实际上并没有秩序,它现在被用作一个普通的剧场(现代的布景在这样一种实体结构中看上去贫乏而且轻浮)。

参观罗马剧场,它显然不对游客开放,但是人们可以透过栏杆观看。在朱丽叶墓上有两块石碑,上面刻有这些文字:

紧邻着圣弗朗西斯教堂,
是一座名为帕格里亚的塔(一座草塔)。
教堂原先用来储存弹药,
某一天被雷电击中,
由于突如其来的熊熊烈火,
它被炸成碎片,
最终导致教堂也坍塌了下来。
1624年

感谢城市以及虔诚信徒的慷慨捐助,
在市政议员赛巴斯蒂亚诺·西孔纳
以及负责建造军事设施的方塔纳府邸的
乔诺拉莫的指导下,
艾尔维斯伯爵依据基础的形式重建了教堂,
1625年[344]

342 但丁广场(Piazza Dante),也称西格诺里广场(Piazza dei Signori),广场中间矗立着诗人但丁的雕像,周边为众多文艺复兴时期建筑。
343 双层敞廊府邸(Loggia del Consiglio),具有早期文艺复兴特色的双层敞廊宫殿。
344 原文用简体古拉丁文书写,与今天意大利语完全不同,在翻译中有可能有错误和误写。感谢瞿海林与Marco Silvestri先生,他们费尽周折在梵蒂冈档案馆查到这段文字的出处,并在维罗纳的圣弗朗西斯科教堂(St. Francesco)找到该段文字的意大利译文,并转译成英文。这段文字用来记载圣弗朗西斯科教堂的一段重建经历,但是经常被人们误认为是朱丽叶的墓志铭。

在威尼斯圣马可广场的立柱上,大理石块垂直排列,四角固定。乘坐晚上 9:20 的火车前往因斯布鲁克[345]。

8月14日 凌晨4点钟到达因斯布鲁克,整晚几乎没有睡觉。在三等候车室研究一张地图,直到6点钟。车站管理员前来将我赶出候车室。

在靠近市中心的地方吃了早餐,步行爬山,在半路上画了一张速写,然后下山吃午饭。

早晨天空晴朗,到中午时分,开始变得多云。

没有心情去画画。

寄了两本导游书给斯奈德。

8月15日 现在开始起没有参观项目了,我原本应该在柏林、波兰和俄罗斯参观的内容随后只能凭记忆了。因为从明天开始直到回家,我将没有导游书。晚上一阵悲伤涌上心头。一个人不可能在阳光灿烂的意大利面对生活而感到失意,但是在北方下雨的地方,这是非常伤感而孤独的,没有心思做任何事情。

一件还算令人愉快的事情就是又可以去参观奥地利和德国的现代建筑。

8月16日

8月17日 在外面参观了夏洛腾堡宫[346](图226)的花园,种满了树。

乘火车前往俄罗斯。

8月18日 路过华沙。波兰非常乏味,唯一的色彩就是妇女的头巾,建筑是奇怪的俄国与德国风格的,道路很糟糕。

下午4点到达尼格勒罗格,在俄国与波兰的边境有一扇木门,它标志着边境,两旁站立着士兵,按惯例要求火车停靠在大门的两侧。

海关官员还不太令人反感,他们并不关心我的手表,也不去找书籍的麻烦,他们却关注于记录:钱(美国的)必须要登记,而且当人们用美元兑换俄国卢布时,必须要登记。

我被分配到一间卧厢,那里已经有3个女人(后来我知道她们是前往中国的外交官,2名美国人,1名中国人)。

我从未想过这样令人窘迫的情形,并且忐忑不安地等待她们将我洗浴的东西收拾干净。但是后来,当我出来前往餐车时,那位较

---

345 因斯布鲁克(Innsbruck),奥地利北部的蒂罗尔(Tyrol)联邦的首府。
346 夏洛腾堡宫(Charlottenburg Palace),柏林最大的宫殿,也是该城市里唯一可以追溯到普鲁士王朝时期(1701—1918年)的宫殿。

为年长的女士告诉我,她们已经将我转移到其他地方。我十分感激,同时责备自己当时对整个事情糊里糊涂。

8月19日 早晨11点钟到达莫斯科,约翰·威利斯在火车站接我。我们在火车站(亚历山大)停留了很长时间,也许等那个哑巴处理完那些遗失了行李票的人(那个女孩是威利斯同一公司的同事的女儿)。最终威利斯将我带到他的公寓,在那里冲了个淋浴(冷的),并吃了他妻子准备的一顿牛排晚餐。

我们前往克里姆林宫,由另一个人陪同。他出生于保加利亚,现在是一名美国人,在同一家公司工作。他会说俄语,对莫斯科很熟悉。

克里姆林宫非常漂亮,有许多塔楼、城门和城墙,同时它也色彩缤纷。红场正在重新铺装,完成后,它将成为世界上最激动人心的地方。列宁墓被封闭起来,似乎正在按照原设计采用黑色和红色花岗岩进行重修。我们未能来得及申请进入克里姆林宫。

圣巴西尔[347](图227)是一座奇特的教堂,它有10个单元,每个单元向上形成一座顶塔。从平面上识别不出真正的建筑,它似乎充满了黑暗的走道和小礼拜室。做工非常廉价,细部也已经腐朽。但是外观却还是完美无缺得漂亮。人们并不表达崇敬之意,他们仍然戴着帽子!而且完全可以触摸任何东西。在一个礼拜室中坐着两名老妇人,禁止参观者去碰古老的灯。

图226 夏洛腾堡宫
　　　Charlottenburg Palace
图227 圣巴西尔教堂
　　　Saint Basil's Cathedral
图228 基督救世主教堂
　　　Cathedral of Christ the Savior

---

[347] 圣巴西尔教堂(Saint Basil's Cathedral),坐落于莫斯科红场,是为纪念1552年"伊凡雷帝"胜利占领喀山而建。1560年教堂竣工。该教堂为东正教教堂,采用最典型的拜占庭式建筑风格,表现为希腊十字平面,以及高高隆起的中央穹隆。圣巴西尔大教堂是莫斯科,甚或全俄罗斯最具体而微的象征,也是俄罗斯最具代表性的纪念建筑。

只是显示俄国人对物理学是多么的无知。他们将一个玻璃栏杆放置在拱顶上（它将开裂得更厉害），两端则是巴黎的石膏！当然石膏破裂，而玻璃完好无损。

莫斯科的灰尘在欧洲是最严重的，我还认为排水沟也是最肮脏的。我确实看到有人很舒适地躺在排水沟中。俄国人对于变革不假思索。任何事情都可以在一夜之间发生改变：街道名称、博物馆和建筑，如果街道由于某个凸出建筑而变得弯曲，那么这个凸出建筑就会被拆平，不管它是什么建筑。

他们买最好的机器，人们会怀疑他们从哪儿弄到钱。通过出口，全体人民都装备了工业化的思想。那就是他们的宗教，无需广告，无需推销员，但是人们可以看到宣传工业化的漂亮广告。

路过托尔斯泰故居，现在是纪念馆，但是没有时间进去，托尔斯泰伯爵夫人是一位中产阶级，但是他们让她住在博物馆中。

莫斯科的住房问题是尖锐的。城市只能容纳100万人，但是现在却有300万人，他们每周工作5天，每天五分之一的人口处在假期。人们缺乏礼貌，他们为任何事情在排队——烟草、食品，甚至为了去世。用于医治病人的医院很匮乏。

我在17号发电报给威利斯，但是19号才收到，是在我到达他公寓的1小时之后。

当我们抵达法国现代艺术美术馆之后（通过询问），时间已经将近4点钟，没有人愿意全天工作，更不用说加班了。因此管理员不让我们入内，争辩也无济于事。因此我们在保加利亚人的坚持下登上楼梯。那里的女士说法语，因此叫她们女士，以此来取悦她们。我在那里花了15分钟，但是我希望是15天。全世界的宝藏都在那儿！整展室的塞尚、凡·高、雷诺阿、马蒂斯、毕加索、高更的作品。世界上没有其他地方可以在一个美术馆内看到如此之多的大师作品。

参观了基督救世主教堂[348]（图228），它建造用来纪念战胜拿破仑对莫斯科的围困。它的外表采用白色大理石，非常简洁。我们爬到顶部，观看了莫斯科全景。在室内有一些精美的镶嵌大理石做工。

下午6:45在西伯利亚火车站乘坐跨西伯利亚火车。

---

348 基督救世主教堂（Cathedral of Christ the Savior）位于克里姆林宫外西南角，莫斯科河河畔。1812年为纪念打败拿破仑而建造，历经50年才建成。基督救世主教堂是莫斯科最宏伟的教堂，庄严而高雅。1931年12月5日，基督救世主教堂在反对宗教的狂热中被炸毁，以便建造50米高的、带有列宁雕像的苏维埃宫，可惜也同样没能实现。1995年1月7日在俄式圣诞节那天，大教堂开始重建，并于1997年9月莫斯科建城850周年前夕建成。

我向威利斯的妻子要了一些食物，但是忘了一条面包。当我们出来坐街车前往车站时，她在后面追赶我们，而且那半条面包确实非常好吃。

与一位年轻的苏俄共产党同坐一间包厢，他很英俊而且聪明，他知道俄国文学中所有的长名称，他给了我一些糖果，而我给了他一个橘子。

8月20日

8月21日 俄国人在维亚特卡[349]下车。

俄国人一般称呼公民或女公民。我的手表停了，而车站大钟在其正反面显示出不同的时间。车站时钟是莫斯科时间。

西伯利亚人显然不洗脸，也不洗他们的衬衣。

8月22日 农妇在车站内卖东西，但是她们沉默不语，而且看上去非常憔悴。她们站在那儿，一言不发，当然也没有人买东西。在这种沉默中，必定隐藏着某种巨大的苦难，然而她们比以往过得要好，因为没有人去鞭打她们。

8月23日 多云，山峦起伏的田野。

8月24日 路过伊尔库茨克[350]，看见后营，然后是贝加尔湖，原始风景，目前还没有被蒸汽船或旅馆所触及。现在是群山。

8月25日 傍晚7点路过赤塔。

8月26日 一大早起床看日出，看见带刺的铁丝网和战壕。早晨7:15到满洲里，进城并看见战争的废墟。

后来我发现应该在满洲里交验行李，或者在满洲里提交检查。因为我的行李被海关扣在满洲里达2天。

8月27日 早晨8:30到达哈尔滨。

---

349 维亚特卡（Viatka），俄罗斯的一个港口城市，含义是："生命之水"。维亚特卡是俄国和波兰的国酒伏特加的故乡。伏特加原文名为Vodka。

350 伊尔库茨克（Irkutsk）是伊尔库茨克州首府，1661年建城。位于贝加尔湖西66公里伊尔库特河入安加拉河河口处，被称为"西伯利亚的心脏"、"东方巴黎"、"西伯利亚的明珠"。

TOUR OF EUROPE

编者注：

　　Tour of Europe(旅欧日记)由童寯先生撰写于1930年5月至8月，时值他离美赴欧、参观考察建筑并绘制大量水彩画作品之际。由于每到一处行程匆匆，所需参观建筑内容很多，童寯先生既要绘画又需赶路，因此日记采用速记方式，字迹潦草且不易辨认，文中也会存有不少笔误、语句不顺、不通等问题，以及只有作者才知道的记号、符号，再加上日记本局部有所损坏，导致页面模糊、缺角断页等现象，读者如直接阅读会感到难于理解。

　　为了方便读者能够较好阅读并理解日记，编译者将日记由手写原稿（英文）转换成印刷体的辨识稿（英文）。在编译过程中，编译者采用如下方式处理日记中可能存在的一些问题。

　　1. 辨识稿文字力图遵照原稿处理，忠实反映日记原初状态。

　　2. 日记中所存有的由于速记所带来的词语省略，语句不顺、不通之处，以及在时态、语态等方面所存在的问题，辨识稿文字不作更动。

　　3. 日记中所存有明显的拼写错误，缺字笔误之处，编译者将根据自己理解力求忠于原文加以完善。

　　由于"旅欧日记"整理工作存有很大难度，再加上编译者学识和水平有限，错误之处在所难免，敬请读者指正。

Apr 26   Left New York on "Europa", 12:30 am.
Apr 27   Atlantic Ocean.
Apr 28   Atlantic Ocean.
Apr 29   Atlantic Ocean.
Apr 30   Atlantic Ocean. Man over Board.
May 1   Landing Southampton, 3 pm.

Southampton – a pleasant town and beautiful country road to Winchester (by bus). Many pedestrians and cyclists on main road. It was very picturesque.

Winchester – arrived after 3 and went into a store (Cusworth, 164~170 High Street), where old maids keep business. They let me leave my heavy Gladstone. So went directly to cathedral. First time saw cathedral of such size. Very enthused. Saw Tablet for Jane Austen & an antique black font. The transept is Norman. The columns in nave are [18] converted from Norman. Nowhere in the world is quieter than an English cathedral close. Birds sign & grass smelled so pleasantly. Made watercolor of west gate. Saw museum. Went to see Wolvesey Palace. A Norman keep. It reminds me of the "Old Summer Palace". The stream echoic quietly goes by.

Had dinner at God Begot, an old inn. Food not so bad but expensive (6s). Gladstone as heavy as a truck, and two arms were tired out, waited long time till 9:30 for train to Salisbury (changed at East Loogh). Arrive at Salisbury at 10:30. Taxi to Old George (2s) and stayed in Room 14. The George Chamber (17) is a double room where Samuel Pepys used to live. The proprietress is Jane Eger Tye. She said there is a room that has plenty of beams but I could have a room with just one beam for 6s.

Sound sleep.

May 2   Chamber maid knocked door

Fig1 On Europa   "欧罗巴"船上即景
Fig2 On Europa   "欧罗巴"船上即景
Fig3 On Europa   "欧罗巴"船上即景

Fig4 Gloucester Cathedral 格罗塞斯特大教堂

at 7:30 when I was asleep. After breakfast went to see cathedral. Beautiful interior, colorful because of black shafts. Good proportion & baroqurious most beautiful cloister. So peaceful. No sound but birds sing. Sketched north gate. Saw St. Thomas Church with wood beams & frescoes. Hall of John Halle is very fine wood timber front. Museum closed. Passed St. Anne's gate 3 times. Could not get into Bishop's palace. Saw outside of King's House. Beautiful gardens & houses everywhere. Delightful stream of Avon runs by the town with arched bridges. On the road to sarum one can see the cathedral at a distance and the meadows form a good cushion for the edifice.

Went to Stonehenge by 7 am. [**19**]

Because the bus company could not find other people going, costs 16s. On the way saw Oliver Lodge's houses. Not interesting, rather off the road & small. The

Fig5 Salisbury North Gate 索尔兹伯里北门

Stonehenge looks much smaller than I imagined. On way back saw abbey church (Amesbury), not interesting at all.

Ate lunch & supper (with cold) at same place near St. Thomas Church. Took trains to Bath at 7:20, arrived 8:40, stayed at Argyll's opposite station. Took a stroll on Stall street. Town more Italian Renaissance than Gothic.

More cyclists in England. Half of them are women. It's a small town, like Salisbury. Windows dressing is quite as good as New York Gimbels. Women are smartly dressed too. Food not so good for its price.

On the mantle piece in my room at Argyll's, there is pictures of the P. of W. The duke of York & the duchess and probably are actress.

May 3 Breakfast at 8. The best ham & egg I ever tested at this Argyll hotel at

Fig6 Salisbury, Street View 索尔兹伯里，街景

Bath. Bus to Wells. Saw cathedral. Between Bath & Wells, nothing on the road is worth look at. Every house is modern looking & cheap. Some old houses are not interesting either. English is the best place for gothic. I don't like Bath, because it is too classic (Italian). Wells is better—at least the houses around the cathedral are very gothic and picturesque. Saw the Dean's eye, the Bishop's eye, the Penniless Porch, and Brown's gate. The Bishop's palace is not open in the morning of Saturday. I could not stay till 3 pm, so I had to be satisfied with peeping them a chink above the gate. The draw angle and the mood are just [20] as mediaeval as they ever were. Such a peaceful & beautiful ground, with little children playing, and ducks swimming in water. The palace ground is strongly fortified with a long wall with portholes. The cloister has no open arcades, all the arches are succeed with stone tracery. One cypress stands in the middle of the cloister. The Chapel House has a wonderful fair ceiling above the crypt, reached from the cathedral.

Fig7 Salisbury, Cathedral 索尔兹伯里大教堂

    The interior of the cathedral is quite horizontal, Saw St. Andrews cross X under tower. The golden windows (East End) have such beautiful glass as I ever yet saw. It is a marvelous picture, which I could have painted it. Went down to the crypt, saw several stone coffins, it smells earth. Went up through a delightful stone stair to Chapel House.

    Went up to tower and viewed whole town. Carved my initials & 1930 near the entrance door on lead roof. Also carved initials on wood door. It's top is reached by a small circular staircase of stone, well lighted with small windows.

    The Dining Hall in Vicars Close is very fine, with wonderfully presented wood work & manuscript. Ceiling is very good, with wood crude tracery & plaster. The pewter pieces were gain by Crownwell. Saw Chapel House at the end of the Vicar's Close, very wonderful wood screen on 1st floor & beautiful ceiling on second floor, reached by a stone staircase move out in some steps.

    The mayfair is in town. Rather noisy near the cathedral, a lively place now. Had lunch near Brood Street.

    Back to Bath by 4 o'clock. Saw Roman Bath. In the museum there is a model showing the rectangular & circular baths. The great pump room has [21] very bad classic style. Had a glass of mineral water. Then bought a ticket (4s) for a bath in the Sulis. Had a wonderful hot bath in the tub, and after 15 minutes the man came with hot towel & sheets & rap me up. First like Emperor Claudius in his Toga, then like an Egyptian mummy lying on the bed. Lying for 15 minutes and then up to get dressed. Sat a while in the cool room.

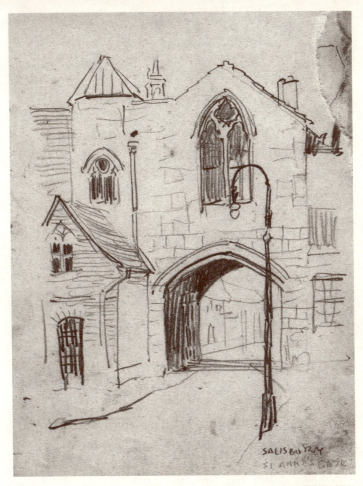

Fig8 Salisbury, St. Anne Gate 索尔兹伯里圣安尼门

Before I took the train went through Victoria Park to see the Circus & the Crescent. Both in Renaissance Style. But somewhat gothic roof & chimneys. Almost lost my way back to Midland station.

Train for Gloucester. Stayed at Midland Royal Hotel. B & B for 8s. Had ham & eggs for supper.

English tea is abominable yet very boring drinks it, as an institution.

May 4 Breakfast at 8. Saw inside of cathedral at 10. Enormous pink Norman columns in nave, gothic ceiling, very fine by decorated ceiling in choir. Wonderful window at E. end. Sunday service prevented me from going into the choir & up to the whispering gallery. Also the cloister was closed. Saw procession of clergy men. Some

Fig9 Wells Cathedral 威尔士大教堂

are mere boys clad in red with white collar & a white jacket over it. The top of the tower (supported underneath in crossing by flying arches) has five tracery like lace, very ornate in general. Outside. S. porch very fine with wood Norman gate. Some Norman arches are seen outside. Had no idea about cloister until saw photograph.

St. Mary de Lode is not worth seeing. [22]

Several old houses are interesting, like the one in which Bishop Hooper stayed in night before martyrdom. The new inn is quite old, and I made a good pencil sketch of it, just while it was raining, standing under a store entrance. Made several miles of walking, but saw nothing interesting. The plan of the town is like Chinese (Roman), streets & gates are named by the compass. The Royal Hotel is very bad for its price. Food is not good either, 8s B.B.

Arrived at B'way by train at 6 pm.

From the G.W. Station to Broadway (the village) the distance is a mile, and I almost despaired to carry the 50# Gladstone. Had to make many stops before I got to the "Swan", exhausted & perspiring. The "Swan" was filled. So I had to go to the Lygon Arms, & what a great pleasant surprise! Such beautiful rooms & everything is clear & so tastefully arranged. It is the best hotel I ever saw.

Made a trip through B'way about 2 miles & half long. Saw nothing worth- while to photo or to sketch. I think the best is in the Lygon Arms. Had dinner at 7:30 in the great dinning hall. Full of fashionable people. The hall is a masterpiece. The hostess in the dinning room is a beauty. She reminds me of K's statue only a trifle stoute. She suggested wine and I took cider, very very good, and she poured it out for me. The dinner is good too (6/s). Made 2 sketches in Dinning Room.

Shown into the Cromwell Room & Charles or [**23**] Oak Room (Charles I).

Both are so old, and very charming indeed. Saw chairs Cromwell sat in. The Lygon Arms has a huge backyard for garage. Had a hot bath. It is indeed a pleasure to stay in such a place, no matter how much it costs. Because it is worth it. All my disgust was long walking with a heavy bag, and over the long train of autos was over, after such pleasant surprise. The guide book says many Americans stay here. I haven't met one. But, the air here may be American. (The number of automobiles & people in street).

There are only 2 B'ways in the world, and they are full of Americans. Just recalled a thing I did at Gloucester.

Went to Police Station to find out whether I needed registration. After 20 minutes they found out if I stay under 2

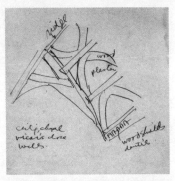

Fig10 Chapel Ceiling, Vicars Close
　　维卡胡同小教堂顶棚
Fig11 Cloister, Salisbury　索尔兹伯里大教堂庭院
Fig12 English Tea Thing　英国茶具

months, I don't have to register. But if over 2 months, it would be necessary.

The man at B'way station smelled liquor. No wander he took half an hour to find out train schedule for Stratford on-Avon.

May 5 Did some sketches in the morning. Had breakfast at 9. At the same table as I took my dinner. Left hotel (bill 1-2-7). Took bus to G.W. Station for Stratford on-Avon. Arrived at 12 o'clock. Stayed at "White Swan".

Saw Shakespeare's birth place, I was thrilled. Saw Scotts & Carlyles names on window on 2nd floor where the poet was born. Took lunch at Judith Shakespeare's House. [24]

Saw "new place" & a wonderful garden with flowers sent by the King Duncan & the Prince of Wales. Saw old well & foundation of part of old house.

Went to see school in which Shakespeare studied, the beam is like chinese 金. Saw Church of Holy Trinity, where Shakespeare was buried near the altar. Then took a long walk to Shottery & had a devil's time in locating Anne Hathaway's cottage. Saw the best bed & line, also the wood bench by the fire place on which Shakespeare did courting. Of course, Anne's parents sat on either side of the fire. The new memorial building is not up yet. Did not go into the library. Saw Avon.

This is the best place I have yet enjoyed seeing. There are not many things but they are so precious. Had dinner at the hotel.

And some man dress for meal. Some old Victorian ladies are simply grotesque.

Saw "Macbeth" tonight and liked the scenery.

Lady Macbeth is outshined by her husband. Bed at 12.

The "Red House Hotel" is a terrible looking place but Washington loving stayed there!

May 6 After breakfast, tried to take 10 am Bus to Warwick, but there was none. Back to hotel to write. Rainy all day.

Took 11:30 bus to Warwick, could not see the town well on account of rain. Just saw the East gate (on which stands the library) & the outside of the church of St. Mary's. Saw part of the interior of the castle. Rooms are enormous & beautifully furnished, many Rubens & van Dykes. Walked to Italian garden, saw a peacock standing in the rain & the Grecian vase in the pavilion. [25] Ject both soaked.

Could not sketch or take photo.

Went on to Kenilworth, in the bus met a handsome old gentleman who has been in Hanchow. He lives at Kenilworth.

The castle at Kenilworth is in ruins and reminds one much of the old Summer Palace in Peking. As it is rainy, there is no splendor falling on the walls. Just took one photo: The great lake as shown on plan (restored) was drained in Crownwell's time. The whole thing must look beautiful in fine weather.

Took "tea", opposite. It is a mile's walk from Kenilworth to the castle, I came back too early & had to sit in the post office to wait for bus. But when I did come out , still thinking it was early, the bus was already running along. Jumped in all right. Back to Stratford on Avon again. This could have been avoided if I had known, to take a train to Oxford right from Warwick to save time & money.

Had ham & eggs in an inn. First time had coffee in England. Took 7:45 train to Oxford, arrived at 9:30.

Fig13 Broadway 百老汇

Nothing enrage me more than to carry a 50# baggage for 2 miles & than find the hotel (mitre) full. Carried the burden still further on & stopped at "East Gate". The place is very gloomy. Rather disappointing.

Feet soaked wet so took a hot bath.

May 7 After breakfast went out seeing, different college. Saw Dr. Johnson's room first. It is [**26**] on the 2nd floor near the gate to Pembroke college. A small sitting room with small fine place, and a very little bedroom. The upper (3rd) story was added later.

Saw great tower, feel on top of tower Christ Church, most of the colleges have quadrangles bare cold & lonely. It undoubtedly has the appearance of age. Some students wear gowns, in most cases mere rags, at new college the wall (like chinese wall) remains, with gate & entitlements. Most of the college is gothic except Queens which is classic, and of cause the Camera.

Finishing sightseeing at 2 pm. Then made 2 water colors & 4 pencil sketches in the afternoon.

Getting myself familiarized with London, by an 1898 edition Baedeker.

English food is expensive and not good. The only course they can made well is fish.

May 8 Took train to Windsor after breakfast. Did not arrive till 12. Castle not open, but saw some interesting timber houses and the North Terrace, & back of Queen's apartment, also saw interior of chapel.

Went to Eton, saw old schools with old desks & flogging apartments (2 steps). Names carved on all places—panels, desks even rail. Saw chapel. In here the uncomfortable wood benches are called knife board by the boys. Saw boys in top hats & also in sporting clothes. The dry boys play circlet, the wet boys play swimming.

Saw an old house (500 years) called cock list at Eton, took tea there, very good hot rolls with jaw. The Queen (Mary) come there often & [27] signed her name once (I did not see it). So I signed more (Asked to do so). Went up stairs to see old rooms, very interesting, like Shakespeare's birthplace. There is another one in Canterbury. Behind the house is the pit where people fought cocks till 50 years ago. The floor is paved with pig's knuckles.

Outside the house on the facade, there are 2 wood figures. Corner window, also on the side walk there are those foot lockers made of wood.

Arrived at London Pattingdon station at 5:30. Took bus to Regent street, but could not get into Regent Palace, nor could I get into YMCA. Finally walked to Grafton & got a room B&B, 8s. Took a bath.

Saw Tussaud's wax work. But too late to see chambers of horrors.

Had a very good steak at the hotel.

London is a big place. In those small towns, I always walk beyond a place, now in London, I never walked far enough to get near. It is a good place if I can take the right bus.

Got films deposited at a Kodak shop at Regent St.

May 9 After breakfast went to cook finding out about near Siberian Rd. open & safe. Went to Regent Street comes place measured for a black suit 8£. Saw outside of St. James Palace, outside of St. Paul, Royal exchange and Westminster. Tonight again went to Tussauds place to see chamber of

Fig14 Stonehenge 石环阵

horrors. But the important [28] I did today was to the British museum, from 1 to 4, and finished seeing everything. Bought post cards for Elgin watches & some Chinese painting in pins. Rather a thrill to see so many precious original things like the oldest paper in the world (Chinese discovered at Tung Huang), auto graphs of famous man & sculpture but not costs. Saw Hyde park and Epstein's sculpture. Also the artillery monuments.

May 10 Gray sky but with sunshine in the morning. Then it gradually became cloudy until it started to rain at 5 pm, till evening.

Westminster, service at 10. Went to see parliament. Saw the king's Robing Room, with carvings (wood) of English history and some painting on wall. It has the throne & opposite is the fire places. The Royal gallery has 2 long paintings, one representing Trafalgar (Nelson's death) & the other Waterloo. I believe it was in this room that King George had his speech before the naval conference.

The House of Lords has beautiful color scheme—red leathered benches with light steaming through high window. But the House of Commons looks very drab, plain & cold. The Lords is about the most colorful rooms, all these rooms have heroic proportions and very well lighted. Some rooms on account of high windows look very theatrical, with plenty shading & few high lights.

The thing I was interested most in was of course the Poets' Corner, [29] never surfeited Longfellow's bust there. The whole abbey is just full of busts, tablets and statues. The proportion of the nave is very pleasing, because of its great high and length. Beautiful light effect from windows. The cloister has very warm color ceiling & cold tracery facing the court, on account of light. There is another delightful little Italian courtyard with fountain, just beyond the cloister. Made a watercolor of the cloister passage.

Saw these two buildings in 2 1/2 hours.

Took a photo of Epstein's statue, at the underground tread office.

Took bus to Windsor. Entered the castle at quarter to 3. Saw the state apartments, most of the rooms are used for the entertainment of state visitors. Every room is beautiful & tasteful layouts, mere photograph don't give the color effect. Those high ceilings and tall rooms, and every door open to an interesting world. The Rubens room & van Dyke room. A room has several Holbeins. The arrangement of pictures & furniture is perfect. 3 painted ceilings-same subject (The book of Esther). Other rooms have beautiful paneled ceiling. Most of the furniture is French and some rooms are Louis 15. The banquet hall is enormous, and it must be a colorful affair during a state dinner, when serving persons stand in their places as guarding theirs.

There are too many visitors and one woman just to [30] show her wonderful sense of touch felt the blue velvet chain cushion with her glove on.

Went up to the round tower saw whole Gr. Windsor.

Went into the Queen's Dolls' House. But it is entirely unnecessary to go into, merely wasting time.

The best way to see the House of Parliament, Westminster abbey & Windsor is on Saturday, like the way I did today.

First time ate supper at Lyons today for 11D.

Took bus 18 to Holborn to see old house. In the bus a baby got "pipied" and the conductor had to stop the car to borrow some sand from the road builder to cover it up. Made a sketched of the old house. Then went to see old curiosity shop– 14 Portsmouth St. Walked along Hut St. in the rain, and then saw the Temple, also walked around Lincoln's Inn & park. But never could locate the actual building of Lincoln's Inn.

On my way back to the hotel, stopped at a night fair near Eastern Road-in the slum-and bought 2 oranges for 3D.

May 11   Saw Tower Bridge and outside of London Tower.

The Nation Gallery contain a good collection of Italian masters. The Dutch, Flemish, French schools are fairly represented, Spanish is scanty, German not many. British School of course is richly collected. The portrait gallery is not worth seeing.

The Tate gallery is very good. The arrangement of sculpture & painting in one big hall, with tasteful wall paper, is very effective. Usually you see a vista of doors [31] and the plan is such that you would see everything. The largest collections of Turner & Sargent I ever saw. Down stairs there is an exhibition of Jugoslav art. Bought a photo of a sculpture. Made a sketch of Bridge & Westminster at dark.

May 12   Made a sketch of the "old curiosity shop " went in to see the shop. Saw two bus full of tourists came by, stopped for a second and never came down to see the inside. Really there is nothing inside except cheap but expensive souvenirs. The neighboring shop is a tailor's.

Saw interior of St. Pauls. In the crypt there are the tombs of Nelson & Wellington. Then went up to the whispering gallery. Also went up to the very top by circular stairs & ladder. From the golden hall through a hole on the floor, one can see the ground floor of the chamber with mosaic clearly shown of course from the top (above 300 ft), one can see whole London, in a very dreamy character, one has to get permission to sketch from Dean Luge! The cost is 2£, I made only one sketch of the side aisle.

Want to see the London Tower, the Bloody Tower is where many murders were done. Where Raleigh was imprisoned and married, where Richard III murdered the 2 princes whose bodies were found at the foot of the stone winding stair. Upstairs is their chamber, with window (through which moon beam was said to have streamed in) was blocked. So was the door through [32] which the assassin entered.

The walls are full of inscriptions & carvings, all of which are so artistic.

The Beauchamp Tower is a small prison chamber with prisoner's names on walls.

The White Tower is the London Tower proper, now full of armors. The chapel upstairs is a good & simple place, in Norman style. The Jewel Tower has all the crowns & staffs.

They are drilling army now on the Tower ground.

Had lunch at the Tower waiting room.

Took subway to Hammersmith & then took Train #7 to Hampton court, the train gets there in one good hour.

The State apartments are much inferior to Windsor ⋯

Shine much but it did shine the effect is very grand. Lost in the maze for

Fig15 Prisons, Edinburgh 爱丁堡监狱

several times, got into the center & came out successfully at last. It helps me to know the definitation—a maze, you can be lost in. But a labyrinth you go into & came out again without mistake or difficulty. The wine cellar & kitchen are not worth seeing.

Saw show "apple cart" tonight at Lyceum. The king is not as good as Tom Powers in New York, nor Orinthia. But the prime minister is better. [**33**]

···15 Cambridge at 5 pm. A town is not so picturesque as Oxford. But the river can runs along the colleges and with picturesque bridges thrown cross makes an interesting scenery. What a blessing to those Cambridge students who can just lie in the grassy bank and talk about the stars.

There are many colleges at Cambridge, some having the same name as Oxford. The plan of the schools are alike too. The cloister plan, with a chapel attached, most of the colleges are Wren. There is more Renaissance than gothic, like Oxford.

Stayed at Garden House Hotel near the water with a large garden, facing which the sitting room stands. A good dinner too. Have a small single room (access) facing a grassy meadow with a murmuring steam.

May 16 Row boat before breakfast. Saw various colleges after breakfast and the museum, which contains Raphael's 7 cartoons and Augustus John's portraits of Hardy & Show.

Cambridge is much quieter than Oxford, and the students have a better chance of studying nature—stream & meadow. It is an ideal university town.

Saw several Chinese students there, at Ely in afternoon, and got to Lincoln rather late, went up hill to see the cathedral. But before the train reached station, a fine view (misty like a dream castle) of the cathedral can be obtained. The cathedral stands on [34] the hill, which makes it more wonderful. Stayed at an old and dirty place, gas light & hot water bottle in bed.

Before going to Lincoln, stopped at Ely between 1 and 6, to see the cathedral, the cathedral has a funny lantern at crossing, sort of a gothic dome. The interior is mostly Norman. Made a sepia rending of Nave, nothing else can be of interest at Ely.

May 17 A very fine morning. Saw the Roman Arch, after breakfast visited the castle, which has only a gate and wall (The other bridges don't look castle-like).

The cathedral has nothing distinguished, I climbed up the tower. The close is too small, and a narrow road divides the cathedral and the houses. The cathedral tower is being repaired.

Saw the Jews House and some other local things of litter interest. Shop windows even display modern furniture.

Arrived at York at 2 pm. Walked outside the wall till I reached the castle, which has only the Clifton Tower open.

The cathedral of York is the best of all. The spacious nave, the wonderful glass, and the lofts ceiling (though painted wood). The chapter house has no central, column and the glass is beautiful. Climbed up tower again, and carved BM, K. M. & C.T. at the battlement opening marked below. [35]

The "five sisters" window are the best I have seen. The whole church is good, outside towers are beautiful too.

City walls are in perfect condition. I walked part of it, sketched gate. St. Mary's Abbey is picturesque. The museum there is not good. Shambles is a very picturesque lane, with butcher shop's on each side. It started to rain in the evening, made a watercolor in the rain, made 7 sketches today.

Arrived at Durham at 10 pm. Saw the cathedral at the hill. No train is going to Edinburgh tomorrow, till 11 at night, so have to go by bus.

May 18 Visited the Durham cathedral, very good towers, outside most of the windows are Norman. The interior is almost entirely Norman, with massive pillars

& barrel vaults. The church is well heated, did not try to see the chapter house & monks' kitchen.

Saw the old city wall near water gate.

It is very imposing the way the cathedral and the castle stand on the hill.

The castle is closed on Sunday, it is a students' dormitory.

Went to Edinburgh by bus. The castle standing on the hill appeals to any ones' imagination, some houses near High Street are 10 or 11 stories high.

Princes Street is very imposing. The monument of Scot, in Gothic, is not good. [36]

May 19 The Edinburgh castle looked from distance, is something that is highly imaginative. But after you get up there and look down, there is no dream or romance at all. A man that is worshipped must be worshipped at a distance, and there is no hero in any household.

The war memorial is new. The other towers are of little interest. The whole castle stand on a solid rock, with one side sloping and other three going straight down to lower level.

Nothing is of particular interest at St. Giles and the Parliament. The University is a cold classic structure with a square court and looks dirty & old. The palace is not open. The Scots' monuments not worth climbing up.

Did much walking but little sketching. The city is too big. Took "Night Scotsman" back to London.

May 20 Canterbury in evening, too late to see things.

May 21 Went to see cathedral early morning. The outside is good but ordinary, with apse. But the inside is wonderful, especially the ceiling over the crossing, made by four spring up from pillars & so clearly decorated with red & blue sparingly by used that the whole effect looks very modern in spirit. The glasses are very colorful. In fact the whole thing has no fault to be found, nothing unusual in the cloister.

The nave is long enough but the choir is equally long, so the cathedral is cut into halves at the choir screen. The plan is almost like 3 crosses, counting the chapels at the apsidal end. St. Augustine [37] , stone chair stands in the apse.

The west gate is interesting, so are the other gates outside the cathedral, could have stayed at this place longer to make more sketches. The streets are much less commercial and houses are very picturesque.

Bakers Temperance is cheap & very good.

The boat crossing the channel is small & I was almost seasick, train from Calais to Paris is fine. The first French I spoke was at the Gard du Nord, asking for baggage.

Paris is just another city, but I think the wide avenue of Champs Elysees & other public monuments save it. If it does not have anything else, it should have some beautiful woman.

May 22

May 23 Museum Cluny, full of old junk. Did not miss 2 chastity belts.

Museum Carnavalet is full of junk, some models of old Paris is interesting.

The most interesting of all is Notre Dame. No English cathedral can hold candle with it. The very mister interior with beautiful glass gives you worlds of thrill, far the best I ever saw.

Saint Chapelle has a rich and wonderful interior, with beautiful glass. It is just a little jem, gold & red & blue, posed together by light. The first floor is not good.

May 24   Sacre Coeur stands high on a hill at Montmartre. It takes labor to climb. Built entirely of white granite. The interior is not wonderful. It is too bright. [**38**]

It took one hour to get to the top of Tower Eiffel and come down again. The service is slow. But when you do get on top, you get a marvelous view of Paris. Everything can be clearly read, especially the garden plots, just like a Grand Prix de Rome. You see whole Paris like a basket of flowers. The river Seine gives a green color, with white bridges thrown across so many times.

Tombean de Napoleon has a beautiful interior, especially at the altar where there are brown glass windows which throw in golden hue onto green marble shafts, very wonderful. Went down to see Napoleon's tomb.

Rodin museum has a delightful garden (where the thinker is) and a chapel, it has same castles too.

The Grand Palais has a salon of 1930 and the exposition of decoration arts, very good, modern interiors, saw salon of painting & sculpture. Took much for 3 hours.

The interior of Madeleine is very mystic, as the whole church is lighted from 3 little lights from the domed ceiling. The best classic interior of a church I have seen, with the exception of St. Paul at London.

May 25   The Louver has so much but I have passed them most of it and the only thing of interest are Mona Lisa, the Venus de Milo and the Wing les Victory.

Luxembourg museum has Bourdelle's archer.

Versailles is not a good place for rainy day, as the [**39**] garden has no walks and trees don't shelter very much. After seeing the interior (starting from garc Invalide trolley), we walked in the woods to find Les Trianons. Found both and feet wet, very disgusting afternoon.

May 26   Went to see Charters. It has beautiful glasses, but the effect is rather monotonous. It does not have the picturesque quality & mystic character of North Dame. But everybody like Charters. I prefer Notre Dame. Saw the small town by walking, only spent 3 hours there.

May 27   Saw church St. Étienne du Mont. It has scrolled façade and interesting interior, with circular stars going up columns, to balcony around ambulatory (inner) & across front between choir & nave.

Pantheon has tombs of Zola, Rousseau, Voltaire in the crypt. On the 1st floor the murals are very good, mounted to top (dome).

Rue Mallet-Stevens is a new development on the boundary of Paris. First time saw modern exterior. It has bright colors some where quite interesting.

May 28   Up at 6 to catch the train at Gare St. Lazare for Rouen, got to cathedral at 10. The "Butter Tower" is very good indeed. But central tower with iron spine is bad. The interior is common as any English cathedral. Saw St. Maclon, wood carved doors are beautiful. Also saw St. Ouen, has a good tower like the "Butter Tower". Both are very good, saw tower of Joan d'Arc.

Took noon time train from Gare du Nord to Amiens, arrived there at 4:30. [**40**] Saw cathedral at once and made a sketch of interior. Also sketched outside. The cathedral has the most beautiful façade I ever saw. The 3 portals have deep reveal. But inside the height of church nave and width deserve a much longer nave. Made a tour through ambulatory & saw the "Weeping Angel", made a tour the town in evening, stayed at "select" on Place René Goblet, very reasonable & clean place.

May 29 Took 9 o'clock train to Reims, got there by 12. Took lunch and saw cathedral by 1 o'clock. The most wonderful façade I have ever seen. It is a gem, save what like Amiens but façade has more color and very much softened and aged and looked just to be picturesque enough. The inside is still being repaired. All the five glasses are same except central Rose above entrance on façade side. The choir now is temporary at the end of nave. The ambulatory is walled off for repairs.

I like the façade so much that I went back to it 4 times to look at it, to worship its beauty, combine the interior of Notre Dame with the exterior of Reims and you have the best cathedral in the world.

Saw new battle monument, very good.

Reims cathedral has one advantage I know and that is, its façade is facing a fairly wide avenue, where you can see it from a far.

Back to Paris evening.

May 30 Saw Museum Grevin, just like London wax works. Wented on tower of Notre Dame in rain, saw all the grotesque [**41**] look at the Rose windows inside again. They are wonderful.

Went to see Theatre Pigalle tonight, wonderful interiors. The façade is not good. The inside (theatre proper) has a red –black-silver scheme, ceiling white plastic, slightly painted & moulded. Red chair is with silver piped bars, balconies all fluted wood painted dark red. The foyer and hall are very German. In the basement there are shops & dinning, show windows and a modern picture gallery. In the vestibule(ticket place), there is a model of interior with seats numbered, so a patron can see where he is going to sit.

May 31 Went to Gare du Nord took 9:40 train for Bruxcelles, but the so called expressed, which stopped at every place never got there until 4 o'clock in the afternoon. The Belgium customs are literal but they demanded visa and I had none. The gendarme finally asked for 30 F for a piece of paper which is called visa.

Explored Bruxcelles a little. Saw Palais de Justice, but did not see the Royal Palace which must be hidden in the woods. Tried to find Stoclet House designed by Josef Hoffman, but nobody know where it is.

Took 5-47 train for Bruges, at a banana & 2 cakes for lunch and 3 bananas, one orange and 3 cake for supper. Hungry at 10, so drank cup of OXO and ate another cake.

Stayed at Hotel Hubert, 25 F for room, wonderful.

Walked around the canals, saw many interesting houses. Saw cathedral built of brick, a very complicated tower. Inside most of stone work is painted. Rather interesting, many paintins, some hung right [**42**] over gothic moulds or tracery. Another instance of painted stone is the ambulatory of Reims, which is being repaired and still closed to public.

Most of the gable are stepped, saw several men & women wear wooden shoes, a day without any sketching.

June 1 The Belgians are up early on Sunday. Tramways and auto work before 7. Postman distributes letters at 7 am. So all some shops & cafés open. You hear hardsoles beat on the pavement.

It kept raining all morning, so sat in a café and made a watercolor of bell tower, also 2 pencil sketches of square, order Munich bear but only drank half glass. As rain did not stop, went on the canal to sketch a bridge & then the Ponte de Canal, in front of which is a steel bridge pivoted at mid stream. Lunched at hotel for 20 F, good food.

Took 1 o'clock train for Bruxcelles, arrived there at 2:30, went by bus to Station Midi to take baggage in Nord. Took 3-42 train to Antwerp, arrived there by 4:30, stayed at Hotel de Handers. 50 F for a dwell room. The towns is crowed with visitors, as the exposition is on.

Went by to exposition, of cause everything is wooden, and very good in execution. It far excels the Philadelphia sesqui-centennial, both in design and workmanship. and the ground & number of buildings are much larger than Philadelphia. I arrived there by 6, and all buildings are closed. So have to go there tomorrow to see inside.

Made a sketch of Hotel de Ville and Cathedral. The river is full of steamboats. Just saw one sailing yacht, did not see any sailing fishing boat at all. [**43**]

A mineral hotel is expensive, 40 F.

June 2 Up at 7, out. Beautiful morning but could not find any subject to sketch. Just walked around, finally did the cathedral spire again. (one last night) Had 4 cake & chocolate for breakfast at 9:30.

Went to exposition again at 10. France Building is open, some modern interior, and fashion shows. Other buildings are not worth looking in, mostly machine products, and marine. The Flemish art Building is not get open, walked on the ground & took photos.

Ate 4 cakes & chocolate again for lunch near station, after seeing the Museum Plantin and having made a

Fig16 Cologne, Exposition Ground 科隆展览会场

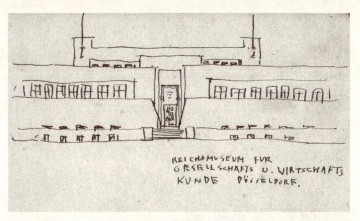

Fig17 Reichsmuseum Für Gesellschafts u. Wirtschafts, Kunde, Düsseldorf
杜塞尔多夫社会与家庭客户皇家 ftqn 博物馆

sketch of the court (very bad sketch). Took 21 train for Rotterdam, arrive at 4.

Rotterdam is a bigger city than I imagined. It has wide streets but no place is picturesque enough to sketch. Along the canals stand matter of fact houses, and no sailing or fishing boats, all steamers (detestable). Finally after walking a long way to look for hotel I chanced to see a windmill standing right in the street. Made a sketch of it and had a large audience. Walked too long & lost my way. By sheer luck found my way back near station. Ate dinner in a restaurant on the boulevard for 2.8 (80 ₡). Then walked to Hotel Europe, very good place & cheap, B& B for 3.5g.

Did not see much modern architecture later. Saw a modern theatre & went there to see a movie tonight (by the way [**44**] a story about London crooks. The theater is nice, ceiling has long parallel lights & could lights with red & blue lights which shine by turns.

June 3 Spent too much time at Rotterdam and saw nothing there. I should have come here (Amsterdam) last night, so as to have whole day here. But instead took train from Rotterdam at 9:30, and got there by 11, stayed at Hotel De Bijenkorf. B & B for 3 guilder. Had lunch in their restaurant & the portions are enormous. Dutch cook make good soup, bought 3 modern books here at Kosmos.

Between Rotterdam and Amsterdam there are many modern buildings & windmills. Everywhere one is struck with the flatness of the country, a typical country sight would be. An avenue of slender trees and a wind mill.

Saw real old Dutch town & villages, with costumed people and narrow streets of 3 feet wide. The places are from Amsterdam to Tolhuus by boat then train to Edam, Volendam, steam boat to island Marken, again stream boat to Brock (Where cheese is made). First time in my life sketched sail boats at Volendam—a thrill. Men wear ear rings and small boys under 5 are dressed like girls, with the mark of a star on the top of the cap. People wear sabots (wood) and leave them outside the door. Women wear lace caps and generally blue dress with a light colored apron. The scenery is very picturesque.

Fig18 Reichsmuseum, Düsseldorf 杜塞尔多夫皇家博物馆

Saw many new building in south suburb of Amsterdam, [**45**] everyone is good. Brick work is exquisite. All wood doors are well designed. A modern church but could not see interior. Even the post boxes on the street are modern in design.

Bought 2 handkerchief at market. In the market, there is a village of six houses.

Caught a glimpse of office life at Amsterdam while in Kosmos. "These are 2 executors & 3 girls (typists). They all have lunch in the office, about 12 o'clock."

In Amsterdam, almost every house has a pulley over the dormer for lifting furniture.

June 4 Took 7:33 train for Cologne, arrived at 12. Walked along some busy streets and made a sketch of the bridge. Saw cathedral as soon as I got off station.

June 5 Went up to church tower. Saw Rome model in exposition remains, across the Rhine.

The cathedral of Cologne is the one finished gothic church. It is quite high and scale looks forced. There is no high choir screen to hide view. Only one window has old glass, the one directly behind the choir.

The silhouette of Cologne along the Rhine at night is something marvelous, though the outline is harsh.

Very black silhouette with light ray & white band of water below. It is very romantic.

June 6 Trip to Düsseldorf. It has modern buildings before the war. Saw a tall office building (WM Mark's House), I went up to tower. It has a lobby of brick, with running elevation cars. The tower gives view of city. Fine brick work.

Went to exposition ground. Saw Prof. Kreis' Planetarium, and art [**46**] galleries. The Planetarium was not open today. Saw the galleries with recent collections, not much of interest.

Düsseldorf is a city worth seeing, as it has some of the best modern buildings in Europe.

June 7 Took photos at old exposition ground and then went to see Stadt und land aus Langen. The exposition contains a large number of photos of modern architecture in the districts around Cologne, like Kalkfeld, Bickdorf and Zollstuck, most of the photos are very good. So also is the architecture, this induces me to go to Bickendorf and saw most of the architecture with my own eyes. Took a large amount of photos too.

Took trolley to Kalk, but did not see anything striking there. Walked from bridge to university and Hinderburg Park. Rode back to see Rathaus.

While at the old exposition ground, this morning, went into the copper church. The inside is all steel & glass with wooden pews. The stair glass is good, concrete roof, behind the altar is the crucifixion with Christ in plate copper. The pulpit stands right in front of the crucifixion.

Also saw a modern church at Bickendorf. The outside is concrete, with pointed arches & a tower. Interior is plaster and red brick hands, very bright. The church has a niche with a cross hang on it, while the white wall is flooded with colored lights through stained glass. The effect is wonderful. There are small chapels on each side of the church & confession [**47**] booths, at the back is balcony.

June 8 Arrived at Bonn from Cologne at 9. Saw Beethoven House, museum and attic where Beethoven was born. Low ceiling (beamed) and old floor. Museum contain Beethoven's letters & manuscripts, violins and his ear trumpets, numerous portraits and busts. Only second to Stratford on Avon in its inspiring atmosphere. The courtyard is nice and has Beethoven's statue, but photo & sketch are forbidden.

Saw Bonn University and took trolley ride through Coblenz strasse. Walked back on bank of Rhine. Had lunch and then saw minister. The inside is very colorful & mystic. Beautiful cloister, where I made a sketch. Also sketched Beethoven's House outside.

Took boat from Bonn to Koblenz. The most beautiful ride I knew. The scenery on the bank is superb, especially when the moon rises and distant spires and castle walls are in dreamy colors. The moon casts its reflection on water, a sailing boat or two purple clouds, blue mountains, black trees, orange water. Saw the Seven Mountains in detail in the afternoon. Never saw such perfect composition of scenes before. Saw many places when I wish I could stop and sketch.

June9 Up at 8. Breakfast at 9. Out to see Kaiser Wilhelms monument, which stands at the corner of the delta where Mosel meets Rhine. There you see different colored water. Mosel being bluish while Rhine is [**48**] yellow. The monument is very baroque and details ugly. But it commands such a fine position and it looks beautiful in silhouette at night and from the air in day time.

The Kastor Kirche is an ordinary Romanesque building. A long walk along more leads to the head of the bridge, where there are some interesting old houses to sketch. Also there stands an old timber house at the intersection of Lohr Str. and Alter Graber Str. The timber has its surface chopped to give texture.

The schloss is ordinary and the museum (including state apartments) are not worth seeing much.

There is a new modern apartment near the Haupt Bahnhof.

Today is a general holiday and all shops are closed.

Left for Mainz at 2:40 by boat. This ride is even more wonderful than yesterday's, as castle after castle rises above hill tops as you sail on. Everyone is a picturesque masterpiece. It brought you back right to the light day period.

Fig19 Bonn 波恩
Fig20 Bonn 波恩

Fig21 Coblenz 科布伦茨

1st castle to be seen is Marksburg, the most sketchable thing I ever saw.

There the twin castle or "2 brothers", Sterenberg and Liebenstein also the "Maus" & Reichenburg.

The Loreley rock is not picturesque, but is historically rich.

The "Caub" is the most picturesque house standing on the water.

After the Caub there are many more ruined [49] castles but not so favorably placed. It is because one has seen the best that one does not care after "Caub". Then the bank become suddenly flat and you see woods & country houses all along, the picturesque middle ages are no more. The moon, though present, stands far low on horizon and does not hang over any old ruins.

Arrived at Mainz at 8:45, made a trip in town, saw outside of cathedral.

June 10 Saw cathedral very simple inside. Made a sketch of outside & market, today being market day. Sketched Holy tower and then Eisenturm, a square stone tower (13th century).

Also sketched St. Quintin.

Saw the outside of St. Stephen's, the palace and the library.

But the best thing is a walk on the bridge, with the moon hanging over the Rhine, the reflection in the water, being a long line of golden sparks.

June 11 Sketched door to palace and saw Gutenburg museum, which has photo-states of page dating middle of 15 century, also modern printing in the show room.

Took train to Frankfurt noon time.

Frankfurt is a large town, with suburbs full of modern buildings. Saw Goethe's House. His birth room, study and dining room. Took a picture at Goethe's desk.

Saw old market place [50] on way to Homburg, there is a large section of

Fig22 Marksburg, Rhine 莱茵河，马克斯山堡

modern buildings.

Went to Homburg to hear music (Beethoven's 9th). The choirs consists of local men & women, simple & intense in nature.

June 12 Made sketches around old market place. Every step new subjects to sketch.

In evening walked towards university.

June 13 Saw new stadium, a large place in the woods. But the architecture of the stadium is very bad.

Went to see St. Boniface church at Holbein St. (car 19). Brick outside very nice and colorfully dramatic interior. Made a sketch of it. The nave is vaulted, choir being vaulted higher. It is concrete painted blue in nave & yellow in choir, with crimson

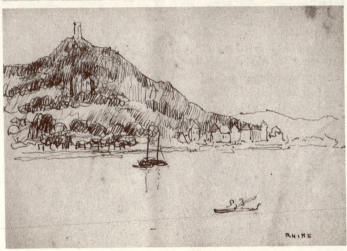

Fig23 Marksburg, Rhine 莱茵河，马克斯山堡
Fig24 Rhine 莱茵河

step & altar, very nice effect indeed.

Went to see Canad Hamish School outside town (cer 18). Brick building with a clock at corner on 2nd story, with white tile in blacks as numerals, white hands.

Not far is the church on a hill, while concrete exterior. Inside has not good proportions. On the balcony stands a special stair case painted that looks like Russian constructure stage setting.

On way back saw gross market hall, very good modern building .

Made a sketch of the stadt hall in the court of Römer. Then went to see Frauen-Friedenskirche at 99 Zeppelin Str.(cen 4). Both interior & exterior are good. Outside made of concrete slabs with 3 deep & tall arches. In the center [51] arch is a mosaic relief figures of the Virgin. In each side arch is masaic (blue & gold mostly) wall. This church has 2 chapels that are effective. The stain glasses are very good in throwing light on white stucco walls & piers.

June 14 Went to Frankfurt Kunstverein, an exhibition of modern architecture(mostly factory buildings) by Walter Gropius.

Saw Kunstgewerbe museum. It has a good collection. In the Chinese section, there is a Han mirror about $4^{1}/_{2}$ diameter, broken through the middle. It is perfectly charming, and the first Han mirror I ever saw. There did not seem to be or in the British museum, with all the cleaver ability of the Englishman to rob us.

There is a small collection of modern art, mostly common piece. One room has old wood panels very good color.

Saw Römer, Kaisersaal, wonderful color. The plan is not a perfect rectangle, the wall facing the square being slant, therefore you have an irregular barrel

Fig25 Mainz 美因茨
Fig26 Rowlano Snyder 罗兰诺·施耐德

vault end. But it is hardly noticeable because the room is long. The floor is polished inlaid, wood & is in perfect condition. The whole effect is so colorful and rich. The rooms Kurfürsten Zimmer and Bürgersaal are also well kept & colorful. Visitors have to put on feet shoes before they go in.

Saw inside of "Dom" very colorful & mystic. The glasses are bad.

Took car 25 from Schauspiel Haus to Homburg, then to Saalburg, to see the Roman remains. The Kastel [**52**] is entirely a reconstructure. German restoration looks hard & awkward. There is no feeling whatever. Saw the museum, in which there are many leather shoes.

From Die Saalburg, I went out in search of Herzberg but got lost in the woods, walked for half an hour and finally came back to the Saalburg. Again went out from the mortuary to look for the round town called Fröh hechenmann Koff, again could not see anything after walking for half an hour. So there one whole hour was wasted. To saw the Mithrum and took a drink of the cold spring water.

Took train way back to Homberg (at 4) and then to Frankfurt, but got off at Dom, back to see a modern school and some modern apartments, made a sketch there.

Saw opera house in evening, an exact miniature of the Paris opera.

June 15 Saw Städel Museum, not much to admire. It has one Millet and several good Degas through. One Van Gogh, and other modern stuff. Saw museum of sculpture. It has a Chinese section, also China Institute 中国学院 , could not get in.

Left for Darmstadt. Saw marriage tower, fine building and 2 good fountains, also a Russian church. Went on top of tower, Darmstadt has some old houses in slum condition.

Got to Heidelberg in evening. Took double room with R.S. with window looking out at castle.

June 16 Sketched bridge head in morning [**53**] and other subjects. Saw inside of ruined castle in the afternoon. After it became cloudy. The restored part of the castle robs imagination. The whole appearance from a far does not look splendid. The color is too red and the thing has no mass. The only thing that saves, it is because it is a ruin. Saw 2 big beer barrels in the cellar.

Took walk on the philosophers' walk up to hill across river.

June 17 Made 7 watercolors altogether. Did not see anything new today. But could stayed here for a good week and make sketches everyday. Delightful little tower. Food is more expensive than other places. Developing & printing of films cost money too. 1 roll (G) for 2.50 marks.

June 18 Fine. Took train at 7:30 to Mannheim. Saw new art gallery modern pre-war (1907). But most of exhibits in there are futuristic, oil, water colors, and sculpture. Good architecture as well as contents.

Saw palaces, the biggest in Germany, a copy of Versailles. The garden has no plan, just like English park. The Jesuit church has rotten interior.

Mannheim has some ultra modern buildings.

Left for Worms at noon. Saw cathedral & Luther monument. The outside of cathedral has atmosphere of age & charm, like Rhine, but inside is bad, looked with Baroque sculpture. The Rhine Bridge is good, made sketch. Saw old wall, St. Paulus Kirche, St. Andrä and Jewish synagogue. Worms is [**54**] a picturesque little town that is worth a day's stay.

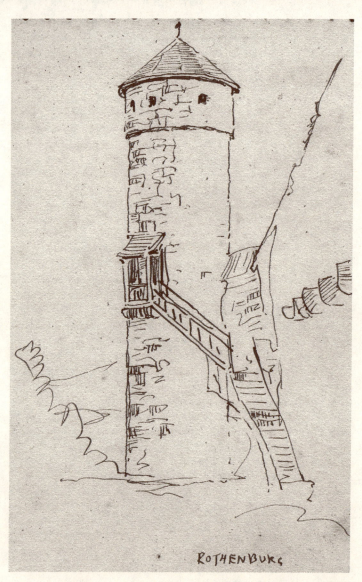

Fig27 Rothenburg 罗滕堡

Went to Lorsch at 5 pm. saw Romanesque church (Michael's Kapelle), also a ruined church behind, sketched both.

Worms & Lorsch are places famous for Nibelungen Saga.

June 19 Overexertion & a little cold made my joints ache & slept very poorly last night. Took 2 pills of quinine sulphate, gave up breakfast.

Took morning train to Würzburg, got there at 1.

Feel much better at Würzburg, after sleeping on the train. Hotel same at Bohnhoff, street is very good.

Saw church (interior is bad taste), not very good in general, just a provincial church.

Saw old bridge on Main, very good and simple. Made a sketch.

Würzburg is very Baroque in architecture. All the Germany architecture I have seen is Baroque.

The Palace from outside is fair. The garden is nothing, a poor imitation of French garden.

Würzburg is not yet frequent by tourists, except German tourists. It has just as much picturesque as Mainz.

June 20 Completely recovered. Had breakfast & went across the old main Bridge, made a tour below the castle, Marienburg, trying to find entrance. Back to old bridge & sketched it again. Went up to castle, made 2 watercolors inside. Did not see inside of houses. Out trying to eat lunch when the guard wanted permit to sketch. Told me to go down near Peters Kirche to get it. [**55**] So I came down building, stopped in a café on my way to eat lunch I bought this morning, 3 boiled eggs, 2 rolls & a bottle of beer, went near Peters Platz but wasted one hour there trying to find where to get permit to sketch, a storm was threatening, so I came back to hotel to make up parcel post for mail.

Had a lot of difficulty at post office in trying to get parcel mailed. Finally I had to wrap parcel in oil paper, bought at 13 Kaiser Street & sealed there. Did not attempt to register. Hope it will get there. It contains all the drawings I made, between Bruges and Würzburg & all post cards bought & photos taken. It is really invaluable, thought I put value down as L 10 RM.

Had an enormous omelette for dinner, the omelette itself costs only 40f, with salad, beer, and a bretzel for 1.50 m.

June 21 Left Würzburg in morning and arrived at Rothenburg before noon. Bought a map of town and walked through main thoroughfare. Very interesting place and picturesque beyond imagination. So many towers, and houses in confirmation with them.

Sketched some of the towers and Rathaus, then went down hill to sketch the old Tauber bridge.

Rothenburg is the most imagination city I have get seen. It is a combination of medieval and modern times, people seem to still have common baking oven, for they carry large pans of pastry on streets. It is a small town, half rural and half city like, with 2 main streets.

Walked towards Detwang in evening. It has a bridge [**56**] several miles, a church called St. Peter & St. Paul, with a gateway in front of it. A picturesque village. Just before going downhill, one saw the wonderful sunset, sometimes through green trees. While going up to Rothenburg, again one heard dogs barking, circlets singing and water murmuring. There are the terrace of Burgtor, the silhouette looked so light and unreal like a dream. A superb sight that.

June 22 Have seen every part of the town and sketched 4 watercolors. Went down to Detwang again, to sketch some house. This little village has a blacksmith shop and a café. It being soundly I heard singing salms. A woman came out with a chair to offer me to sit down which I did not.

Went back to Rothenberg to the market place, waiting for 12 o'clock to see the clock. Sure enough, after the hour struck, the windows on each side of the clock flew open, and a full sized figure, dressed like real, started to move. One drank a big mug of beer and the other seemed to smoke a pipe, for duration of 2 minutes, then the windows closed.

Went down to see the double Roman Bridge again.

Rothenburg is such a small town and is so easy to get around. The air is delicious.

Left for Nürnberg at 7, but on account of getting on the wrong train did not get there until 11:30 pm, got into hotel and went to bed at quarter to one.

June 23 Walked through town between station and Kaiser's Tor. Sketched one watercolor there, came down and sketched Henkersteg. Then the weather became cloudy after lunch on bread & beer, went to see Dürer's House. Very charming [**57**] interior, museum on 3rd floor, kitchen on 2nd floor is interesting. Some furniture came down from Dürer's time.

Did much walking. Nürnberg is picturesque, but every subject is painted or illustrated, and you can do nothing new. Things have become so obvious, some of the colored prints of etching in shop windows are remarkable.

Walking towards the seven rows of weavers houses in the evening. On the way saw Hans Sachs' House ("Meistersinger"), a timber structure. The 1st floor must be an alteration.

June 24 Saw nothing new of the town today. Rather tired of doing watercolors. So did pencil drawings.

Saw Germanic museum this afternoon, the room 125 is the famous "Nürnberg Madonna" in bronze. The museum is a monastery with several cloisters and a chapel. The collection of any interest is tomb tablets and stone sculpture, the rest being junk.

June 25 Saw modern church at Bamberg St. Heinrichskirche (Dr. Goerty arch.). The outside is of good stone work, with brick at the arch reveals. The inside has a good wood paneled ceiling, the rest being concrete & plaster.

Went to see Priesterseminar way beyond town, concrete exterior with pleasant court, a pillar stand in front of building.

Went up hill to Die Altenberg, nothing but a view there on way back, sketched the cathedral from the hill. The cathedral looks hard, though old. It does not have the soft quality of age. The Rathaus is very baroque, so are the "old" & "new" Residences. The interior of cathedral is good.

The other churches have nothing special, except St. Michael's church, which stands on a hill & has a view. On the whole Bamberg is an ante choice [**58**] after Rothenburg & Würzberg. It can very well be omitted on the trip.

June 26 Rain almost whole day. Saw Rathaus and Cathedral, Luther's cell, and Krämer Brüke.

The cathedral is the best in Germany, even better looking (from outside) than Cologne, very perpendicular in style. Also it has a large open space behind and can be viewed from afar. Its approach is nice, a flight of steps. The inside is filled with

Fig28 Leipzig, Russian Church 莱比锡，俄罗斯教堂

Baroque monument. The nave & aisles are equally wide 3 equal parts, or the nave is perhaps ever narrower than the side aisles. The glasses are poor. The cloister is rather nice. The choir is screened off, and there is no depth to the church, on account of its square effect produced by the proportion.

St. Severi is close to the cathedral. Its towers form a false front, as the roof is detached from them. The roof is of red tile and looks like a big private residence. The color is very rich and silhouette very charming. Did not go inside.

St. Martinstift is a new church (rebuilt). Luther's cell looks old. It might be a fake, with the burnt Bible. So much for Erfurt.

Weimar is full of 19 century. Walked in garden in the rain, saw Goethe's summer house, Shakespeare's monument, and then walked towards Nietzsche's house. The museum is on first floor. Nietzsche's sister living upstairs. The rooms are newly furnished, with new books, including Spengler's "Decline". Full of portraits, and busts. Spengler is a friend of the house and comes often; his portrait being on the wall. Nietzsche lived here from 1897 to 1900, when he died.

Saw Liszt's house, his bed, study room, portraits, busts [59] and manuscripts. Liszt as a young man resembles Charles Dickens very much, although in old age he was rather grotesque.

Saw Goethe's house, much bigger and more pretentious than the one at Frankfurt am Main. The nature history collection is very big and physics laboratory looks much up to date. I believe it has been enlarged every year. His bed room looks humble, with only one little window to the garden. The arm chair by his bed is the one in which he died.

Schiller's house is not as palatial as Goethe's. It has many busts and portraits. Also it contains the poet's bed chamber, with writing desk.

The achieves contain letters and books. Goethe's Faust, written are there, also so many letters written to & from Goethe, Schiller etc. Carlyles, Byron's letters to Goethe, Beethoven's letter to Goethe, Goethe's dairy and his work in different languages.

Saw the outside of the theatre palace, and saw von Stein's house.

Took train for Leipzig at 6.24, arrived at 7.50.

June 27 Saw outside of new theatre, not good. The museum looks imposing. The university too. There are two new skyscrapers (about 10 stories high) spring up at the square.

The Auerbachs Keller, source of Goethe's "Faust", is now a nice restaurant and is very much torched up. The philosopher's furnace now is lighted by electricity, like a stage setting. Everything looks fake. But there are several Goethe's handwritings, framed & hung on the wall. [60]

St. Thomas is the church in which Bach sang in the Choir. The inside has nothing to look at. I sat on the pew to read Baedeker.

The Rathaus is new. The old one stands at the market, a colorful tower it has. Near the Church of St. John, there is a modern building which houses the Grassi museum. The museum has a good collection of modernistic & old art, mostly kraft work.

Went to out skirt of the town (car 32 from station) to see Deutsches Bucherei. There is also a modern Russian church nearly, built in 1913, with an onion dome, which is well built up inside. The bronze hand work of religious art is good. The exposition ground has modern buildings. The clinic of the university is modern and is also nearby.

Ran through whole town to get a bath.

Heard good concert at the Conservatory, by students, between 6 & 8.

June 28 Saw museum at Augustus platz, it contains some popular paintings and a good collection of Max Klinger's woks. Klinger sometimes used colored marble in different figment in figures. His Beethoven is there. His painting has new idea of compositions too. The current exhibition of painting and sculpture is very good.

Saw Austeilung Gelände again. This time went in to see from exhibit, of which I was not interested. Went to sketch the Völkerschlacht Denkmal, but did not go up. Sketched Russian church and saw the new market, which has two domes.

The new theatre has the same appearance as the [**61**] New York Metropolitan and the Philadelphia academy. Only it has a smaller capacity.

June 29   Thomas church has a good choir. Most of the boys are under ten. Organ is good and the orchestra plays with it.

Have seen enough of Leipzig, and are sick of it.

The Zoo has about twenty bears & a number of peacocks. It has some modern architecture for the elephants & to bears. The planetarium is modern, but is cheap & is closed.

June 30   Got to Magdeburg, about 10 in the morning. Saw cathedral, not very interesting, the façade is all right but it is a very false front, the central gable stands way above the roof over navy. Also the 2 towers don't have anything behind.

The exhibition ground is very interesting. Saw the inside of the Stadthaus, an auditorium for concert. The organ screen is made of vertical fins covered with blue velvet tripn need with red. The interior is lined with horizontal hands of wood. The windows are made of relief glass and are heavy. The arrangement of light fixture is very interesting. Color scheme very effective. The best modern interior I ever saw.

Saw market and Rathaus, not much to like.

Arrived at Potsdam about 5 pm. Started for Sanssouci garden, walked till I saw the windmill.

Made a sketch of the town palace.

July 1   Made a sketch of the windmill, walked towards the Ruinenberg, an artificial work of imitation of Roman grandeur, but very terrible when looked at close. Strolled in garden for a while, then took trolley to Glienicker Brücke. Saw gothic castle at Babelsberg at a distance.

Tried for a hour to find [**62**] the Einstein Tower and finally when I got there, the old lady at the gate would not let me in. I was so eager to see the thing that I walked around the property of the observatory far enough to catch a glimpse of the top. The photograph usually shows the tower as being dark. It looks white & clean in reality.

Started for Berlin at 5, got there half an hour later, stayed near Friedrich Street station. Hotel Victoria.

July 2   Did not see anything till 5, going about to get way through Russia (an ex. look and Legation).

Saw zoo at 7 & planetarium at 8. The equipment of the planetarium is wonderful. A projection of sky map, with all the stars on it, looks like real.

July 3   Saw national galley, which does not contain much. Saw old & new Rathaus, rotten architecture, especially the old one.

In the afternoon walked along Kurfuerstendamm & saw Universum Film Theatre.

July 4   Saw old & new museum, plenty of Greek, Roman, Egyptian collections, mostly sculpture. In evening went to Universum Film Theatre. The outside has very good lines & movement. The theatre proper has red color scheme, people get in from side aisle doors, no central aisle. The foyer has blue color scheme.

July 5   Saw Pergamon("Pergamon Museum"), superb and unique, beyond words. The museum is not yet ready, but we got in through the American Institute. The Pergamon altar is housed modern glass roof. The relief ("Gigantomachia") is

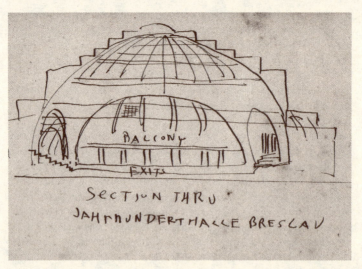

Fig29 Breslau Jahrhunderthalle 布雷斯劳，百年纪念堂

a purely fragmentary state and no restoration made. The [63] architecture of the temple above is a restoration, with origin at fragments shown clearly. Better than the way, it is done in the British museum, where the fools try to plaster the relief and make it more whole, thereby destroying imagination. Besides Pergamon alter, there is a Romanesque like door at Sion, also fragments from Milet. The proportion of the antiques are perfect.

Saw Kaiser Friedrich museum. It has a good collection of Dutch. Also many Rubens and a few Hals & van Dyke. But the treasures are those Italian painting & sculpture. Renaissance masters like Della Robbia (over 50 pieces), Donatello, Sansovino etc. also one Da Vinci and 2 Michelangelo. One Raphael's Madonna is also here. It is 5 Raphael's altogether.

Saw Crown Prince museum. It has modernistic paintings & sculpture on the top floor. Superb thing. Cézanne, Degas, Henri Matisse, Kandinsky, Some are very radically modern.

July 6 Saw flying field at Tempelhof. Then took train for Breslau. Saw Rathaus at Breslau, very charming & red. Made sketch.

July 7 Saw almost every church in town (not inside) including the cathedral. They are all made of red brick and are rather picturesque. The cathedral is especially colorful.

Saw the modern group called Jahrhunderthalle, a great auditorium with stepped dome of glass, very effective inside. All of concrete & glass. Don't know how the acoustics works.

July 8 Saw Clemens Maria Hofbauer kirche, south west of town. The outside is conservative, only the top of the tower has modern note, all the arches are elliptical. But [64] the inside is nice & colorful, although there are no side aisles. The church is on second floor, as you go up the stair there are colored terracotta relieves, set in wall which look interesting. The note of decorating is red, very much like a theatre.

Saw Stadium, which consists of tennis courts, field & swimming pool.

Went all the way to Oswitz on trolly (15) to see Kaiser-Wilhelm-Gedächtnisturm, which appears good in photograph. But in reality the color is horrible, a cheap kind of red brick & gray stone tower. So I just made a pencil sketch. On way back went into a cemetery to see a new crematorium, very good.

Germans are after all people of sound habit, women especially take gigantic strides in walking and are fond of carrying things on their back, men put a lot of junk on their bicycles & almost convert motorcycle to auto mobile.

Germans are fond of carrying their own lunch everywhere, sandwich and pastry, men and women alike.

July 9 In the morning at Breslau in the station. Saw a chimney sweep with a silk top hat on, a double institution that ought to be abolished.

Saw Picture gallery at Dresden, very good collection. Saw Raphael's Sistine Madonna, Andrea del Sarto's Holy Night, Titian's Tribute Money. Raphael's Madonna has good composition & drapery but the color is drab.

Dresden is a good Baroque city, as it is the cradle of Rococo art.

The modern section of the picture gallery has some radical paintings. Wassily Kandinsky uses geometric forms (globe etc.).

Lyonel Feininger passes planes through objects.

Paul Klee uses Egyptian forms in line drawings, and sometimes [**65**] the pattern, looks like children's drawing.

Ernst Ludwig Kirchner paints not radically in forms but uses green and purple on people's face.

There is not much traffic in Germany, but they are particular about lights and usually a police stands and controls the light signal. Also there is no demand for hurry but every town (even morning) has an automat, which sells more beer and wine than sandwiches.

July 10 Saw Porcelain museum, which has a good collection of Chinese things.

Saw industrial art museum, which has one 宣和御笔之鹰, 文徵明 and 刘石庵题字。

July 11 Saw sculpture gallery, which has some original Greek masters like Praxiteles. Saw academy exhibit, price for entrance 1 mark. But it does not have much good stuff in it.

In the picture gallery there seem to be copies passing as original. There are 2 Ruben's Drunken Hercules in the same room. One must be a copy. Another Rubens looks like a copy too. The only genuine ones are Raphael's Sistine, Giorgione's Sleeping Venus and Correggio's Holy Night.

In front of the Johanneum, there are two sculptured boys, one of which is a Chinese. Took a photo of it.

July 12 Saw Hygiene exhibit. The exposition is so arranged that to it is more of an architectural exhibition than Hygiene. There are so many photographs of building (houses, factories, hospitals) and models too. Several crematoriums are shown in photo.

One model shows a living town of circular plan. Blocks are divided in concentric circles, and streets radiate from center, dividing the city into 8 sectors. This perhaps would solve the problem of facing the sun more equally all round, as they call it the [66] gesunden grosstadt. (Recovering or "convalescence city".)

The Russians put up a living show and their idea about, it is very radical. On the balcony there are albums of photographs & information. The whole ceiling is covered (pasted on) with placards of propaganda.

The Japanese have a section also. The architecture is imitating German to the last detail. You cannot tell the difference.

The Hygiene museum is very good in architecture & contents. On the 1st floor back there is a chapel-like with ambulatory, a statue in the center. Statue that has celluloid body & organism inside, every part being lighted by turns and corresponding names grave on panels on table. The salon on top floor has a good color scheme (blue) and is in good proportion.

In the Russian hygiene exhibition the poster says visit Russia. It takes 6 weeks to get a visa and you can't have camera or books when traveling. The Russians must have good sense of humor.

July 13 In Prague at noon, saw Mozart house in west suburb of town. It has a garden, rather unkempt. There is nothing particularly interesting about the house, except during 1787—1791, he lived there as guest of Duschek.

There is a ground for stadium, which is yet to be built.

Near Karl's Bridge there are many kinds of interest, like the Rathaus and bridge towers. Very sketchable like Würzburg.

Prague is rather gray in color. In a garden the red flowers look exceedingly red became the surrounding are so drab. The modern building lack refinement. The Y.M.C.A is rather good.

Bohemian life is rather cheap to live, food seems [67] to be less expensive than Germany.

Saw Beggar opera at new German theatre. The music is half jazz—good jazz at that. I suspect the musician is a corrupted one, standing place costs only 4 Krone (12'/2fp or 3¢)

July 14 Sketching whole day.

The Bohemian are less sophisticated people, don't dress much. But some girls are awfully beautiful.

Bohemian cooking is wonderful. It has the flavor of Chinese dishes. The meat balls in soup is just like Chinese. Also the gravy.

The old town of Prague is as picturesque as any good German city.

(Spengler's address at Munich is Widenmayerstr.2).

July 15 The street cars and automobiles, keep to the left. Pedestrians are also supposed to keep to the left. But some people do not seem to know what to do. Some insist on keeping to the left even if you keep to the right.

The natural museum has nothing to see, full of botanic and physiological collections. Art treasures there are few or none.

Went up to the Burg in late afternoon, and saw cathedral St. Vitus. The 2 towers look like Cologne, only smaller. The inside is quite good. The nave proper is very sober. The choir and chancel has some Baroque sculpture. Some glasses are passably fine. Everything seems to be in good taste. The whole interior is open without screen of kind. This is probably the best Gothic in Bohemia.

The Burg commands a good view of the city.

Almost lost my umbrella, forget to take it after finishing [68] a sketch. In about 3 or 5 minutes, recalled & run back for it, it still stood there.

Got into a Bohemian restaurant in the evening, the wine is cheap & good. Food is cheap but not wonderful. Pasty is very bad. After evening the waiter took away the wine glass and nodded, I nodded too. So he brought another glass of wine, I refused but he said I ordered it. I did not take it anyway.

There are plenty of beggars. Woman beggars usually have babies with them. Need another day to finishing sketching & sightseeing. 2 days are really too short for Prague.

The city hall has tricky clock like Rothenberg. There are many figures passing behind the windows. The astronomical instruments are also supposed to work. But did not see them.

The Bohemians are up early, shops open at 8.

Architects advertise with photos of works at entrance door.

July 16   Arrived at Vienna from Prague at 1 pm.

Stephan dom has good Gothic exterior, towers similar to cologne. In strong sunlight the effect of the tower is charming, the upper part being a white shaft with black dots and lines and the tower part is dark gray with cream colored patterns

Saw the outside of Kunsthistorische museum, near Burg and garden. Rode trolley to Schönbrunner and Schloss park, modeled after Versailles and similar to Sansoucci (really not) garden, on a smaller scale.

Vienna cooking is just good as Bohemian and very cheap. Besides Prague, Vienna is a place to live cheaply.

Went to Maxer Gasse and found No. 1 with difficulty, for it is on the other side of the bridge. Rang the bell and a man came out. [69] He rang for the janitor, an old man. I persuaded him to show me where Ernst Pischke was. He climbed up and I followed, 5 or 6 stories, right to the top floor. Stairs had no light. Then finally be opened a series of what looked like closet doors, and knocked at the front. Pischke came out without shirt and a bear foot, which had a hurt toe. So he hopped on the floor. He said the work was busy but not much prospect (nor perhaps reward). The drafting room is just like anyone in America, dirty & disorder, all the drawings are modernistic, of course. He showed me photos of his work. They look good. Then we talked about sight in Vienna. He came down with me and to the bridge. I did not know how he felt, but I felt some pathos about what once we had hear. There is a strange feeling when you meet some one again at a different place after a while.

On the route between Prague and Vienna, the scenery is good, with rolling hills, black trees (cedar & pine) well grouped and fleeting clouds. At Eggenburg (Austria) there stands a church (nice color, red roof & white straw walls) much ruined fortifications. It is quite picturesque.

July 17   Went to Kunsthistorisches museum. It has some good things but cannot compare with other big European museums. There are many Rubens, van Dykes, Rembrandt & Titians. But I suspect some are copies. One Raphael may be a copy too. It is Madonna with child & St. John. A small picture. There are many small objects of art, and many armors.

Modern gallery is very good. There are not many pieces (painting & sculpture), but what is there is good. There are [70] 4 or 5 by Gustav Klimt. His costumes are original (black, silver and gold) and compositions are wonderful. The sculpture is not good in general but same is quite praise worthily.

(In the modern gallery, every room has a different color scheme. The general arrangements is tasteful)

The modern gallery is in the Orangerie, and on the other axis of the Belvedere is the 19 century museum, which is very poor and does not have a simple thing of note except one or two Renoir. The Salvator Rosa's are terrible.

There is an exhibition on Karlsplatz on book building & home art. It is quite worthwhile, with all the Viennese craftsmanship on display. Part of the exhibition is also devoted to architecture.

Saw Haydn museum. The house has only 2 chambers on view, the inner one full of portraits and busts, the outer one has a piano & furniture. The old drawing shows the house as having thatched roof, alone in the countryside. Now the street is only a slum.

Saw interior of Stephan dom, which has same of the mystic quality of Notre Dane. The glasses are not good but they do well in a dark church. This church and the St. Vitus at Prague use low gothic arches very effectively at the main entrance in the interior.

Walked all the way to the Danube, could not see its color (probably green) on account of the dark night.

A Viennese would take the trouble to help you to find the way even to the extent of dogging you.

July 18 After breakfast went to Heiligenstadt on stadtbahn [71] to see modern apartments. They are good. Found one from the milk shop about Beethoven house, got there and saw two houses near each other where Beethoven lived. But both are private. The one at Pfarrplatz has a nice court. It is when one stands beyond the threshold that imagination plays free. Made a rather good sketch of the white stuccoed exterior.

Saw Schubert house on way back. It also has a nice court, but the gate is facing a busy street, instead of being like Beethoven houses which are rather secluded.

Ate near Schubert house, in a restaurant where the mother cooks (she looks dreadful) and daughter waits on table, while the son serves wine and beer. The cooking is very good and I ate a big dessert, besides a glass of bear.

Crossed the Danube under an impending storm in the afternoon. It is like Beethoven's music, Sturm und Drang. The Danube is light green in color. The water looks shallow now but the dykes are very far from the main bed.

July 19 Went to see Secessism museum. There is something good there, not much radical stuff.

Went to district III to see modern apartments. Where you pass from one court to another and to streets. Very well planned and good architecture also.

Walked in stadt part. Saw court of the Burghof. Saw Rathaus at close range in the evening, then went to Wurzbach Str. to see modern apartment. There are nice tile fountains [72] in arcaded courts.

July 20 Arrived at Salzburg at noon time. Went up to see Mozart's little house (which was moved from Vienna) on the hill. It is just a wood cabin filled with impossible pints.

Sketched the castle. The castle looks very English. It has a good composition from the river. Saw most of the landmarks.

Salzburg is such a small town. It is easy to get around.

Beautiful landscape between Veinna and Salzburg. Rolling hills and distant mountains (snow clad), with black trees grouped very architecturally. Houses begin to assume the Tivolian character, with hard looking boarded roof, eaves over hanging on all sides.

July 21 Saw Königsee and took motor boat to Bartholomae and Obersee. There is nothing to see at Obersee. But Bartholomae has a nice little building with restaurant. The best sketching subject. Mountains are beautiful, with their waterfalls and glassy lake. At one place the man on board blew the bugle and the echo was distinct as the original, only a little fainter. Made a sketch at Bartholomae and a pencil at Konigsee, very beautiful scenery on the way and mountain air is delicious. The water looks cold. I had sweater on.

Went up to the castle, the most picturesquely composed and there are so many sketchable spots. Better than English castle in composition and picturesqueness, but details are bad (Baroque). On the whole it is the best in Europe. The mere fact that if stands in the town on top of hill is dramatic. Two good terraces are taken by [73] restaurants. Those who dine there can enjoy the best scenery one can ever wish. It is superb. Distant mountains with beautiful outline, strange clouds

Fig30 Actors in Passion Play 苦难剧演员
Fig31 Country Woman at Passion Play
   苦难剧中的乡下妇女
Fig32 Audience in Passion Play 苦难剧观众

and fields and houses. Who would not have appetite.

Could not have time to see Mozart house. Nor the Festival house. But went to Marionette theatre tonight. The first marionette I ever saw and the best. The first one is "Bastien und Bastienne" which is a mere comic opera. But the second one is "Wolfgang and Der solcher Meister", which illustrates Mozart as a little boy defying the new music teacher, who did not ever know what minute was. So he left. Mozart is very sweetly played and the others are cleverly done too. It is really better than some of the stage plays.

Spengler, 26 Wiedenmayer Str. Munich.

July 22 Up early (5:30) for Munich train, arrived at 8. Found room near station, and looked around town. Saw Prince Royal Theatre when Wagner's operas are given. The lowest price there is 15 m. At the Residents theatre, when Mozart operas are given. In one of the poster photographs, I saw a series of plays named Li-Tai Pe, when I imagined it was given 2 years ago. First time drank Munich bear—Löwer bear, very mined and rich and does not make you feel thirsty. Saw Spender's house, top floor.

Took train for Oberammergau at 2, arrived at 6. Stayed at house No.119 Hauptstr., Maria Klamme the landlady, is an excellent cook. The room has an 8 foot ceiling and 4 windows, very nicely furnished. It has a narrow winding stair to the 1st floor, you go thought the house to the vestibule. It is a simple white stucco house with blue blinds. The dining room has pearplanks for ceiling. Probably the underside of floor above. [74]

The whole congregation are American except myself. One woman from Washington D.C. had a long argument with the landlady in German. I thought she was German too, so I called her a damned nuisance. She turned around and looked at me. I knew that she knew it. So I determined to be angry, and not to talk to anybody. Two young girls from America sat at the end of table and probably have rich parents the way they talk. Silly heads both. R.S. tried to entertain them.

The meal is excellent but it seems to be out of place, in a little village like this, to have table manners and politeness. It kills the fun. Women make one feel uneasy to start with. I never was nervous with women in America, but they made me here nervous. Because they are not interesting and carefree.

What one notices as soon as one came out up the station are the horses-carriages and men with beard and long hair. The children and boys also grow their hair long. Some say they do it 3 years before the event of Passion Play. But they make the village look very picturesque indeed. The horses are very alpin. With overhanging ever on all sides, white stuccoed usually, or brown.

The place is full of Americans, some dumb English people are also there. They of course are not of place. Ever the Germans themselves look out of place in that matter, if they do not live at Oberammergau.

This is the only occasion perhaps I come in direct contact with American tourists. They are so ignorant that to speak to them means wasting breath. It is a kind of blessing to sleep in this little quiet village. Anticipating one of the greatest events that only happen at long intervals. [75]

July 23 The weather today is very clement cloudy in the morning and sunshine in the afternoon, while the rain in the evening is too late to spoil anything.

Had very satisfactory breakfast, with plenty of rolls and fresh butter, jam, and mountain honey. The coffee also tastes good.

The Passion Play starts at 8 am. In the theatre which has hidden orchestra and open stage. I sat too low in front, but I believe those up behind can see the distant mountains.

All the tableau vivants are good, music, costumes, acting, can be said leaving nothing to be desired. The music is given only when those is prologue. It is simple and pure and as great as any great opera music.

Judas acts very well. Although a little too forcibly. But on the whole he knows what he ought to do. On the other hand Christ is rather uncouth, peasant-like and none too gentle. He does not even have a carefree face, which is very rough. His voice is too strong, and movements and gestures are not up to the standard.

Mary is quite good, anyway she does not have much acting to do. She is a beautiful woman.

The play starts from Christ entering Jerusalem to the Ascension or transfiguration. It takes 8 hours schedule time, actually it starts at 8 am, ends at 5:45 pm. With intermission at noon time between 11:30 and 2 pm.

Ate a good lunch of chicken and a marvelous nachtisch, like melted cream made of eggs and banana. Excellent indeed.

In the afternoon the sun shines and serves as a [76] light source for the stage. The effect is very good. Some of the characters stand in shade and some in light. It is really stage lighting at its best.

The whole performance makes the Bible alive. I think for a long time, hereafter when I see a crucifix or anything that has to do with christianly I will be reminded of the Passion Play. It really makes you live the life young and I think it is true especially with the villagers.

The Germans are fond of using flowers in a long row to make their count as ornament.

July 24 Back to Munich in early morning. It rains whole day at Munich. Saw Bavaria museum, full of junk. Then went to see old Pinakothek, which has many Rubens, van Dyke, Rembrandts, 2 Raphael Madonnas, and some very good Titians. I never yet saw so many Murillos. There are also some Goyas, Dürer's 4 apostles are also there, together with other good works by him. His own portrait I have seen in almost every museum and don't know which is copy and which is not.

Went to Prince Regent Theatre in the evening to hear Wagner's "Flying Dutchman" (15 marks for cheapest seat) which starts at 7, and ends at 10. The setting is excellent, music is simple and singing very much better than any I heard at metropolitan. It is the best Wagner I enjoyed besides Lohengrin.

July 25 Went to see Nymphenburg palace, just a group of Baroque building, with park. Not worth a trip at all, it is not far from Munich. Trolley takes 15 minutes from station. [77]

The hospital near the Palace is modern and is not bad.

Saw exhibition at glass palace in the afternoon. The collection is good in quality and quantity. It is to my mind even better than the salon at Grand Palais in Paris. Some of the watercolors are inspiring too. It is a show of painting, and

Fig33 Alps 阿尔卑斯山

sculpture, with lithograph and prints and etchings. It is quite worth seeing.

Saw new Pinakothek. It is entirely impossible, not only in quality but there is very scanty painting indeed.

Saw State gallery, which is wonderful in its French collection. The other rooms are all right but the French room has van Gogh's self portrait. Cezanne's self portrait. van Gogh's till life (some flowers and Landscape). Cezanne's landscape and landscape. Also there is one Pisaro, one Matisse, 2 Gaugins, and 2 Renoirs, One Manet. The museum in this respect is worth a trip.

Went to Theatre museum. It does not have many. But a unique thing. Photographs models and prints of dancing and drama, also masks and costumes.

Saw Deutsche museum on the island. It is purely scientific. I just walked through all the parts that are open and came out.

Saw Ausstellung park buildings, modern, with colored terra cotta figures lined on the path.

July 26 Did not see any museum today. But sketched 5, the Rathaus old & new. The tower of Ausstellung building, and a terra cotta figure there. Also a street scene.

Heard Beethoven's moon night Sonata and Serenoade [**78**] tonight in the courtyard of the Residenz. It is excellently done. In between, the program some wind instruments were played on the tower, with light flooded on the pointed roof, and the musicians are just discernable. The effect is very theatrical. Candles are used in most of the lamps and in window sills in the entrance court. It looks like middle ages.

Oswald Spengler must be easy to see, as R.S. sent up a letter of self introduction and got an interview. Spengler is described as a man about 50, bald headed but with handsome or sharp-feathered face. He had a kind of smoking jacket on. And soft slippers. His rooms are comfortably furnished with long rows of books and old pictures. Spengler must be playing on the piano, which he has, and his "Decline" shows his knowledge of music. He lives on the main floor, with a maid & a house keeper apparently.

Spengler does not like Richard Strauss nor modern jazz. He thinks Liszt, especially Wagner, was the last great musician, modern architecture to him is not yet agreeable. In the tribune tower competition he likes the building built and 2nd prize (Saarinen). The German competition drawings he does not think much at all.

I rather would not see him. What after all can an interview do? If he is too great, we would not understand him. If he is not great at all, we better wait till he comes to see us. A man has no business to intrude on another just for the sake of curiosity.

July 27 Arrived at Augsburg from Munich in the morning at 8:30. Went to cathedral at once [**79**] during service, with organ music and choirs, very beautiful. Baedeker mentioned "a" huge candelabrum of the middle age. But there are 4 or 5. No one knows which is. The interior is rather nice, not much Baroque. The south brogue door is good.

On the south side of the cathedral there is a grand with excavator remains (Roman?), Baedekers does not mention it. Probably very recent, to me it looks like a Roman Bath.

The Rathaus is very poor. So is the Perlachturm. Went to Jakober Str., looking for Holbein's house. But saw an old house and Vogel Thurm & sketched both. There was a fair going on, and circus for children. Several boys led me through Fuggerei, but no one knew where Holbein's house is. Instead one boy called out a Chinese.

The boy must have thought I was looking for a country man. There were 4 or 5 Chinese merchants (Vagabonds). They talk aloud and play mal-junp on the beer table. Fortunately the place is full of people, who eat with their knives (even a woman did that). They are a disgusting lot any way. So I never saw Holbein's house.

Arrived at Ulm at 2:30. Ulm is an old town on the Danube. Saw the cathedral. It looks like an American skyscraper in silhouette. The inside is quite plain and nice, with double aisle on each side. Took trolley to go across Danube to see a modern church (Kath Stadtpfarrkirche). The outside is a modern version of Romanesque. The inside is very wonderful (almost cubistic). By Prof. Dominikus Böhm. There is not much color but the light and shade playing [**80**] on whole plaster is very effective. There are several chapels and each is different. The only fault perhaps is the low ceiling.

Sketched the water-tower on the Danube. The Danube has reddish green color.

I imagine the train passed through the Black Forest region. But the forest is not different from others in south Germany.

Arrived at Stuttgart at 7:15. The new train station is beautiful. I never saw such a good thing. Probably the best station in existence.

Saw the palace at night and some of the modern buildings. The old market

Fig34 Alps 阿尔卑斯山

has many old houses. The Rathaus is too new to be good.

July 28 Raining morning. Saw Schocken Department Store. The best department store (architecturally of course) I have ever seen. It has combination of brick horizontal lines and stucco. The use of shop name on huge light box letters is effective.

Opposite Schocken is a tall building (about 15 stories) (newspaper press), the tallest in Germany and perhaps in Europe. Made sketches of both.

Left Stuttgart at noon time for Friedrichshafen, which is on Lake Constance. Took boat (St. Gallen) to cross the lake to Romanshorn.

Constance has green water, glassy. Felt a thrill to see the distant Alps for the first time. The weather is cloudy. But one can see distant mountains in sunshine. Some mountains are hidden by clouds, of others only the peaks are visible. It is very much like Chinese painting, which always [81] produces the greatest effect with the most simple willows.

Had to wait at Romanshorn for the train to Zurich. So went to an old church (which I saw from the lake) and made a sketch of it. Romanshorn is a small town. So is Friedrichshafen. The dirigible hanger is visible from the lake.

Train left Romanshorn 6:24, arrived at Zurich at 8:05.

Went into a gay place tonight by mistake. It is a restaurant with "Konzert". On the platform women dressed in fairy costumes and lace caps to play instruments. Men dressed in black with tight coat and ample trousers. Colorful lace around neck and chest. One has to pay 30 centinies for the concert.

As I could not get a room at hotel Limmathof, I left my baggage there and came to the place. After I got the room, I said I was going for baggage. It did not take long to get it. The hotel keeper was suspicious and demanded payment. He asked if I came from another hotel.

Had all kinds of weather this day, Swiss landscape in a cloudy day is like Chinese painting.

July 29 Up very early. Out to see the Zurichsee. All Swiss lakes appear to be the same.

Saw Lindenhof, site of old Roman Palace, now an elevated [**82**] ground with trees and benches. No remains of any kind.

Saw statue of Pestalozzi. Sketched covered wooden bridge and old museum.

The Bahnhof Strasse of Zurich is the main street, and on both side early in the morning there are lined with stales for fruits. It is a market street.

Lucerne is on the Vierwald Stätter See, which is more beautiful than Zurichsee. Made sketch of covered bridge on the Reuss. Then went to see the famous Lion of Lucerne, Also saw glacier Park. The only museum of its kind in the world, and marvelous things. Worth while to see, especially the palm impressions on stone, glacier mills and round stone. One is set at work by waterfall.

Went up to Gutsch tower but the view is very ordinary.

Arrived at Basle at 5:30 pm. Right outside the station there is the markethall, modern but not very good, got to Spalen tor by mistake. But from a shop (Post card place) near there found out the location of the modern Antonius Kirche. Walked to there at once. The tower (concrete) is the best I saw. Inside is also very sober and very theatrical. But the proportion does not see right. The section of it is a barrel vault over nave and flat ceiling over aisle. All ceiling is treated with square panels sunk in concrete. The stained glass windows are modernistic and have figures besides Cubistic designs. The choir is on the balcony facing the chancel. The pulpit is made of copper and has [**83**] a flat hood over it. This church is very worth seeing. I believe the new building now under construction is Sunday school.

Saw Rathaus, which has a fresh pink color and rich by decorated roof. St. Martin is close by and its tower is good from certain angle. The cathedral is of red stone and is rather nice to look at.

Stayed at Basle only for 2 hours and yet saw many things although did not make any sketch.

Took train for Bern, a nice evening with crescent moon.

Too dark to see Bern tonight, while in the train saw picture of Chillon, near Montreux, just on way between Lausanne and Milan. So determined to stop at Montreux.

Did not have time for dinner, so bought 2 bananas and 3 prices of party to eat on the train.

July 30 Up and out to see Käfigturm, the Minister, which looks new (gothic), and Rathaus, which has no tower but stairs of stone with shelters stand outside, very unusual.

Berne is famous for its numerous fountains. But Zunich has just as many. One good thing about Berne is its covered sidewalk or arcades on all principal streets. It is an old thing but modern architects are dreaming it for the being metropolis of tomorrow.

The Bernese Alps are not clear from terraces on account of clouds. Also could not see the "Alpine glow" which must be see in clear evening.

Saw an accident. A trunk was turning street corner [84] and hit a motor cyclist. I don't know what because of the victim. But he seemed to hold his own, an old man too.

The Rhine has light yellowish green color and has swift current.

Arrived at Lausanne at 2:00 Pm.

Up to Berne people speak German, from Berne on they talk French. Railway language change accordingly.

Saw Rathaus, very insignificant with painted cornice.

But the cathedral restored by Violet-le-Duc is the best gothic in Switzerland and is better than any church in Germany. The tower is dwarf and has a spine. But the main portal is excellent.

The interior is marvelous for its simplicity. The Rose window recalls Chartres Saint Chapelle. There are few glasses, but they are all splendid. The details as well as proportions are superb. Because of its being a litter squatty, it's better than any forced height (false because it is misleading to give sense of height by narrow width). It is wide so one has sense of space.

Saw Chateaux. Excellent because it is a good combination of brick and stone. Nice mellow pink brick.

It is low and massive.

Went up to the signal for view, but it is no better than the view from the train. Another view [85] from Promenade de Montbenon, saw W. Tell's statue.

Walked down hill to see the lake. Better than any other Swiss lake. Sailing boats and swans adorn the water, sunshine too, made sketch of sailing boat.

Took train for Montreux. As soon as I got there, went to see the Château of Chillon in the evening light, it looks splendid, and grows bigger as you approach it. Must go there tomorrow morning. Made sketch and took photos. It is in tonight must like the "Island of Death", very imaginative. The air is delicious, swans swinging in water and frequently submerge.

I like to hear French. At Berne people speak both German & French. But at Lausanne & Montreux, they only speak French, which charms my ears. One sees more beautiful women too. The food is more French in form any way.

July 31 Saw inside of Chillon. Views from the windows are superb, even from the prison cell. There are torture chamber, justice room, dining hall, knights hall, etc. The medievalism about it is very unique. In Bonivard's cell, I looked for Byron's name. Could not find it on the column. But there is a modern tablet (1924) on the wall, opposite to that column.

The Dent du Midi was hidden in clouds all morning. The top is clear in the evening, but main body is cloudy. Also saw snow capped shafts behind.

Aug 1 Took train in morning to Martigny, there took bus to great St. Bernard. [86]

The train before arriving at Martigny passed St. Maurice. The church probably looks fine. The bus has a good driver, we arrived at great St. Bernard at 12:30, passed many villages. The houses have fully the rugged character of the mountains. Also the inhabitants have hard and worn faces (dry looking). At Bourg St. Pierre, there is a hotel where upstairs Napoleon had breakfast, it has a good carved wood ceiling. The church looks very aged and the tower has stone spine. Good character. In the wall of the church yard stands a Roman mill stone. After passing Bourg St. Pierre, we saw what I thought was Mont Blanc. It looked extremely grand. Waterfalls snow-capped mountains. The road winds itself upward the top and as you look back, it really like a snake.

The bus almost had an accident. Another truck came. Both stopped just on time to avoid collision. Beyond is the deep ravine.

The sky is very clear, and the air cool. But when the bus stops in the village, the sun is fierce.

The party consists of 3 Americans (husband & wife with daughter) , 2 French or Swiss (man & wife) and myself. The American only counts the height of mountains.

St. Bernard, when you reach it, is a disappointment. The best part of the ride is before you reach it, when the mountains rise one after another.

The St. Bernard Hospice is very common plan looking (commercial looking too). It has an bad chapel and all the rooms are numbered, [87] like hotel. The dining room is on the first floor. The priest eats with the guests. The Hotel du St. Bernard is opposite and is connected with a bridge. The food is fine. Wine is the best I ever drank. The looking is excellent except the beef, which no wonder, they call it l'anglaise. The white wine is called L'Etoile, and is so rich and fragrant, besides some power.

The famous St. Bernard dogs, I only saw three (behind the Hospice) they look like a cross between a bull dog and wolf.

Crossed the Italian border, photograph forbidden.

It is very mild up there, the lake is not frozen, though some snow never melts.

One has to use a good deal of imagination to see St. Bernard in summer time as winter snow, there can be no danger, and the dogs are taking long rest.

On the return trip, I felt tired and took several winks.

The train for Milan was one half hour late, crossed the Simplon Pass at 8 o'clock. It took about 2 minutes to cross the 3 major ones, and the other short tunnels together with Simplon took about one hour.

On the north side of the Alps, the sky was blue, on the Italian side, it was cloudy, though the crescent moon once a while share through the clouds.

It is a thrill to see Italian villages the first time. They are all charming things.

At Stresa a middle aged French woman welcomed a couple of young people of the station. Not only their French charmed my ears, [88] but also their manner and grace and some beauty.

Aug 2   Saw St. Fedele. The first thing the outside is very charming. The brick work reminds one of modern German brick, with bands horizontally run sunk & raised. The façade is splendidly proportioned (Renaissance store).

Saw museum of the La Scala, the inside of the opera house (which looks so small,) and the stage, the ceiling is high enough to distinguish itself from the medieval opera house at Philadelphia & New York, Leipzig and Prague. The general color scheme is dark red. The façade is fine. Leonardo's statue stands in the square. The cathedral does not looks as well as the photograph. But the interior is extremely fine. Like Notre Dame and much bigger.

The windows are good, and they are placed to advantage on account of the dark interior of the church. The high nave and double aisle. The whole thing is very simple looking indeed.

Saw city from tower and roof. Atmosphere not clear and the Alps are not distinct.

Saw the coffin of St. Charles. It is made of silver. The whole chapel ceiling is silver ornamented. The coffin has crystal windows, so you can look in and see the skull, with clothes intact. An ornament in the coffin by Cellini. The skull is dark brown. Hand severed with white gloves and rings.

Palazzo Ambrosiana has collection of Renaissance painting. Like Leonardo's drawings and some paintings. Raphael's cartoon of the [**89**] school of Athens.

Piazza Mercanti has Palazzo della Ragione, part of which is Roman remains. This is the center of old Milan.

Biblioteca Ambrosiana has a picture gallery, the most important thing being Raphael's cartoon for the school of Athens. Leonardo has a cabinet too, with albums & all kinds of line drawings. Also there are some small painting attributed to Leonardo.

San Satiro has a choir in perspective (sculptured), Baedeker says it is painted. But the modeling is of stone. It is very original (on account of narrow street) beyond it is impossible to have a choir.

Santa Maria Presso San Celso has a good atrium – the first atrium I have yet seen in front of a church.

San Lorenzo is the most ancient church of Milan. It is Romanesque and has good coloring inside. Outside is the row of Roman columns with architecture of brick and stone. The columns are Corinthian and are weather worn.

San Ambrogio has an atrium also. Romanesque and according to tradition Augustine was baptized here.

The most charming church, no doubt, is Santa Maria delle Grazie. The dome is after Bramente's design.

The chief thing there is Leonardo's last supper, in the monk's dining room of the Dominican Monastery. The whole picture was restored and the door opening which appeared in some of the prints is blocked up and painted over, with trace left to be seen. A wonderful thing it must have been to look at when new! Now [**90**] it is damaged to such an extent that it is only like a cartoon. Christ's face is barely visible. The composition is something grand and original. The 12 disciples are grouped 3 and 3. The colors are very simple. The Lunettes are also painted by Da Vinci.

The church has a very nice portal. The inside looks old. That's all I can remember.

I must confer the seeing of the Last Supper did not give me any thrill, it looks like an old friend and seeing it merely means identification.

The Castello looks grand. The Lombardic tower has an original composition and character. It reminds one of the Kremlin (?) at Moscow. The round towers at the corner reminds me of the towers at Nürnburg, only those in Milan have stone rustication, and look better. The buildings surrounding the castle are very good and civic, some of which are in Florentine style.

Saw outside of Palazzo di Brera and Pal. Crespi. Di Brera has a fine court and good picture gallery, which I am going to see tomorrow.

I have finished seeing all the thing outlined by Baedeker. The inside of museums at Di Brera and Castello remains to be seen tomorrow. Made only one sketch of the cloister of Santa Grazie.

Aug 3 In the morning went to the castle, saw museum. The best thing there is the ceiling by Leonardo. It is the most original thing one can imagine. The coved ceiling, penetrated by arches, is treated as a covered bowl of green tints [**91**] leaves, with shields of blue and gold at four sides, and brown branches coming down to the cornice. It is very rich and simple, and restful to the eye. The wall is covered with red silk, and dark brown wood panels on seats. The floor is again a wonderful design of black & white marble in the most interesting pattern. The whole conception is almost modern.

There is a collection of China (Ming and Kang Hsi) and some Jap art.

The museum at Brera is very good, and rivals with Dresden and Munich. It has Raphael's "The Nuptials of the Virgin". The Titians I did not see.

Took train for Como from station Nord at 1:02, arrived at 2:02. From there took boat (Milano) to Bellagio (arrived at 4:30). But in 5 minutes took return (salvia) boat back to Como)

From Como on the first half hour is very dull, with uninteresting houses on both banks. But as soon as one gets to Nesso, the houses suddenly look fine and they pile up so picturesquely, with an old hunch-backed bridge and a big waterfall. Next good place is perhaps Leno, where on the hotel wall the trees or vines are so trained as to climb in trunk and rest in leaves.

But before that there is Argegno, where there is a charming old Romanesque tower and a horrible new [**92**] grey Romanesque church.

Bellagio is nothing but a pill of living villas, in block form. It is not picturesque. The church of San Giovanni I could not have time to see or sketch, but I saw it from distance on boat. It is gray stone. Maybe sketchable.

All those lake towers and villages are good to look at from the water. But when you get inside it looses its charm.

Stayed at Bellagio only for 10 minutes and took next boat back. On the return trip the west side of the lake is already in shade.

On the train from Martigny to Milan, on the Italian frontier, there was a customer officer who looked like B. Mion. In a restaurant yesterday noon, I saw another person who looked more like him, even to the gesture and way of eating.

In Germany the panel doors are often like this.

But in northern Italy, the door panels are often horizontal, recalling the stone joints.

Aug 4 Left Milan 9:22, arrived at Certosa 9:50.

In the train, an old woman put 9 pieces of large baggage overhead, the others having nothing to occupy the space.

Two French women are traveling to Certosa and on presenting their tickets to conductor, who got so excited that the women thought they took the wrong train. But they only had to pay extra for express train.

At the station of Certosa, a driver has his rail- horse carriage waiting for the [**93**] (these pages were written while I was half drunk, head swimming anyway) monastery.

But on seeing we walking along the track without taking his car, he pointed me the wrong direction, which I followed and walked a complete circle around the wall.

The central gem is the chapel with tower. Such perfect inlaid marble work on the façade, of different colors. The façade is white marble and the rear axis is red brick. The combination is most charming. The tower builds up very well also. The interior of the church looks grand. Every chapel is a gem, with a fine attar of fine inland marble. The choir is a little Baroque. The cloister of the fountain is grand. So is the grande chiostro, which is surrounded with the monk's cells. Each monk has three rooms on the 1st floor, with a fire place and a food converge (dumb waiter turned).

The Entrance and guide and checking of articles require no fee, to my wondering.

This no doubt is the fine early Renaissance work in Lombardy.

Nearby is a restaurant, where one dines in the open, sheltered by tree and vines. No place is more cool and peaceful. The hostess is charming and speaks French. The wine is excellent and puts me into that forgetful condition, from which all the thirty souls are reluctant to return. The food is equally good, and two monks beside me are having as good an appetite as any earthly creature.

Took train (1:15) to Genova. On the way first passed Pavia. Its excellent dome and bell tower stand out with the [**94**] covered bridge (the arches are different in width). It is a little gem again, and the Italians are as incapable of doing it now as any other race at all times.

I forgot to mention the fact when one enters the court towards the chapel on the right wall, the windows are painted also. The door way has painted order in stucco.

Arrived at Genova 5:20 (Took train from Catosa at 1:15). The weather is cloudy, and the whole town does not seem to be interesting, except the old winding narrow streets with tall houses on each side, bannered with clothes just washed. All the palazzos and churches Baedeker praised are nothing at all. The best part of the town is along the harbor, where houses of ten stories high pile up most picturesquely, like a miniature New York, only more artistically.

The harbor is far different from what I imagined. I expected sail boats (at least some), but there are nothing but steamships.

Had dinner on the quay, under a long arch-spaghetti, wine, beef and fruit for 8 lire.

Stayed at hotel Bellevue, on the hill near station for 15 L.

Aug 5 Up very early (4:45) caught train for Pisa at 5:25, and arrived at 9:15, went towards the river, sketched Torre Guelfa, saw San Paolo, which has a fine façade resembling the Duomo. There is a stair going down near the church to the river bank, where the smell of human deposits is unbearable and my sketch was made right there.

Santa Maria della Spina has a curious gothic [**95**] façade of hi-part composition, and is the smallest church I ever saw.

Saw the university, a very classical façade. San Frediano has ancient columns inside. Palazzo Augustini is in Venetian style. Santa Caterina has fine glass inside. The feeling of proportion is almost modernistic. Horizontal blue hands too, suggest modernism. The ceiling of dark wood painted (blue pattern) is fine.

Saw the Leaning Tower, entirely of white marble, so are the cathedral and baptistery. Therefore in the sun, the white stone reflects light and dazzles you eye.

Went on top of the tower and took a photo of myself.

The cathedral is very good, although the dome from outside looks funny. Horizontal blue marble hands used freely. The mosaic by Cimabue over the altar (gold background) is so bold that it looks very modern, especially the treatment of Christ's face.

The baptistery has the finest dome one can imagine. The outside looks superb. The inside is again so bold, and simple that any modernistic architect would be inclined to do. The gem there is Nicola Pisano's pulpit. The workmanship of marble is superb.

Did not have any breakfast, so had lunch at Pisa, near the cathedral.

The Campo Santo has frescoes and tombstone.

The monuments at Pisa are such as to suggest the vigor and simplicity of an age which just realized its greatness, without yet any sophistication.

Took train for Florence at 1:30, arrived at 3:30, stayed at pension Martellini, 13 Via dell'alloro. [**96**]

Saw outside of Palazzo Pitti. Also saw Santa Maria del Carmine and San Spirito, Sketched Ponte Veccio, the best bridge I yet saw.

Aug 6 Went to the cathedral first, saw inside, rather bare, but very monumental. The glass windows in the dome are the best, sparkling and full of mystic quality. The choir is under the dome which is quite novel, and good.

Inspected the doors of the baptistry. They are very simple in modeling and that is why they are good, just enough and not too much to be Baroque. The inside of the baptistery is just like Pantheon at Rome, very simple, and impressive. Did not go up the campanile, but saw Donatello's "Zuccone", way up in the air.

The cathedral museum has Luca Della Robbias.

Going gallery and Donatello. There are perhaps the only outstanding collection there.

Palazzo Vecchio has tower (high) that looks like a castle and swallow-tailed battlements (ghibilline), very impressive.

The rooms upstairs seldom have square or rectangular shapes. They are just haphazard and form sided rooms. This amazingly frankness recalls the irregular streets, by which the palace is bound. The interiors are better than another palace that is open.

Saw bronze slab (in the Piazza della Signoria) about Savonarola's being burnt to death on the stake there.

Loggia dei Lanzi, a copy of which is in Munich, far surpasses that in beauty. The number of sculptures there is amazing and [**97**] most by masterpieces. It is a little open-air museum.

Saw Uffizi gallery. It is on top of a U-shaped columnler, and has an important collection, but not as good as Pitti, though here they have a combination of painting and sculpture.

The national museum has more Donatellos than any other place, also there is Michelangelo's Drunken Bacchus. His unfinished building is also here. The della Robias are also numerous.

Spedale degli Innocenti has medollious by Andrea della Robia, with blue ground.

Santissima Annunziate has numerous frescos.

Palazzo Medici is not worth seeing at all. The apartments are very poor in taste, the museum is not any good either.

Monastery of San Marco has many frescoes in the cloister, and the cells upstairs. Some of the cells were once occupied by Savonarola.

Gallery of the Academia di Belle Arti has Michelangelo's "David", and is unfinished Prigione Group, very much like the finished work of Rodin. David has nothing particular except it is big and vigorous.

San Lorenzo has an unfinished façade. Saw the Medici chapel, the whole thing being marble of different colors inside. It gets Baroque. The marble floor (mosaics) begun at 1888, is now only half done, with 3 people working on it.

The new Sacristy was built by Michelangelo and contains his famous Medici tombs. One for Giuliano and the other Lorenzo [**98**] "il Penseroso".

Palazzo Strozzi has fine iron work, and unfinished cornice.

Palazzo Pitti is the most impressive and grand building in Florence, with its monumental garden. The picture gallery contains Raphael's Madonna della Sedia (also his Granduca) and also numerous portraits of pope & ladies by him.

Fiesole is about 25 minutes ride from the Duomo. As one approaches the hill, the view of Florence looks very grand, with the Dome and Campanile in the mist, and cypresses stand up like sentinels, black green against silver gray of the olive leaves.

Aug 7 Went up the Dome in the morning. The fresco in the ceiling can be seen in detail. The inner dome follows the contour of the outer dome. The detail of marble of the lantern is very fine. From there the view of whole Florence is superb. It is quite different from the view obtained at London from the dome of St. Paul. There one saw smoke and ugly drab buildings. Here the houses and churches and cypress trees blossom before your eye.

Or San Michel has a very flowery Gothic 1st story. The niches are filled with status (outside). The interior is not wonderful.

Santa Croce has Michelangelo's Tomb. The murals by Giotto in the chapels are good.

Casa Buonarroti has fine interiors and the museum is all right, though not much. [**99**]

Santa Maria Novella has unequal bay inside. Saw the frescoes in the Spanish chapel.

Aug 8 Rain in Venice.

Saw inside of San Marco. The first impression of it is grand, with so much color and such rich silhouette. It is the best church I have seen.

The mosaics inside (examined from the gallery) is grand. The atmosphere is excellent as a church. The floor is very old and has hills and valleys.

Saw inside of Doge Palace, very good interior. The prison reminds one of Chillon. Only this is on a bigger scale. Walked inside the Bridge of Sighs.

The academy of Fine Arts has collection of Titian. But it otherwise is full of junk. Titian's assumption of the Virgin, said to be here. I could not find. But there are many Titian.

Aug 9 Glorious weather in the afternoon, and at night the perfect moon over the Adriatic.

In the morning it was still cloudy. But made several sketches of sailing boats.

Walked over the Rialto, a wide bridge with 3 open passages and 2 rows of inclined covered arcades in between. It is a beautiful thing.

Went to where Marco Polo used to live. A court with a square tower (much altered) which is the sole remain of his home. The court has an old door way of carved stone. Beyond is the Marco Polo Bridge, not different from any other.

Walked all the way to the public park, the extreme end of the island. Made 7 sketches.

Aug 10   Another glorious day. Went to see Colleoni's statue. The church nearby [100] (San Giovanni e Paolo) is somewhat like San Marco in exterior. The inside is nothing.

Went to Marco Polo's court again, found with difficulty, through maze of streets. This time found a house marked with tablet, saying the site to be Marco's house. The house is too new to be original, which was built down in 16 century.

Walked through most of the street in the afternoon and after all even in Venice most of the streets are alike.

Heard music in Piazza San Marco, very common.

In the morning I climbed up the Campanile, one sees the whole island and the main land. Made 6 sketches.

Aug 11   Went to Lido in the morning, very common place. The bathing is the main thing.

Saw international art exhibit in public park. Paintings representing France, Germany, Czechoslovakia, Russia, U.S.A. , Belgium, England and Italy, which last has a large collection of futuristic paintings and some goldsmith works along modern lives. All the other counties send in very scanty and bad examples.

The exposition building are mostly modernistic, in very poor taste.

Bathed for 1/2 hour on the Lido beach in late afternoon. May go there tomorrow again.

Made six sketches.

On way back from San Marco to station, just close to San Georgio Maggiore, the moon shone on the water and the dome & campanile of San Giorgio stood in silhouette, male and female sing (extremely good)was heard from either the [101] gondolas or small boats. The whole thing looked so much like a dream and very romantic.

Aug 12   Walked a long way in the morning, made 2 pencil sketches. Took a gondola ride on the grand canal, seeing Palazzo Vendramin. The stone slab has Wagner's profile and some Baroque ornament, there carved the following words:

F.T. Cadorin F.
IN QUESTO PALAGIO
L'ULTIMO SPIRO DE RICCARDO WAGNER
ODONO LE ANIME
PERPETUARSI CAME LA MAREA
CHE LAMBE I MARMI
   GAB D'ANNUNZIO
+XIII FEBBRAIO
MDCCCLXXXIII
IN MEMORIAM

Went to Lido to bath again, there being hardly any sunshine.

Made 3 watercolors at Piazza San Marco.

While taking dinner at the usual place. A man and a woman played music-mainly Romano. The woman reminded me so much of 白居易琵琶行.

Aug 13   Took train for Verona at 7, arrived at 9.

Porta Nuova is very good in proportion. Porta Palio, which Goethe praised, does not look as good as Nuova.

San Zeno Maggiore is the best Romanesque church I ever saw. The wood ceiling over the Nave (14C.) is grand, made of carved, wood ribs forcing little square panels, on which faint painting can be seen. The effect is very modernistic.

The font supported by an inverted capital is also in modernistic form. The whole aspect of the interior [**102**] is good, and the choir is original in treatment, with marble rail on which stand Christ and his disciples. The little windows with orange light through them, look effective. The outside Romanesque portal is very charming and colorful, besides being graceful. The whole proportion of the façade is fine. The doors are covered with separate bronze plates of sculpture in the most archaic manner.

Porta Borsari has lost its entablature. There are two arches on the street and above them 3 rows of windows, or open arcades.

The view from the bank looking towards the fortress, across the old bridge (Ponte Pietra) is very fine, with beautiful pile of houses. The thing reminds one of Würzburg.

The cathedral has nothing particularly good, the ceiling is painted blue with gold stars, and the general aspect is Baroque. The new addition (looks new) of the Campanile is very poor.

The garden of Palazzo Giusti is good, with steep slope, treated with niches & probably cascades, with cypresses lined on both sides, very impressing, visitors not admitted.

Saw supposed house of Juliet's parents (13C.) with balcony very high (on 3rd story). The other balcony was removed with brackets remaining. The courtyard is square, with long rows of railed balconies. The place is being remodeled.

Then saw Juliet's tomb, an open stone coffin with admission tickets collected in it. It lies in the little loggia of Romanesque arcades. It looks too well turned to be true. All fictitious any way. Shakespeare's [**103**] bust stands on the backwall.

Saw the group of building around Piazza Dante, La Loggia (Palazzo del Consiglio) is gracefully proportioned.

The arena is still in good shape (Roman), and has practically no orders. It is being used as a regular theatre now. (The modern setting looks bare and papery in such a solid structure.)

Also saw the Roman theatre, apparently closed to visitors. But one can see through the railing.

On the wall of Juliet's tomb are 2 stone tablets.

With these words.

① Sacras Aedes

Seraphico Patri Addictas
Turris Cognomento a Palea
Nitrati Pulveris Cadis
Abunde referta
Qno Fulgurito
Incendi vi Subitari
In Lapidum Fragmina Arietata
Faede Tritas Illisit Terras
(I). I). c. XXIV

② Easdem Aedes
Co. Aloysius Turrianus
Basilica Urbis Stipe et Pierum
In Havce Angustam Speciem
Ex Redivivis Excitavit
Sebastiano Ciconia a Consiliis.
Hileronimo Cafontanio ab Aedif
(I). I). c. XXV

In San Marco, Venice, on the pillars, the marble slabs are laid vertically with feather joints at the corners.

Took 9:20 pm. train for Innsbruck.

Aug 14 Arrived at Innsbruck at 4 o'clock in the morning, without much sleep the whole night. Look a map in the 3rd class waiting room when at 6. The station guard came and chased me out.

Took breakfast at a place near the center of the town, walked up to the mountain, half way made a sketch and came down to [**104**] lunch.

Weather in the morning is fine. Towards noon, it becomes cloudy.

Have no more desire to sketch.

Mailed 2 guide books to Snyder.

Aug 15 No more sight seeing from now on. The things I shall see at Berlin (of any) and Poland and Russia will be recalled later on, as I must part with the book from tomorrow till I reach home. A sad feeling came over me in the evening. One cannot get sick of life or anything in sunny Italy. But in the north what with the rain, it is very miserable, alone and to have no desire to do anything.

One delightful thing is to see Austrian and German modern architecture again.

Aug 16

Aug 17 Saw Charlottenburg garden from outside.
Full of trees. Took train for Russia.

Aug 18 Passed Warsaw. Poland is very drab, The only color is the scarf of a woman. The architecture is strangely Russian and German. Roads are bad.

Reached Niegoleroje at 4:00 pm. Between Russia & Poland there is a wood gate, which marks the boundary, on both sides stand soldiers, and the formality requires the train to stop on both sides of the gate.

The customs are not very nasty. They did not care for my watch, nor did they bother with books. They did look after writing, money (American) must be registered, and when one changes American notes for Russian Rubbles, registration is necessary. [**105**]

I was assigned to a sleeping compartment where there had been 3 women (whom later I found to be missionaries to China, 2 Americans & one Chinese)

I never thought of the embarrassing situation and was impertinently waiting them to clean things from my bath. But after, I came out from the dining car, the elder woman told me they had moved me to another place, I was thankful and at the same time reproached myself for being so absent-minded about the whole thing.

Aug 19 Reached Moscow 11 am. John Willis at Station to meet me. We stayed in the station (Alexandra) for a long time, probably waiting for that dumb give who lost their baggage check. (The girl is daughter of a man in the same firm with Willis). Finally Willis took me to his apartment, there took a shower (cold) and had a steak dinner prepared by his wife.

We set forth to the Kremlin, accompanied by another man, Bulgarian by birth, now an American and working in the same firm. He speaks Russian and knows Moscow pretty well.

Kremlin is very wonderful, with its many towers and gates and walls. It is also colorful. The Red Square is being repaved, and when it is finished, it is going to be the most impressive thing in the world. Lenin's tomb is enclosed as it is being rebuilt in black and red granite in the old design. We were late in applying for entrance to the Kremlin.

St. Basil is a curious church. It has 10 units, and each unit goes up to be a tower. The plan cannot be read from the actual building, which seems to be full of dark alley and small chapels. The work is cheap and detail are rotten. But the exterior ensemble is [**106**] perfectly beautiful. People don't show any reverence. They have their hats on! And one can touch anything at all. In one chapel there did sit 2 old women forbidding visitors to touch an old lamp.

Just to show how little the Russians know about physics they put a glass bar, on the arch (which is going to crack worse) with both ends in plaster of Paris! Sure enough the plaster cracks leaving the glass unbroken.

The dust in Moscow is the worst in Europe. And also the gutter into which I fell. I actually saw people lie comfortably in the gutter too. The Russians think nothing of change. Anything can change over night – street names, museums, and buildings. If the street is curved on account of the projection of a certain building, the projection can be torn down, no matter it belongs to what building.

They buy the best of machines. One wonders where they got the money. By export, the whole population is industrial minded. That is their religion, no advertisements, no salesmen. But one sees good posters advocating industrialism.

Passed Tolstoy house, now museum, but had no time to go in. The countess Tolstoy is a bourgeois but they let her live for the museum.

The housing problem in Moscow is acute. The city can only take care of one million but now there are 3 millions. They have 5-day week. Every day one-fifth of the population are on holiday. People have little manners. They line up for [**107**] everything – for tobacco, food, and even for dying. There are so few hospitals to take care of the sick.

I telegrammed Willis on 17th and the telegram arrived on the 19th, one hour after I arrived at his apartment.

When we reached the modern French art museum (by inquiry), it was nearly 4 o'clock. No people are willing to work full time, much less overtime. So the custodians refuse entrance. By argument we won't win. So we just ascended the stair by Bulgar insistence. The women there spoke French. And calling them madams pleased them. I spent 15 minutes there, but I would wish 15 days. The treasures of the whole world are here, whole rooms of Cezanne, Van Gogh, Renoir, Matisse, Picasso, Gaugin. Nowhere else in the world can one see so many masterpieces in one museum.

Saw church of Christ the Savior built to commemorate the siege defeat of Napoleon on Moscow. It is of white marble outside, very simple. We ascended the top and had a good panorama of Moscow. There is some good inlaid marble work in the interior.

Took Trans Siberian train from the Siberian Station at 6:45 pm.

I asked some food from Willis's wife, but forgot the loaf of bread. She ran after us after we left for the street car to station, and that half a loaf did do some good service.

Shared a compartment with a young Russian communist, handsome and intelligent. He knows about all the long names of Russian literature. He gave me some candy and I him an orange.

Aug 20

Aug 21   The Russian went down [**108**] at Viatka.

The common address in Russia is citizen and citizenness. My watch stopped and the clock at the station showed different times on both sides. The station clock is Moscow time.

People in Siberia apparently stop washing their faces, much less their shirts.

Aug 22   The peasant women sell things at the station. But they are so silent and look so dumb. They stand there saying nothing, and of course nobody buy anything. In that silence there must be concealed an immense suffering anyhow they are better than before, as there is no one to whip them.

Aug 23   Cloudy, hilly country.

Aug 24   Passed Irkutsk, saw barracks and then Lake Baikal. First scenery and not yet exploited by steamship or hotels. Mountains now .

Aug 25   Passed Chita 7 pm.

Aug 26   Up early to see dawn, saw barbed wires and trenches. Reached Manchouli at 7:15 am. Went into town and found war ruins.

As I found out later baggage should be checked to Manchouli, or attend to baggage examination at Manchouli, as mine was held at Manchouli for 2 days by the customs.

Aug 27   Harbin 8:30 am. [**109**]

所 绘 与 所 摄

童寯先生在旅行途中同时还拍摄
了部分建筑照片,本书在此将其
部分所绘速写与所摄照片并置,
以为读者还原当时历史原貌。

（英）温彻斯特，西城门 Winchester, West Gate

（英）索尔兹伯里，圣安妮街景 Salisbury, Saint Anne Street

（英）格劳塞斯特，大教堂 Gloucester, Cathedral

(英)埃文河畔斯塔德福德,礼拜堂街 Stratford on-Avon, Chapel Street

(英)埃文河畔斯塔德福德,绵羊街 Stratford on-Avon, Sheep Street

(英)埃文河畔斯塔德福德,莎士比亚诞生故居 Stratford on-Avon, Shakespeare's Birth-Place

〔英〕伦敦，老古玩店　London, Old Curiosity Shop

〔法〕夏特尔，大教堂门廊　Charters, Portals of Cathedral

〔法〕夏特尔，城门　Charters, City Gate

(法)鲁昂,教堂远眺 Rouen, Cathedral

(法)亚眠,主教堂 Amiens, Cathedral

〔法〕兰斯,大教堂 Reims, Cathedral

〔荷〕沃伦丹姆,帆船 Volendam, A Sailing Boat

〔德〕杜塞尔多夫,天文馆 Düsseldorf, Planetarium

（德）科隆，比肯多夫现代教堂 Cologne, Bickendorf, Kirche St. Dreikönigen

（德）波恩，波恩大学 Bonn, Bonn University

（德）美因茨，埃森纳塔 Mainz, Eisener

(德)美因茨，城门 Mainz, City Gate

(德)美因茨，王宫 Mainz, Palace

(德)法兰克福，市政厅广场集市 Frankfurt, Market in Römerburg

（德）法兰克福，城塔 Frankfurt, City Wall Tower

（德）法兰克福，城内望楼 Frankfurt, Bockenheimer Warte

（德）法兰克福，圣伯尼费斯教堂室内 Frankfurt, St. Bonifice Church

(德)法兰克福,老市政厅 Frankfurt, Römer

(德)法兰克福,贝特曼大街 Frankfurt, Bethmannstrasse

(德)达姆斯塔德,展览馆 Darmstadt, Exhibition Building

(德) 达姆斯塔德,婚礼纪念塔 Darmstadt, Wedding Tower

(德) 洛希,修道院教堂 Lorsch, Klosterkirche

(德) 罗滕堡,郊区代特旺 Rothenburg, Detwang

(德)罗滕堡,克林根门 Rothenburg, Klingen Tor

(德)罗滕堡,双层古桥 Rothenburg, Doppelbrucke

(德)布雷斯劳,郊外堡门 Breslau, A Gate Tower

（德）德累斯顿，格奥尔根门 Dresden, Georgentor

（奥）维也纳，卡尔·马克思大院 Vienna, Karl Marx Hof

（奥）维也纳，贝多芬故居 Vienna, Beethovenhaus

(奥)萨尔兹堡,街景 Salzburg, Street View

(奥)萨尔兹堡,国王湖 Salzburg, Konigsee

(德)慕尼黑,手风琴手雕像 Munich, Sculpture of an Accordion Player

(德) 奥格斯堡,老房子 Augsburg, Old House

(德) 乌尔姆,城塔 Ulm, City Wall Tower

(德) 斯图加特,肖肯百货大楼 Stuttgart, Schocken Department Store

（瑞士）卢瑟恩，河边古堡 Lucerne, Castle by the River

（瑞士）卢瑟恩，瞭望塔 Lucerne, Watch Tower

（瑞士）苏黎世，廊桥 Zurich, Covered Wooden Bridge

(瑞士)洛桑,洛桑湖 Lausanne, Lausanne Lake

(瑞士)西庸堡城堡 Chateau de Chillon, Castle

(瑞士)西庸堡 Chateau de Chillon

(瑞士)西庸堡远望 Remote View of Chateau de Chillon

(瑞士)圣伯纳德救济院 St.Bernard Hospice

(意)米兰,卡斯泰罗广场 Milan, Piazza Castello

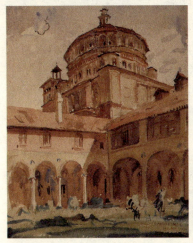 

(意)米兰,圣玛利亚感恩修道院 Milan, Santa Maria delle Grazie

(意)佛罗伦萨,街景 Florence, Street View

(意)佛罗伦萨,维奇奥桥 Florence, Ponte Vechio

(意)威尼斯,圣马可广场 Venice, Piazza San Marco

(意)威尼斯,总督府 Venice, Palazzo Ducale

(意)威尼斯,叹息桥 Venice, Bridge of Sighs

（意）威尼斯，里亚托桥 Venice, Ponte Rialto Bridge

（意）威尼斯，贡多拉 Venice, Gondola

（意）威尼斯，民居大门 Venice, A Gate of a House

(意)威尼斯,圣乔瓦尼广场,巴托洛米奥·科勒奥尼雕像
Venice, Campo Santi Giovanni e Paolo, Statue of Bartolomeo Colleoni

(美)费城,宾夕法尼亚大学,学生宿舍入口 Philadelphia, University of Pennsylvania, Approach to Students' Terrace

(美)费城,贝西玫瑰屋,第一面星条旗在此制作 Philadelphia, Betsy Rose House

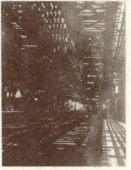

(美)纽约,高架铁路桥面 New York, Elevated Railway

北京,北海团城 Beijing, Beihai Roundcity

上海,豫园湖心亭 Shanghai, Pavilion in Water, Yu Garden

童寯年谱

1900年10月2日 童寯诞生于奉天盛京（今沈阳）附近东台子村。童寯祖先属满族正蓝旗，原姓钮牯录，曾随努尔哈赤征战于辽东平原。清政权奠都于盛京后，全家就在沈阳东郊东台子村定居下来。

童寯祖父名为郎德祥，一生务农，在童寯出生之前即已去世。父亲名为恩格，为家中独子，也是家族所供养的第一个读书人。他在考中了沈阳县秀才之后，于乡村开办私塾，弃农从教。恩格勤奋好学，通读经史古籍，精于小楷。

童寯兄弟有三人，童寯为长子，二弟童廎早年留学日本学电机，1928年回国后在沈阳电灯厂和兵工厂工作，曾任沈阳电业局总工程师。三弟童村，北京协和医学校1929年毕业，1941年前往美国霍普金斯大学留学进修，参加过该校首次青霉素临床试验。新中国成立后在上海曾主持我国首次青霉素的研制生产工作。

1903年 童寯祖母病逝。是年时值日俄战争期间，两军在沈阳附近展开激战，乡间闾里鸡犬不宁。恩格带领全家迁入奉天省城沈阳的浩然里，住进一位喀姓的官僚地主家中，做家庭教师。童寯在这所封闭的深宅大院里，开始了童年生活（图1）。

童寯自小受到家规的严格管束，塑就了日后严肃内向的性格。在他的记忆中，所犯的唯一严重错误就是往水井里撒了一把土。

1908年 童寯被送入奉天省蒙养院，由一位日本侨民女教师进行启蒙教育，教授他手工艺术、剪纸、拼贴图案、搭制积木模型等。童寯曾经在制作火车模型时，不慎在左手食指上留下一道刀痕。

1910年9月 童寯进入奉天省立第一小学读书，开始学习四书五经。父亲对他严加督促，命其背诵不甚理解的古文。这为童寯日后的古典文学修养打下了坚实的基础，同时也养成了他惜墨如金，千锤百炼的治学方法。

1911年（宣统三年） 童寯的父亲恩格在43岁时，以奉天府学禀生资格考取岁贡，通过保和殿复试（通常由皇帝面试），被列为当年二等第十一名进士，钦点七品。从京师回到家乡后，恩格就开始从事志愿中的教育事业，先后任劝学所所长、女子师范学校校长和奉天省教育科科长等职。

1917年9月 童寯进入奉天省第一中学读书，直至1921年毕业。这一期间童寯已经受到新型学制的全面教育，经常前往基督教青年会听取科学和艺术讲座。教师中有多人系留日归来，他们所讲授的

课程,特别是世界地理和世界历史使他视野开阔,从而开始接触西方文明。

从此,童寯开始全力学习英文,订阅上海出版的英文周报,前往青年会聆听英文演讲。同时他也开始学习西洋油画、铅笔素描等(图2)。

童寯在中学的学习刻苦努力,成绩名列前茅。他的中学同学后来大多成为张学良的属下和谋士,如同窗好友苗剑秋作为张学良的政治顾问,是后来西安事变的主谋之一。事变后苗剑秋亡命香港,途经上海时曾经藏身于童家。另外还有一位著名的伟人周恩来,他比童寯高二班,于"五四"前夕离开沈阳,前往天津就读。

1920年 童寯在父亲的完全做主下,按照封建婚姻的传统,与女子师范学校的高才生关蔚然(满族)结婚。他们结婚后才开始互相了解、互相恋爱,尽管在随后大部分时间里,童寯都是在外求学或者工作,俩人长期分居两地,但是夫妻感情却愈来愈深。童寯在晚年时回忆到,这桩婚姻是

图1 与父亲恩格于沈阳浩然里
图2 奉天省第一中学读书,学习油画
图3 天津车站,前往天津新学书院进修英文

图4 清华园大门
图5 1923年，清华高三年级
图6 1923年，清华担任年鉴美术编辑
图7 1925年，清华学堂毕业证书

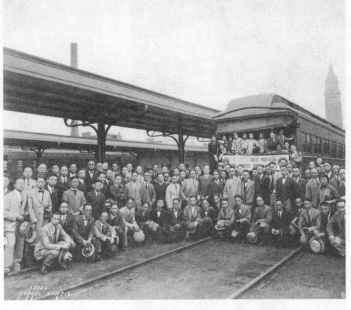

图8 赴美途中,与清华同学在渡洋客轮上
图9 赴美途中,西雅图火车站

图10 赴美途中，于东京作短暂停留
图11 西雅图大北方火车站
图12 宾夕法尼亚大学入学登记照片
图13 留美护照照片
图14 在宾夕法尼亚大学

美满的,他是幸运的,因为在包办婚姻的情况下是不可能找到像关蔚然这样的女性。关蔚然于1956年的早逝给童寯在精神上带来巨大打击,在他的床头总放有一幅她的肖像。

1921年7月 童寯中学毕业。当时正值以收回旅大为导火线的"五四"运动时期,这场运动给东北的学生带来了极大的激奋。童寯决定接下来攻读土木工程专业,以建设家乡。于是他欲往投考唐山交大。就在此时,新任奉天省教育科长的父亲恩格在北平出差,了解到清华留美预备学校于该年准许接收东北籍的考生。在恩格的鼓励下,童寯决定参加竞争。为了提高英文水平,他于暑假特地前往天津新学书院进修英文(图3)。随即回来参加唐山交大的入学考试,接着又赶赴北平报考清华。当时考生有三四百人,这次激烈的角逐是他一生中的重要转折。结果童寯在唐山交大名列第一,在清华名列第三。最后,童寯选择了清华(图4)。

1921年9月 童寯进入北平清华学堂高等科学习(图5)。在与之交往的同窗好友中,有比他高二班的梁思成、陈植和黄家骅,有同班的蔡方荫,低班的过元熙、哈雄文、梁衍、王华彬等。童寯在校期间,美术功课出色,并积极参加学校美术社的活动,与社中的闻一多、梁思成和张治中等交往。在斯杜女士(Miss Storr)和加瑟尔女士(Miss Gauthier)的辅导下,童寯在钢笔画、水彩画方面有了长足进步,全校闻名,并举办过个人画展。后来他担任了三年清华年鉴的美术编辑(图6)。同时,童寯在清华也接受了大量新思想的洗涤,经常前往聆听梁启超、胡适、王国维的讲座,并受教于英文教师王文显,物理教师梅贻琦,生物教师秉志,体育教师马约翰(图7)。

1925年9月 童寯受高班杨廷宝的影响,选择留学美国宾夕法尼亚大学建筑系。童寯由上海出发,途经东京、西雅图至美国东部费城,途中记录有"渡洋日记"(图8)(图9)(图10)(图11)(图12)(图13)。

宾夕法尼亚大学建筑系在当时正处于一个黄金时期,不仅在全美国拥有一流的师资队伍,而且云集了一批艺术天才,著名建筑师路易·康此时也正在这里学习。同时而来的中国留学生也显得格外的才华横溢,其中有已毕业的杨廷宝、朱彬、赵深,在读的陈植、梁思成、过元熙等人(图16)(图17)。

图15 宾夕法尼亚大学建筑系设计教室
图16 宾夕法尼亚大学艺术学院大楼

图17 宾夕法尼亚大学学生宿舍入口门廊
图18 在宾夕法尼亚大学图书馆
图19 1926年于费城工作
图20 童寯在宾夕法尼亚大学作业：园林小品

图21 在宾夕法尼亚大学绘图教室:童寯、过元熙、陈植(从左至右)
图22 在宾夕法尼亚大学绘图教室:童寯、陈植、Rowland Synder、Alice Warin、John Richard（从左至右）
图23 在宾夕法尼亚大学绘图教室:童寯、过元熙、陈植(从左至右)
图24 在宾夕法尼亚大学绘图教室:陈植、童寯(从左至右)

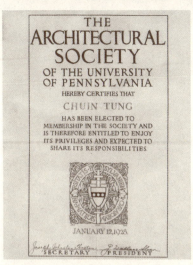

图25 宾夕法尼亚大学建筑社

兹此证明童寯当选本社会员,享有本社各项专许,并期分担其责。
1928年1月12日
社长:华莱士·肖(J. Wallace Shaw)
秘书:约瑟夫·约翰斯顿·胡顿(Joseph Johnston Hooton)

图27 童寯在学生作业竞赛获得奖章。左上:1927年全美大学生建筑设计竞赛二等奖;右上: 1928年全美大学生竞赛一等奖;下:1928年的亚瑟·斯佩德·布鲁克纪念奖竞赛金奖。原奖牌在"文革"期间的抄家过程中遗失。图片为童寯保存的拓片

图26 在学生作业竞赛获奖的新闻报道

费城咨询报
Jefferson R. Carroll, Jr., 童寯: 宾夕法尼亚大学建筑系学生在纽约艺术设计学院建筑系所举办的第三届全国竞赛中获得奖项。来自中国沈阳的学生童寯获一等奖,卡罗尔等四人获二等奖。

  杨廷宝刚毕业不久,已在其导师保罗·克雷[1]的事务所中工作,星期日常与童寯相聚。而梁思成则更是童寯在宾大期间的同屋室友,情如手足(图13)。

---

1 保罗·克雷(Paul Philippe Cret, 1876—1945年),出生于法国里昂,曾在巴黎美术学院接受系统教育,1903年前往美国,执教于费城宾夕法尼亚大学建筑系,并将布扎教育体系带入美国。保罗·克雷同时也是一位出色的职业建筑师,自1907年开始,完成过许多重要的纪念性建筑的设计。我国著名建筑师杨廷宝在宾夕法尼亚大学留学期间曾受教于克雷,并在毕业后前往其事务所实习工作。

宾夕法尼亚大学建筑系的教学是按照巴黎美术学院的"图房"（Altelier）传统模式进行的，也就是几个学生编为一组，在一位教师（称房师 Patron）的指导下进行设计，所有不同年级的同学均在一个大通间上设计课，由克雷巡回指导、评图和改图（图15）。全系学生有150人左右，学制五年，授学士，研究生院一年授硕士。由于童寯的学习成绩优异，才华出众（图20）。在设计导师毕克莱（George Howard Bickley）（"法国国家文凭建筑师"）的指导下，仅用三年时间完成本科学业，再过一年获硕士学位，并被选为美国丁字尺三角学会（T Square Society）会员（图14）（图18）（图19）（图21）（图22）（图23）（图24）（图25）。

童寯在学习期间曾多次参加建筑设计竞赛，数次获奖，其中包括全美大学生建筑设计竞赛，1927年获得二等奖（博物馆），1928年获得一等奖（教堂）。在1928年的亚瑟·斯佩德·布鲁克纪念奖（Arthur Spayd Brooke Memorial Prize）设计竞赛中，童寯更是获得金奖第一名，该竞赛在全美有近五十所大学建筑系参加，评委主席为芝加哥著名建筑师雷蒙·胡德（Raymond Hood），而宾夕法尼亚大学此前仅有克雷和哈伯森教授曾获此奖（图26）（图27）（图28）。

与此同时，童寯的绘画天赋也得以充分发掘，接受美国著名水彩画家道森（George Walter Dawson）的指导，奠定了日后杰出的绘画功底。

1928年6月—1929年6月 童寯自宾夕法尼亚大学毕业（图29）（图30）（图31）（图32）。毕业后前往美国费城本科尔（Ralph B. Bencker）建筑师事务所担任绘图员、设计师（图33）。

1929年6月—1930年4月 在美国纽约高层建筑权威伊莱·康（Ely J. Kahn）建筑师事务所任设计师，并参加华尔街120号商厦设计。

自1929年起，童寯开始接受现代建筑思潮的影响，决心毕生致力于探索和创造中国新建筑的道路。他开始接触并研读包豪斯、柯布西埃、构成派、风格派的理论。

1930年5月~1930年8月 童寯离开美国赴欧洲参观考察古典建筑，游历英国、法国、比利时、荷兰、德国、瑞士、意大利等国，最后途经东欧、苏俄回国。在这短短4个月的时间里，童寯完成了大批绘画作品，同时也目睹了新建筑运动的成就，并撰写《旅欧日记》（图34）（图35）（图36）（图37）（图38）（图39）（图40）（图41）。

图28 童寯在布鲁克纪念奖设计竞赛中的作品,一座新教教堂

图29 童寯在宾夕法尼亚大学毕业证书

宾夕法尼亚大学教务长、副教务长及教授谨向文件之收受者致敬:

以恰当之学位表彰在文学、科学与哲学等领域之勋绩,在公共福祉之贡献,乃大学之古老权利与传统。童寯先生已荣符学业各项要求,我等于此仅凭学校董事会所赋之权,授其建筑学硕士学位,以及相关之所有权利、荣誉及专许。
经我等之手与董事会印信

我主1928年2月18日
宾夕法尼亚大学第188年于费城
教务长:约赛亚·H.潘尼曼(Josiah H. Penniman)
院长:沃伦·鲍尔斯·莱德(Warren Powers Laird)
秘书:爱德华·W.芒福德(Edward W. Mumford)

图30 寄给父母的毕业照
图31 毕业照（最后一排左二为童寯）

1930年9月 童寯回到家乡沈阳。应当时东北大学工学院院长孙国锋的邀请，出任沈阳东北大学建筑系教授。当时已经在东北大学建筑系任教的还有梁思成、林徽因、陈植、谭垣、蔡方荫等，阵容强大（图42）。童寯在执教期间，写著《建筑五式》、《各式穹窿》、《做法说明书》、《北平两寺塔》等文章，并积极编撰建筑教材。在他给学生所列出的参考书单中，就有柯布西埃《走向新建筑》一书。在东北大学任教期间，童寯还曾参加梁、陈、童、蔡建筑师工程师事务所。1931年2月，陈植辞去在东北大学的教职，到上海与赵深创办事务所。1931年6月，梁思成、林徽因赴北平任职中国营造学社，童寯继任东北大学建筑系主任。此后不久即发生"九一八"事变，在这紧急时期，童寯慷慨资助学生进关逃难。在举家避难北平的途中，他仍然不忘携带东北大学建筑系的教学资料和幻灯片，在抗战期间在辗转大后方的过程中，从未损坏。直到新中国成立后，如数归还东北工学院。

1931年9月 童寯利用在北平停留期间，参观考察河北易县清陵、北平大正觉寺塔、碧云寺塔。

1931年11月 童寯应陈植之邀，赴上海加入赵深、陈植在上海正在组建的"华盖建筑师事务所"。该事务所后来于1932年元旦正式挂牌成立，由赵深负责外业，陈植负责内务，童寯主持绘图房设计工作（图43）。华盖建筑师事务所在20世纪30—40年代完成了大量建筑设计作品，在当时盛行的复古潮流中，始终坚持新建筑

图32 毕业照
图33 本科尔建筑师事务所工作推荐证明

拉尔夫·B. 本科尔
建筑师事务所
费城，栗树街1601号

1933年2月28日
敬启者：

兹此证明童寯先生从1928年6月至1929年6月受雇敝事务所，任建筑绘图员与设计师。其行止方正，工作卓有成效。
我等满意他于事务所之表现，对其离走费城深感遗憾。

您忠实的，
拉尔夫·B. 本科尔

图34 旅欧途中,在欧罗巴邮船上
图35 与大学同窗Rowland Snyder同游欧洲
图36 在欧洲游历途中,科隆大教堂前
图37 在欧洲游历途中,从阿姆斯特丹至科隆的火车上

图38 在欧洲游历途中,在莱茵河游船上
图39 在欧洲游历途中,在日内瓦湖畔
图40 在欧洲游历途中,在西庸堡前
图41 在欧洲游历途中,在威尼斯贡多拉船上

图42 东北大学师生合影(前排左二为童寯)

方向。华盖建筑师事务所的成就代表着中国建筑师在近代史上的崛起(图44)(图45)(图46)。

1931年 童寯加入中国建筑师学会,并被选为首届常务理事。

1932年 东北大学建筑系部分三、四年级学生流亡来沪,童寯呼吁建筑界好友与他共同义务为学生补习功课,并在家中组织讲课和考试,历时两年。在授课完毕后,通过事先磋商,由上海大夏大学发给文凭,从而造就我国第一代国产建筑师(图47)(图48)。

1932年 设计南京国民政府外交部办公大楼。这是童寯来沪后所参加的第一个实际项目,该设计先由赵深作出平面,童寯、陈植与其讨论外形处理,根据功能需要决定总体布局,同时在檐口采用简化斗拱来体现民族风格。建筑立面渲染图由童寯即兴完成。南京国民政府外交部办公大楼是中国近现代建筑史中的一件里程碑式的作品,它既体现着对于中国传统建筑文化的

图43 华盖建筑师事务所标准照
图44 与赵深在一起

图45 与陈植及友人
图46 与陈植及友人
图47 与杨廷宝在一起
图48 与杨廷宝在考察江南园林途中

继承，也体现着不落俗套的创新精神。该建筑现为全国重点文物保护单位。

1933年 童寯完成具有极强现代感的大上海大戏院、南京首都饭店、南京下关电厂、南京孙科住宅等设计。

1932—1937年 童寯利用在上海的工作余暇，遍访上海、苏州、无锡、常熟、扬州以及杭嘉湖等地，考察江南园林。他不辞辛苦，独自一人徒步踏勘、调查、摄影、测绘，又广为收集资料文献。当时交通工具很不方便，而且社会局势较为动荡。童寯在调研昆山、吴江两地时，曾先后被误认为日本奸细而入警察局。由于当时珍贵的园林文化日益凋零，而地方的富商巨贾又恣意兴作，童寯在目睹了这些现实状况之后，深感传统园林艺术所面临的灭绝境状，他怀着坚韧的毅力和刻苦的精神，着手整理我国传统的造园理论，并于1937年完成《江南园林志》一书。

《江南园林志》是我国近代最早一部运用科学方法论述中国造园理论的专著，也是学术界公认的继明朝计成《园冶》之后，近代园林研究最有影响的著作之一。

在书中，童寯非常精辟地通过对于"園"字的析解，诠释了中国园林的实质内含："囗"代表围墙，"土"代表屋宇的平面，也可代表亭榭，"口"字居中代表池塘，"衣"字在前既可表示为石，也可表示为树。同时童寯提出了造园的三种境界的观点：1.疏密得宜；2.曲折尽致；3.眼前有景。这些观点日后又成为现代园林研究的入手点。

在总结古人造园经验的基础上，童寯也为这门传统的建筑技艺纳入了现代科学的方法。他曾经批评古人："除赵之璧平山堂图、李斗扬州画舫录等书外，多重文字而忽图画……昔人绘画……谓之园林，无宁称为山水画。"因此，童寯在上海、苏州、无锡、常熟、扬州及杭嘉湖一带花费大量的精力进行园林的调研测绘，大都是一个人进行踏勘。无法测量，就用步量，而且与别人后来用皮尺量的尺寸，八九不离十，非常准确，可见其艰辛。在《江南园林志》一书中，许多园林今日早已荡然无存，其测绘图纸和照片都显得格外珍贵（图49）。

该书完成后即经营造学社刘敦桢介绍出版。梁思成看后在致童寯信中说："拜读之余，不胜钦佩。"后因芦沟桥事变，出版计划随营造学社南迁而中辍,直到1962年,才由中国建筑工业出版社出版。

在20世纪30年代,近代研究中国园林的著述甚少,用外文介绍中国园林艺术成就更属阙如,致使外国人得出东方园林有以日本为代表的错误认识。有感于此,童寯在林语堂、全增嘏主编的英文刊物《天下月刊》上连续用娴熟的英文发表《中国园林》、《满州园》、《建筑艺术纪实》、《中国建筑的外来影响》等文章,其后还发表关于园林建筑风格、形式,中西建筑影响和中西比较方面论文多篇,不仅奠定了他对于中国园林、中西建筑比较和当代中国建筑学术研究的基础,而且对西方学术界针对中国园林的认识和理解产生了重大影响。

1932—1937年 童寯开始着手"中国建筑史"、"中国雕塑史"、"中国绘画史"、"西藏建筑"、"日本建筑"等资料收集整理工作,该工作一直持续到20世纪70年代。

1935年 陪同他在纽约工作时的事务所老板伊莱·康,1936年陪同克莱伦斯·斯坦因[2]及其著名演员的妻子艾琳·麦克马洪[3]参观苏州园林。

1935年 应邀参加南京故宫博物院设计竞赛。

1936年 在上海会晤柏林大学教授鲍希曼[4],后者曾在中国营造学社工作,著有《中国建筑》、《中国之塔》,两人在中国建筑很多问题上观点一致。

1936年 设计南京中山文化教育馆,该作品在融会古今中外的尝试上具有示范意义。教育馆右方屹立一个柱塔,形成不对称的立面。上部嵌以琉璃花砖,气势宏伟,以形传神地表达了浓厚的民族风貌。

---

2 克莱伦斯·斯坦因(Clarence Samuel Stein, 1882—1975年),美国著名城市规划师、建筑师,美国花园城市运动的先驱者,曾与刘易斯·芒福德、本顿·麦凯耶等等共同成立美国区域规划联盟(Regional Planning Association of America)。他与另一位著名建筑师亨利·莱特合作成立事务所,是纽约雷德朋住区的主要设计者。

3 艾琳·麦克马洪(Aline MacMahon, 1899—1991年),美国著名电影、电视演员,曾于1944年因在《龙种》影片的演出而获奥斯卡女配角奖。

4 恩斯特·鲍希曼(Ernst Boerschmann, 1873—1949年),德国汉学家,他在1906年开始在中国作旅行考察,穿越了中国的十二个行省,行程数万里,拍下了数千张古代皇家建筑、宗教建筑和代表各地风情的民居等极其珍贵的照片,并著有《中国的建筑与地景》一书。在营造学社成立之初,鲍希曼曾经受邀加入其中。

5 叶恭绰(1881—1968年)广东番禺人,字誉虎,自号遐庵,清末举人。叶恭绰毕业于京师大学堂仕学馆,擅长诗词书画,精于考古鉴赏。早年追随孙中山先生进行革命斗争,1921年任交通总长。1920年,叶恭绰以交通部所属几所院校为基础成立上海交通大学,并任校长。

1936年4月 叶恭绰[5]在上海发起举办中国建筑展览会。其中华盖建筑师事务所的作品因其简洁洗练而别具一格。在展览期间,童寯发表题为"现代建筑"的演讲,华盖建筑师事务所被建筑界誉为求新派。

1937年 完成南京资源委员会及地质矿物陈列馆建筑群设计。

1938年5月 抗日战争爆发,随着江南业务萧条,童寯应邀赴重庆从事西南地区的业务。随资源委员会叶渚沛博士驾吉普车辗转赴重庆,主持资源委员会重庆炼钢厂的规划。在途经武汉时,曾经结识白求恩医生和美国记者斯诺。

1939年冬—1940年春 途经越南、香港返回上海,与家人团聚。1940年,参与《中国文化系列》研究,负责"中国绘画史"和"中国园林设计"等主题的写作(图50)。

1940年春—1944年 童寯赴重庆、贵阳建立事务所分所,此时赵深于昆明开设分所,而陈植留驻上海。在这期间童寯还晤见过王明、博古,外国记者篡丁、艾黎、比兰道尔、史密斯及美国大使馆文化参赞费正清等。

1940年—1944年 监督建造资中酒精厂,贵州筑县政府,华溪清华中学等工程,在这过程中,童寯经常跋山涉水,有时步行数日,亲临施工现场,一丝不苟。

1944年秋 应中央大学建筑系主任刘敦桢邀请,抵重庆任该系教授。同时期还有许多其他著名建筑师应聘中央大学建筑系,一时人才荟集,蒸蒸日上,成为中央大学建筑系"沙坪坝黄金时期"。

童寯从1944年在中央大学建筑系兼职任教一直到1951年,专任教学工作,他认为"建设我们这样大国,仅靠几个建筑师不行,要通过教育培养出成千上万的建筑师。也只有通过教育才能使人们对建筑有科学的认识"。童寯在教育园地上辛勤耕耘,培养出一大批建设人才,许多后来成为教授、学者以及著名的建筑师。

1945年8月 抗日战争胜利,国共两党和谈,组织政治协商会议(约50人),童寯应邀代表无党派人士出席,但和谈未果,内战再起。童寯从此谢绝和远离所有政治活动。

1944年 撰写《中国建筑艺术》、《古代中国时尚》等文。

1945年8月 抗日战争胜利,华盖建筑师事务所返回上海,重新整合为一。童寯随即赴南京负责华盖建筑师事务所在南京的工程项目,

图49 在安徽滁州醉翁亭

同时兼任中央大学教授。期间完成的主要设计工程有：南京交通部公路总局办公楼、南京美军顾问团公寓、上海新业银行、南京新街口百货商场等。

1949年　梁思成在北京清华大学成立营造系，邀童寯北上任教，被他婉言谢绝。

1950年　随着新中国建设的展开，赵深发起成立"联合顾问建筑师工程师事务所"，该事务所包含华盖事务所在内的沪宁建筑师11名，结构工程师2名和设备工程师1名，由赵深任主任，在上海、北京、山西、榆次、乌鲁木齐等地承接多种业务。童寯与其他13位建筑师、工程师共同工作。

1952年　"联合顾问建筑师工程师事务所"随着公私合营的进程而解散，从此童寯中止建筑设计创作，全心投入在学校的理论研究和课程教学之中。同时大约在20世纪50年代初，童寯一次在南京东郊画水彩写生时，被一解放军粗暴制止，他也因此再未重拾过画笔。

1952年　全国院系调整，童寯任南京工学院建筑系教授，从此主要从事教学和建筑理论研究，著作甚丰（图51）。

童寯治学严谨，对学生严格要求，教学中特别注意对学生独立工作能力的培养。他精通英文，通晓德、意、法多种文字，又能博闻强记。博大精深的知识，深邃睿智的见解，使童寯成为学生和老师的"活字典"，不时为师生答疑解惑。

1956年　童寯妻子关蔚然因冠心病病逝，这对他的精神打击很大。

1960年11月　成立南京工学院建筑设计院，童寯任首任院长。

1961年　发表文章《亭》，系统研究各种类型的亭（图53）。

童寯20世纪60年代初开始着手系统性研究西方现代建筑理论，虽与当时政治气候不合，但仍然独自一人不懈进行专题研究，例如"西式园林"、"密斯万用空间"、"巴黎城市规划史"等。他数十年如一日，端坐南京工学院资料室之中，博览群书，精心研读，为我国现代建筑理论研究作出了开拓性贡献。

1962年　童寯经检查发现膀胱癌，手术后病情稳定，身体基本康复。

1966—1976年　童寯经历"文革"浩劫，曾数次被剥夺教学和科研的机会。1968年经历数次抄家，并被派往长江大桥工地敲石子，进行劳动改造。

在"十年动乱"期间，童寯受到一定的政治冲击，但是他仍然坚持不懈地从事理论研究和教学工作，每天坚持从家步行半小时到学校查阅资料，刻苦钻研。

1978—1979年　研习中国水墨山水画（图52）。

1979—1983年　在《建筑师》杂志上陆续发表《外中分割》、《北京长春园西洋建筑》、《随园考》、《悉尼歌剧院兴建始末》、《外国纪念建筑史话》、《新建筑世系谱》、《建筑设计方案竞赛述闻》、《巴洛克与洛可可》、《建筑科技沿革（一～四）》、《中国园林对东西方的影响》等文章13篇（图54）（图55）。

1981年　出版《童寯水彩画选》和《童寯素描选》。开始集中研究"建筑教育史"。

1982年　出版《苏联建筑》。

1982年7月　童寯接受膀胱癌手术。11月，赴北京肿瘤研究所继续进行治疗。

1983年3月28日　病逝于南京。

图50 与夫人关蔚然在一起
图51 在南京工学院与学生合影
图52 晚年与赵深在一起
图53 在南京紫金山

童寯在病逝后，仍然有许多著作在不断整理出版，其中有：

1983年　出版《造园史纲》，《日本近现代建筑》。
1984年　出版《新建筑与流派》。
1986年　出版《近百年西方建筑史》。
1993年　出版《童寯建筑画》。
1997年　出版《东南园墅》。童寯于晚年撰写的"Glimpses of Gardens in Eastern China"（《东南园墅》），是他在病榻上完成定稿的呕心沥血之作，反映他对中国园林艺术的挚爱和在园林研究上的成就。

《东南园墅》一书采用英文写作，于1981年杀青。1982年在病重住院期间，乃至转诊北京之时，童寯仍然以顽强的毅力精心修改，直至1983年3月中旬还在病榻上口述结尾，两周后，即溘然长逝。我国建筑史学家郭湖生教授对于童寯在园林研究方面如此评价说："童寯先生是近代研究中国古典园林的第一人。"他还写道："依愚所见，具备如童寯先生的渊博知识，足以胜任这样复杂课题的，目前似无第二人。"

童寯天性澹泊宁静，很少参加社会活动。他不为世俗名利所惑，有着自己极其坚定的文化立场。在他深层的精神世界里，时刻秉承着与生俱来的文人传统，不向现实政权靠拢，不依附政治权势，不以时俗为转移（图57）。

因此在这种角度上，学术研究的自由独立精神在童寯身上体现得尤为强烈，这也相应使他采取了更为冷静的态度来对待文化和历史，而这种精神又激发了更为全面的文化慎独（图56）。

在童寯一生的学术研究中，充盈着大量的微观课题：从对中国文人园的考证，到东西方园林的比较；从假山叠石，到文人禅宗；从比例分割，到学史分析；从文人生活，到古代时尚。而童寯对于中国传统园林的挚爱，也更加显得丝丝入扣。"至于园林，对其中几个最著名的，我几乎熟悉它们的每块石头。"这种对传统文化的迷恋，也反映了他的文人品位与理想（图58）。

从这点意义上，童寯的处世态度也决定了他的学术思想和学术品位，在大半生的学术生涯中，他一直避讳大道理，而潜心于具体的学术文献。在他生命最高潮的时候，能够把自己生活的圈子、视野缩小到中大院的一张书桌上，以至于常年终日埋头于书写文字中，

图54 晚年与杨廷宝和刘敦桢夫人陈莲在一起
图55 与天文学家张钰哲及其夫人在一起
图56 在南京文昌巷家中读报
图57 在南京工学院资料室看书

而无只言片语。但他的眼光却相应地拓展到世界的高度,这是一个伟大的学者所具备的人生历程。

图58 晚年在清华

童寯的职业认知、自我认同及现代性追求

赖德霖*

清华大学建筑学院有一张历史照片,那是几位老教师与一位老者的合影。教师当中有汪坦、吴良镛,还有他们在中央大学时期的校友和清华工作中的同事胡允敬、辜传海,以及当时建筑系的系主任李道增。这些久在杏坛、成就卓著、桃李满天下的学者们正在与自己的老师或老师的老师相聚。他们站立着,表现出在老师面前的虔敬;他们欢笑着,表现出与老师久别重逢的喜悦。然而与他们形成对比,照片中端坐的主角却双唇紧闭,眉头微锁,表情严肃,默然于这个欢快的场景之外。他与周围的人们近在咫尺,却又形同路人;他身在空间的中心,心却毫无参与之意。这位老者就是童寯(图1)。

童寯给大多数认识他的人们的印象更像是一位独来独往、特立独行的隐士:他没有同学梁思成对复兴中国传统和参与现实活动的热情,也不同于挚友杨廷宝的随遇而安、无可无不可;如同事刘敦桢对学术的执著,但视野宽广,绝不囿于中国建筑;他具有深厚的中国文化修养,但却与事务所的同仁相约摒弃"大屋顶";对西方

---

* 赖德霖,1992、2007 年分别获清华大学建筑历史与理论专业和芝加哥大学中国美术史专业博士学位,中国近现代建筑史研究专家,现任美国路易维尔大学美术系副教授。曾主编《近代哲匠录:中国近代重要建筑师、建筑事务所名录》(2006),主要论著和文章有《中国近代建筑史研究》(2007)、《解读建筑》(2009)、《梁思成"建筑可译论"之前的中国实践》、《构图与要素:学院派来源与梁思成"文法-语汇"表述及中国现代建筑》、《中山纪念堂——一个现代中国的宣讲空间》、《文化观遭遇社会观:梁刘史学分歧与 20 世纪中期中国两种建筑观的冲突》等。

图1 童寯与清华大学建筑系教师合影（后排左起：胡允敬、汪坦、吴良镛、辜传海、李道增、童诗白（童寯长子），1982年。图片来源：童明，杨永生．关于童寯．北京：知识产权出版社，中国水利水电出版社，2002. 无页码和图号。

文化有着广博的了解，却绝不"崇"洋；受到过正统的学院派建筑教育，却积极引介现代主义；出身满族，却以"戴红顶花翎，后垂发辫"讽刺古代建筑要素在现代建筑上的不合时宜；反对中国建筑的"传统复兴"风格设计，却又对江南园林情有独钟；精湛于西洋水彩画，却又嗜好中国水墨山水；博览群书、学富五车，却又惜墨如金、慎于立论；更突出的是，他从事于建筑师职业，却鄙夷商业习气，毕生坚持士人本色。如此多的对立集中在童寯身上，使得他既令人熟悉又令人陌生。在他逝世之后，人们写了无数的回忆文章表达对于他渊博的学识和崇高的人品的敬意，但是这些敬意本身就来自高山仰止的距离感。人们可以毫不怀疑他作为一位建筑家在设计、历史、理论乃至绘画各方面所取得的杰出成就，也可以对他为人、教学与治学的事迹如数家珍，可是对于他在中国近现代建筑史上的特殊地位却又感到难以把握。

童寯到底是一位什么样的人？他如何认识自己？又是如何认识自己的职业、社会和时代？的确，童出身满族家庭，幼年受过中国传统教育，青年负笈留洋于西方，中年执建筑师业，后半生改任大学教师，一生经历晚清、民国和共和国三个时期，这些曲折的经历造成了他性格、思想，乃至文化认同的复杂性。但是毫无疑问，他的设计作品、著述，以及后人们的回忆都清楚地说明，他的一生都表现出对于科学和技术的信奉、对于艺术的热爱、对于建筑的现代主义的探求，以及对于一种独立的人格的自觉。所有这些都反映出作为一位个人，童寯在中国近现代社会转型的复杂背景下对于职业和人生的现代性追求。因此要认识他就必须认识他的现代性，而要认识他的现代性就必须认识中国近现代的建筑专业史语境以及社会文化和思想史的语境。

一

童寯首先是一名建筑家。他做过建筑师，也当过建筑教师。在诸多后人对他的回忆中不乏关于他恪尽职业操守和师道的故事。不过最能反映他的专业追求的还是他在"文化大革命"期间说的一句话，当时针对"工宣队"裁撤建筑学专业的决定，他毫不含糊地说，"我爱建筑学，除非地球不转，只要还在转，我下世投胎也还要学建筑。"[1] 这一表述掷地有声，听之凛然，是因为它已经超乎职业的选择而近乎对于信仰的捍卫。那么童是如何选择这一职业的？他对于这个职业的认知又是如何？

童寯成长在中国一个大变革的时代。据清史学者阎崇年，辛亥革命以后，满人经历了在政治、经济，以及社会地位等多方面的巨大变化：八旗军队被解散，贵族学校被裁撤，满人官员不再领取俸禄，八旗兵弁不再支放饷银，满族百姓甲粮被停发，王庄旗田被丈放，先前的特权民族转而成为一个普通的民族。种种变化导致满族开始受到汉人的歧视，许多满人的生计也遭遇了空前的困境。如一些王公贵族只能靠典卖祖产度日，甚至有王爷后裔以拉洋车为生。很多满人被迫改变姓氏，隐瞒民族成分。满洲八旗原来"不农、不

---

[1] 童寯长孙童文在 2010 年 5 月 2 日给笔者的信中说："他的确是在不计代价地捍卫自己的信仰，因为他很可能会因此被关押起来……1969 年，在南京工业学院中大院建筑系入口大台阶上，红卫兵命童手持红宝书在毛主席像前下跪。三百年前，在梵蒂冈圣彼得教堂大台阶上，经过 20 年的教庭审判，伽利略下跪，双手放在《圣经》上对教皇朗读自己的拉丁'认罪书'，当这位 69 岁老人站立时，轻轻自语一句传世名言' Eppur si mouve' ——'地球仍在转动'。如果没有这样的精神信仰，我觉得他是难以活动'文革'的没顶之灾，所谓'士可杀不可辱'也。"

工、不商"，此时也不得不农、工、商皆务[2]。童寯出生于辽宁奉天（今沈阳），父亲恩格为满族正蓝旗，原姓钮祜禄。对于改朝换代和社会变迁，童家的感受虽然未必像北京满人那样强烈，不过作为满族的一分子，家庭成员们对于民族地位的巨大转变很难无动于衷。目前童家放弃钮祜禄这一满族大姓而改汉姓的确切原因尚不清楚[3]，但这一变化无疑标志了家族自我认同的一个极大改变。而童氏子弟们的职业选择也清楚地体现了他们的现实考量。多年后童寯说："我选学建筑专业动机，主要是为解决生活问题。我争取'自食其力'，靠技术吃饭，尽量不问政治。"[4] 他的两个弟弟童麐和童村则分别选择了电机工程师和医生作为各自的职业[5]。并非偶然，建筑界与童寯持相同想法的还有出生于清朝两广总督家庭的张镈。有感于"宦海沉浮，为官不义、不易。改朝换代，必受牵连"和"家有良田千顷，不如薄技在身"，张也选择了与医师和律师并称自由职业"三师"的建筑师专业[6]。

中国古代视建筑为匠作，建筑师的地位远逊于今天，但20世纪20年代以后却有越来越多的青年，包括许多仕宦子弟、名门之后选择了这一专业。对此笔者曾在《学科的外来移植——中国近代建筑人才的出现和建筑教育的发展》一文中分析指出，"对建筑的科学性以及艺术性的新认识使它摆脱了传统匠作的低下地位而获得了中国现代社会精英们的认同。"[7] 同样，童寯选择建筑学除了因为它是一门可以"吃饭"的技艺之外，还因为这项职业体现了技术与艺术的结合。他说："单单学技术，固然也可以饿不死，但我认为只有技术的人，生活有点单调，需要调剂，而用艺术来调剂生活则是最理想的。"[8] 20世纪10年代正是中国现代美术从萌牙走向蓬勃发展的一个重要时期。据"童寯

---

2 阎崇年. 北京满族的百年沧桑. 北京社会科学，2002（01）：15-23
3 童寯幼孙童明在2009年12月28日回复笔者的信中说："曾祖父即有汉姓，我爷爷这辈取其'葆童'的号而为姓，只是后来进关将童字固定作为家庭姓氏。按家谱，我父辈应姓林，我辈好像是'业'，再下辈是'家'。我伯父童诗白好像原名'林伟'，后入关后改现名，取'思北'之意，但跟下来姓童。"
4 童寯. 童寯文集（四）. 北京：中国建筑工业出版社，2006：375
5 童寯. "文革"材料 // 童寯文集（四）. 北京：中国建筑工业出版社，2006：374
6 张镈. 我的建筑创作道路. 北京：中国建筑工业出版社，1994：1
7 赖德霖. 学科的外来移植——中国近代建筑人才的出现和建筑教育的发展. 艺术史研究，2005（07）；赖德霖. 中国近代建筑史研究. 北京：清华大学出版社，2007：115-180
8 童寯. 童寯文集（四）. 北京：中国建筑工业出版社，2006：394

年谱",童早在中学时期就是艺术的爱好者,"常往基督教青年会听取科学和艺术讲座"。他对艺术的兴趣在他1921年进入清华学校之后又得到进一步的发展,他加入了学校的美术社,进修素描和水彩,还曾因美术功课出色而担任校刊美术编辑[9]。而在清华,与他相似因爱好美术而最终选学建筑学的还有吕彦直、朱彬、杨廷宝和梁思成等多人。到美国之后,童对艺术的兴趣又扩展到音乐。他不仅自己在生活中追求技术与艺术的结合,还把二者当作培养孩子的目标。他的三个儿子都是出色的科学家,又都深具音乐修养[10]。显然对于童寯来说,艺术是人生的一个重要部分,而建筑学就是一门可以使他同时兼顾生活需要和人生理想的专业。

用艺术改善人生和社会还是20世纪初中国许多文化精英们的一种现代理想,而这种理想在清华学校的师生中尤为突出。清华学校注重美术的传统可以追溯到办学之初。早在1914年,学校中等科一、二年级就开设了图画课。1920年10月1日,《清华周刊》发表"征求艺术专门的同业者的呼声",提出"艺术是社会的需要","艺术是改造社会的急务"。同年12月1日,闻一多、杨廷宝、梁思成等学生还组织成立了以"研究艺术及其与人生的关系"为宗旨的"美司斯"(Muses,即缪斯)社团。宣言称"生命的量至多不过百年,他的质却可以无限度的往高深醇美的境域发展。生命的艺化,便是生命达到高深醇美的鹄的的唯一方法。""我们既相信艺术能够提高、加深、养醇、变美我们的生活的质料,我们就要探搜'此中三昧',并用我自己的生活作试验品。"12月10日在"美司斯"社召开成立大会,著名艺术家陈师曾、吴新吾、刘雅农、江少鹣等到会演讲,最后由著名学者梁启超讲"中国古代真善美之理论"[11]。由此可见,

---

9 童寯年谱 // 童寯文集(一).北京:中国建筑工业出版社,2000:388
10 有关童寯的音乐修养,见童诗白.回忆与怀念——建筑学家童寯工作、生活片段 // 童明,杨永生.关于童寯.北京:知识产权出版社,中国水利水电出版社,2002:103-110。童文还告知,童寯感情丰富,他会在听完古典音乐后兴奋几天。他曾经把贝多芬遗像的面模放在枕边。(童文致笔者信,2010年3月27日)
11 闻立鹏,张同霞.追寻至美——闻一多的美术.济南:山东美术出版社,2001:5,153-155。笔者据《清华周刊》第202、203期(1920年12月10日、17日)校对。此外,梁启超还曾在1922年给北京美术学校和上海美术专门学校师生讲演"美术与科学"和"美术与生活"(见《饮冰室文集(38、39)》)。另据闻著,清华学校中等科一、二年级的图画课分别由两位美籍女教师斯塔尔(Starr)和里格卡特(Lyggate)教画静物和写生。1918年2月16日斯塔尔还曾为图画特别班讲演"建筑上之美术"。

在童寯1921年入校前,清华学校的一些师生就已经在教育和学习中引入了用艺术改善人生和社会的思想。

　　清华学校艺术教育传统兴起的原因尚待进一步深入研究。不过,除梁启超的支持和宣传之外,20世纪中国的国学大师和美育的先驱王国维担任学校导师这一事实应该也是一个不可忽视的重要原因。包莉秋在讨论王国维和主张"以美育代宗教"的杰出教育家蔡元培时曾指出:他们关注人自身内在的精神世界,希望在一个社会剧变,世人纷纷"逐一己之利害而不知返"的时代,通过宣扬并依靠美育陶冶国民情操,从而改造国民精神。她说:"正如美育之父席勒所言:'有促进健康的教育,有促进认识的教育,有促进道德的教育,还有促进鉴赏力和美的教育。这最后一种教育的目的在于,培养我们的感性和精神力量的整体达到尽可能和谐。'王国维、蔡元培正是继承了这种精神,在重视感情的前提之下宣扬美育思想的,认为美育的首要宗旨就是要培养人具有一种超越精神——超越利害、超越名禄、超越物欲。超功利性是审美的最高精神境界,也是美育精神品格的'内核'。"[12]"童寯在清华期间还常听王国维讲座"。他对艺术的热爱以及毕生对于名禄和物欲的淡然即使不是直接受自王国维思想的陶冶,也与王对于一种现代理想化国民的期盼相一致[13]。

二

　　作为建筑师,童寯在作品风格上也以追求现代性著称。1931年日本侵华的"九一八"事变发生后,他从沈阳移居上海,并加入了赵深、陈植两位建筑师的事务所,该事务所也在1933年1月改名华盖建筑师事务所。三位建筑师共同创作的作品包括南京国民政府外交部办公大楼及官舍(1932—1935)、资源委员会南京地质矿产陈列馆(1937)、南京首都饭店(1933)、首都电厂(1933)、南京公路总局办公楼(1946)、

---

[12] 包莉秋.论王国维、蔡元培美育思想中的审美与功利性.扬州大学学报(人文社会科学版),2007(103):47-50

[13] 童寯年谱 // 童寯文集(一).北京:中国建筑工业出版社,2000:388;解放前我参加过哪些组织? //《童寯文集(四)》.北京:中国建筑工业出版社,2006:382

图2 华盖建筑事务所：大上海大戏院，上海，1933年。图片来源：中国建筑，1934，2（03）

下关交通银行（1946）、下关工人福利社（1946）、西藏路大公寓（1946），苏州市青年会大戏院（1932）、上海恒利银行（1932）、大上海大戏院（1933）（图2）、中央大戏院改造（1933）、金城大戏院（1934）、合记公寓（1934）、华懋公寓（1934）、林肯路中国银行公寓（1934）、江西路北京路口浙江兴业银行（1935）、叶揆初合众图书馆（1940）、浙江第一商业银行大楼（1947），昆明兴文银行（1940）、南屏街住宅（1940）、南屏街银行区办公楼（1941）、南屏街聚兴诚银行（1942），贵阳贵州艺术馆（1942）、贵阳儿童图书馆（1943）、贵阳招待所（1943）、贵州省立民众教育馆（1943），等等。正如陈植总结所说，华盖的作品"格调严谨，比例壮健，线条挺拔，笔法简洁，色彩清淡，不务华丽，不尚修饰[14]"。它们体现了三位合作者追求现代主义和"相约摒弃大屋顶"的理念[15]。而相对于中国近代著名的基泰工程司杨廷宝建筑师作品的细腻和典雅，这些设计强调了建筑立面的点线面构图、整体的体积感，光影效果和材料的质感，因而也更具阳刚气质。

除作品之外，童寯还是同辈中少有的一位明确用文字宣传现代主义建筑、反对他所认为的中国现代建筑中的保守主义的建筑师。1941年他在《战国策》杂志上发表了《中国建筑的特点》一文。针对中国近代以来一种用钢筋混凝土材料仿造古代建筑风格的"古典复兴式"设计方法，他在结尾质疑说：

"以上中国建筑的几个特点，是否也是其优点呢？无疑的，在近代科学发达以前，中国建筑确实有其颠扑不破的地位，惟自钢铁水泥盛行，而且可以精密计算使其经济合用，中国建筑的优点都变成弱点。木材不能防火耐震抗炸，根本就不适用现代。中国式屋顶虽美观，但若拿钢骨水泥来支撑若干曲线，就不合先民创造之旨，倒不如做平屋面，副[附]带的生出一片平台地面。我们还需要彩画吗。钢骨水泥是耐久的东西，彩画是容易剥落的东西，何必在金身上贴膏药？……中国建筑今后只能作世界建筑一部分，就像中国制造的轮船火车与他国制造的一样，并不必有根本不相同之点。物质文明在不停的进化，……因此以后建筑物的权衡尺码，恐又要改观。"[16]

1945年10月童寯又在《我国公共建筑外观的检讨》一文中重申了上述观点。他说：

"中国木作制度和钢铁水泥做法，唯一相似之点，即两者的结构原则，均属架子式而非箱子式，惟木架与钢架的经济跨度相比，开间可差一半，因此一切用料权衡，均不相同。拿钢骨水泥来模仿宫殿梁柱屋架，单就用料尺寸浪费一项，已不可为训，何况水泥梁柱已足，又加油漆彩画。平台屋面已足，又加筒瓦屋檐。这实不可谓为合理。"[17]

在《中国建筑的特点》一文中，童寯还批评了当时以大屋顶为特征的"中国式"现代建筑。他说："以宫殿的瓦顶，罩一座几层钢筋水泥铁窗的墙壁，无异穿西装戴红顶花翎，后垂发辫，其不伦不类，殊可发噱。"无独有偶，童寯在另一篇题为《建筑艺术纪实》的文章中更毫不客气地将所谓的"复兴式"建筑贬称为"辫子建筑

---

14 陈植.意境高逸，才华横溢——悼念童寯同志.建筑师，1983（16）：3-4
15 同上。
16 童寯.中国建筑的特点.战国策，1941（08）；童寯文集（一）.北京：中国建筑工业出版社，2000：111
17 童寯.我国公共建筑外观的检讨.（内政专刊）公共工程专刊（第1集），1946；童寯文集（一）.北京：中国建筑工业出版社，2000：118-121

艺术"[18]。童寯的这一比拟值得注意，是因为他本人出身满族，在此他竟然以近乎嘲讽的态度视满族的官服和发式为落后的象征。更值得注意的是，他少年时期曾在辛亥革命之后三年拒绝剪辫，并为最终不得不留短发而痛哭不已。[19] 对比当初的固执和此时的反叛，这一变化就不可谓不大。

童寯曾在1930年的一篇教学笔记中这样写道：

"现今建筑之趋势，为脱离古典与国界之限制，而成一于时代密切关系之有机体。科学之发明，交通之便利，思想之开展，成见之消灭，俱足使全世界上 [之] 建筑逐渐失去其历史与地理之特征。今后之建筑史，殆仅随机械之进步，而作体式之变迁，无复东西、中外之分。"[20]

中国近代建筑史学者王敏颖认为，童的这一思想反映出他对于"建筑普世化"（architectural universalization）的信奉，即他认为现代建筑将最终消除历史和地理的差异[21]。王所说的"普世化"也就是全球化，它表明了童对于一种建筑的发展趋势所抱有的积极态度。不过从立论的基础来看，我们又可以把童的观点称为建筑的"科学观"或"时代观"，如他在这些文章中的基本立论都是，科学技术是建筑发展的基础，随着时代的进步，建筑的功能、材料和结构都发生了变化，所以建筑的形式也必须随之变化[22]。他在《中国建筑的特点》一文最后使用的"进化"一词格外重要，因为这个在今天已经近乎俗语的词在20世纪初却代表了中国一个颇具革命性的思想。1898年，由严复翻译的赫胥黎著《天演论》在中国问世，它所阐明

---

18 童寯.李大夏，译.建筑艺术纪实 // 童寯文集（一）.北京：中国建筑工业出版社，2000：85-88
19 童寯."文革"中思想汇报，1968年1月—1969年5月；转引自朱振通.童寯建筑实践历程探究（1931—1949）：[硕士学位论文].南京：东南大学，2006年。感谢葛明博士帮助笔者核查这一史料。
20 童寯.建筑五式 // 童寯文集（一）.北京：中国建筑工业出版社，2000：2, 118-121
21 Min-Ying Wang. The Historicization of Chinese Architecture: The Making of Architectural Historiography in China, from the Late Nineteenth Century to 1953: [Ph.D. dissertation]. New York: Columbia University, 2009: 311.
22 另参见赖德霖.文化观遭遇社会观：梁刘史学分歧与20世纪中期中国两种建筑观的冲突 // 朱剑飞.中国建筑60年（1949—2009）历时理论研究.北京：中国建筑工业出版社，2009：246-263

的"物竞天择,适者生存"的进化论思想曾给中国人"一种当头棒喝"[23],一切有识之士都不得不把中国的传统与西方的近代文明放在"优胜劣汰"的天平上衡量。童寯从小学起开始接受新式教育,青年时期到天津新学书院进修英文,后又入清华学校接受留美预备教育,继而留学美国、环游欧洲。必定是对西方文明的了解和对进化论思想的服膺使他能够站在文明进化的立场,顺应时代的发展,最终接受清王朝垮台的现实,甚至不再认同满族固有习俗。对时代的认同和对科学技术的强调也使他能够在专业中倡导现代主义,毫不隐讳地批判中国现代建筑中他所认为的保守主义。

三

在其职业生涯之中,童寯始终表现出对于世界建筑发展新潮流的极大关注,这种关注在与他同时代的大部分中国建筑师中极为少见,即使在他的后辈之中也属前卫。他的长孙童文告诉笔者,即使在抗日战争期间,童寯仍在订阅美国重要的建筑杂志《建筑实录》(*Architectural Record*)。20世纪40至50年代,他继续让在美留学的儿子按照他开列的书单寄回南京20余种建筑书籍和出版物,其中就有柯布西耶(Le Corbusier)的著作《模数制》(*Le Modulor*, 1948)和著名现代建筑史家吉迪安(Sigfried Giedion)的经典著作《空间、时间与建筑——一种新传统的成长》(*Space, Time and Architecture: The Growth of a New Tradition*, 1941)的1954年版[24]。而这种关注早在他留学归国之前,从1930年4月26日至8月27日在欧洲的旅行中就已有所表现[25],如他的日记有如下记录:

5月31日:"在布鲁塞尔逛了一会儿。……试图寻找由约瑟夫·霍夫曼设计的斯托克莱住宅,但是没有人知道它在哪里。"(《童寯文集(四)》,331页)

6月2日:"10点钟又去了[安特卫普]博览会场,法国馆开放了,其中有一些现代风格的室内和时尚展览。……"(332页)

---

23 胡适.四十自述.转引自陈越光,陈小雅.摇篮与墓地.成都:四川人民出版社,1985:61
24 童文致笔者信,2010年3月9日。
25 童寯.童明,译.旅欧日记//童寯文集(四).北京:中国建筑工业出版社,2006:315-373

6月3日:"在阿姆斯特丹南郊参观了很多现代建筑,个个都很棒,砖作很精致。所有的木门都设计得很好。有一座现代教堂,但却没法参观室内。甚至街头的邮箱设计得很现代。"(333页)

6月6日:"前往杜塞尔多夫。在战前它有一座现代桥梁。参观了一座很高的办公楼(WM马克楼),爬到楼顶。它有一个砖砌的大厅,其中有运行的电梯轿车厢。从楼顶能看到城市全景。很精致的砖作。……杜塞尔多夫是一座值得一访的城市,因为它有几座欧洲最好的现代建筑。"(334页)

6月14日:"前往法兰克福手工艺馆,这里有一个沃尔特·格罗皮乌斯的现代建筑展(大多数是工业建筑)。……乘火车回到霍姆堡(4点钟),然后再去法兰克福。在大教堂下车,回去参观一所现代学校和一些现代公寓,在那里画了一张素描。"(337~338页)

6月18日:"晴天。7:30乘火车前往曼海姆,参观了战前(1907年)新艺术现代美术馆,但是大多数展品是未来主义的,油画、水彩画以及雕塑。好建筑加上好内容。"(339页)

6月25日:"在班贝格参观了现代教堂,圣·海尔里希教堂(建筑师为高蒂博士)。……"(341页)

7月1日:"花了一个小时去寻找[波茨坦]爱因斯坦塔。最终当我到达那儿时,门口的老妇不让我进去。我非常急迫地想看上一眼,因此围着观察站(按:或可译为天文台)的周边走了很远,才看到它的顶部。爱因斯坦塔在照片上通常是黑色的,但是现场看上去却是白色的,而且很洁净。"(344页)

7月18日:"早餐后乘轻轨前往海雷根城去参观现代公寓,它们很棒。"(350页)

7月19日:"前往参观分离主义美术馆,那里有一些好东西,没有太多激进的内容。前往三号街区参观现代公寓。在那里,你可以从一个庭院穿行到另一个庭院,直到路边。规划得很好,建筑也很棒。"(351页)

7月27日:"7:15抵达斯图加特。新火车站很漂亮。我从未看到过这么一件好东西。也许是已建成的最好的车站。晚上参观了王宫以及一些现代建筑……。"(356页)

7月29日:"下午5:30抵达巴塞尔。在火车站外面就有市场大厅,虽属现代风格但不是很好。误打误撞走到了斯帕棱城门,但是在一家商店（明信片上的地方）的附近找到了现代的圣安东教堂，立即步行前往那里。钟塔（混凝土的）是我所见过最好的。"（357页）[26]

童寯对现代建筑的关注无疑与他留学的时代有关。20世纪20年代后期正是发源于欧洲的现代建筑运动开始得到美国响应之时。如《建筑实录》杂志在1928年介绍了荷兰的现代建筑（2月），德国格罗皮乌斯（Walter Gropius）、考夫曼（Oskar Kaufmann）、施耐德（Karl Schneider）等建筑师的作品（4—6月）、法国现代装饰艺术展览（5月），德国德骚包豪斯的工艺商店（5月），1925年德国德累斯顿的国际艺术展览（6月）等。此外，还在1月发表了年轻的建筑史家希区柯克（Henry-Russell Hitchcock Jr.）所写的关于法国建筑家柯布西耶（Le Corbusier）的著作《走向新建筑》（*Toward a New Architecture*）的书评。希区柯克自己的系列文章《现代建筑》（*Modern Architecture*）也从4月起陆续在该杂志上连载。这些文章后来汇集成《现代建筑：浪漫主义与再整合》（*Modern Architecture: Romanticism and Reintegration*）一书在1929年出版。这本书首次从建筑形式方面论证了现代建筑发展的合理性，刚一问世便很快成为一部建筑经典。

童受教的宾夕法尼亚大学虽然是巴黎美术学院在美洲的大本营，但在20年代后期包括著名建筑家克瑞（Paul Philippe Cret, 1876—1945年）在内的教师都已在尝试用简洁的现代建筑语汇去诠释古典的建筑法则，从而发展出一种"摩登古典"（Modern Classic）或"简洁古典主义"（Stripped-Down Classicism）及"简洁摩登式"（Stripped

---

[26] 不可忽视的是，当时他还不失时机地观看了许多现代派绘画，如他在日记中写道：7月5日"参观了皇冠王子（按：或可译为太子）博物馆，在顶层它拥有现代主义的绘画和雕塑。棒极了。塞尚、迪亚兹、亨利·马蒂斯、康定斯基，其中一些非常前卫现代。"（345页）7月9日："[德累斯顿]画廊的现代部分有一些先锋的绘画作品，瓦西里·康定斯基采用几何形式（球形等等）。莱昂内尔·杰宁格将平面穿过物体。保罗·克利在线描中，有时也在模式上采用埃及形式，看上去就像儿童绘画。恩斯特·路德维希·奇切内的绘画在形式上不算激进，但是在人们的脸上采用绿色和紫色。"（346～347页）7月17日："[维也纳]现代画廊很棒，里面没有多少作品（绘画和雕塑），但那里的东西还是不错的。有4～5件是古斯塔夫·克里姆特的作品。他的服饰很原创（黑色、银色和金色），构图也很美妙。"（350页）

Modern)的新风格[27]。据美国建筑史家 G. 赖特(Gwendolyn Wright),克瑞还强调让学生根据法国考古学家、建筑历史学家和工程师舒瓦西(Auguste Choisy,1841—1909)的建筑分析图去分析以往纪念性建筑中的要素,但不吸收那些风格和纪念物的程式。舒瓦西曾任巴黎国立土木学校(École Nationale des Ponts et Chaussées)的教授,他将建筑结构而不是风格视为建筑的本质,他曾说:"新的结构是逻辑学在艺术上的成功。一座建筑成为一个经过筹划的整体,其中每一个结构构件的造型不取决于传统的范式,而仅仅取决于其功能。"[28]而童寯反对将新的结构用古代式样作为表现显然与舒瓦西的这一思想一脉相承。

童寯毕业后到纽约实习所跟随的伊莱·康(Ely Jacques Kahn,1884—1972年)也是一位追求摩登风格的建筑师。康初学于纽约哥伦比亚大学,1907年入巴黎美术学院,师从著名的象征主义画家欧迪隆·雷顿(Odilon Redon)的兄弟伽斯敦·雷顿(Gaston Redon)。在巴黎他还接触到了布拉克(Braque)、德雷恩(Derain)、毕加索(Picasso)等立体派画家的作品。他于1911年回到纽约,加入了以设计百货商店闻名的巴克曼-福克斯事务所(Buchman & Fox),1915年福克斯退休后,巴克曼与他合作,改事务所名为巴克曼-康事务所。新的事务所仍以设计商业建筑著名。康本人则成为与曾设计芝加哥论坛报大厦和纽约洛克菲勒中心的胡德(Raymond Hood, 1881—1934年),参与设计洛克菲勒中心的哈里森(Wallace K. Harrison, 1895—1981年),以及设计了纽约克莱斯勒大厦的凡·阿伦(William Van Alen, 1883—1954年)等人齐名的现代摩天楼建筑

---

27 克瑞在1929年设计的华盛顿的佛杰尔莎士比亚图书馆(Folger Shakespeare Library, Washington, D.C., 1929—1932年)就是这一风格的代表作品。
28 转引自 Hanno-Walter Kruft. A History of Architectural Theory from Vitruvius to the Present. p. 288. 中国现代建筑家童寯对于仿古的中国风格建筑的批判或许就受到了舒瓦西思想的影响。如童在总结中国建筑的特点后说,这些特点,"是否也是其优点呢? 无疑的,在近代科学发达以前,中国建筑确实有其颠扑不破的地位,惟自钢铁水泥盛行,而且可以精密计算使其经济合用,中国建筑的优点都变成弱点。木材不能防火耐震抗炸,根本就不适用现代。中国式屋顶虽美观,但若拿钢骨水泥来支撑若干曲线,就不合先民创造之旨,倒不如做平屋面,附带地生出一片平台地面。我们还需要彩画吗。钢骨水泥是耐久的东西,彩画是容易剥落的东西,何必在金身上贴膏药?"见童寯.中国建筑的特点.战国策,1941(08);童寯文集(一).北京:中国建筑工业出版社,2000:109-111

师。1928年4月康曾在《建筑实录》杂志发表题为《摩天大楼的经济学》(Economics of skyscraper)的文章,还曾在5月撰文介绍法国的装饰艺术展览。童实习期间他正在设计建造纽约斯奎伯大厦(Squibb Building)这栋装饰艺术风格的著名建筑[29]。童日后与事务所同仁赵深和陈植所作的一些主要设计都有摩登古典和装饰艺术风格的影响,强调立面线条的表现,但这些设计更加简化,也因此更接近现代主义风格。

现在我们尚不知道童寯如何计划他的欧洲之行,他选定参观目标的信息来源又是什么。他的日记虽然提到斯图加特火车站等个别被希氏著作用作插图的建筑,但所记其他参观对象大都不见于该书,显然他并没有以这本现代建筑经典作为导游。不过日记确实显示,他是带着极大的兴趣,甚至常常是专程去探访一些现代新作的。童的欧洲之行对他日后创作有何影响也是一个引人思考的问题。如他在1933年在设计南京资源委员会及地质矿物陈列馆的外墙时将面砖间隔凸出,从而使墙面具有图案性且又有丰富光影效果,不知这一手法是否借鉴了"砖工很精致"的阿姆斯特丹新建筑。又如他在1933年为大上海大戏院的观众厅设计了平行光带天花,其效果就令人想到他在1930年6月2日的日记里记下的一座鹿特丹现代剧院,他说:"剧院很棒,天花是很长的平行光带,可以依次由红、蓝色光进行照明。"[30]

四

童寯对外国近现代建筑的研究可以追溯到抗日战争爆发之前。有记载表明,他曾于1936年4月16日在当时正在举办的中国建筑展览会上作题为"现代建筑"的讲演[31]。但他存世最早有关西方近现代建筑的著述则是他在1964年写成的《近百年新建筑代表作(资本

---

29 David Garrard Lowe. Art Deco New York. New York: Watson-Guptill Publications, 2004:70. 他的作品还包括2 Park Avenue (1926), Indemnity Building on John Street (1928), 261 Fifth Avenue (1928) 等。

30 童寯.旅欧日记 // 童寯文集(四).北京:中国建筑工业出版社,2006:332

31 上海通社编.旧上海史料汇编(下册).北京:北京图书馆出版社,1998:480

主义社会）》一文[32]。当时中国建筑学会的核心刊物《建筑学报》所发表的文章内容大都是工业厂房、社区规划和住宅设计，而有关国外建筑的介绍也仅局限于与中国友好的亚洲和拉美国家。对比这一情况，后人便不难看出童在介绍西方"资本主义社会"现代建筑时所具有的眼光和勇气。

《近百年新建筑代表作》一文的开篇即说："新技术新材料促使建筑演变，大量铁制构件及玻璃应用于1851年伦敦水晶宫建筑，使结构初次脱离笨重的砖石。"显然此时他仍坚持自己在20世纪30年代就已经形成的建筑科学观，继续视建筑技术和材料为建筑发展的动力。非常值得注意的是，英国著名建筑史家佩夫斯纳（Nikolaus B. L. Pevsner, 1902—1983年）在4年后出版的《现代建筑与设计的源泉》（*The Sources of Modern Architecture and Design*, 1968年）也把水晶宫当作现代建筑的开篇之作，并称之为"19世纪的试金石"[33]。两位建筑史家分别在东西两方，但他们都视科技的进步，尤其是工业化和钢材料与钢结构的出现为现代建筑的主要特征，这一观点使他们在现代主义起始这一问题上获得了共同认识。

1978年完稿的《新建筑与流派》一书是童寯有关西方现代建筑发展的最重要的著作。该书的叙述以工业革命为开端，既延续了他自己视技术和材料为建筑发展的动力的一贯认识，也与佩夫斯纳有关现代建筑历史的论述角度颇为一致。在名作的介绍方面，童非常强调建筑的结构和材料，也即建筑外观造型的来源和内在逻辑。如他在介绍柯布西埃的著名作品朗香教堂（The Chapel of Notre Dame du Haut, Ronchamp, 1954年）时写道：

"结构用钢筋水泥支柱，砌毛石幕墙，粗犷水泥盖面；上覆双层钢筋水泥薄板屋顶。屋顶、地坪、墙身多作斜线曲面形。屋檐与

---

32 见：童寯文集（一）. 北京：中国建筑工业出版社，2000：170-193。童的长孙童文在2010年3月9日致笔者的信中说，这篇文章是他为南京工学院建筑系图书馆编写的一份资料。由于当时大多数教师和学生不能直接阅读英文原文，从20世纪50年代开始至其逝世，童编写了数百份类似资料供师生参考。但今天这些资料的收藏情况不详。
33 Nikolaus Pevsner. The Sources of Modern Architecture and Design. New York: Frederick A. Praeger, 1968:11

墙顶有一条空隙隔开，形成横窗，使屋顶似乎漂浮上空。屋檐向上翻卷，可使院内布道声音反射给听众。这座教堂各部分尺寸都由模度决定。柯布西耶把这得意建筑视为掌上明珠。造型首次冲破他在战前惯用的机械几何直角而用大量曲线，手法近乎古拙。这也不是突然决定而是来源于1928年柯布西埃与奥赞方纯洁画派的抽象造型，作为新表现主义作品。"[34]

这里童寯着重介绍了朗香教堂的结构和材料，而没有特别强调那设计独特并颇具神秘感的室内空间。而在介绍柯布西耶的另一件著名作品萨沃伊别墅（Villa Savoie, Poissy, 1928—1930年）时，他仅仅强调了它对柯氏在《走向新建筑》一书中所归纳的现代建筑五特点的表现，而没有进一步介绍这栋建筑所体现的新的空间概念，即吉迪安在《空间、时间和建筑》一书所提出的"空间-时间"一体概念和他对萨沃伊别墅的赞扬——"一个在空间-时间中的营造"[35]。同样，他在介绍赖特名作鲁比住宅（The Frederick C. Robie House, Chicago, 1908—1910年）与落泉庄（Fallingwater, Bear Run, 1934年）时也是着眼于二者的结构而对它们的空间不置一词。重视现代建筑的结构技术而"忽视"空间问题或许是因为童寯并没有机会考察和体验这些建筑的内部，不过更为根本的原因应该还是他在介绍现代主义建筑时所采取的一种取舍态度。

如前文所述，童寯的建筑思想与宾夕法尼亚大学克瑞所推崇的结构理性主义思想有很大关联。这种结构理性主义的观点在童的校友梁思成的中国建筑史写作之中有十分明显的表现[36]，因此，童对现代主

---

34 童寯.新建筑与流派.北京：中国建筑工业出版社，1980；北京：中国建筑工业出版社，2001：71

35 Sigfried Giedion. Space, Time and Architecture: The Growth of a New Tradition . Cambridge, MA: Harvard University Press, 1941: 518

36 梁思成在自己的《图像中国建筑史》（*A Pictorial History of Chinese Architecture*）一书的前言中说："研究中国的建筑物首先就应剖析它的构造。正因为如此，其断面图就比立面图更为重要。" 有关结构理性主义与梁思成中国建筑史写作的关系，详见汉宝德.明清建筑二论.台北：境与象出版社，1969；夏铸九.营造学社——梁思成建筑史论述构造之理性分析.台湾社会研究季刊，1990，春季号，3（01）：6-48；赖德霖.梁思成、林徽因中国建筑史写作表微.二十一世纪，2001, 64（04）；设计一座理想的中国风格的现代建筑——梁思成中国建筑史叙述与南京国立中央博物院辽宋风格设计再思.艺术史研究，2003, 5.见赖德霖.中国近代建筑史研究.北京：清华大学出版社，2007：313-330，331-362

义建筑的介绍偏重材料结构也就不难理解。此外，1949年以后，中国建筑界在历史写作方面对马克思主义唯物主义的重视和强调也是一个不容忽视的原因。按照这种史观，生产力和经济基础是历史发展的主要动力。童寯的同事刘敦桢主编并于1964年完成的《中国古代建筑史》一书就曾试图体现当时这一正统的历史思想[37]。童以建筑科技的进步而不是空间观念的进步为现代建筑起源的观点便与唯物史观相符。

在近现代建筑史上还有一些重要思想和重要建筑师，它/他们在《新建筑与流派》中有所提及，但并没有被深入讨论，其中包括花园新城理念、芬兰杰出的现代主义建筑师奥托作品的"民族特点"，"新建筑后期"所主张的"联系历史并注意与地方特色相协调"[38]等等。童在介绍外国近现代建筑时的取舍态度很可能还与他对中国建筑现实需要的认识有关。20世纪30年代，童寯曾从以建筑的"科学观"批判当时中国建筑中他所认为的保守倾向。在"文化大革命"期间，他又用这一观点反对极"左"思想和强调建筑阶级属性的"社会观"对于介绍和研究西方现代建筑的压制。他在1970年11月写成的《应该怎样对待西方建筑》一文中说："我们批判崇洋思想，其要害在于'崇'，不在于'洋'。必须认为：尽管西方建筑是为资本主义服务，掌握在资产阶级手中，追求利润，剥削劳动人民；尽管设计思想有时故弄玄虚，尽情研求享受，追求个人名利，为设计人自己树立纪念牌[碑]，这种种无疑应加以批判，但西方建筑技术中的结构计算，构造施工和设计法则等等，虽也夹杂一些烦琐哲学，空谈浮夸，绝大部分还是科学的，正确的，而应该于[予]以肯定。"[39] 在这篇文章中他列举了西方建筑结构力学、现代钢铁和玻璃等材料、钢筋混凝土结构、薄壳结构、三角屋架、功能布局、建筑类型、建筑设备、施工仪器、图式几何等15个方面的优点，指出它们对中国来说"可以接受、应该学习"。

童寯还在1979年完成了专著《近百年西方建筑史》，并在1982

37　赖德霖. 文化观遭遇社会观：梁刘史学分歧与20世纪中国两种建筑观的冲突 // 朱剑飞. 中国建筑60年（1949—2009）：历史理论研究. 北京：中国建筑工业出版社，2009：246-263
38　童寯. 新建筑与流派 // 童寯文集（二）. 北京：中国建筑工业出版社，2001：80，90，99
39　童寯. 应该怎样对待西方建筑 // 童寯文集（一）. 北京：中国建筑工业出版社，2000：227-230

至1983年间发表了长文《建筑科技沿革》[40]。在《近百年西方建筑史》的结尾他继续以科技的发展作为衡量建筑进步的标准展望"现代建筑发展方向"。在他看来,这些方向就是"大跨度大空间"、"薄壳"、"球体网架"、"拖车住宅"、"抽斗式住宅"、"张网结构"和"充气结构"[41]。而在"建筑科技沿革"一文的前言里他还强调说,西方对于建筑三要素中的"坚固"问题有着久远的探求,至今已达高度的科学水平。建筑设计、结构和设备三个专业应该互相重视并合作,而新的结构技术还有助于节约资源。这些思想既包括了他从科学观的角度对于学科发展的展望,也体现了他对于正处于工业化初期的中国建筑现代化程度的判断以及它所要面对的现实问题的深切关注。

童寯对外国近现代建筑的研究还包括日本。1983年他出版了《日本近现代建筑》一书。在介绍日本建筑现代化过程的同时,他也触及了一个对于中国建筑具有重要意义的问题,这就是传统与革新的关系。他在前言中说:日本现代建筑"利用钢筋水泥可塑性,形成屋顶微妙曲线和传统形式呼应,在结构上显出露明梁头和发挥抗震特点,建立日本独特风格"。他最后说:"在现代建筑的创作中,我国能从日本得到很多启发;但在共同追求先进目标,摸索东方民族风格道途中,也不应忘记英国史学家汤因比近来所警告的'西方文明本身就埋下自戕种子',而要有选择地对待西方的成就。"[42]总之,通过介绍日本建筑,童为当时正在努力探索建筑的民族风格的中国建筑师指出了一个目标,这就是材料、结构与造型的统一。

五

童寯1930年的《旅欧日记》内还有多处他对欧洲建筑、雕刻、

---

40 童寯.建筑科技沿革.建筑师,1982(10-12,14),1983(03);童寯文集(二).北京:中国建筑工业出版社,2001:171-206
41 童寯.近百年西方建筑史.南京:南京工学院出版社,1986;童寯文集(一).北京:中国建筑工业出版社,2000:171-206
42 童寯.日本近现代建筑.北京:中国建筑工业出版社,1983;童寯文集(二).北京:中国建筑工业出版社,2001:350,461 在《新建筑与流派》一书中,童特别指出丹下健三"总是想用日本固有艺术结合新社会要求,把传统遗产当作激励与促进创作努力的催化剂,而在最后成果中却看不出丝毫传统痕迹,这是他的创作秘诀(童寯文集(二).北京:中国建筑工业出版社,2001:104)"。

绘画、戏剧、音乐，以及人和事的品评。其中最引人注意的是他在佛罗伦萨看到米开朗琪罗的著名雕刻"大卫"之后，竟然毫不客气地说"大卫除了它很大，而且有力，没什么特别之处。"[43]在他德国之行的日记中还有这样的话："奥斯瓦尔德·斯宾格勒必定很容易见到，因为R.S.递上一封自荐信并且见了一面。……我宁愿不去见他。这种会面又能怎样？如果他太伟大，我们将不会理解他。如果他一点也不伟大，最好等他来见我们。一个人没有必要仅仅因为好奇而去打扰另一个人。"[44]这些反权威的话语显现出童的极其自信甚至孤傲。

孤傲的内心在童25岁时所写《过洋日记》也有所流露："一大群男女老少前来给我们送别。可怜的姑娘们最先开始放声大哭，……离开中国时最好不要看见女人，她们总是控制不住自己的眼泪。""船上大约有150名中国人，其中有十几名妇女。感谢上帝我没有被介绍给她们其中任何一位，她们出国没有任何目的。""这样的海上生活必然是现实的，而且也是虚假的。我对这里的每件事情都感到厌烦。如果不是感到孤独，就是感到无聊。""吸烟室变成了一间赌博室。我们的学生一边叼着烟卷，一边搓着麻将。我远远躲在监护办公室里，把他们画下来。"[45]这些叙述再次体现出童在空间场景上与周围人们的分离与拒绝认同，而他永远是一位远离中心、目光冷峻的旁观者；在更多情况下他的旁观还表现出他男权主义的立场[46]。

如果说童寯为了"自食其力"而选择建筑专业的目标是出于经

---

43 童寯.童明，译.旅欧日记 // 童寯文集（四）.北京：中国建筑工业出版社，2006：366
44 童寯文集（四）.北京中国建筑工业出版社，2006：355.据童文调查，R.S. 即 Roach, F. Spencer, 是童寯在宾夕法尼亚大学的同学，生于1906年4月，大学毕业后于费城 Harbeson, Hough, Livingston & Larson 建筑师事务所任建筑师，美国建筑师学会（AIA）会员。
45 童寯.童明，译.渡洋日记 // 童寯文集（四）.北京：中国建筑工业出版社，2006：239-240
46 如1930年5月10日他在"旅欧日记"中写道：温莎城堡"参观者太多，有一名妇女去那里仅仅为了带着手套，去感受蓝色天鹅绒坐垫的美妙感觉。"（《童寯文集（四）》，324页）；7月22日，他记述在德国奥伯拉马岗旅社的晚饭"除了我之外还有一大群人，都是美国人，一名妇女来自华盛顿特区，她与德国的主妇在高谈阔论，我想她也是德国人，因此我称她该死的家伙。……两名来自美国的年轻女孩坐在桌子的端头，并且从她们的谈话中可以看出她们的父母可能很有钱。两个愚蠢的脑袋。"（《童寯文集（四）》，352页）7月30日在瑞士蒙杜，他写道"我喜欢听法语。在伯尔尼，人们既说德语也说法语。但是在洛桑和蒙杜，他们只讲法语，这使我的耳朵很舒服。也可以看到很多漂亮的妇女。"（《童寯文集（四）》，359页）

济上的独立,那么他为人处事上的孤傲性格则体现了他对于自身在社会上的独立人格和自由精神的强烈追求。"文化大革命"期间,他曾用当时常见的"个人主义"一词自我批评说:"我解放前最大问题:我是一个十足的个人主义者。不管别人,不闻外事,'独善其身'。求学时是这样,毕业后工作也是这样。"[47]

童寯孤傲性格应该来自他的成长环境和成长经历。他出生于一个传统文人兼官僚家庭。父亲恩格是家中的独子,也是家族中第一位读书人,他曾经以奉天府学廪生资格考取岁贡,殿试为二等十一名进士,钦点七品。归乡后,他先后担任了"功学所"所长、女子师范学校校长和省教育厅长[48]。这样的身份和地位使恩格不仅充当了一个传统伦理、礼教和文化精神的代表,还充当了一个家庭,一个女性世界,甚至一个社会中更多家庭的权威。童寯是家中的长子,有着极强的家庭伦理观念。"文革"中,当他知道祖坟被掘时,痛心疾首,曾在父亲遗像前长跪不起,并对长孙童文说"死不瞑目"[49]。而在他的家人与学生对他的回忆中令人印象最深的就是他的严肃与严格。他的这一品性就令人追想到他的父亲曾经担当的家庭和社会角色。

孤傲的性格还可能体现了童寯的一种"遗民"情结。历史上改朝换代每每出现许多遗民,诸如周初的伯夷、元初的钱选和清初的朱耷。他们无力抗争社会的变化,但为标明气节,便如孔子所说,"隐居以求其志"(《论语》第十六,"季氏")。隐居在空间上可以有郊隐、市隐,甚至朝隐,但在心理上它们都体现为一种自我的边缘化,即对于新朝的不合作态度。刘光华教授曾经告诉笔者,童寯不讲满语,认同汉族,不过他反感推翻清朝的国民党,私下经常贬称孙中山为"孙大炮"[50]。必定是对历史上遗民那种气节的崇尚使得童难以认同梁思成到张学良主持的东北大学任职,正如他说:"我

---

[47] 童寯."文革"材料 // 童寯文集(四).北京:中国建筑工业出版社,2000:377
[48] 童文,童明.童寯年谱 // 童明,杨永生.关于童寯.北京:知识产权出版社,中国水利水电出版社,2002:148-157
[49] 童文致笔者信,2009年12月29日。
[50] 2004年8月21日采访刘光华教授。

永远也不明白,为什么两年之后他会去沈阳,就在那位杀害他岳父的元帅眼皮下创办建筑系?"[51]如此,他所说"我争取'自食其力',靠技术吃饭,尽量不问政治"这句话就有了更深的含义,即他试图通过从事技术性的自由职业,逃避因其他人文、社科专业而出仕民国政治的可能。

在更大的思想史范围内,童寯性格的形成还可能受到了中国近代新文化运动和无政府主义思想的影响。1915年新文化运动的主将陈独秀曾在《新青年》杂志创刊号上发表《敬告青年》一文,阐述其著名的"青年六义",其中第一条就是"自主的而非奴隶的"。他说:"我有手足,自谋温饱;我有口舌,自陈好恶;我有心思,自崇所信;绝不认他人之越俎,亦不应主我而奴他人。"[52]而无政府主义(亦曾译作"安那其主义")盛行于19世纪后半期的欧洲,20世纪初伴随着中国的反帝制革命传入中国,"五四"运动前后在追求平等和自由的中国知识界广为传播。其基本主张是:相信智识完备和人格健全的个人是现代社会的基础,反对一切权力与权威,否认一切国家政权与社会组织形式,主张绝对的个人自由,所谓"人宜自治而不肯被治于人","人贵为主,他人来主我者何为?"(张继《无政府党之精神》),要求建立无命令、无权利、无服从与无制裁的"无政府"社会[53]。无政府主义在个人层面上强调个人作为社会的最基本要素和社会改造的原点,追求独立、平等和自由的人格。在社会层面上反对政府的管治,提倡志同道合者之间的互助。在价值观方面,无政府主义者相信科学的公理,而反对种种政治的和宗教的权威。无政府主义思想是近代中国反封建、反专制的一个武器。童寯的青年时代适逢这一思潮在中国兴盛之时。这种主张在他身上也有很多的体现,如他虽然加入了朋友互助性质的"曦社",但不

---

51 童寯. 致费慰梅信,1982年5月10日 // 童寯文集(四). 北京中国建筑工业出版社,2006:431-432
52 陈独秀. 敬告青年 // 陈独秀文章选编(上). 北京:三联书店,1984:74。陈的"六义"分别是:一、自主的而非奴隶的;二、进步的而非保守的;三、进取的而非退隐的;四、世界的而非锁国的;五、实行的而非虚文的;六、科学的而非想象的。
53 参见陈寒鸣. 论近代中国无政府主义思潮 [EB/OL]. (2004-08-16). http://www.xslx.com/htm/sxgc/sxsl/2004-08-16-17166.htm

入政党，不奉宗教，甚至不坐人力车轿[54]。

尽管建筑师职业的服务性质使得建筑师必须重视社会关系，而童寯也需尽量保持"人缘"[55]，但在事务所里，他主要负责技术性的设计工作而不是需要经常交际应酬的业务承揽[56]。孤傲的性格和对于独立人格的追求使他对唐柳宗元在《梓人传》一文中所道出的"梓人"职业操守极为赞同。晚年他曾将这篇文章指定为自己研究生的必读材料，不仅作为一种古文训练，而且也作为一种人品教育[57]。柳宗元在这篇文章中说：

"或曰：'彼主为室者，傥或发其私智，牵制梓人之虑，夺其世守，而道谋是用，虽不能成功，岂其罪邪？亦在任之而已。'余曰：不然。夫绳墨诚陈，规矩诚设，高者不可抑而下也，狭者不可张而广也，由我则固，不同我则圮。彼将乐去固而就圮也，则卷其术，默其智，悠尔而去，不屈吾道，是诚良梓人耳！或其嗜其货利，忍而不能舍也，丧其制量，屈而不能守也，栋桡屋坏，则曰'非我罪也'，可乎哉？可乎哉？"

1952年后，政府进行公私合营，取消了自由建筑师职业，而在设计方针上又提倡"社会主义内容，民族形式"，这些都与童所坚持的职业自由性和设计理念的现代性相违背。《梓人传》或可视为在新的政治环境之下，童下决心离开建筑设计领域而转入教育领域，并谢绝梁思成来自首都的邀请，"悠尔而去，不屈吾道"的自我明志[58]。也正是出于对一种理念的坚持，他会批评日本现代建筑元老村野藤吾。

---

54 如中国无政府主义的主要倡导者刘师复曾在1916年发起组织"心社"，规定十二条社约：不食肉、不饮酒、不吸烟、不用仆役、不坐人力车轿、不婚姻、不称族姓、不做官吏、不做议员、不入政党、不做海陆军人、不奉宗教，完全履行者为社员，部分履行者为赞成人。出处同上。
55 童寯. "文革"材料 // 童寯文集（四）. 北京：中国建筑工业出版社，2006：403
56 曾经在华盖建筑事务所工作过12年的职员丁宝训在谈到童寯时说："所有草图、透视图等均出其手，且能高速高质量地完成。赵、陈两位老师常参与研究讨论。"见丁宝训. 1937年前华盖建筑事务所概况 // 赖德霖，主编. 王浩娱，袁雪平，司春娟，编. 近代哲匠录——中国近代建筑师、建筑事务所名录. 北京：中国水利水电出版社，知识产权出版社，2006：232
57 方拥. 跟童寯先生读书 // 童明，杨永生. 关于童寯. 北京：知识产权出版社，中国水利水电出版社，2002：82-88
58 童寯的长孙童文在2010年3月14日致笔者的信中还说，解放以后江苏省政府还曾请童出任建厅厅长一职，省委书记也曾邀童参加宴会，但都被童谢绝。在笔者看来，童后来的读写乃至治学方法还令人想到元末明初以及明末清初的大学者陶宗仪和顾炎武。

村野在设计大阪新歌舞伎座（1959年）时因屈从使用者要求而采用了"帝冠"风格和传统装饰。童寯说这是"把平生抱负付之东流，而丧失一贯的信念。"[59]

六

孤傲的性格和对于独立人格的追求也必定是童寯在反对建筑中的保守主义、提倡现代主义的同时，能够认同于中国传统的士精神和士文化的一个原因。他的一些遗诗就从一个侧面反映了他的文人气质和理想。

1937年日本侵华战争全面爆发，华盖建筑师事务所不得不在西南后方开辟新的业务，童寯也因此于1940年至1944年滞留贵州。其间他在业余与一些友人多有诗词唱和，留下了诗集《西南吟草》[60]。诗集封面由黄竹坪题签，内容为童寯毛笔手书。包括封面，诗集原有17页，其中第17页为5首诗的草稿或原抄稿，而9、10两页已失，所以正文尚存14页。全集共有诗41首，童本人的作品占15首。他的这些诗表达有对战争胜利的憧憬[61]，对妻子的思念[62]，以及对于朋友离散的伤感[63]，但更多的是他在一个动乱的时代里远离尘嚣、寄情山水，对于诗书耕读、渔樵江渚生活的向往。如：

扁舟不系亦生涯，愿据高枝饱露华。孰令成名看竖子，宁为谋利问盈赊。知农悔较知书晚，遣兴年来解爱花。归计满怀催鬓老，烽烟何处好为家。（和淦芝湄潭寄省）（1942年？）

---

59 童寯. 日本近现代建筑 // 童寯文集（二）. 北京：中国建筑工业出版社，2001：361
60 诗集由童寯的幼孙童明保存。与童唱和的友人包括"葆老"、"淦芝"、"湄潭"、黄竹坪、"敬第兄"、李仲昭、萧庆云、张驹昂等，但他们的生平待查。其中"敬弟"也为陈植叔父陈叔通的字，但童在此称"兄"而非"父"，故当另有其人。黄竹坪在20世纪70年代仍与童有书信交往。其寄童二诗见《童寯文集（四）》456页。
61 童寯："避警过文昌阁"诗："攀登画阁仰崔巍，每感失群与俗违。军垒清笳征戍众，边关重税旅人稀。沈腰马齿惊花落，蜗角牛车羡鸟飞。孤馆夜郎风雨阻，故园何日见旌旗？"（1943年）
62 童寯："甲申寄内"诗："对镜青丝白几根，最贪梦绕旧家园。西窗夜雨归期误，羡听邻居笑语温。"（1944年）
63 童寯："癸未新正题赠李仲昭画"诗："乱中易隐不才身，屈指西南几故人。梦醒空悲灯对客，意闲每喜鹤为邻。云升江表招青眼，日落峰头剩绛唇。生计哪堪兵火劫，书城尚在未全贫。"（1943年）

图3 童寯"得砚歌"手迹,1943年。图片来源:童寯《西南吟草》,童明藏。

肥马轻车不羡人,山中风雨最关情。芒鞋破伞花溪路,版筑声中已半生。(和淦芝湄潭寄省)(1942年?)

南明碧色透柴扉,十里江流罢钓归。邻叟力田加麦饭,村姑汲水浣寒衣。尘扬隔岸驹争还,香葱穿花蝶乱飞。几度五湖为范蠡,不如高卧旧渔矶。(敬第兄避兵烊河,得郡城负郭河边基地,邀予小为区划,鸠工庀材,朝夕经营,新居落成,爰涂鸦奉赠,并占即景一律,壬午冬)(1942年冬)

愁城未破入书城,唱和声杂板筑声。远客思家畏路断,老农盼雨喜云生。丹青小试因山绿,膏火迟煎赖月明。何日归乡为钓叟,蓴鲈斗酒一身轻。(癸未春题萧庆云兄画)(1943年春)

为避兵戈留夜郎,恣情山水益猖狂。好游兼有丹青癖,不计芒鞋路短长。某夕乘兴过书肆,若叟待沽砚一方。索金高至三百余,付钱未半已空囊。相约翌日备补足,抱砚归途意彷徨。晚食无策惟梏腹,顽石宁能饱饥肠。走过屠门唤奈何,始悔误识张驹昂。张君授我辨砚诀,此砚张君应谓良。入室案头得小束,有人招宴饫高粱。(得砚歌,癸未未定草)(1943年)(图3)

作为教师,晚年的童寯还试图用中国传统的士精神和士文化去教育、影响自己的学生。除《梓人传》外,他为研究生指定的古文名篇还有《马援诫兄子严敦书》、《圬者王承福传》、《种树郭橐驼传》,以及《兰亭集序》、《归去来辞》、《桃花源记》、《滕王阁序》、《陋室铭》、《阿房宫赋》、《岳阳楼记》和《醉翁亭记》[64]。它们不仅代表了童的职业准则,还体现了童严谨自守、淡泊宁静、重义乐道的人格理想。

七

反映童寯文人气质和理想的还有他的中国画作。1933年至1937年,就在他创作了大量现代风格的建筑的同时,他开始师事汤涤,潜心学习中国画。据胡佩衡,汤涤(1878/1879—1948年)"字定之,小字丁子,号乐孙,亦号太平湖客,双于道人,武进(今江苏常州)人。清季名画家贻汾曾孙。山水学李流芳,以气韵清幽见重于世。又善墨梅、竹、兰、松、柏,用笔古雅,自成一家。书法隶、行并佳,题画字与画笔相调和。善相人之术,自谓生平相法第一,诗第二,隶书第三,画第四。在北京画界任导师多年,晚寓上海。"[65] 由此可见,汤画延续了宋元以来中国文人画的传统,即强调诗书画的统一,风格的古雅,题材上对于士大夫品格的象征以及一种对于出世思想的表现。童寯对中国画的审美与汤涤颇为相似。"文化大革命"期间,他曾自我剖析说:"至于我的个人主义,倒不是为名为利,而是比名利更自私的个人主义;是放在名利上的,名利之外的'遗世独立','孤芳自赏','

---

64 方拥.跟童寯先生读书//童明,杨永生.关于童寯.北京:知识产权出版社,中国水利水电出版社,2002:82-88
65 胡佩衡稿《枫园画友录》,载《美术年鉴》,转引自俞剑华.中国美术家人名词典.上海:上海人民美术出版社,1981:1088

图4 童寯：水墨山水图，1978年6月12日。画上的引首章印文为"童寯建筑师"，压角章印文为"言不在画"。图片来源 童明提供。

落落寡合'，'不随流俗'等的资产阶级知识分子所视为评定人格的标准。为名为利的个人主义还是入世的，不能离开群众；而不为名利的个人主义则是超然的，脱离群众的。……我的逃名鄙利思想是由欣赏元朝绘画和晚明文学而来。……这是当时士大夫的风气。"[66]他特别提到倪瓒的山水画，"从来不见一人，只二三棵枯树，几块乱石，有时加一亭子"，并说"我就是陶醉于这种画中的人。"[67]

童寯的中国画作传世不多，1978年他为友人林同济所画的一幅山水图是他少数遗作中的一件（图4）。林（1906—1980年）是中国

---

66 童寯."文革"材料 // 童寯文集（四）.北京：中国建筑工业出版社，2006：419
67 童寯."文革"材料 // 童寯文集（四）.北京：中国建筑工业出版社，2006：419。另据童文，童寯"热爱西餐，他不喜欢（可以说讨厌）中式宴席"。（童文致笔者信，2010年1月8日）在笔者看来，除口味的偏好之外，童的这一好恶可能还因为西餐可以分食，而中餐宴席是群聚

现代史上一位重要的政论家和学者。他出生于著名的福州东瀚镇林家，其曾祖、祖父均为清朝进士，并任知县。父亲曾任北洋政府大理院和南京政府最高法院的法官。母亲也出身于福州望族。其堂叔林澍民为中国近代著名建筑师，林斯登为著名地质学家。同辈中还有林同骅、林同棪、林同骥、林同奇等，均为著名的科学家和学者。林本人1926年从清华学校毕业后赴美留学，初在密西根大学学习国际关系和西方文学史，1933年获得加州大学伯克利分校政治学博士学位。归国后任教于南开大学和复旦大学等校。为了表示对中国文化发展的态度及积极的入世精神，以古代的谋臣或策士自诩，1940年他与云南大学、西南联大的教授陈铨、雷海宗、贺麟，以及何永佶、朱光潜、费孝通、沈从文、曾昭抡等26位"特约执笔人"在昆明共同创办了旨在重建中国文化的《战国策》半月刊。该刊抨击官僚传统、检讨国民性、提倡民族文学运动，在当时的学术思想界颇有影响。这些作者也因此被称为"战国策派"。林对尼采十分崇拜。在他心中，尼采的"超人"是一种"把宗教家'超于人'的高度认合于道德家'入于世'的热力，再透过苏格拉底以前希腊异教的自卫精神，唯美精神，而烧烤出他心目中所独有的理想人格型"[68]。1949年以后他转向研究莎士比亚和李贺。由于林性格直率，1958年他被打成"右派"，继而又在"文化大革命"中受到迫害，直到1978年12月的中国共产党"十一届三中全会"之后才获得平反[69]。

童寯是林在清华学校时的室友，也是《战国策》杂志的26位"特约执笔人"之一。他的《中国建筑的特点》一文就发表在该刊1941年第8期[70]。尽管1949年以后他与林分别在南京和上海工作，且林又因言获罪、身处逆境，但童并没有中断与他的交往，1964年5月

---

68 林同济.我看尼采——《从叔本华到尼采》序言 // 雷海宗.从叔本华到尼采.重庆：在创出版社，1944；转引自李琼.林同济传略[EB/OL].http://www.xschina.org/show.php?id=1550
69 见李琼.林同济传略[EB/OL].http://www.xschina.org/show.php?id=1550
70 童寯在"文化大革命"中所写的"交代材料"中曾说："'中国建筑的特点'一篇短文，刊登于《战国策》1941年的一期，这刊物是云南大学教授林同济主持印行的不定期刊物，其中讨论当时抗战情势和关于其他杂事。1941年我由贵阳回上海过春节时，路经昆明，林同济说这刊物缺乏稿件，要我写些文章充数，这文的内容讲中国古典建筑与西方不同点和将来的趋势。"见解放前写了哪些文章 // 童寯文集（四）.北京：中国建筑工业出版社，2006：389

还曾将自己的新著《江南园林志》寄赠这位老友[71]。童的长孙童文回忆，1976年"四人帮"被打倒后，林曾到南京探望童寯，这是二人自1949年以来的第一次见面。他们相聚后紧紧拥抱，落座后童意味深长地背出了林肯的一句名言："You can fool all the people some of the time, and some of the people all the time, but you cannot fool all the people all the time."（汝可欺众人于有时，亦可欺有人于时时，然断无法欺众人于时时。）此时林尚未获得平反，出于谨慎，二人交谈使用的是英文，但他们兴致之高，畅谈竟两天两夜[72]。

根据题记，童为林画的山水图作于1977年6月12日。该画采用的是挂轴式的竖向构图，强调了山水景色的高远和深远效果。画中的远景是一座孤立峻拔的峭壁，中景是自画面左侧斜出的几座山峰以及山谷中的瀑布和溪流，近景是掩映在古松之下和修竹丛中的房舍和房舍前的两个身着长袍的隐士，应该代表了画家自己与老友。整幅画墨色恬淡，而山势构图奇曲，又使画面充满动感。从用笔看，童画以雨点皴为主，与李流芳和汤涤擅长的披麻皴并不相同，但童所表现的出世思想却与两位文人画家异曲同工。他更在题记中表达了这一思想，他说："每当忆及早岁同舍同砚席诸彦鸿飞东西，良晤难再，感念无已，比游黄山，观始信峰，颇思结庐其下，餐霞饮露，嘲月吟风，时得良朋，觅句叩扉，流连话旧，岂非至乐？同济年兄想具同感，亦必笑可爱，戏涂其意以赠，戊午夏长至前十日，亥末寯。"

值得注意的是，童寯也是一位非常优秀的建筑水彩画家，他在20世纪20和30年代曾写生过大量中外建筑。不过50年代以后他便放弃了这方面的练习和创作[73]。如果说西洋风格的水彩画要求画家去描绘现实景色并常常需要在公众的注视下进行，中国传统山水画作为画家的"胸中丘壑"则使他可以更专注于自己内心理想和情感的

---

71 见林同济致童寯的四通书信（1964年5月19日、20日，1965年6月15日、18日）// 童寯文集（四）. 北京：中国建筑工业出版社，2006：445-446
72 童文致笔者信，2010年3月14日。
73 据童寯的助手晏隆余，南京刚解放时，童在街上写生，未料竟被一解放军战士制止，童从此罢笔。见杨永生. 淳朴而杰出的童寯 // 杨永生，明连生. 建筑四杰：刘敦桢、童寯、梁思成、杨廷宝. 北京：中国建筑工业出版社，1998：33

表现，并在创作过程中避开外界的干扰。这些可能性正是童寯在生活中所希冀的，而他为林同济画的山水图也完成于"亥末"——一个夜阑人静的时刻。

八

也正是在向汤涤学习中国画的时期，童寯在工作余暇开始了对于江南园林的系统调查和研究。他于1936年发表了自己第一篇关于中国园林的论文《中国园林——以江苏、浙江两省园林为主》[74]，次年又完成了自己的第一部书稿《江南园林志》（图5）[75]。今天中国建筑学界普遍认为，童是近现代研究中国古典园林的第一位学者。在笔者看来，更确切的说法或许应该是他在中国建筑师中首先重新"发现"了中国古典园林。这是因为，任何研究都起源于对于研究对象的特别关注，正是这种关注使得历史过往重新进入人们的视野而与当代产生了联系。人们或许很难想象受教于以轴线构图为基础的西方学院派建筑传统，外表严肃、行为近乎刻板的童寯能够"心有戚戚焉"于以林泉山野著称的中国古典园林。那么童是如何"发现"中国古典园林的？他最初的研究动机是什么？刘敦桢在1963年为《江南园林志》所写的序言中说，童著书的动机是因为"目睹旧迹凋零，与乎富商巨贾恣意兴作，虑传统艺术行有澌灭之虞"[76]。

图5 童寯《江南园林志》封面（北京：中国建筑工业出版社，1963年初版，1981年第2版）

---

74 原文标题为 Chinese Gardens, Especially in Jiangsu and Zhejiang, 发表于《天下月刊》(Tien Hsia Monthly) 1936年10月. 方拥中，译 . 中国园林——以江苏、浙江两省园林为主 // 童寯文集（一）. 北京：中国建筑工业出版社，2000：62-74
75 童寯 . 江南园林志 . 北京：中国建筑工业出版社，1963；第2版，1981
76 刘敦桢 . 序 // 童寯 . 江南园林志 . 北京：中国建筑工业出版社，1963

他的话无疑是想强调童作为一名爱国的知识分子在民族文化遗产面临毁灭时所表现出的社会责任感。然而，童并没有像刘本人以及梁思成那样研究同样有"澌灭之虞"的寺庙及宫殿等"官式"建筑，如同他为人的卓尔不群，他在学术上所关注的也仅仅是一个当时中国学者中并无人介意的边缘领域，其中缘由便不能不令人追问。

事实上童寯天性上就对自然山水情有独钟。除了他在20世纪40年代所写的诗，他在1930年所写的"旅欧日记"中也有多处对于河流山水与自然环境的赞美描写。如他对英国剑桥这样评论说："这座小镇不如牛津那么漂亮。但是河流可以流经各个学院，许多如画的桥梁跨越其上，形成了一道有趣的风景。剑桥的学生们真幸福啊，他们可以躺在河岸的草坡上，谈论着天上的星星。"（326页）而到德国后他又写道："沿着莱茵河的科隆夜景剪影非常壮丽，尽管轮廓有点粗糙。非常深的剪影加上单桅小船，还有下面的白色水滩，真是太浪漫了。"（333-334页）"乘船从波恩到科布伦茨，这是我所知最美丽的航程。两岸的风景无与伦比，尤其是当月色升起时，远方的螺塔和城堡的围墙笼罩于梦幻般的色彩之中。月亮在河水中投下倩影，一艘航船或两朵紫色云彩，蓝色山脊，黑色丛林，橙色水光。下午详细参观了七座山，以前从来没有见过如此完美融合的景色。有如此之多的地方我想停下来画画。"（335页）这些描写文字优美，生动地表现出童面对自然所获得的愉悦，也使人得以领略童冷峻孤傲的外表之下那颇富诗情的内心。

引发童寯关注中国古典园林的因素可能还包括一些西方学者对中国造园艺术的记述与评论。从13世纪开始，西方人就已经从《马可波罗游记》中得知中国皇帝在拥有蔬果湖沼的园林中生活，16、17世纪又有传教士和荷属东印度公司的使节在报告中描述中国园林。18世纪以来，受浪漫主义哲学与艺术思想影响，西方更出现了对于崇尚自然的中国园林的赞美甚至模仿。其中英国宫廷建筑师钱伯斯（William Chambers, 1723—1796年）就是这方面的一位代表人物。除了为王太后主持过一座具有中国趣味的花园——丘园（Kew Gardens）——的设计之外，他还出版了《中国建筑、家具、服装和器物的设计》（*Designs of Chinese Buildings, Furniture,*

Dresses, Machines, and Utensils,1757年)和《东方造园艺术泛论》(*A Dissertation on Oriental Gardening*,1772年)两部著作,介绍中国园林艺术[77]。童寯在《中国园林——以江苏、浙江两省园林为主》一文中曾提到钱伯斯的《东方造园泛论》,他对钱氏著作的了解当在更早。

童寯最初接触到的江南园林是上海豫园。1931年移居上海后不久,他在陪伴家人逛城隍庙时参观了这座名园。他的长孙童文说:"他为这个不大的园子所震撼,那里的一切布置既令他心仪,又令他困惑。从此他便开始了对于园林的研究,并惊喜地发现沪宁沿线尚有许多私家园林。他很快认识到了它们巨大的建筑和文化价值。他作出计划,争取利用周日探访各园并进行测绘。"[78] 豫园创建于明嘉靖年间(1521—1566年),占地70余亩,明代著名书画家董其昌曾写诗描述道:"森梢嘉树成蹊径,突兀危峰出市廛。白水朱楼相掩映,中池方广成天镜。"园中的大假山更是一处胜观,据传出自著名叠山家张南阳之手。但入清以后豫园便逐渐破败并沦为城隍庙的庙园。庙内还有一个占地仅2亩的内园(又称东园),厅楼亭廊和山石池沼俱全。不过经过鸦片战争、小刀会起义之后,全园又相继被外国军队的兵营以及21个工商行会的公所占用。至民国时期,虽然故园的山石池沼犹在,但环境和景物已非,除内园外,其余大部已变为茶馆酒楼林立,商贩游人云集的庙市和商场[79]。

1932至1936年华盖建筑事务所在苏州承接的工程又使童寯有机会接触到更具代表性的江南园林。根据苏州城乡建设档案馆档案,这些工程项目有:观西青年会大戏院(1932年6月至1933年2月;铁瓶巷50号朱兰孙先生住宅(1935年4月2日至5月7日);天锡庄景海女中校舍(1935年6月至1936年12月)和景海女子师范学校礼堂(1936年2月至1939月1月)。青年会大戏院的设计由童寯

---

77 详见窦武(陈志华).中国造园艺术在欧洲的影响 // 建筑史论文集(三).北京:清华大学出版社,1979:104-166
78 童文至赵辰信,2001年1月1日。童文提供,本文作者译。
79 参见童寯.江南园林志.第2版.北京:中国建筑工业出版社,1981:34;顾启良.上海老城厢风情录.上海:上海远东出版社,1992:50-52

图 6 华盖建筑师事务所：苏州青年会大戏院（设计方案之一），苏州，1932—1933年。图纸来源：苏州城乡建设档案馆。从这一设计可以看到童在1933年设计的大上海大戏院正立面的雏形。

接负责（图 6）[80]，该建筑地处玄妙观西，与拙政园、狮子林和留园等著名私家园林相距不远。[81]

  我们可以想象童寯在"九一八"事变和相隔不久日军轰炸上海的"一·二八"事变之后游览这些园林时的复杂心情：面对城隍庙攒动的人流，他或许会想到苏轼的"笑渐不闻声渐消，多情却被无情恼"，林升的"暖风熏得游人醉，直把杭州作汴州"，甚至杜牧的"商女不知亡国恨，隔江犹唱后庭花"。而漫步在那些颓败的私园里，他或许有杜甫般"感时花溅泪，恨别鸟惊心"的伤感，或许有司马迁般"低回留之而不忍去"的孤寂，还会有王羲之那样对于"事殊事异"的兴怀。当然，他还可能会有一种如欧阳修因"朝而往，暮而归，四时之景不同"而获得的无穷之乐和归属感。简言之，颓废的私园难免令他触景生情，更加忧虑战乱之中的故土家园，并平添身在异乡的孤独。同时，封闭的园林空间或又可以使他"躲进小楼成一统"，暂时摆脱或忘却纷杂动乱的现实。所以他在1937年春为《江南园林志》所写的序言中写到："吾国旧式园林，有减无增。著者每入名园，低回噱唶，忘饥永日，不胜众芳芜秽，美人迟暮之感。"而同年，他又在另一篇文章"满洲园[按：即拙政园]"的开头说："避开大城市喧闹的一种美妙方式是游赏苏州——一座以女性媚人和园林众多而享盛名的城市。……[拙

---

80 这些图纸现在保存于苏州城乡建设局档案馆。
81 其中拙政园在清同治时被改为八旗直奉会馆，至1928年仍旧。所在位于玄妙观北"不过里来路"，"进内要费一毛小洋"。见胡儿. 苏州. 贡献，1928,3（03）:34-48

政园]特别使我着迷,提及这名字对我就象一种神灵的召唤,在其宁谧的怀抱中悠闲地待上几个时辰,便是我的完美度假方式。我能无数次回到那里而毫不感到乏味,并非它每天能散发新的魅力。岁月磨砺的醇美和超脱沉浮后的安详,使这块迷人土地具有一种独特的宁静象征。"[82] 两种表述情绪不同,语调也不同,但它们都流露出一种"遗世独立"和"不随时流"的态度。我因此更倾向说,是童寯内心对于自然的眷恋和性格中孤傲的气质使他获得了对于江南的私家园林的空间环境的认同。

这种认同也使童寯对中国园林有了与钱伯斯不同的看法。出于浪漫主义美学对"惧畏感"(horror / awe)的重视,钱氏认为中国园林的景色给人三种体验,即愉悦(pleasing)、惧畏(horrid)和着迷(enchanted)[83]。童寯则强调了中国园林的亲切感。他说:"中国园林旨在'迷人、喜人、乐人'(原文:to charm, to delight, to give pleasure),同时体现了某种障蔽之术。笔者无意说游人确知自己被障蔽。但一旦从游'园'而入'画',他便不再感受到现世的烦扰。世界在他眼前敞开,诗铭唤起他的遐想,美景诱发他的好奇。的确,每件景物都恰似出现在画中。一座中国园林就是一幅立体山水画,一幅写意的中国画。……中国园林不使游人生畏,而以温馨的魅力和缠绵拥抱他。"[84]

九

《江南园林志》首志"造园",次志"假山",再志"沿革",

---

[82] 童寯. 方拥, 译. 满洲园 // 童寯文集(一). 北京:中国建筑工业出版社, 2000: 77。这段话令人想到他的诗句"几度五湖为范蠡,不如高卧旧渔矶。"
[83] William Chambers. Designs of Chinese Buildings, Furniture, Dresses, Machines, and Utensils. New York: Benjamin Blom, Inc., 1968: 15
[84] 童寯. 方拥, 译. 中国园林——以江苏、浙江两省园林为主 // 童寯文集(一). 北京:中国建筑工业出版社, 2001: 64。译文在此略有修改。童文在2010年5月2日给笔者的信中说:"苏州园林乃至江南园林是童的梦幻之境,应该说他的最后一次访探是在上海沦陷之前。他再也没有勇气重返故园,虽然只有咫尺之遥。但他一但有机会就会不断打听它们的现状。他太怕这些国粹毁于日军炮火,国共内战,'土改','文革'的浩劫。这些园林的存在,似乎比他自己的存在还要重要。即使是这些园林安然无恙,它们的美丽与趣味如果受到损害对他来说依然是一种灾难。他生命中的一个希望就是保持它们的遥远与梦境。"

再次志"现状",最后附"杂识"。作为总纲,"造园"一章实际是童寯园林审美思想的概括。他谈到布局之妙,"在虚实互映、大小对比、高下相称",为园的三种境界依次是"疏密得宜,曲折尽致,眼前有景"。他还强调了植物的重要性,"园林无花木则无生气",他还赞同计成所说"旧园妙于翻造,自然古木繁花",因为"屋宇苍古,绿荫掩映,均不可立期"。他继而谈到了园林屋宇,认为它们"方之宫殿庙堂,实为富有自由性之结构"。对于围墙,他欣赏"式样变幻",墙洞外廊"任意驰放,不受制于规律",漏窗能以日光转移而"尤增意外趣"。而铺地则能"形状颜色,变幻无穷,[材料]信手拈来,都成妙谛。"[85] 他反对墙因嵌砖刻人物而"欠雅致",也反对镶琉璃竹节或花砖而"难免俗"。正是因为强调自然变化与古朴,童在"现状"一章里将拙政园列于苏州园林的首位。他说:"惟谈园林之苍古者,咸推拙政。今虽狐鼠穿屋,藓苔蔽路,而山池天然,丹青淡剥,反觉逸趣横生。……爱拙政园者,遂宁保其半老风姿,不期其重修翻造。"[86]

童寯还在全书最后的"杂识"一章里引用文献进一步佐证他的园林审美。其中有《红楼梦》中贾宝玉的话"古人云天然图画四字,正畏非其地而强为其地,非其山而强为其山。即百般精巧,终不相宜,"袁学澜《吴中双塔影园记》中所说的"今余之园,无雕镂之饰,质朴而已;鲜轮奂之美,清寂而已",李渔所说的"未有真境之为所欲为,能出幻境纵横之上者",还有庄子所说的"覆杯水于坳堂之上,则芥为之舟",以及晋简文帝所说的"会心处不必在远,翳然林木,便自有濠濮间想"等等。童寯的中国园林审美远追庄周、王维,近趋李渔、计成,体现了中国文化中的出世思想。如果说在20世纪30年代以梁刘为代表的中国营造学社研究者们首先关注到的是以宫殿和寺庙为代表的官式建筑和它们所体现的中国古代建筑法式,那么童寯则在中国现代建筑家中最先发现了古典园林所体现的中国文人建筑的美学追求。[87]

需要指出的是,虽然身为一名建筑师,童寯《江南园林志》的写作关注的却不是传统园林与当下创作的关系,而是它们的审美、

85,86 童寯.江南园林志.第2版.北京:中国建筑工业出版社,1981:7-14, 28-29
87 童在《江南园林志》"杂识"一章里引用的前人文字,今天已经为大多数中国园林史学者所熟知,但它们在当年却应是童"发现"的结果。

相关的叠石技艺、历史沿革和重要遗存[88]。虽然童接受的是西方学院派建筑学教育,这本书关注的却不是法式而是"不拘泥于法式"。虽然童追求的是建筑的现代主义,但是他却并没有从现代建筑的角度对中国园林进行解释和阐发,尽管他已经注意到了中国园林空间的疏密曲折和"眼前有景"等特点。更重要的,虽然该书出自一名接受过全面现代教育,熟谙西方文化甚至语言传统的学者之手,并且配有按照现代建筑学标准绘制的平面测绘图和摄影插图,但它的写作方式无论从体例还是从风格上却更接近中国传统文人的笔记、丛谈和杂录而不是严格西方经院传统的论文或论著,甚至作者为选用的字体都是古雅的小篆而不是现代的印刷体。除此之外,他在相关著作中还常常加写一些中国文人们的逸事,如晋王子敬游顾辟疆园、元倪瓒赏荷、明文徵明的手植藤等等。总之,《江南园林志》和童寯其他有关中国园林的文章更多地体现的是他对于一种中国文人传统的认同和追摹,这种传统见之于元朝绘画、晚明文学,以及明清江南园林,而他所追求的独立人格就与这种传统若合一契。

《江南园林志》的书稿完成后由刘敦桢介绍,拟交中国营造学社刊行,但排印方始,日本侵华战争爆发,学社南迁,书稿的文字图片也因保存地点遭遇水灾而至模糊难辨。1940年学社将原稿归还童寯。直至中华人民共和国成立,1953年刘敦桢创办中国建筑研究室,才又有机会促请童将旧稿重新移录付印。尽管此时中国园林研究已经成为一门"显学",更有一些学者试图运用西方现代建筑的最新概念解释中国园林的设计[89],童寯却无意去更新自己这部旧作的观点甚至文言文字。所幸1959年5月建筑工程部主持召开"住宅标准及

---

88 童寯.江南园林志.第2版.北京:中国建筑工业出版社,1981:3
89 空间问题从20世纪60年代起成为中国园林研究的核心问题之一,其中代表性研究有郭黛姮,张锦秋.留园的建筑空间.建筑学报,1963(02)。另外陈薇还指出,早在1956年10月,刘敦桢在南京工学院第一次科学讨论会上宣读的论文中也提出了关于园林空间和层次的见解。(见陈薇.《苏州古典园林》的意义//杨永生,王莉慧.建筑百家谈占论今——图书篇.北京:中国建筑工业出版社,2008:115-122。刘文即.苏州的园林//刘敦桢文集(四).北京:中国建筑工业出版社,1992:79-129)笔者认为,这种研究的新趋势应该是当时现代主义建筑理论新发展影响的结果。其中吉迪安在1941年出版的《空间、时间和建筑——一种新传统的成长》一书中提出的"空间-时间"一体思想在20世纪50年代已经成为解释现代主义建筑的经典理论。中国的一些大学建筑系在这一时期也在教学中引入了"流动空间"概念,这个概念随之启发了中国学者和学生对于传统园林的新认识。(参见杨永生,王莉慧.建筑史解码人.北京:中国建筑工业出版社,2006:280-286)

图7 喻维国摄：童寯像，1982年夏。图片来源：杨永生，明连生.建筑四杰——刘敦桢、童寯、梁思成、杨廷宝.北京：中国建筑工业出版社，1998：24

建筑艺术座谈会"之后，全国范围的建筑思想又得以活跃，1961年3月《建筑学报》还发表了题为"开展百家争鸣，繁荣建筑创作"的社论。1962年3月副总理陈毅在全国科学工作会议上讲话，给知识分子行"脱帽礼"——即摘掉"资产阶级知识分子"的帽子，肯定"人民的知识分子"和"为无产阶级服务的脑力劳动者"[89]。这一切都活跃了当时的出版环境。而刘敦桢也不无苦心地为这部书写了序言——他不仅尽力论证了这部旧著在新社会的意义，还试图去抬高作者的"思想觉悟"[90]。该书终于在1963年正式出版。

1952年以后童寯放弃了建筑设计职业而改从教学，以一名建筑教师的学识替换了他在建筑设计上的"技术"。他后半生的大部分时光都是在两点一线中度过。两点分别是他在20世纪40年代为自己设计的住宅和工作所在的南京工学院，而一线则是连接二者的一条两公里的路。建筑系图书室的一套桌椅和家中起居室靠窗的一个躺椅是他在这两个空间中的个人领域。在学校陪伴他的是书，在家里，除了家人和书外，他还有一只猫、一台留声机和庭院中四季常青的花草树木。一张摄于1982年夏天的照片可能是他辞世之前留下的最后一个影像。照片中的童寯表情依然严肃，他身着无领短衫，胸襟半敞，脊背微驼，孑立于庭院内种植的瓜果前。摄影者说，此情此景，令他想到了东篱采菊的陶潜[91]（图7）。

---

89 承杨永生先生告知这一会议的情况及其对当时建筑出版的影响。
90 除了说童原初的研究目的是为了保护和拯救传统艺术之外，刘还说书的出版可以"有裨于今日学术上求同存异之争鸣"。他还不失时机地借用一些时代新词，通过说园而称颂了新社会。他说："至若解放以来，各地园林起堕兴废，不遗余力，而新建之园，数量规模均迥出昔日私家园林之上，且能推陈出新，使我国园林艺术有如百花怒放。"最后他巧妙地抬高童寯的思想觉悟说："以今观昔，隔世之感，不期油然而生，岂仅著者一人引为欣慰而已耶？"见刘敦桢．序 // 童寯.江南园林志.北京：中国建筑工业出版社，1963：1-2

人们也记得他出现在公共场合的一些情景：那是在教室里给学生的妙手改图，"文革"中面无表情地跳"忠字舞"、背语录，"文革"后带着孙子看卓别林电影时的哈哈大笑，还有他在1979年出席南京金陵饭店的方案审查会——对于熟悉他的人来说，这是一个异乎寻常的举动，面对这个当时颇有争议的现代主义风格方案，他旗帜鲜明地说："这是第一流设计。"[92]

这就是童寯，一位一生都处在中国现代转型的动荡与矛盾之中的建筑家和知识分子。他用自己的作品、著作，乃至人生表明了自己对于彷徨于历史与现实、东方与西方冲突的中国建筑和一个中国人的现代化目标的认识。虽然不得不放弃自由职业而重操教鞭，但终其一生，童寯没有放弃自己对于技术与艺术结合的人生理想的追求，没有放弃对于建筑的科学性和时代性的追求，更没有放弃对于一种体现为独立人格的士精神的追求。他靠技术和学识得以自食其力，通过艺术摆脱了庸俗，他用建筑的科学性和时代性抵制中国现代建筑中他所认为的保守主义，又凭士精神默默抗拒着来自社会和现实的种种动荡和专制压迫，坚持自己在专业上的理念。这些追求，我相信，就是童寯作为一名中国现代建筑师的现代性所在。

2010年冬于路易维尔

致谢：在本研究调查过程中原苏州科技学院尤东晶教授、陈卫潭教授、苏州城乡建设局邱晓翔副局长及其同事们给予我巨大帮助。写作过程中童寯先生的文孙童文、童明博士以及东南大学建筑学院葛明博士曾给予我史料的支持。罗圣庄教授、杨永生先生、王明贤先生、朱剑飞博士、李华博士、林伟正博士和彭长歆博士阅读了初稿并提出宝贵意见。对此我表示衷心感谢。

91 这一联想来自摄影师喻维国本人。见杨永生，明连生.建筑四杰——刘敦桢、童寯、梁思成、杨廷宝.北京：中国建筑工业出版社，1998：37
92 童明.忆祖父童寯先生 // 见杨永生.建筑百家回忆录.北京：中国建筑工业出版社，2000：221-222；黄一鸾.童先生的人格魅力；童文，童明：南京童寯故居 // 童明，杨永生.关于童寯.北京：知识产权出版社，中国水利水电出版社，2002：97-102，141-147。另据童文告知，1980年3月，童寯曾出席南京金陵饭店的奠基典礼，这大概是他在1949年后唯一一次在这样的场合露面。邀请他的是设计师香港巴马·丹那建筑师事务所，其前身即20世纪30年代在上海最为著名的外国事务所公和洋行。童文认为，这一邀请体现了建筑师对童的尊重，而童的出席则体现了他对建筑师的支持，因为他预见了中国重新回到了现代建筑的主流之中而不是继续纠缠于"民族风格"的争论。（童文致笔者信，2010年3月27日）

读童寯先生画作有感

金允铨[*]

凡熟悉我国近代建筑史的学子和同道,都知道童寯教授。他是一位精通中国历史、传统文化,而又熟练掌握英、德、法等诸国文字的建筑大师、学者、教育家和画家。

八十多年前,童先生信手画成的素描和水彩画,即使陈列于当今建筑美术画坛,仍是无与伦比的优异之作。

在我们这代人的心目中,童先生是智慧、才学、默默奉献的典范。我们发自内心地尊称他为"夫子",把他喻作中西文化铸造的"大钟",有求必应,有问必答。

近几年,我有幸能反复拜读童先生的数百幅绘画原作。每次读后不免赞叹!这些素描和水彩画精品,竟然多数创作于20世纪30年代前后,正当也是先生的"而立之年"。

现在以成稿顺序,暂把它们归成三部分:

一部分作于留美期间,是先生绘画风格形成的佐证。

绝大多数作于1930年5月至8月,赴欧洲考察文艺复兴时期的建筑……此时,先生日以继夜忙碌。绘画成就也正处于炉火纯青之巅。

此后,也有不少描绘中国古建筑与民居的题材问世。它们与前述遥相呼应。

---

[*] 金允铨,1934年生,浙江义乌人,东南大学建筑学院教授。1958年入南京工学院建筑系(现东南大学建筑学院),从事建筑学科的美术教学工作。曾得到童寯先生的指导。

这是一笔巨大的精神财富。

从整体上拓宽了建筑的地域、文化、空间；

从绘画上拓宽了艺术、审美视野；

从学术品位上，让人们领略到先生的治学方式、艺术才华以至人格魅力。

这些多半以建筑为题材的绘画作品，并非是一般意义上的建筑画，而是地地道道扣人心弦的艺术精品。它们不仅如此，并且还为后人研究不同国度、不同时代、不同建筑形态与内核，提供了极其珍贵的历史篇章。

尽管建筑与绘画有所不同，但在它们的灵魂深处，却有着诸多相同或相似的文化内涵。无论是建筑设计或是绘画创作，它们的精神支柱必是高尚的文化，必是作者的思想、才学、情怀、审美、境界的总和与倾向。

如今就绘画与建筑的关系而言，童寯先生仍然不愧为前述二者和谐统一、诗情画意的形象大师。

先生那些以建筑为题材的数百幅水彩画，就其实质，是他融会中西美术、依仗建筑、真诚阐述各种建筑文化的结晶；同样也是他借助绘画与建筑的巧妙结合、潜心赞美各种艺术情态的写照。

就画应当论质。先生的基本绘画风格是写实的，但也借鉴写意、装饰之类的多种表现方式，旨意塑造完美的形象；有时也根据景色和情愫的需求，酌情选用铅笔、色纸与色粉笔之类的画具，指望丰富画面形式，拓展画中情意空间。

绘画是写形、传情、表意的艺术。

先生作画，首先关注形象的整体神韵，以画好"这座"建筑的特殊性为前提，随后朴实地写生、探索建筑真谛。画好每座建筑的个性，这是区别画面形式的首要条件。否则，远离建筑个性，光玩空乏的形式，与建筑师有何相干？

凡参观过先生画展的画家，无不赞誉先生的艺术才华，以及情与景高度统一的境界。

先生作画，思维敏捷、热情洋溢、笔法精到、技法娴熟。"每染一色都是最后一色，不再重复……"可谓言简意赅，恰到好处。

我每次精读先生作品，都有新的收获，至今留给我的印象是：

气势恢弘、形象真切、语言质朴,浓浓的书卷气不时荡漾于画面内外。几乎每幅作品均处于某种氛围之中,或叙事、或沉思、或吟咏、或高歌……

一幅写实绘画,其立意、构图、造型与色彩,必将决定全画的整体格局。一般来说,画中各种形式规律都是交替、综合使用的。若取其一点加以强化论述,总不免有些勉强。现将我对先生作品的读后感,罗列如下:

一、顶天立地

这个"顶天立地",不光指画面形象,也指作者的气质。先生选用的画幅普遍不大,但仍然拥有气贯长虹的大家风采。

如《维也纳,圣斯蒂芬大教堂一》(图1),其尖顶越过画框,矗入云霄。

又如《乌尔姆,大教堂》(图2),借助环境烘托主体,又利用主体建筑两侧透视斜线与运笔方向,强化锥状形态而成撑天之势。

二、内涵外延

画中的节奏、韵致和气息,必须依靠形象与形式的完美组合才能如愿以偿。如《伦敦,圣保罗大教堂侧廊》(图3)和《亚眠,主教堂室内》(图4),这两幅描绘室内的题材,气势十分雄伟。前者向纵深重重推进。后者向四周拓展,同时在画面上端形成回荡之势。尤其这些"点彩"起着画龙点睛的作用。先生根

图1 维也纳,圣斯蒂芬大教堂一 Vienna, St. Stephen's Cathedral, I
图2 乌尔姆,大教堂 Ulm, Cathedral
图3 伦敦,圣保罗大教堂侧廊 London, Side Aisle of St.Paul
图4 亚眠,主教堂室内 Amiens, Interior of Notre Dame

据画面需要，又通过强弱、虚实、增减的艺术处理，使其更富于形式美感。

三、浑然一体

不少建筑师作快图，甚至画效果图，都习惯在建筑周围加上粗线或深色块突出建筑。像《萨尔兹堡，城堡三》（图5）这样采取虚实相间的方式，展示建筑文化与艺术情趣，实系罕见。此画将天地、树木、建筑全融于同一色调、同一氛围之中。其中自有奥妙和韵味，须要细细品味。

四、岁月如歌

《林肯，古堡城门》（图6）与《浙江南浔，风安桥》（图7），若把视线集中于"古"、"安"二字，它们仿佛像两首叙事诗。前者运用大笔触记叙岁月如歌的境界，后者似乎情理结合：一色的天、缓缓的水、四周空无一人，甚至连标题也用上一丝不苟的楷书。

五、斗转星移

先生笔下的《柏林，勃兰登堡门》（图8），其横线和竖线正沉酣在深蓝色的夜幕之中。上下对应的雕塑和人群，似乎与天籁之音构成美妙的和声，更衬托出一派宁静而无眠的沉思。

然而斗转星移，《约克，大教堂远眺》（图9）却是另一番情景。远处的建筑聚焦而撑天，迷人的色调令人心醉！两个人影自远而来……

图5 萨尔兹堡，城堡三　Salzburg, Castle, Ⅲ
图6 林肯，古堡城门　Lincoln, Castle Gate
图7 浙江南浔，风安桥　Nanxun, Feng'an Bridge
图8 柏林，勃兰登堡门　Berlin, Brandenburger Tor
图9 约克，大教堂远眺　York, Remote View of Cathedral

六、一挥而就

"时间往往是匆忙紧迫的……",《洛桑,大教堂》(图10)是先生分秒必争、一挥而就的上乘之作。此画给人的感觉:一笔不能增,一笔不能减,笔笔都是真情的流露。

七、清明纯真

诗是由情与景锤炼而结晶的语言。

这两幅《大西洋舟中》(图11)、《维也纳,贝多芬故居》(图12),它们的意义在于纪念价值,共同的特点是"纯真",如同雨过天晴荷中明净的雨露。

八、琳琅满目

闪闪烁烁、琳琅满目的"点彩"结构,用于表现中国古建,在当年国内画坛,尤其水彩画界,少之又少,难得一见。画家面对像《清东陵》(图13)这类强烈的色调,若不善于观察和组织,那些绿树、红墙、斑斓的彩画,实在难以取得和谐的效果,也难以取得如此动感的场景。

九、删繁就简

这幅近似装饰性的《萨尔兹堡,山居一》(图14)整体色调先生概括成三大块,形成中心明、四周暗的基本格局。画面两侧建筑透视与斜面台阶,将观众视线引向纵深,并留下一个悬念——在迎光墙外那边,究竟还有什么?

除此之外,值得关注的是:暗部墙中和阶上的各种反光(面与线)、各个窗框、右上角

图10 洛桑,大教堂
　　　Lausanne, Cathedral
图11 大西洋舟中
　　　In the Atlantic Ocean
图12 维也纳,贝多芬故居
　　　Vienna Beethovenhaus
图13 清东陵
　　　Eastern Mausoleum
　　　of Qing Dynasty

的编号，以及窗台上的盆景、檐下的天沟等等，都是经过先生随意而又精心组织的。即使从形式美的角度去分析，也十分有趣。

十、腾腾冉冉

从笔意判断，《约克，老街》（图15），是一幅无拘无束的速写。此作聚焦而向上的气韵，主要依靠两点：（一）位于画面中心的建筑顶层，相互向内倾斜；（二）天上似云似烟的运笔，形成腾腾冉冉之势，使古老民居在时空岁月中，又唤起爽朗生机。

十一、古趣盎然

先生对《美因茨，教堂广场早市》（图16）有一段题记："这类建筑群构图参差高下，古趣盎然，具极大吸引力。早晨阳光随日影不断变化以及人流来往不停，真使写生工作兴奋紧张，笔不停挥。"

这段文字，有情、有景，还有繁忙的工作与心情，值得领悟和深思，先生是以何等热情治学的。

十二、继往开来

上世纪童先生旅欧考察，实际上是建筑与绘画的双重考察。在此期间，绘画上涌现出留美时期不曾有过的许多新形式，以至新内涵。

如《莱比锡，圣阿列克西纪念教堂》（图17），为了能让环境与主体建筑相协调，刻意把天和树画成各种块状与三角形——似规则又不规则的节奏和韵致，使画面形式与时代气息相呼应。

图14 萨尔兹堡，山居一 Salzburg Houses on the Hill, I
图15 约克，老街 York, Old Street
图16 美因茨，教堂广场早市 Mainz, Morning Market in the front of Cathedral
图17 莱比锡，圣阿列克西纪念教堂 Leipzig, St. Alexi Memorial Church

与前述不同的是《威尼斯,圣马可广场钟塔》(图18),该画以极简练的笔法和色调,构成钟塔与环境的鲜明对比。尤其那些装饰趣味的层云,先生是否也在叙说音乐感呢?

在欧洲画坛上,曾经有人主张绘画回归平面中去。这幅《维也纳,卡尔·马克思大院二》(图19)几乎全部由平面色块与不同程度的补色关系所组成。画中最具视觉冲击力的是这堵经过夸张的大型钴蓝墙面,似乎正在向东西两侧延伸。此外,正对着我们的拱券大通道,同样也在向纵深步步推进。从此平面的画面也就成了全方位的艺术空间。

这幅作于灰褐色纸上的《萨尔兹堡,街景二》(图20),整个画面近似浮雕。墙上几处提光的同种色与类比色,其中某些角状块面,经过加工,部分成了弧状,且与凝重、沉稳、含蓄的色调相默契,仿佛在记叙建筑文化的积淀,也在记叙先生的艺术感受。

童先生的艺术表现,一般都是根据题材、风情、触目兴怀,有感而发的。《萨尔兹堡,城堡入口》(图21),整体气息明朗、清新。全画采用直线、弧线、三角等形状构建形象的框架。其中建筑垂线微微内斜,窗画成错落有致的倒梯形,甚至连门前两个人物体态,也作了相应的变形调整,使人耳目一新。

唐代诗圣杜甫云:"读书破万卷,下笔如有神"。

童先生博览群书,除中文经典外,还阅读了大量西文图书,这在一般中西画家中,都是屈指可数的。先生笔下的神,也是经过中国书画反复熏陶的神。

中国书画有其系统的哲学、艺术体系,历

图18 威尼斯,圣马可广场钟塔 Venice, Campanile of Piazza San Marco
图19 维也纳,卡尔·马克思大院二 Vienna, Karl Marx Hof, II
图20 萨尔兹堡,街景二 Salzburg, Street View, II
图21 萨尔兹堡,城堡入口 Salzburg, Entrance to Castle

来注重一个"写"字,以民族气质写形、写神、写意境。先生的水彩画,或多或少都含有中国书画的笔意。

《沃伦丹姆,帆船》(图22),可堪称写意的代表作。

《因斯布鲁克城郊区,阿尔卑斯山乡村风景》(图23),先生运用了干、湿、浓、淡、皴、擦等多种技法,写出了山雨初晴、草木滋润的山村气象。

《剑桥,郊区住宅(雨中作)》(图24),画面形式近似"泼墨",气韵生动。

《布鲁日,城门运河铁桥(阴雨中)》(图25),桥傍建筑与水面倒影,既像"泼墨"又像"泼水",仿佛环绕主题的协奏曲。

《海德堡,石券门》(图26),铁门的作法,如同篆刻白文,有顿性、有刀味。

关于水彩画的色彩,童寯先生在自撰"引言"中有一段精辟论述。我以为,阅读时要联系他的作品(甚至创作方法),细细品味其中的奥妙与精微。可否归纳为下列方方面面?

(一)不以光顾景色表面真实为满足;

(二)重点研究色彩的艺术价值及其文化价值;

(三)选择最纯粹的色彩语言,用于表达

图22 沃伦丹姆,帆船
Volendam, Sailing Boat
图23 因斯布鲁克城郊区,阿尔卑斯山乡村风景
Innsbruck Surburb, Alps View
图24 剑桥,郊区住宅(雨中作)
Cambridge, House in the Rain
图25 布鲁日,城门运河铁桥(阴雨中)
Bruges, Ponte de Canal & Steel Bridge
图26 海德堡,石券门
Heidelberg, A Stone Arch Gate

对景色的独特感受。

一般而论，水彩画应根据自身特点和颜料性能，"宜取低调，不求水彩的'彩'，而求彩外之彩"。

绘画沿革至今日，人们早已认识，任何一种颜料，都可通过增光与减光的方式列出若干个色阶，用于艺术造形，表现数以百计的色调。这不仅素描是如此，中国画运墨是如此，甚至连黑白胶卷——遵循科学原理——同样也是如此。

童先生的赋色理念，能否看作色彩学的"色"与中国画的"墨"二者高度统一呢？我以为，是先生弘扬了"运墨而五色具"的论断，根据艺术需求和景色实际，选择精湛的色调达到造形、传情、喻义和审美的目的。

这篇读后感于此告一段落。

真诚感谢：杨德安教授、童明教授、白颖博士的协助和指点。

这次我的主要收获归纳为三句话：

无论就读、治学，研究众人智慧，其真谛在于不断净化灵魂，寻求创造空间，实践人生价值。

无论何时、何地，无论自我水准如何，在大师群贤面前，要勇于承认自己只是刚刚开始……

尽管众说纷纭，流派纷呈，惟有学问、思维、顶天立地的气概，才是永恒的。

图书在版编目（CIP）数据

赭石：童寯画纪/童明编．—南京：东南大学出版社，2012.04
ISBN 978-7-5641-2523-3

Ⅰ.①赭… Ⅱ.①童… Ⅲ.①日记–作品集–中国–当代 Ⅳ.①I267.5

中国版本图书馆CIP数据核字（2010）第223199号

出版发行：东南大学出版社
社　　址：南京四牌楼2号　邮编：210096
出 版 人：江建中
网　　址：http://www.seupress.com
电子邮箱：press@seupress.com
责任编辑：戴　丽　魏晓平
印　　刷：利丰雅高印刷（深圳）有限公司
经　　销：全国各地新华书店
开　　本：880mm×1230mm 1/32
印　　张：15.375
字　　数：486千
版　　次：2012年04月第1版
印　　次：2012年04月第1次印刷
书　　号：ISBN 978-7-5641-2523-3
定　　价：80元

若有印装质量问题，请同读者服务部联系。
电话：025-83791830